D1713206

Myth of the Moon Goddess

The Aradia Chronicles— Books One, Two, and Three

April Rane

iUniverse, Inc.
Bloomington

Myth of the Moon Goddess
The Aradia Chronicles—Books One, Two, and Three

iUniverse books may be ordered through booksellers or by contacting:

iUniverse
1663 Liberty Drive
Bloomington, IN 47403
www.iuniverse.com
1-800-Authors (1-800-288-4677)

ISBN: 978-1-4759-4147-0 (sc)
ISBN: 978-1-4759-4148-7 (hc)
ISBN: 978-1-4759-4149-4 (e)

Library of Congress Control Number: 2012914012

Printed in the United States of America

iUniverse rev. date: 10/1/2012

Author's Note

Years ago when I read Charles Leland's accounts of the Goddess Aradia, in *Aradia, Gospel of the Witches*, it shook me to my core. Reading about Aradia opened doorways into past-life memory that I had only touched upon up to that point. And though I had no idea why his book or stories about Aradia created a need to explore the lives I had lived, I pursued that track as well as many other deep approaches to spiritual growth.

Leland claimed that Aradia actually lived on earth somewhere around the year 1350 A.D. From that point alone, it should be noticed, seeing as the *Aradia Chronicles* begins more than 300 B.C. that my books are not in any way a historical document of her life. Leland's book has since been debunked, creating quite a bit of controversy. My book is neither a claim that Aradia actually lived, nor is it a statement that she did not live.

I channeled the **Myth** portion of this book in 1994 and put it aside and forgot about it. It was in 1998 that I began to channel the stories. They came to me fast and furious and were fun and exciting to read because, as I was writing, I never knew what was coming next.

It was through the dream-time that I recognized it was consecutive lives and soul lessons that I was writing about. And it was in a deep meditation that I connected the **Myth** that I had written in 1994 to the stories that were flowing through me. It was at that time that I decided that Aradia's archetypal presence was guiding me, and that I needed to honor that fact by keeping her name alive.

I truly believe that it matters not what spurs us forward on our spiritual path, but that if we can continue to *know ourselves* then we are participating fully in life. So no, what I have written is not a declaration about when or if Aradia lived. It is about her impact on me as an individual that I wish to acknowledge because *she lives in me*, just as she lives in many of you who have connected with her through the written word, dreams, visions, or perhaps through this book.

Blessed be, *April Rane*

Acknowledgements

I don't believe in coincidence. Every single event that has happened in my life led to writing *The Aradia Chronicles*, and every single person I have ever come across has added dimension to the stories and imagery that have always been in my head.

The names and faces of the people that have edited, read or commented on this book weave together like a colorful kaleidoscope with each turn of the wheel adding to the next amazing improvement, filling my senses with awe at just who I should thank first. So I will try and list them as I remember the events taking place, because each one was essential to the whole. If I have neglected someone I should have mentioned, please forgive me and know that I appreciated every bit of help I got along the way.

My **Aunt Connie** rolled up the pages of one of my stories after reading it and wacked me on the head saying, "These stories are great because they have a message! They belong in a book. In fact they belong on television like *Xena the Warrior Princess*! If you don't publish them I'll come back and haunt you when I die!" My aunt was no spring chicken, so picturing her glued to the T.V. watching Xena gave me a chuckle, but I really had to laugh when she *insisted* that her husband, my wonderful Uncle Larry, who didn't enjoy reading at all, actually perused a few pages so he could encourage me also.

Next, my best friend **Patricia Mulraney,** an avid reader, read through the original manuscript (bless her,) complete with every grammatical mistake possible, an over-abundance of commas and tons of semicolons, my favorite form of punctuation, thrown in everywhere, in spite of which, she declared it to be a f _ _ _ _ _ _ page turner! That got my attention!

And then there was…. **Jorie Eberle** who pointed out all the spelling and grammatical mistakes, which as a dyslexic didn't surprise me, but it did make me more determined to see it through. Her not being able to *read it* allowed me to verbalize Aradia's story. Hence, we talked about chakra lessons, which opened another door. Thanks for listening between the lines!

Tomara Hotary LeMieux, upon reading a couple of the stories, and loving them, has constantly encouraged me to continue with the series. Thank you my beautiful daughter-in-law and thanks also for giving me my intelligent and wonderful grandson **Taylor**, who cooked and shared so many meals with me as he was growing up. It is hard to realize that he is now in the service. I love you Taylor!

My friend **Ron Sabatino** patiently began to do some editing just before he left for a job overseas. It was he who suggested that I needed to add a bit of background at the beginning of each story. He also, *not so patiently*, being shocked that I did not know how to use it, taught me about the micro-soft office editing program.

Life happened and I put the books down for some time until my friend and teaching partner for Reiki classes, **Antoinette Parato**, asked if her mother, **Margaret LePrine,** who loved to read could review the books. And she, very Aries-like, not only critiqued me but gave me some good solid advice about additions to the endings; she then told her daughter how much she like them.

Donna Brewer, my dear and wonderful Sagittarian friend upon hearing Margaret's opinion through her daughter, called me out of the blue and asked if she could read Aradia's stories; after doing so she enthusiastically encouraged me saying! "I love it! *I love Aradia's feisty spirit* and her multifaceted personality. I would be glad to offer my time to do some preliminary editing and polishing to get these stories on the market, because I truly believe it will make a great book!" *Donna I will be forever grateful for your hard work and your belief in me!*

Meriann Schneble, an avid reader and longtime friend, was elected to be the word-master, researching redundant words and replacing them with more interesting ones. After attracting a few more helpers, we named our little group 'The Dream Team,' and I believe all of us benefited from the creativity of working on this project together.

After all the basic editing, my cousin **Kyah Mull**, my Aunt Connie and Uncle Larry's daughter, excitedly joined our group. Her job was to help me clarify situations and shore up places that lacked consistency.

She was a hard task master determined not to let me throw in my famous semi-colons anywhere I thought they looked pretty! She was an absolute blessing in an endeavor that became more and more difficult, rather than easier, as it went along. For me as a writer the initial story comes through so rapidly that it is hard to type fast enough, but the editing is grueling.

My sweet and loving friend **Jackie Kopie** gave me an opinion from a more youthful perspective, loving it she mentioned that perhaps her mother, **Ronna High**, being an avid reader could help. Thanks for joining the Dream Team Ronna!

I asked my dear friend **Gayle Phillips**, who is a psychologist, to critique it from her perspective, and it was she who encouraged me to trust myself and add *more* information about the color rays, as she found that concept fascinating. Thank you, Gayle.

Maggie Schultz, my friend *and* real estate agent, after reading it sent out some query letters and **Donna Jo Young** brainstormed with all of us in the beginning before she moved away. Both were great additions to our Dream Team. Donna we miss you!

Thanks to my loving friend **Carol Nelson,** for reading and commenting on my efforts. Also **Betty Fair,** my new neighbor and condo mate for her quick eye as she read through many of the changes and additions that were taking place as the book was being prepared for market.

I love my spirited and funny daughter-in-law **Beth LeMieux** for many reasons, but at the top of the list is the fact that she gave me two incredible grandchildren who have always been close to my heart. My grandson **David LeMieux** was terrifically helpful on this project with his knowledge about computers. But more than that, he encouraged me by cheering me on and making me laugh! Thanks, I love you David.

Catherine McClure, 'Kat,' Beth's daughter, now a beautiful young lady in college and one I am delighted to call my grand-daughter, has been a blessing! Having the benefit of her delightful company, laughter, and precocious views on life through the years has kept me young! She's delighted to have an author in the family. I love you Kat!

My friend **Mark Anthony**, author of the best selling and award winning book *Never Letting Go*, has greatly encouraged me to get my books in print. Thanks Mark, you are a terrific friend!

Caroline Connor, grand dame of Radionics, author of numerous books, and informative friend has applauded me in many arenas. Writing is just another area in which she believes I will thrive, thank you Caroline for your support over the last twenty-five years.

Robin Bowen Seibold, PH.D., an old friend and author of the book *To Divorce or Not,* a great counselor, has always been supportive, thanks Robin!

There are some other ***very special people*** that have applauded my writing and my efforts to be an author in one way or another throughout the years. A great big thank you goes out to **Jerry Venuti,** for his laughter, support and belief in my ability. **Tommy C.** for his faith in me, and our wonderful talks about string theory, quantum physics and torsion field energy! Eternal thanks to **Dave** *'MacGyver'* **Buckowski**. I think the 'MacGyver' says it all. And also **Joe Dow**, who I think will be most surprised when the book finally hits the market.

~And then of course there is my dearest and longtime friend and companion **John Sarno**, who has always been there to catch me when I fall! He, I am sure will be happy about this book, and that my feisty, determined nature has been put to good use for a change!

Howard David Johnson, my cover artist who puts his heart and soul into all of his work, cheered me on when he learned about the subject matter of my book. His taking the time to write me a meaningful letter meant a lot to me. Thanks David!

Geri Mach, February 9, 1940- April 2, 2011, thanks for the unexpected blessing!

Mary Linn Roby comes last, but most certainly not least! As I neared the end of assembling all of the components that make up a novel, I realized that, after all the hard work everyone had put into accomplishing this project, they deserved to have their work honored. I decided to have Mary, a professional editor then working on my memoir, read a few chapters. I was impressed by her work, she was quick witted, brutally honest and insightful. After reading *Myth of the Moon Goddess*, which she truly loved, Mary encouraged me to get it on the market as soon as possible. It was after Mary did a professional edit for me I found out that she was an award winning author of fifty two novels, who in her *spare time* labors over manuscripts of fledgling authors like me. Boy I lucked out! Thank you Mary~

-I was blessed to have a loving mother who always encouraged me and two incredible sons that were proud of me. I am sorry that they are not here on earth to share in my accomplishment, but I am aware that they encourage me with love and laughter from the other side. -

Rose Burns - Jan. 20, 1908- June 22, 1999
Russell LeMieux April 5, 1963 -March 29, 2000
David LeMieux August 7, 1964- May 29, 2010

Foreword

In **Myth of the Moon Goddess, April Rane** breathes new life into color with her fascinating and in-depth knowledge of the '*Seven Sacred Rays.*' While reading this book you'll discover a whole new way of looking at the power of color and its effect in your life. Enjoy her spellbinding story-telling as you learn about past lives and karma, *and...* discover more about yourself on every page!

~**Mark Anthony**, *best-selling author of,* **Never Letting Go**~

I am the Goddess Aradia, and this is my journal

As you read my epic tale perhaps you will find that truth is a destiny
that lies somewhere between virtue and immorality. In these pages I share
with you three lives in which I lose, and then slowly piece together my
heart and mind, to regain some hold upon the heavens and my immortal soul.

The words written here are not so much a book but an experience,
a journey if you will, deep into the core of my being. I've come from a mystical
golden sphere called the Moon, with a sworn oath upon my lips to free
women from oppression and fear.

As a traveler to your Earth I find it lush and inviting. But your world,
unlike mine, is a polarized world of black and white, male and female, good
and bad. It is balanced by karma, and love is the key.

It is possible that you will find a bit of yourself and a glimmering of truth
within these pages, for the facts of my sorcery and magic are laid bare. You
will see that in the confusing intricacies of love, hate, resentment and guilt
that are part of Earth's precious lessons, I lost my way.

Perhaps in reading this, you will be spared the mistakes I have made, as
knowledge applied, becomes wisdom. So…look well for truth; it sometimes
gives the impression of landing, when it is forever in flight, looking to find its
precarious place in the wind.

The Myth

Diana, goddess of the moon, parted the mists between the worlds and looked sadly down upon the wondrous fields of earth. Before her lay, the extraordinary blue green oceans and resplendent mountains of the once peaceful planet. With sorrow in her heart, she beckoned her daughter Aradia, and after composing herself, looked at her daughter with deep love in her eyes.

"The words I speak today are the most difficult words that will ever be uttered from these lips," she said. "Many of our women have gone to Earth and have become caught in an outrage of mistreatment from those that carry the seed. Because of this, I ask you, Aradia, to join the mortals and live among them, even though you were born unto a great royal line that hold the womb and all females that spring from it as sacred. You will be subject to their laws, and you will, at times, forget who you are. Yet, that which you will accomplish upon the Earth will spread until it cannot be denied.

"If you agree to this, you will be initiated in the temple of the Sorceress until such time as you are ready for the task ahead of you. You are a great priestess, my daughter. You are not to feel you must do this, because unless this is your *heart's desire* you will fail. Go now and listen to your innermost stirrings. Gaze into your cup of ambrosia until the answer comes."

Diana sat watching from her window seat, high above the pristine courtyard, as the newly chosen novitiates, called doves, were filing into the temple for their first lesson. They were honored to be chosen, but couldn't quite contain their excited whispers and quiet laughter as they began their dedication in the Temple of the Dove. As novitiates, they would be expected to pass a series of seven tests designed to eliminate those that would not be fit for temple life. Diana's gaze fell softly upon her daughter. Aradia moved gracefully, stopping every now and then to observe the young doves in training.

Aradia's heart was heavy, yet her head was held high. A silent tear slipped down her cheek. As she slowly climbed the spiral stairway leading to her mother's mystical chamber, she looked longingly over her shoulder at the laughing young women playing at the water fountain. Reaching the top of the stairs, she walked gracefully and knelt in front of the one who gave her life. Her heart was leaden, but her words earnest.

"From you I received the breath of life, and unto you I would give over this breath... for any reason you ask," she told her mother. "I tell you this out of the deepest love and admiration for the queen you are, and the mother you have always been. I will go gladly upon the mission set before me, because until I give over this life to the cause of the goddess, I do not have the right to fully declare myself your daughter."

"I had a vision of Arcadia in a dream many eons ago," Diana murmured in response. "She was the high priestess who led us here to the moon, to begin our lives of freedom. In the dream she spoke of you before you were born. She knew you would be a great teacher. Arcadia gave you her crown. Here, let me show you, exactly as she showed me."

Rising, Diana went to the etching box made of sand. Gracefully picking up a long ornately carved writing stick she wrote the name *Arcadia*. Taking the letter 'C,' she erased it from its place and put it above the name *Aradia*. Now, resting above the name as it did, the 'C' appeared to be a crescent moon, looking for all the world like a crown glistening in the morning light.

"Know that this mission is what you were born to do," Diana went on. "Arcadia named you. She gave you her crown, to show that you carry her name forth. Go now and shine like your name. Wear the crescent moon as a reminder of the one who gave you this gift, and with pride of your ancestry, bring this name to Earth. Many will tremble at your knowledge, and woe unto the man who tries to still your hand of magic, for your spells will be stronger than evil."

Taking her daughter's hand, Diana spoke of the life that Aradia would embrace in her journey upon earth.

"Teach and gather women to you to learn the ways of the old path, to protect them from those who would do them harm. Teach them of sisterhood and magic herbs for healing. Teach them to speak their truth and hold their ground. Teach them pride in those who came before them and awe for those who yet follow.

"Your mission on earth is to teach *heart's desire*," said Diana, "to those who cry out in the night against a system patriarchal in its nature and brutal in its actions. For all earthlings are losing sight of the goddess, as they strive to be heard above the din of war, poverty, and ignorance. I bless you, The Goddess Aradia. Hold fast to this name, for there are those who will try to eradicate it. Go forth and teach them well."

Thus began Aradia's preparation to move through the galaxies and heavens on her sacred passage to Earth, carrying with her a strong sense of duty and the belief that she was, as her mother had put it, " to make war on men," for it was those of male breeding that looked disdainfully upon those who had wombs. They lusted after them, craving their softness, yet fearing their strength. They made light of women's feelings, for such things led to *heart's desire*. This they somehow knew, although they did not truly understand. So men burned and pillaged temples and villages alike, killing women or making them slaves, changing the face of the Earth from a peaceful society to a warring one, in the name of religion and in the name of God.

After much time spent on the astral realm in preparation for her descent, Aradia was called to the Temple of Knowledge.

A great hush came over the temple as a tall, sleek goddess, wearing a shimmering turquoise robe, drifted into the room. A touch of glitter extended across her high cheek bones and flowed up into her raven hair, splashing it with twinkling stars. Golden flecks of color danced in her deep sable eyes and a smile crossed her lips as she studied Aradia.

As the two proud and beautiful goddesses stood in quiet assessment of each other, Aradia bowed her head momentarily showing respect toward her elder.

"My name is Desimena," said the goddess, her lilting, musical voice matched her ethereal beauty. "I am to be your *spirit guide* once you descend to earth. There I will assist you whenever you need guidance, advice or direction. I will never *tell* you what to do, for that would hinder your free will. I will simply, *guide.* Planet Earth is breathtakingly beautiful, but it is none-the-less a difficult school, for it is a place of polarity, choices and karma. It is my duty to inform you of the manner in which you will complete the lessons you will choose for yourself." The goddess paused, her eyes blazing with intensity.

"You have shown great courage and perseverance in your training as an initiate," she continued, "both in the Temple of the Sorceress on the Moon, and here on the astral realm in the many halls of study that assist souls in their evolution. But the initiation of the Goddess on Planet Earth is most difficult because the *Veil of Forgetfulness* is heavy upon the Earth. It is entirely possible that you will feel separated from your celestial beginnings, and it is for this reason that you have undergone such stringent instruction here on the astral realm. You have, I see, chosen your earthly family. Now it is time to choose the lessons you are to learn in Earth School."

Aradia fidgeted, aghast at the suggestion that she was to *learn* anything, as she had been under the impression that she was to be a teacher during her earthly sojourn. She was about to protest, but Desimena's commanding voice continued.

"Giving up your immortality means that you will be subjected to the laws of karma," said Desimena, "and you will not be allowed to return to your heavenly abode until you have learned your lessons *through and with* the help of the spectrum of the Seven Sacred Rays. I must ask, are you entirely sure that you wish to journey to the Planet Earth?"

Aradia tried in earnest to be reverent, but feeling that Desimena was attempting to deter her from her mission, she spoke boldly.

"I have given a pledge unto my mother. I am anxious to fulfill that promise and I am ready to descend, despite the fact that I have just learned I am going to the *School* of Planet Earth."

There was impatience and signs of rebellion in the look Aradia cast on Desimena, but in the end, she decided discretion was the better part of valor. "Will you speak to me of the Sacred Rays?" she asked, reluctantly lowering her eyes.

"I shall give you a basic understanding of the Rays. The light of the Goddess expresses itself in seven tones," said Desimena, "seven vibrations or frequencies which hold distinctive qualities. These tones move out in *waves* from the Goddess toward each soul that chooses to inhabit Planet Earth. Like attracts like; therefore the lessons that are desired by individual souls attract the most appropriate frequency to aid them with their intentions.

"The *frequency* of the *wave* determines its *color* and each frequency holds specific characteristics such as honor, faith, charisma, self-esteem, dignity or the power to command. These attributes can be used for good or ill, and can either challenge or aid individuals to evolve toward enlightenment.

"The Karmic Council," said Desimena, turning to acknowledge the colorful array of goddesses that had quietly joined her, "recommends that you begin with the Red Ray and move systematically through each ascending ray. In this way you will progress more quickly and have additional understanding of the evolution of the soul. We will now outline the Red Ray for you." And with that Desimena proceeded to summarize the first ray.

*"**Red is the color of the Ray of Sacred Purpose and Will.** The Goddess of this Ray is called* **Enchantress of the Wheel of Life and Death.** *It is the objective of this Ray to supply power and passionate intensity to evolve all beings upon Planet Earth. The **life force** of the human body is emanated from the frequency of this ray. Entities born under this ray have the ability to ignite others with passion and to assist them in finding a purpose or direction in life."*

~ "**The lessons** that will be offered to you if you choose the Red Ray will be of the nature of security. You will need to learn to accept your family such as they are, recognizing that your family of origin was picked by you to assist you in the lessons of the Red Ray. You will need to learn to express a passion for living, and recognize you will be challenged in some way to learn survival skills. You will need to discover how to become responsible, and to live an honorable life. ~ **On Earth,** if you refuse the lessons offered by this ray, you will negate life and chooses anger over love-lethargy over passion- malice over honor.

"The Key words associated with this Ray are ~ Do unto others as you would have them do unto you. After hearing the qualities of the Red Ray, do you agree with the council that you should begin there?" asked Desimena lovingly.

"Yes, as I am to *teach* when I descend, I would think that passionate intensity would be helpful," said Aradia. "Also you mentioned learning survival skills. Seeing as Earth holds a *karmic frequency,* obviously I will need to learn to survive without creating karma, as I don't intend to spend more time than I need away from my celestial home."

"Yes," said Desimena with a glint of mischief in her eye, "that *is* the challenge. But I am sure you will not spend any more time than you *need to...* on earth. No matter what, remember I will always be with you. And so, it is time-let us descend. We have made you ready for Planet Earth; I do hope Earth is ready for you!"

*There is a difference between the *soul ray* (derived from the day and time you are born,) and the *personality ray* which is fashioned by a combination of residue karma, your name and birth date, thereby creating the dominate color in your aura. It is the latter that is referred to in this book.

**The description of the remaining rays can be found in the back of the book.

Book One
Aradia, Daughter of Diana

There is a fine line between pride and humility. If you are too humble you lose yourself in meekness. Too much pride becomes arrogance, and in arrogance you lose yourself, just as surely as you do in humility that serves no purpose. ~ Desimena, spirit guide to Aradia

Our story begins approximately two thousand four hundred years ago in the city of Volsinii, a beautiful wide open plateau on top of the greenest hills in the ancient country of Etruria.

Chapter 1

"Grandmamma, where are we going?" Aradia asked, gaily skipping circles around the ageless figure leading her down the village path. "How come Sardiana can't come?"

Her grandmother could hardly keep up with the flood of questions. These were just two more in the torrent that had followed since they left home.

"We are going to see the widow Leana Figante because I am teaching you the craft and your sister doesn't have the gift," the old woman told her.

"What gift? Maybe I could give it to her."

"Yes, you would if you could child, but it doesn't work that way. Either you are born with it or not. Do not get me wrong child. Everyone has a bit of the gift. But most are afraid of things they do not understand, or cannot see. You know how you see the little people dancing around you? Have you ever seen them dancing around anyone else?"

"Yes, Grandmamma," Aradia said, squinting her eyes. "I have seen them around you. I see colors around other people, not fairies! Most of the time the colors are pretty and bright like a rainbow, but sometimes they are quite ugly. They look like the pea soup mamma makes me eat. Yuck! Or sometimes like dreary dark clouds."

"Yes, of course around me," explained Grandmother with slight impatience, yet smiling with pride at the gift her granddaughter possessed, "but what I am asking is when you go to the woods or the river and see the little folk, are they different from what you see dancing around you and me?"

"Yes…" Aradia hesitated, realizing for the first time how different they were.

"The ones at the river are gnomes, elves, and fairies, and they work with the trees and flowers to make them grow," explained her grandmother. "Then there are the special ones that you see dancing around us. These are "elementals." They work with humans and do their bidding. When you work with them, learning as you have to use the proper words and intonations, you form a special bond between the two worlds."

"What do you mean? Do their bidding?"

Grandmother shifted her weight from side to side. "Remember how nasty old man Gramaldi used to behave?" the old woman asked her.

"Oh yes, he scared all of the children. He would hide behind his bushes and jump out with an ugly mask covering his face and nothing else on. I remember the time I ran over and pulled on his...well, you know..."

"Yes, child, all of the city knows, as well. Gramaldi told all of his old cronies he would hurt you because of that! Ha! I hope you pulled it hard enough to hurt the old *bastido*. I sent the elementals to sour his cows and poison his pigs," she added, touching Aradia's hair lovingly. "But best of all, his chickens flew the coup! Furthermore, I warned him that if he harmed one little hair on your head, he would not awake to see the new day. And if he jumped out at the *bambinos* again, his manhood would turn black and fall off. These, my child, are the things the elementals can help you with."

"How can they make his, you know...turn black and fall off?"

Grandmother looked at her beloved granddaughter through blue-green eyes that seemed to hold the depths of the ocean. Her long dark silver streaked hair worn braided on top of her head had a mind of its own and she was forever tucking stray strands behind her ears. Her slightly hunched back and shoulders were the only evidence of her years. Smooth olive skin, unlined except for the crinkles at the corners of her eyes, radiated health and vigor, giving the impression of timeless youth.

"Ah, we are here. Not one moment too soon," she said as they entered a house which was like any of the other houses in Volsinii, long, narrow and dimly lit.

"Come, child, it is your time. Let us go in. You will do the spell. You will use the words I have taught you and you will call on the elementals. Be firm in your intentions when you call them to dance, and strong with your words when you send them to do your bidding."

The widow Figante, a short plump woman dressed in the customary black of the village widows, warmly welcomed them and chatted like a magpie as she led them to a small room in the back of the house. Her thin brown hair, streaked with gray, was pulled back in a bun revealing a roundish face. Her deep brown eyes darted expectantly to grandmother and then granddaughter. Tools for the garden hung on the wall, and the room smelled of animal dung.

"Leana, Leana," said grandmother, wrinkling her nose, "This is the first spell my granddaughter will make. Is it necessary that we use this unpleasant room?"

"But...it is for privacy we come to this room," huffed Leana, irritated at the rebuke. "You told me *privacy*!"

"I did not tell you animal dung, huh?" spat Grandmother, while sniffing the foul air with disdain. "No matter. We have wasted enough time. Leana, tell the child what it is you need. I have taught her well!"

As the widow Figante woefully recited the tale of her un-betrothed daughter, Madeline, to Aradia, Grandmother noticed the deep look of understanding in her granddaughter's eyes and she nodded in approval. Aradia decisively stepped toward her grandmother who was holding the brightly colored bag she always carried. Aradia's precocious manner slipped as childish glee lit her radiant face when she excitedly drew open the ribbon and removed a sprig of basil, a pinch of sea salt and a vial of sacred rose oil used for making love spells, all nestled amongst the many herbs and potions within the colorful sack.

With a quick wave of her hand Aradia motioned the two women to step back. Casting a protective circle of salt on the crude, dusty floor, she stepped into the center, preparing to open the veil between the worlds. Her small voice became deep, confident, and full of arcane mystery as she proceeded to call upon the lofty ones. Using the secret and sacred names of the mysterious leaders of the elementals, her special friends arrived as always colorfully dancing in the light as she chanted her spell.

"Gob of the mighty earth, protect us and hear our plight.
Paralda of the mighty air do not make Madeline wait.
Dejin who dances in fire of might, place Madeline in her lover's sight
Necksa bind together these lovers and for all time hold them tight."

Turning slowly and then more rapidly, her gaily tinted robe became a swath of color as she danced in the middle of the circle. Casting basil into the air, she conjured the protective genies of the four directions. Holding fast to the rose oil, Aradia passionately sang out the ancient Etruscan words that her grandmother had taught her. Kneeling down in reverence, as if taking a sacred vow, she placed drops of rose oil ever so lightly onto the palms of her hands. The warmth of the oil permeated the whole of her body, traveling ever so slowly up her arms, reaching and going through the top of her head. Closing her eyes, she continued rocking back and forth, forming words that became a chant.

"Dejin, who dances in fire of might, place Madeline in her lover's sight.
Dejin, who dances in fire of might, place Madeline in her lover's sight."

After a few moments had passed, she opened her eyes and looked directly at the widow Figante. "Place mallow in a colored pot outside your door. Shortly a man of honor will come to court your daughter." She lowered her eyes. "It is done. So be it."

Chapter 2

"Aradia, you frightened me! What are you doing up in a tree?" exclaimed Sardiana in shock, as she peered out of the library window.

"I am watching a spider weave her web, and reminiscing about Grandmamma. Although it has been many years since she passed, I still miss her so. It was she that taught me that the spider web is to remind us that life is eternal. Then again, I believe it also teaches us not to weave yarns, or we might get caught up in them." Aradia's eyes misted over with rich memories. For a brief moment she gave herself over to the past.

"Well…no matter; back to your problem. By the way, where has he gone?"

Sardiana turned her head with an air of insouciance that didn't quite suit her. "Whom do you speak of?"

"The statesman of course! You know perfectly well to whom I refer. Trying that look of indifference is not getting you out of this conversation!"

"He's looking for Father. He caught me…unaware," stammered Sardiana, her face blushing with embarrassment. "I did not know that there was anyone in here. I – I know that he was being condescending, but I… "

"Mother has taught us well," interrupted Aradia. "You carry the royal blood and as such, never act subservient to anyone! So he is a councilman with haughty airs. I do not care."

Then, realizing she was sitting in a tree speaking to her sister about etiquette, she fixed an errant curl and brushed her dirty robe. Searching to regain some dignity, Aradia looked adoringly at her younger sister.

Deep rich mahogany hair and dark twinkling eyes framed her lovely expressive face that exploded into dimples when she smiled.

Yes, she thought. Sardiana will make a good wife for a rich and loving landowner who wants many children.

"I am going to the river to study my letters. Tis up to me to carry forth such matters, as you have no interest in them," she teased her sister, as she climbed down close enough to pull on her sister's long, shiny braid.

"You hide my lack of studies because I am the only one that knows of your comings and goings," Sardiana replied quietly. "If Mother knew you secretly went to the river, she would be frantic! It is a long way and very dangerous. Whenever you decide to go traipsing around the countryside on a whim, I pray to Vulcan to protect you and to Minerva to give you the sense not to do it."

Now it was Sardiana's turn to place her hands on her slender hips.

They glared at each other for a moment, and then together burst into uproarious laughter. Aradia reached in through the open window to hug her sister, both of them laughing so hard that tears came to their eyes, tears that brimmed with memories and the great love they shared for one another.

"I do not use the river road," Aradia said briskly. To hide her emotions she paused to tuck her flute and the scroll she had been reading more securely in her tunic's belt. "I have a special way. It is much shorter."

"What other way could there be?" questioned her sister suspiciously.

"Come. Must I teach you everything?" Aradia teased.

Together the two girls went out through the sitting room where they encountered one of their three brothers.

"Kouros, *mea bambino*, what are you doing here? The others have left to view the metal works," said Aradia chidingly to her youngest brother as they sauntered gaily through the room.

"Do not speak to me like that or I shall call Mother and she will set you right," Kouros said bravely, sticking his tongue out and squeezing his eyes so tight that his outrageously long lashes feathered his cheek

"*Mea bambin*o," Aradia taunted, as she and Sardiana headed for the front door in gales of laughter. "When father sees that you are given a long robe like the rest of us, to cover those ugly chicken legs, then I will stop calling you my baby boy."

"It is good that he knows that you tease the older boys as well, or he would take it to heart and cry his eyes out. He loves you so much," she said with an unusual show of boldness. "We all do, but you test our reserved nature. We often wonder if you were dropped on our doorstep when you were a child."

As Sardiana walked beside her sister, she thought once more of the heavenly scent of colorful wildflowers she would gather from the garden to decorate the table for the evening. They always sat for their heavy meal at the end of the day. Flowers and a brightly colored cloth, made the evening a memorable occasion. Dinner conversation was truly engaging, touching, as it did on many subjects. Mother did not care for debating issues nor did Sardinia, but Aradia loved to air what were sometimes outrageous views that enlivened the meal, baiting her brothers and inevitably besting them at their own game, something Sardinia always enjoyed watching. She also enjoyed watching her father nod in approval as Aradia spoke, and smile with support when she was done. Aradia would be stoned to death in some cultures for her ideas, thought Sardiana. It's good that our people have such a high regard for our women.

Sardiana shuddered at the thought of Aradia getting married and having to live in another land. She had heard of other cultures in which it was commonplace for women to be beaten, and goddesses to be berated, something she found difficult to understand, for her people worshipped both gods and goddesses alike. They were always equal one to the other.

Aradia slowed her natural step and cocked her head to one side. Seeing her sister's grave concern she asked, "What are you thinking about, *bella sorella*?"

"I am thinking *lobatz*, it's crazy to go with you!" said Sardiana, tapping her head as she spoke. Yet hesitantly she followed Aradia and they meandered unhurriedly out of the main gate of the city and began making their way down the sloped road that led to the river.

Looking back over her shoulder to see if anyone was watching them, Sardiana was awed, as always, by the sight. Volsinii, the small village in which they lived, was built on a citadel of rock that reached high into the clouds. Flowers gently swaying in the breeze and brightly colored flowers sprouted from the pots that decorated every balcony. Sardiana realized she was holding her breath at the ennobled sight.

The beloved faces of Jupiter, Juno, and Minerva were sculpted upon the gate with terra cotta, and they were awash with lively colors that pleased the eye, each color depicted the dynamic energy of the god or goddess it represented. The sculptures told the tales of their wonderful, but sometimes errant, gods and goddesses. These deities had taken the place of the olden gods of Etruria when Rome had begun encroaching upon their territories. To keep peace Volsinii had succumbed to the changes. After all, the gods and goddesses hadn't changed, just the names they were openly called.

Bright red was for the power and passion of Jupiter; guardian of the law and protector of justice who dealt out harsh punishment in order to serve truth though it was rumored that he tended to stretch the truth in matters of philandering against his wife Juno, who presided over marriage and childbearing. Tinted the same lush green of the trees and grass was Juno, the earth mother whose expressive face bejeweled the wall. Seldom was it mentioned that she had a jealous nature, only that she railed at her husband on occasion for his indiscretions. The Daughter of Jupiter, Minerva, emblazoned the triad with radiant gold, reminiscent of the early morning sun. Minerva's strength, evident in the chiseled contours of her face made it easy to believe the rumors that she sprang from the head of Jupiter, fully armored and ready for battle.

When they came upon a tall, thin fieldstone wall, Aradia moved behind it quickly, not wanting others to see the trail she had found.

"Here it is," she whispered, pulling her sister after her.

"Oh, no, on the head of Juno I shall disown you!" Sardiana cried. "Are you mad? I will never go down that path!"

So seldom did her sister raise her voice, that it gave Aradia pause to look down the narrow path that seemed to plunge straight down to the winding river. For a moment, she doubted her own sanity, but then she yielded to her spontaneous nature, and laughing, she turned toward the path.

"Life is a journey," she said." If you are not willing to take the first step, then the journey ends before it begins."

"I intend to live my life, not end it foolishly!" Sardiana exclaimed nervously, looking at Aradia in dismay, only to see her sister suddenly clasp her head in both hands.

"What is wrong?" she demanded. "Was it a vision? What did you see?"

Aradia had many visions but they usually did not cause pain. As the vision intensified she steadied herself and sat down on the ground.

"Are you all right?" asked Sardiana as she bent over her sister.

"Yes, you are right," her sister told her, removing her sandals. "Never follow me on this path. It is very dangerous!"

"Then why do you go?" pleaded Sardiana, sitting down beside her.

"Sar, I want to tell you how much I love you," Aradia said earnestly. "The gods blessed me when you were born. You are all that is good. You put me to shame at times with the things I do, but I have this lust for life. It goes so deep, that I cannot believe it began in this body. I know that you do not believe we live many lives. Father is patient, not pushing his ideas on all of you. He allows you to search your hearts for what feels right. But I have seen the sacred writings of the priests and I know in my heart that life is eternal. Our bodies are just specks of dust in the wind. Some lives we gather much to us, and other lives we blow hither and to, with nothing to anchor us. I want you to know, Sardiana, that you have been my anchor."

"This sounds so final!" her sister said, cautiously looking over the steep incline. "You are not running off, are you? Perhaps I should go with you."

"I am not running off!" Aradia said, rising. "But I do not want you to come with me."

"Then you must promise not to put any spells on anyone when you are gone. I heard about the mysterious curse you put upon Sobona. Her ox keeled over and died. According to Mother, it was because her ox knocked over our gate, trampled our flowers, and scared our donkey."

"There was much more to it, *dolce sorella*," Aradia assured her. "Latna Sobona is a vicious woman who hurts young children. She put a curse on…well, it does not matter. Rest your mind, for I only repay what has been given out. If I use magic for my own revenge, it will come back to me threefold."

"Yes, I know you are not evil," Sardiana said. "It's only that I worry about your powers, about the things you…well, all of it."

"I will walk you back to the main gate." Aradia hesitated, thinking about the vision.

"No, I will be fine," Sardiana said, smiling radiantly as she embraced Aradia. "You teach bravery in your wake, do you know that? Yet, I'm not brave enough to traverse that incline with you. Although, I will certainly look our councilman in the eye upon his next visit. You know, I love you too! I know not why you spoke so just now, but I always have known how much you love me."

As soon as she was gone, Aradia moved deftly and steadily down the dangerous path. It was mostly rock, though there were places that were sandy and slippery where she had to travel slowly with the surefootedness of a mountain goat, carefully wedging each foot in crevices found only by memory. Taking care that her flute did not slip into the darkness of the cavern below, she remembered the time when her father had presented it to her and the sweet surprise in his eyes as she played him a mysterious and soothing melody. It had helped, he told her later, with the unease he was feeling about allowing Vetus, the Greek statesman, to visit their home in hopes of setting a marriage between him and Aradia. When the song came to an end, she remembered, Vetus had entered the room in search of her father to firm up the arrangements. When he was told that it was not up to Aradia's father alone, that she needed to agree, the statesman was shocked and could not believe she had any influence in the choice her parents would make for her future.

As she continued to clamber down the rock face, Aradia remembered how her father had told Vetus bluntly that many women of Etruria were not only educated, but were allowed to take part in choosing a husband. Outraged, Vetus had strutted around the room like a rooster, puffed up with his own pride and his belief in his own importance. His stately face turned an angry bright red and his dark brown eyes narrowed as he made his pronouncement.

"It goes beyond being outside convention," he declared. "It's shocking, and will cause moral decay for the Etruians."

Vetus may have been a handsome man, with his muscular frame, arresting, deep set eyes and thick wavy brown hair, and he may have been a well versed scholar, but Aradia would have nothing to do with a man who did not treat his woman as an equal…or revere her!

Well no, she mused. If a man puts you upon a pedestal, eventually he will become disillusioned, as pedestals are precarious places. *How my mind is wandering today.*

Peering down the steep incline, she was so glad she had not let Sardiana come. The vision she had had of her sister sprawled on the ground must have been a warning.

Thinking of the vision as she continued down, she tried to remember visions she'd had that had not come true. But only those in which she saw herself as a bit older and in a different land had not yet come to pass. *I must stop these maudlin thoughts!*

Instead she began looking forward to the quiet time she would spend at the river. She called it the Tiger River, although she knew its real name was the Tiber. She wished someday to see a tiger. No, she thought, I *wish to see it all!*

When she emerged from the path at the bottom of the incline, she looked furtively to see that she was alone. Yes, today there was only welcoming silence and the sparkling, meandering river.

Smiling, she walked to her special spot, hidden from view by trees and tall reeds. Here, she could watch the sunset at day's end; then as usual, she would have to climb hurriedly up the incline before dark. She knew she took chances, and many times she ripped her clothing as she bound up the path, trying to make it to the city gate before it closed for the night. More than once the gate was closed and she had to climb over the large sculpted stones on either side of the gate.

Settling comfortably into the nook of her favorite tree, whose branches hung low out over the water in the bend of the river, she reached up and undid her braids which were wrapped around her head like a crown. Removing the pins that held her rich, titian hair and pulling her hands through its softness, she stared at her reflection in the river. She enjoyed gazing at herself here. Her remarkable blue-green eyes flashed back at her with vitality and animation. Vetus had told her they were the color of the Mediterranean. Sea green, he had called them. He said they were the same color as the eyes of the sirens, mermaids that lured sailors to their death with their sensual song.

He had asked her if she could sing and she said she could, and then in order to amuse herself and perhaps to frighten him, she droned a lullaby loudly and quite off key for although she could not sing a single true note, she loved to play her flute, not in a conventional manner, but making sounds that took her dreamily to faraway places.

Aradia always felt refreshed when she came away from the river. It restored her. Its mystery filled her. The calm of the river, the sounds of her flute, and the little ones, the elementals that came to dance for her, were all balm for her soul.

Sardiana had recently asked how she could put spells on people, but the elementals were Aradia's secret, eager to do her bidding. Aradia was glad that no one was here today. Many times her afternoons were gobbled up by women willing to walk down the long dusty road, to beg for her attention. They came to her with small matters to be taken care of: a husband that was not paying them attention of late; a child whose bed was wet; a maid who had stolen something. Only when she had performed her spells would they leave her in peace to hide the coins they gave her in her special place under the snarled and half buried tree roots, where she kept a bronze box. Her mother would be angry if she knew of her small business. But stop Aradia could not as she knew somehow it was her mission to help women with such matters.

Chapter 3

Undressing and slipping silently into the cool refreshing water, Aradia allowed the river's crystal clear silkiness to enshroud her in a vestment made of undines, the elementals of water. She called them water fairies, and they delighted in the fact that she could see them. Joyfully adorning her body in a blush of azulene blue and sheathing her in safety, they carried her effortlessly along the serene, tranquil current of the river.

After her swim, lying hidden from view, she dried her lithe and agile body in the sun. Looking up, she noticed the slant of the golden orb in the cloudless sky, and knew that sunset was not far behind. Realizing with reluctance that her day at the river would soon be over, she decided to get dressed and meditate a bit before leaving.

Aradia slipped back into her slightly smudged but comfortable robe and settled back in, snuggling against her special tree as her eyes followed a large crow circling in the distance. Somehow, it brought back a memory from last year, when the priest had come to do the *haruspices*, a clairvoyant reading on the liver of a bull sacrificed each year before harvest. Since she was now of an age to take her grandmother's place in the pre-harvest festivities the priest had asked her to do a special reading.

Shivering, she remembered the deep trance she had gone into and how strange it felt. She had been shocked by what the priest had recounted, that perhaps she had prophesized some kind of invasion, but he was not quite sure. After all, since this was her first time, the priest had assured her that she could be mistaken. Shrugging his shoulders, he had told her not to worry, although he had made sure every word of her prophesy was written down on the scrolls of sacred parchment he carried for just such a purpose. The words of the prophecy came back with a jolt!

"Down from the north in the month of the bull,
Men with false faces will come through the gates.
Just before sunset on a fair and fine day.
False faces on the inside; true faces on the outside; no faces on the
gate."

Had that portent of disaster been tied to the vision of her sister sprawled on the ground of the city that she'd had earlier. Chills racked her body and pure terror permeated her being, as once again she saw in her mind's eye that same vision of her sister. This time, she knew…her vision of today was tied to the clairvoyant reading the priest had written down on the day of her prophecy.

Suddenly remembering that the men had taken the sons of the city to the metal works and that they would return before sunset, she was overwhelmed by the certainty that she must warn her father. Struggling to her feet, she cried, "Oh, Goddess! Not Sardiana!"

No longer capable of thinking clearly, she ran blindly toward the incline and started to climb quickly up the path and found relief when, reaching the top and looking to the city gate, all seemed to be quiet. Perhaps she was just being foolish, but she ran anyway, forgetting her sandals. Her breath was labored as she reached the gate, and at first she saw no one.

And then she saw a man looking down at her from the top of the wall. It was not a familiar face. She let out a terrified scream as a dark, grisly warrior jumped down, landing heavily beside her. She felt a sharp blow on the top of her head. Inky blackness followed, deep as a cave and dreamless.

Slowly regaining consciousness, Aradia was shocked at the menacing pandemonium taking place in her once serene city. Strange brutal warriors in dark, torn britches and light colored robed men and women from the city were locked in battle. She had no idea how long she had lain by the gate. Struggling to get to her feet she found herself tripping over something. In utter horror, she saw that it was a body. Wiping away the blood pouring into her eyes from her head wound, she saw bodies lying all around her on the ground.

One of the foul smelling warriors pushed her, knocking her into the wall. Frantically, she began to run, rushing past houses heading towards her own. As she pushed open the partially ajar front door, she saw her mother and brother Kouros crouched together in a corner. Her mother's long dark hair had fallen over her still face. She sheltered her son to her breast. As if in a daze, she walked toward them, knowing that they were dead.

Aradia knelt down. Brushing aside her mother's dark wavy hair, she softly kissed her forehead and touched the silken hair of her baby brother's head as she kissed him as well. Then, as if in a dream, she walked purposefully to a heavy chest in the corner of the room where the swords were kept. Running her hand over the triple golden braid that surrounded the family crest, her heart ached with the knowledge that things would never be the same again, that she would never hear her mother's voice or her brothers' laughter.

Finding that the swords were gone, she squeezed the edges of the chest with every bit of strength she could muster and slowly walked out back to the donkey pen. In the back of the pen they kept a large knife for butchering the animals. It was still there. Hesitantly, she reached for it.

For a long moment, she thought of using the crude, cold knife on herself, because the reputation of the violent and depraved warriors from the north had preceded them. In the end she would be raped, killed or taken as a slave. Aradia gingerly pointed the blood stained rusty knife toward her heart, but then she thought of Sardiana. *I must find her!*

Hiding the knife in the folds of her robe, she bravely went through the front door, back into the clash of swords and the groans of dying aged men that had come out to fight. She knew they wanted her alive, and that gave her an advantage. Perhaps there was time for her to warn the men coming from the metal works.

Frantically running toward the gate, she raised one strong leg and violently kicked a lunging warrior in the groin; he hunched over in pain giving her time to escape.

Heading again for the gate, wiping the blood from her eyes from the still bleeding head wound, she spotted a robe of soft saffron the color Sardiana had worn that day. Expecting the worst, she ran toward the prone lifeless body. Her eyes blurred as tears coursed down her cheeks. The vision she had seen earlier plagued her mind, as she knelt down beside the body of her beloved sister. Placing the knife she had hidden under her robe on the blood drenched entrance of the city, she looked to the heavens for a moment, fully aware at last of the immensity of the atrocities taking place.

Hugging her sister to her breast, Aradia wept. Rocking the slender body as she had done when she had witnessed her birth, she tried to sing a lullaby but only a guttural moaning escaped her trembling lips. She reached blindly for the knife she had placed on the ground. Plunging it into her heart could not be more painful than this. But when she raised it high, her vision became blurred as her shaking hand moved closer to her chest. She was awed by the thought of death and became mesmerized watching the progress of the chipped and rusty knife as it slowly moved toward her heart. Ashen, her breath became shallow and she collapsed over the body of her fallen sister.

The city was quiet. It seemed as if a black cloud had descended from the heavens, causing a deep sleep upon the people. Like a plague the dreaded dark warriors from the north had nearly obliterated the emerald city of Volsinii.

The matronly women and the old men were dead, and the few young boys who had not gone to the metal works had also been killed. Only the girls of marrying age were still alive, huddled together on the dirty floor of the meeting hall, the largest building in the city that until now had been thought of as a citadel of safety.

Frightened and in shock, blood on their bodies and garments, the girls huddled together. Their hands were tied tightly with hemp rope behind their backs like animals being readied for slaughter; their feet loosely bound allowed them the slightest of movement, and each girl was chained by rope to one other girl, making it impossible to run away.

At sunset, when the men of the city came home from the metal works, they were indeed, just as Aradia had seen in her vision, taken by surprise by the warriors with false faces, and although they fought valiantly, they had no chance. A few of the invading warriors from the north died, but in the end the city was awash in a sea of the blood of its inhabitants.

The thunderous brooding warriors had plundered every house, pillaging and ransacking anything of value. They screamed words at the girls that were held captive, their guttural language nearly impossible to follow.

Aradia, after fighting her way through a bleak hallway of darkness, was stunned to awaken and find herself in the meeting hall with seven other girls. Slowly as if in a dream, a nightmare that would not end, she clawed her way into the light of consciousness. Knowing that her life depended on it, she valiantly strove to clear her head, and despite the hot acrid blood that ran down her forehead to her cheeks and into her mouth, she resolved to show no weakness.

With large calloused hands, the warriors gruffly prodded the girls toward the cistern in the center of the town courtyard, commanding them to drink and wash. Lattia, the girl tied to Aradia, crumpled into hysterics, her tear streaked face awash in terror, but Aradia could not hold or comfort her, as her hands were tied behind her back.

When the warrior came back again, reaching out menacingly to grab Lattia, Aradia kicked him in the groin. Cursing, he doubled over in pain before righting himself. He then grabbed Aradia, shaking and slapping her violently. And when she spat and shrieked in his tongue, calling him bastard born and a coward as well, he pulled out a knife, reached down and cut Aradia and Lattia apart, although leaving Aradia's hands tied.

He would, he told her, receive extra spoils for bringing such a luscious piece and one who could speak their language to the attention of the captain.

"This is one that speaks our language!" he told the Captain puffing out his chest and pushing Aradia roughly in front of him. "A tasty bit, don't you think? She is yours!"

Aradia, straining at her ties, desperately tried to free her hands while spitting furiously at the captain. He became enraged that she showed no fear, and fiercely grabbed her arms and shook her menacingly while shouting, "You stupid bitch! You whore! You'll not do that again!"

She spoke in Etruscan, gritting her teeth, ignoring his words. "You think to use me against my own people? It will not happen!"

The captain's hands bit into her shoulder as he shook her severely, but once again, she spoke only in her language.

He gruffly barked to his man, "She speaks not our language. Take her away!"

⁓⁂⁓

The next morning the invading warriors, their vests and britches bulging with copper plates and cups, were loading as much plunder as the donkeys could carry. A few men came into the city leading at least fifty horses, one of which Aradia and Lattia, still lashed together, were told to mount.

Leaving the dead of the city exposed to the elements made Aradia's heart wrench. They had not been given the benefit of the grand ceremonies and eulogies that were part of their customs, and as they passed through the gates of the city, she saw that the faces of Juno, Jupiter, and Minerva had been destroyed. *False faces on the inside, true faces on the outside, no faces on the gate.* She shuddered at the absolute truth of those words.

When she saw the bodies of both of her elder brothers lying on the road slashed nearly beyond recognition, she had no tears left to shed, although she could feel them in her heart.

She did not see the body of her father, which was a good thing since she knew by now that she could not take any more pain. She would always remember him as he was, all of his five and one half inches in height, alive and smiling, proudly standing straight and tall. She had thought him the most handsome of men, with his broad shoulders, and sinewy build, hair the color of a raven in flight, and deep dark eyes that held both merriment and kindness. Thinking of him, his last words vibrated through her whole being.

"You are taller than I," he had told her. "It is your grandmother you take after. She was the formidable matriarch of our people. She told grand tales about female warriors who came from the sky eons ago, and she claimed that she was a part of the royal bloodline that issued forth from these female warriors. You come from great beginnings. You, like her, shall not be tied to convention. However, my dear, I do hope that you shall not be hung, as she was, for your unconventional life."

He had chuckled when he had said that, no doubt, Aradia thought now, because he had not been able to imagine such a thing happening twice in this quiet hamlet.

20

Aradia looked down at her garment. There was so much blood on her robe, blood caked in her hair and underneath her nails! But the knife, she questioned in her mind. Try as she could, she could not piece together what had taken place.

They rode for hours. By the time they stopped, she was stiff and sore. When one of the men came to her horse and tried to help her down, she kicked him in the face, at which he yanked her off her horse, ripping her away from Lattia, and started to beat her.

"Stop!" yelled the captain. "You will disfigure her and we will not get the highest price!"

The captain then came over and slapped her hard across the face with an open hand. "Do it like this," he said, laughing as she fell to the ground. "Like this, it heals and leaves no scar."

Holding her cheek, Aradia sat up and began to call on the elementals. She was not sure if she could do magic, for the secret was in the breath. Being focused was, she knew, essential and when there was anger, it took the focus away. Struggling to focus she began to breathe deeply, and then she chanted softly the names of the powers.

"From the east I call to you Paralda, bring your Sylphs to me
From the south I call to you Dejin, bring your Vulcani to me
From the west I call to you Necksa, bring your Undini to me
From the north I call to you Gob, bring your Gnomes to me"

Glancing at the captain, Aradia thought, it would be more powerful if I could have a bit of his hair. If it became necessary she would get it. But, for now, this would suffice. She began chanting again in earnest.

One of the warriors, hearing her, came over and kicked her. "Quiet!" he roared, and Aradia shut out the outside world and went deep inside. She could see the weakness of the one who had just kicked her. He was frightened of water. She would remember that.

Aradia concentrated on the captain. She asked herself. What is his weakness? She could not make it out. Every time she concentrated on him, it became dark. Perhaps he is frightened of the dark. I will see if he sleeps near the fire tonight, or keeps a torch going. I will then know, as it is always good to know the weakness of your enemy.

"I thank the rulers of the elements for giving their aid," she said as the elementals began to dance about her. She motioned towards the captain. "He is why I called you. I bid you bring him misery. Go and have it done," she added as she closed her eyes and murmured, "It is done, so be it."

The burly captain sat on his haunches, raising a metal cup containing brew to his thickly bearded face. A deep white scar ran across his forehead and over to his left ear, which had been partially severed years ago. Suddenly, he bent and clutched his stomach, as he went running toward the bushes pulling down his britches. He was gone a long while, and when he returned, his ruddy skin was ashen, and he stooped as he walked.

Next Aradia concentrated on the man who had beat her because she was chanting. As she watched him moving toward the water to fill his pouch, she summoned the elementals and whispered, "That man is frightened of the water. Use that against him." And then, closing her eyes, she said, "It is done, so be it."

She watched the man trying to get clean water. Cautiously stepping in to the cold wet pond, he suddenly stumbled, sank to his chest, panicked, and started flailing around, which made him sink deeper.

The men milling around began laughing and no one helped him. In a panic, he grasped for a log just barely within his reach, but it was slippery and he slid deeper into the water.

Only then did the captain call to one of his men to go and help, saying, "We have lost enough men in battle. We do not need to lose another due to his own stupidity."

Oh, Minerva, great Goddess of Wisdom, Aradia prayed silently, help me to use my powers only when it is deserved. I ask that you keep me strong through this time so I may aid these girls, for they are terrified and frightened of death. They do not know as I do that we will never die, and that the eternal wheel of life continues.

An abyss of sadness washed over her. Sardiana, my loving sister, you will never know what it is to marry, to have children. I will never again see your smiling face, nor that of mother and father. I will never be able to feel the love between us, or hold you in my arms.

Aradia remembered the trusting face of her little brother in the arms of her mother, as she comforted him. Her mother had shielded him, comforting him as she faced the warrior bravely.

"Ah, Mama, you had such strength, such love for your bambinos," she whispered before dismissing the elementals. "Your work is done," she told them. "Be gone until I call upon you again to do my bidding." She reached her hands to the sky.

"Unto the air I give you yours,
Unto the fire I give you yours.
Unto the water I give you yours,
Unto the earth I give you yours."

She touched the earth with her hands, giving back the power unto the earth. "I give thanks. It is done. So be it."

Chapter 4

Aradia fell into a deep sleep. When she awoke, she found food in her lap, scraps of dried meat and a root of some sort. A dark hulking warrior came toward them, rubbing his short grizzled beard. Aradia recoiled from him in disgust as he approached her with lust in his eyes. Powerfully built, he would be a formidable enemy in battle. He was one who enjoyed the kill.

As he tied her to Lattia, she whispered to him in his language, "You are bastard born, as is your mother." Her accent and words were perfect.

He shook her and said, "What game do you play? You speak my tongue perfectly, but only to me?"

"I will bring much gold to you. I am good luck. If you tell your captain, he will keep all the gold for himself. I will line your pockets. Keep me in good care."

Her voice was low and promising. She knew his weakness was greed, and was not surprised when, at the mention of gold, he licked his lips.

"I want to ride by myself, not with her!" Aradia said, throwing back her head and looking him directly in the eyes. "Loosen my hands. I will tell you later how it is that I am worth immense wealth, and that it would do you well to take great care of me."

Slowly taking out his small knife used to cut his food he made a show of scraping the dirt out from underneath his filthy nails. His voice became a low menacing growl. "If you deceive me I will kill you!" he warned her.

"Yes, I can tell how powerful you are," Aradia told him in a low voice, stealing a glance at the captain. "We must be very careful. You deserve great wealth, not just a small share of what the captain chooses to gives you." Aradia spoke softly, so that he would lean forward. She knew this would allow him to think he was conspiring against the captain.

"If your captain learns I speak your language," she continued, "he will demand a great price for me and give you only a small pittance. I will tell you of my lineage and how you can gain by it when I feel I can trust you."

During the afternoon, Aradia managed to ride up beside all of the girls who, because of the discomfort they were suffering were in various stages of depression and fear until she told them that she had a plan to free them once they were brought into the city.

"Be brave and beseech the Goddess Minerva for strength and wisdom. We are warriors, just like our captors, and must use strategy if we plan to escape," she said with whispered assurance. "We will otherwise be sold, and bought by Malakas, the desert nomads, who will subject us to their rule and treat us cruelly."

At the same time that she was spreading the word, Aradia watched every move their captors made. She observed how they rode and she listened to them talk. She spoke to the dark warrior again and found out his name was Zantaunt.

The day's ride had come to an end and as the meal of roots and dried meat was being served, there was a large amount of noise within the camp. Aradia looked at the setting sun and prayed to Juno to show her the way. She prayed to Vulcan to give her courage and of course, to Minerva for wisdom. She refused to eat. She felt if she partook of their food she would submit. She had fasted before, and was used to going without food to make her powers stronger. Instead, she drank lots of water and went into a deep trance to seek out a vision, only to find that nothing would come to her. Perhaps on the morrow she would see more clearly what she needed to do. This was her last thought before falling into a deep undisturbed sleep.

After many hours of riding, the hot sun directly overhead alerted the warriors it was time to stop for their midday meal. As they began to dismount, one of their outriders rode toward them excitedly. Aradia was close enough to overhear what was being said.

Aradia felt relief, for they were just north of the town of Norchia, which was close to the city of Tarquinia. Norchia was noted for its tombs of the city's nobles, and temple of Mythris. She had been to Norchia once before with her father and remembered that the tombs were particularly impressive. Aradia thought of her people, and once again, became saddened. They deserved dignified burials! They had a stately family tomb waiting for them! Still, it did no good to think of these matters. She knew she must concentrate on her plan for escape.

When they mounted again, she noticed that they were now following the Marta River leading west. Was it possible they were headed for the seaport of Tarquinia? Since it was an active seaport and a city with thousands of people where, surely, selling slaves would be no trouble, that would make sense. When they had skirted around the city of Bolsena, she thought it had been because it was too close to Volsinii perhaps, and the warriors feared some of the sheep ranchers from the area would recognize one of the girls. Their captors from the North came from the upper Po Valley, which was north of the great cities of Etruria.

The warriors from the Po Valley felt they owed no allegiance to the original twelve cities of Etruria. In ancient times it was believed that the twelve cities were sacred and that hence no one would dare to attack one of them because all would retaliate. It was also understood that the oracles would know who the bandits were and that they would not be safe anywhere. Although those beliefs had lessened over time, Aradia noticed that the men from the Po Valley did seem to be taking some precautions to hide what they had done, but more to protect the goods they had stolen and the profit they would get from the girls than for any other reason.

Aradia cringed as she thought of the girls and how much they had suffered already, and every time she thought of the family she had so cruelly lost, she ached inside. A vivid picture of the desecration of her city, preoccupied her thoughts. The remembrance of the heavy reek of blood, the aroma of flowers and the smell of fear as she rode away from the only home she had ever known, haunted her.

In order to keep herself from drowning in sadness, Aradia tried to distract herself by naming the twelve cities. The first was Tarquinia, which she thought in ancient times had been called Tyrrhen, after the brothers who had founded it. The story of how the cities of Etruria were founded had always fascinated Aradia. So she busied herself remembering what her father had told her about the beginning of each: Veii, Bolsena, Vulci, and Arezzo…

After her self-induced history lesson, which was, she realized, simply putting off the inevitable, she steeled herself to what had to be done. Riding close to Zantaunt, she spoke to him in a low voice.

"I am of the same blood as King Torintia, who is a direct descendent of the great King Tyrrhen," she said. "King Torintia will pay well for my recovery, but I will not cooperate if you do not free all of the girls. I will tell you exactly how to present yourself to the king's court so that you may get an audience. But this I will not do, until you see to it that all the girls are free. I care not how you accomplish this. When this is done, then I will tell you what you need to know. My decision has been made. I will speak not a word if you do not release all of us. You can torture me but it will not work for I would rather be dead than to have the blood of these girls on my hands."

"I will think on this," said Zantaunt. "I need to have one other man with me. I will see who I can trust, as this is not an easy matter. The Capitan watches us like a hawk."

"I see that this is true, but you will outsmart him. I know that you are very strong and brave, and deserve much favor. I will tell the king how you rescued me, and may' hap he will have a place for you. Would that itself not be worth your trouble? The rewards can be so great!"

Leering at Aradia's breast, he said, practically drooling with lust. "You could reward me with a taste of you."

"Then I would not be worth much to the king," Aradia told him, daringly. "All for nothing, wouldn't you say? He would not reward you for tarnished goods."

Her mind was in a jumble as she thought of the horrors inflicted on her people. Shaking with rage, she could see on the faces of the girls that they carried a deep shame from the dishonor they had suffered at the hands of the soldiers.

Aradia could not understand how she had escaped without being raped! The girls could not look each other in the eye. They cowered each time one of their captors went near them. She hated to see these vibrant young women, who had once felt equal to all men, trained to speak on any subject, in the sad state they were now in. Her heart ached as she looked around at the girls. Their hair was wild, and their clothes, torn and dirty, barely covered them. Each girl had unfathomable shame in her eyes, and their hearts seemed devoid of all feeling. Aradia knew that she must not evade her duty to them. She must set this right.

Zantaunt came up beside her again. "I have one soldier that I can trust. He is the one responsible for feeding the girls. He told me that you have not been eating."

"That is true. I care not for food at this time. We will break bread once this is over. So let us expedite our plan as soon as we get to the city."

"Yes, there is a plan in motion at present," he told her, glancing at a man with a tousled dark beard who was watching them with a look in his eyes which told Aradia that his weakness was young girls. He liked it when they were tied up.

"You must see to it that he does not rape them," Aradia spoke boldly, seeking out his eyes.

"This matters not. The damage has already been done! No sense locking the gate after the bull is out," he argued, raising his voice a bit and laughing in a vicious manner. "That was not part of our bargain. They are no longer virgins, so it matters not what happens, as long as they go free."

"Did you promise him his pick, or all of them?"Aradia demanded furiously through clenched teeth. "Well, tell me!" She demanded, as he leered at her.

"No, it is off!" she hissed. "They will not be abused anymore! I will go to your captain and tell him what you have planned!" With a brazened toss of her head Aradia began to turn her horse toward the captain.

He stopped her in a panic. "No, no! I will see to it that they are harmed no further. I will go with him when he has charge of them, and offer him coin from what I receive from my gain. Is that to your liking?" he whispered angrily. "I can tell from your arrogance that you are of royal lineage. You think that I am beneath you and I won't have it!"

When he struck her, the sound echoed loudly and the captain's second in command, Phesoj, came up beside them and demanded to know what was wrong.

Aradia was silent, not knowing how to deal with this development. She could continue with her plan and take the chance the girls would be abused again, or...

"Capitan, e dos, estru ta danya. I wish to speak to you." said Aradia, her diction flawless.

Phesoj noticed her horse was not tied to Zantaunt's.

"Come, follow me," he spoke sternly to Aradia, and ordering Zantaunt not to break formation, took her aside and asked her how she had learned his language.

"That is not important," said Aradia. "I have something of the utmost importance to tell the Captain!"

Regarding him with a slow measured look she noticed he was quite handsome, with firm smooth skin that held no beard or moustache. He was tanned and vibrant, but did not have dark ruddy skin as the others did. His dark hair, almost black, was cropped just below the ears. His eyes, a warm chestnut, were gazing at her with an unexpected kindness which she found disarming. Medium height with a muscular build, he appeared slightly older than she.

Aradia had been taking stock of him since they had left Volsinii when he rode in with the horses. She had watched his interactions with the men, observing that they seemed to respect him. He had stayed alert to signs of quarrelsome behavior amongst them, and would intervene in a way as to disrupt the tension before it could escalate. When he was not taking care of the horses, or seeing to the needs and comforts of the men, he kept to himself. He had kept his distance from her and the girls, which had made it hard to talk to him before now.

She spoke again in his tongue, deciding to take a chance on the things she had observed about him and on her intuition.

"You do not belong with these animals. It is not in you to rape, and I believe you would only kill if your life was threatened. How did you become second in command to such a tyrant who rules an army of savages?"

"How do you know of my nature?" Phesoj said, clearly surprised at her courage. Aradia could also tell by the way that he looked at her, that he was fighting the impulse to take her in his arms.

"You could be mistaken. Anyway, it does not matter," he added gruffly. "I will ask the questions. And with that he demanded that she tell him what had been going on as he approached her and Zantaunt.

For moment, Aradia looked at him with an affixed stare but did not answer. Then her gaze began to soften, her breath becoming even and light as she very slowly went into a trance.

When she began to speak, it was in his mother's voice. His mother had been dead a long while, and he still missed her and now here was this beautiful young woman with her red gold hair and sea green eyes, speaking of things that she could not have possibly known about him. At first he was completely dismayed, and then, slowly his head began to nod up and down and a tear formed in the corner of his eye.

In his mother's voice, Aradia told the soldier that he should not be responsible for the slavery of these girls and that he must listen to his heart in this matter. Through Aradia, his mother told him he was her favorite child, and that he must flee from these brutal men for they did not worship the goddess.

Aradia spoke with a soft rhythm, while tears poured down her lovely face.

"T' is sorry I am that I had to leave you my son. The next time ya hear someone sing of sea-maidens, think of me swimming with the best of them, and know that I am free."

Phesoj was a child again, waiting for his mother to finish baking so that they could walk to the sea and search for shells and listen to her talk of graceful sea-maidens. His mother had come from a place of emerald beauty where the goddess reigned and all spoke with a lilt in their voice that could charm the hardest of brutes. It was this he heard coming from the mouth of Aradia and it left no doubt that his mother had spoken through this fascinating girl. He was right, destiny was calling.

When Aradia awoke from her trance, she could see that this man had been shaken to the core, although she did not know what she had said. Still dazed, she slowly began to tell him the bargain she had struck with Zantaunt, and why she had changed her mind. She told Phesoj she was only a distant cousin to King Torintia, but the king would embrace her nonetheless. Once again, she made it clear that the most important thing was to see that all the girls go free.

"I will help," he assured her. "I have sisters and I understand." Phesoj let her know that when he first joined this group, it was very different. Back then, he told her, the leader was a good man. Though they sometimes plundered small towns, they never raped, and only killed if it was necessary. Now, however, this *one* was in charge because their leader had been killed, and things were different. Phesoj had become second in command, albeit begrudgingly on the captain's part, due to his knowledge of the territory, and the fact he was able to speak many other dialects beside his tongue of the Upper Po Valley. He also knew horseflesh. Phesoj hoped that this might be in their favor, as this could help with their plan for escape. "When we get to town," Phesoj said, looking around to make sure no one was listening, "I will slip away and have the king send troops back with me."

Phesoj hung his head in shame as he continued to speak. Barely able to look her in the eye he said, "It … it was I that brought the horses into town when … when it was all over."

She watched him closely as he appeared to be gathering his courage before raising his head to look her fully in the eyes.

"I saw you on the ground," he said. "You had picked up a knife and I was afraid you were going to kill yourself. I quickly hit you on the back of the head, knocking you out, and then took the knife, which I still have. After that, I carried you to the main hall and left you with the other girls."

Aradia looked at the aura surrounding Phesoj which was the color of a cloudless sky except for the gold and violet around his head, and knew that he had spoken the truth. This was a man she could trust. Clearing her throat she quickly wiped her eye as if the problem was a bit of dust. She wanted desperately to take his hand in friendship, but knew she could not. "You are a very good man. I so wish we had met under different circumstances."

"I must go now," he replied, flushing. "My name is Phesoj, in case I have not told you. The meaning of my name is *loved but brief journey.*"

Digging his heels into his spirited horse Phesoj rode away swiftly, creating a cloud of dust which helped Aradia hide the tears her jumbled emotions had caused her to shed.

Moving back into formation, she found herself wondering why he had shared the meaning of his name with her. When she again became aware of her surroundings, they were getting close to the town of Norchia where, if she remembered correctly, they would go by the next turn and head towards the city of Tarquinia.

The tombs of the town lined the left side of the road. They were so magnificent that her eyes lingered over every detail. Ornately carved lintels framed the buildings, and stately white marble columns lined the entranceways. Winged horses rode on top of each corner of the buildings. Fleet stallions in motion, allowed the mourners to feel the promise of safety and quick passage for their loved ones. The abundant faces of the gods and goddesses upon the tombs assured those left behind that their ancestors were well looked after.

Just as she thought! They had turned towards the seaport city of Tarquinia, and her heart began to pound as she realized that it would not be long now before she could attempt their escape. She was fearful of things going wrong, and knew it was a possibility. What if she were costing them their lives, instead of keeping them from slavery? To calm herself down, she began taking deep breaths.

Phesoj reigned in his horse beside her. "It has all been arranged," he muttered. "When we get to Tarquina, we are to put you girls into a room reserved for slaves. The last auction of the day will take place in the market square shortly before sunset. As you can see, we are now picking up speed. The leader wants to be done with the sale as soon as possible. He does not want to wait another day. This will make it nearly impossible for me to get to the king, but I will try. Keep looking straight in front of you. I am giving you your knife back. I will make it look like I am angry with you. In the interim, take the knife and hide it well."

Feeling the knife through the wrap, Aradia wondered how to disguise it. Realizing she could make it look like she had an injured arm, she placed the cumbersome blade under her left forearm. Ripping off a strip from her dirt encrusted robe she used it to cover the knife, and instantly felt safer, even though she realized she could not get to it quickly.

Chapter 5

Zantaunt, glaring at Aradia, rounded up the girls. Her indifference to his murderous look infuriated him and he kicked the horse he was working with. He had seen to it that he and Zonoff would be the ones responsible for escorting the girls into the inner city; then they would guard them until the sale began at the slave market. Taking his eyes off her for a moment, he covertly searched the now restless warriors for Phesoj. He distrusted Phesoj, yet he had no choice but to let him in on the deal. She had seen to that, he thought, giving her another poisonous glance. If the Captain were to find out he would not, he knew, be given a second chance. He would be dead.

Zantaunt wondered why Phesoj, the do-gooder, would get involved. His eyes wandered back to the warriors and he located Phesoj busily talking to Zonoff. Phesoj... he's a strange sort, he never really fit in. Maybe he wanted in so that he could get away from this life, one he certainly didn't seem cut out for. No matter, he was getting too old for this. With his share of what they would get from the king he could settle down and live the easy life.

They entered the city of Tarquinia, passing under a roughhewn archway, made to entice the weary travelers with its sculpted promises of the many delights that were offered within its boundaries. It was obvious that all types of entertainment were available from street jugglers trying to make a living, to the urchins paid to tout the wares of the ladies of the evening. Hawkers announced the sale of slaves at market, and busy taverns lined the streets where a man could slake his thirst.

A cacophony of noise reached Aradia's ears, street vendors bartering their goods, wooden wheels on hardened dirt streets, donkey hooves echoing off the buildings, clanging bells and other sounds overwhelming her senses. The stench that wafted around Aradia was palpable. She had been craving the smell of the ocean. Instead, the ocean breeze carried foul odors, which greeted her like a brackish wall and turned her stomach.

Looking down from her position on her mount, she eagerly took a deep breath just as one of the peddlers took freshly baked bread out of the oven. Inhaling greedily, she attempted to remember its taste only to have the odor of it stifled by the smell of fish.

Leaning over as the retching started she heaved, deep dry heaves that created spasms in the pit of her stomach. Clutching her middle and gagging she tried not to call attention to herself. Murky nebulous feelings washed over her. Slowly panic threatened, as she realized she could no longer stave off her fears that their plan of reaching the king's ear would work. She knew she needed another plan but could not think straight as a deep leaden hunger, and a thirst worse that the torment of Tantalus drained her body.

Aradia slowed her horse as a wizened old woman approached her, walking with slow faltering steps. Her plain brown garment was shabby but clean and her white hair was tied in a simple knot at the nape of her thin neck. When she came up beside Aradia, she showed her a green leaf while looking deep into the girl's eyes. Her own held secrets and enigmatic mysteries of old flowed through her finger tips as she placed the leaf in Aradia's hands. It tasted of mint. Smiling and nodding weakly with gratitude Aradia continued along. Taking a deep breath she realized that the mint had fortified her spirit but when she looked back to thank the old woman, she found that she had disappeared. Aradia would have thought she had been an apparition, but for the taste of mint on her tongue.

Most of the men had moved on, anxiously in search of a taverna to wash the dust from their mouths. Zantaunt ordered the girls to get down from their horses. As soon as they dismounted Zonoff led the horses away. They stood in front of a low building that had a wide oak door with a wooden beam on it so that it could be locked from the outside. He ordered the girls inside, wielding his knife with an ugly laugh.

"Shush, it will be all right," whispered Aradia to the girls. "I have a knife. I will protect you. Let us go inside."

As soon as they were all inside, the door slammed. As they hastily gathered around Aradia, she undid the wrap from the knife that she had hidden earlier and began cutting the girls free from their bindings.

"Let me think," she said. "I need quiet."

The girls gathered themselves a distance away from Aradia, at the far end of the nearly empty room. They had come to respect and honor her in the short time of their captivity, marveling among themselves of her valor, and looking to her now as their only hope.

Aradia paced the floor for a few moments, pausing now and then to look at them. How they have suffered these young women, she thought, but how much more will they suffer if I do not act decisively.

When she asked them if Zonoff had been disrespectful of them, none would meet her eyes.

Not hesitating, Aradia looked out through the small hole in the door. Just as she thought, Zonoff was finished with the horses and it was he that was outside as their guard. Knowing that she must work fast before Zantaunt returned, she motioned to Lattia, choosing her because of her large breasts, moon face, and extra weight.

"Lie down on the bed," said Aradia, "and start moaning as if you are in much pain. Go do it now! The rest of you move to the other side of the room!"

"It is a baby, a baby!" Aradia screamed when all was in place. "Someone come quickly! Something is wrong. She will die!"

Zonoff could not believe his ears. A baby is coming? He did not know if he cared. But if he let one of the girls die, it might not go well for him when the king's men came. He hesitantly opened the door, ordering Aradia to step aside and saw that the rest of the girls were huddled on the other side of the room. He went over to Lattia, and seeing her clutching her large belly, he leaned over. Aradia moved behind him as stealthily as a cat, grabbed him and wrapped her left arm around his throat as her right hand forcefully plunged the knife down into his heart. His body contorted with pain and he clutched for the knife as he slithered to the floor.

"Here, help me get him onto a cot and cover him with a blanket," she told the others. "I'm going outside to watch for Phesoj. He is helping us. I promise all of you freedom. Do you understand me? You will be free, but you must do as I say. I will stay out of sight until Zantaunt comes back."

Anxiously, Aradia searched out the two oldest girls. "Lattia, Tona, I am counting on you both! Keep looking out this hole. When Zantaunt comes back, somehow get him to enter the room. When he does, I will come in from behind, and if I must, I'll kill him. Do you understand me?"

Aradia knew this was difficult for Lattia. Taking note of her dazed expression, she had to shake her to get her attention. They have already gone through so much, she thought. Witnessing one of their own commit murders could well push them to the brink of their fragile existence.

"Lattia," Aradia spoke soothingly. "You are stronger than you know. You must do this or we will all die. Tona, I am counting on you. You can speak a few words of the Upper Valley. You must not fail! We have one chance."

"I want to die!" raged Lattia, sobbing uncontrollably.

But Tia, who was small and slight, stepped forward and said, "I will do it. Go. Tona and I will make a good team."

Outside the room, Aradia hid under the shadowy eaves of the stark buildings. Zantaunt, counting his money in his head no doubt, did not at first see the wooden bolt on the ground. When he did he cautiously opened the heavy door and peeked inside. Tia, with a shaking hand, pointed to the cot, "Zonoff is very sick. He is scaring us. Come help!"

Dashing out the shadows, Aradia hurled herself at his bulk, knocking him into the room. As all the girls grabbed for him, Aradia moved forward with her knife pulled, but Zantaunt was much stronger than Zonoff; this time it was harder.

Fighting for his life, Zantaunt pulled his knife and lunged for Aradia. But when Tia kicked him from behind, he lost his balance, giving Aradia the chance to plunge her knife into his throat hitting his jugular, causing blood to gush out with such force that it spattered her and the walls. Feeling queasy, she covered her mouth and pushed away the threatening darkness. Shaking she asked for help to turn him over to make sure he was dead. His eyes agape, his last breath was a noisy rattle. Some of the tension in the room eased.

"Come," Aradia spoke, hearing her own voice as if from a distance. "Let us leave here. We need to be careful. Do any of you have anything of value?" Aradia, with a voice raspy from all the effort, spoke barely above a whisper. "I need to get us some clean clothing in the market place. We must blend into the crowd in order to escape."

Lattia undid a pin, well hidden deep inside her robe. "My mother gave this to me. It is gold." She reluctantly handed it to Aradia as fresh tears coursed down her face.

"Good! This will get us new clothing," said Aradia, as she hugged Lattia. "Come. Let's get out of this room."

Nearby, Aradia found a deserted alleyway. Whispering and motioning with her hand for them to be quiet, she hissed, "Stay here! Hide behind these barrels. I will be back soon."

Cautiously she rounded the corner of the buildings, and peeked out at the busy market place that filled the hard packed dirt street. Spotting a merchant who was selling colorful robes, she vigilantly approached his stall, and removing the pin she had been given from under her robe, showed it to him. His eyes glistening, he bit and tasted it, after which, he told her to take anything she wanted. Aradia's eyes widened as she pointed to the pouch of water hanging by his side. He hardly had it untied from his shoulder before she was drinking thirstily.

Later, when the others had drank and washed before donning their new garb, Aradia urged them to braid one another's hair so that they would blend in with the natives.

"Good," she said when they had finished. "Now we are ready. Come. ...No wait! I have left the knife. We may need it. I will go back. Go to the end of the alley and mix in with the people on the street. Pretend to look at the wares the vendors are selling. I will catch up with you shortly. It is not safe here in the alley! If we get separated, use my name to get an audience with the king. Go now. ... I will join you soon."

As the young girls reluctantly walked out into the street, Aradia crept back to the small room where they had been held and found her knife. But before she could slip away, strong arms engulfed her and a man clamped his hand over her mouth.

"Shhh, it is I, Phesoj! Do not scream. I am not going to hurt you."

She nodded her head to let him know she had heard him, and he let her go.

"I could not get an audience with the king as he is away, nor could I get anyone who would listen to me," he explained. "I was told to come back in two days. We must make haste and leave here quickly. Soon they will be coming to get you for the sale in the town square. Where are the girls?"

As they dashed out of the room and down the alleyway she began to tell him of the events, but they were not quick enough. Five men she had never seen before, dressed as those who rode the sea, gave pursuit with knives drawn, cornering Phesoj and Aradia before they could reach the marketplace. Aradia fought like a wild cat, kicking and hacking at them with her knife, while Phesoj wielded his with skill. But it was soon clear that these men did not want to kill her. She hoped that their hesitation would offer a chance to help Phesoj get away.

Looking over at him, however, she froze. Two men held him as another cut his throat. She staggered backwards, putting her hand over her mouth as a silent scream hung in the air. The men took that opportunity to seize her and quickly tie her up.

Seeing the brutal murder of her friend drained her of all energy. She thought of the girls and bit her lip until it bled to keep from crying out. She could tell that these men would have no mercy. Horrified as she was, she kept reminding herself that at least the girls were safe. Her mind raced as she thought of how to escape. What would Grandmother do? she wondered.

When she began to act *lobatz*, flailing around and talking gibberish, they did not seem to care. One of the men grabbed her hair and laughed. "Made it easy for us, didn't she?" he roared. "With this red/gold hair and her evil eyes, she stands out like an apple in a fish market."

Yes, she thought, her hair was unusual, even in her province where brown or dark red are more common. The comment about her eyes made sense also, as green eyes were thought of as evil in many areas where darker eyes were prevalent. She tried listening again so that she could understand more of what was happening and heard one seaman comment that the other girls must have already gone to the auction block at which her heart began to sing. *The girls were free!*

"No loss," said another. "It was only this one our captain paid for. One of the kitchen maids told the baker that kin to the king was sitting in one of the slave cells and that she has extensive knowledge of the world and many languages to her credit. Our captain knows of a man that will pay highly for her talents."

"By Zeus, she is a hellcat! Can't see why anyone would pay for that!" another cried.

Zeus? That is the Greek name for Jupiter, the father god, thought Aradia. Becoming more upset, she fought all the harder realizing that they might be taking her to Greece.

"I hear she speaks the language from the Upper Valley. I wonder what other languages she can speak."

"Our tongue maybe," said one of them, chuckling as he prodded her. "Can you speak to us, miss? All that knowledge in a woman is a bad thing. It makes them crazy."

He pointed to his head and snorted with laughter as he shared the joke with his motley group.

Hanging suspended between two large men, Aradia raised her feet off the ground and kicked the man who had poked her. Hissing and cussing, spitting and pulling, she tried to get free, but the men held on tighter, laughing at the man she had kicked.

Aradia saw that they were heading for the dock. She had heard of women who had disappeared on ships, never to be heard from again, and fought all the harder. *Goddess, help me,* she prayed. *I cannot go to Greece for it is a place of evil, where men love men and treat women as slaves. Please,* she begged the Goddess… *I would rather die!*

Suddenly someone pressed a dirty rag, which smelled sickly sweet over her nose. She tried not to inhale but it was overpowering. Coughing, and gasping, Aradia slumped soundlessly to the ground.

When she became conscious, Aradia could tell from the rolling motion beneath her that she was on a ship. Looking around at her surroundings, she saw that she was in a small room. As her mind cleared, she tried to think of what her grandmother would do. What spells might she use to protect herself? What potions might she use?

Finding a small earthenware bowl with salt on a weathered table near a chair in the corner, Aradia placed some of it near the door and circled herself with the rest, chanting, *"Scongiuro il sale suona notte giorno."*

Hesitating, for she had not needed this spell before and the words did not come easy, she started again, in a singsong tone using the power of her voice as she had been taught by her grandmother. Speaking the sacred words in the ancient tongue brought back the memories of her childhood and she recalled with a pang that, up until these last few days in her life, she had always felt safe. Aradia threw salt above and beneath herself, and spun around in the circle of salt as she recited the words to the ancient spell over and over. As she spoke the meaning of the words from her heart, it wrenched her very soul. She called out to the spirit world to know her fate.

> *"I do conjure thee, salt, lo! Here at night,*
> *Above me, beneath me, and around me*
> *I take my place in the order of the world,*
> *Likewise the moon and stars, your children all*
> *I yearn to learn the very truth of truths.*

> *I call upon you Goddess, for you are sooth*
> *To know my future, what comes my way?*
> *Earth, air, fire and water, what do you say*
> *Wilt good or evil come, protect me where I lay."*

Finally, exhausted, weak from lack of food and water, dazed by the terror she had felt during the past few days and the heartbreak of losing her family, Aradia collapsed in the middle of the sacred circle, and somewhere deep in the blackness a voice spoke.

"Child, come join me. Rest in my love for a time. You have done well in protecting the young ones. But you are just a child yourself."

Feeling compelled to lift her eyes upward, she saw a stunning goddess in a turquoise robe with intricately carved symbols on the cuffs, and embroidered down the front. Her features were fine and her lips formed a perfect bow; her dark olive skin with deep rich blue-black hair set off golden sparks in her sable eyes.

As the goddess came closer, Aradia noticed that across the expanse of her high cheekbones was a touch of glitter that ran to her temples, splashing her hair with starlight. Her soft curly raven hair was piled loosely on top on her head, and was held with turquoise and diamond combs that sparkled when she moved.

It was a compelling sight. As her radiant blue/green gown, a color more wondrous than the sea, furled around her, the rich deep hues made Aradia want to crawl inside the magnificent cloak for protection. Golden white light shimmered around the lithe form. The Goddess seemed to transport Aradia to a realm where only light existed. Changing from white to gold, and back to white, the light gave Aradia a feeling of tranquility. That... and the glowing smile the gentle goddess wore was a welcomed blessing after the last few days.

"You seem familiar somehow," Aradia murmured. "Do I know you?" As quickly as that thought came in another one followed. "Have you come for me, then? That is good. I am through with this body."

"You... finished... with your lust for life?" said the lovely goddess, "You have just begun. You have much yet to accomplish. Your mother, Diana, Goddess of the Moon, has sent you on a mission. It fits well with the journey of your soul that I am to help you with. You are not done with this life yet."

"You are not here to take me?" asked Aradia.

"No, it is not time. You wanted to know if you would encounter good or evil."

"Yes, that is so."

"What if I told you, that you would encounter only what you need to hasten your spiritual growth, only the things you have called into existence? Would that be so very hard to believe?"

"Yes." Aradia answered, "I cannot believe that I would have wanted my family to be butchered, or that I wanted to be held captive on a ship. I hate the water! No, I love the water but I hate ships!"

*"Be very careful of the word hate," replied the goddess. "It carries with it so much emotion, therefore bringing that very thing into your life. **That which you most love and that which you most hate, you call into existence.**"*

"What I hate, I bring it into my life?" asked Aradia.

"Yes, that is so. Are you not curious as to my name?"

"No. Well perhaps."

"My name is Desimena," she said smiling, "I am a guide to you on your journey as a soul, and will help you on your earthly sojourn. You have

chosen this worldly existence; therefore your soul is now expressing itself in a body. Do not be puzzled, my child. We will talk more of your soul at another time."

"You mentioned my mother's name. It is not Diana, yet the name is so familiar. How is that?" asked Aradia.

"I speak not of the mother you were born to on Earth but of the Goddess of the Moon. I know this is hard to follow, but it is my duty to remind you. When you first came into a body, though it was an etheric body, it was with curiosity and an enormous lust for life. You were born to a great being, Diana, Queen of the Moon. She sent you on a mission, after you had been trained in the art of witchcraft. Your assignment was to come to Earth to help the women who were being abused, beaten and taken as slaves. Your promise was to use the methods you had learned to better the life of all women on Earth. On this life's journey, you will meet many women needing your help."

For a moment the goddess hesitated and it seemed to Aradia that, when she continued, it was with a certain difficulty in phrasing the words.

"This is the difficult part," she said. "In order to better understand the pain these women are in, you have chosen as a soul to experience loss and cruelty at the hands of men. This can only happen in the body. So your soul chose the life you now live to give you the experience needed to understand on the human level, degradation and fear. If you hold onto these things alone, you will become bitter and will close yourself off to love, which could cause you to misuse your power. If you hold onto anger, you will use your power for ill."

Desimena's heart wrenched at the pain she knew Aradia was experiencing. Knowing her last words were essential, she leaned in toward Aradia and whispered softly.

"Your soul cries out to grow. Your soul needs to find a balance between love and power. It will be offered in this life. Will you take it, or push it away?"

"I feel no power. I only feel anger!"

"Yes, when you are angry you give your power away," she was told.

"You speak in riddles," cried Aradia. "Why are you here? If it is not to take me, then why have you come?"

"You asked for me. You asked from the depths of your soul. You wanted to know what awaits you. I come to teach you, for I am your teacher."

"I do not want lessons!" cried Aradia, "I want help. I want to know my future!"

"I have told you that with each thought you bring the future into existence. Watch your thoughts. These words are the most important teachings I can give you on your journey at this time."Desimena's image began to fade.

Aradia cried out, "No... do not leave me! Please, I have many questions."

But deep, all encompassing darkness was her answer.

Chapter 6

Opening her eyes, Aradia, hoping against hope that she would find herself on shore, was soon aware that such was not the case. Feeling movement under her feet reminded her just how much she disliked ships. Rummaging through a chest searching for a knife, she heard a door open and jumped to her feet as the Captain of the ship slammed through the door, his portly body dwarfing the room.

Glowering down at the circle of salt and the signs of disarray in the room, he frowned with displeasure. His weary face, deeply creased at the eyes and mouth, and unsavory beard gave him the look of a man much older than his forty-five years.

"Clean up this mess you've made!" he told her. "Do they think they do me a favor putting you in here? You are not my type. There's nothing good between those legs!"

Aradia rushed him and jumped on his back, beating him with her fists.

Backing her up against the wall, he pushed hard until, feeling her chest constrict, Aradia stopped hitting at him.

"I want you out of my cabin, now," he told her, and going to the door roared into the hall, "Get this witch out of my cabin! Put her in the hold. Before you brought her aboard my vessel I should have been informed of her wicked ways."

The first mate, Arapolis, came quickly upon hearing the Captain's harsh voice. Grabbing Aradia, he drug her out of the cabin, kicking and scratching. She did not know what the hole or hold was, but it sounded dreadful and she wanted no part of it.

Leering at her he smacked his dirty lips over his toothless mouth. "We'll take a bit of a stop on the way so I can sample your wares," said Arapolis. "Tol'em not to put you in the Captain's cabin. He likes young boys. Never did have a woman!"A sinister rattle came from the cavernous opening in his face; Aradia supposed it was a laugh.

When Aradia, overcome with the evil odor of the man, began to retch, he thrust her through an open hole in the floor. The sound of a door closing over the opening left her to strain her eyes in the bleak darkness. Unable to tell whether or not she was alone, she spoke first in her language, then in the tongue of the Upper Valley, and when there was no reply, tried Greek. Still no reply. And then, as her eyes adjusted to the darkness, she saw that three of the men who had been her captors, men responsible for the death of her family, were huddled in a corner, clutching their robes tightly about them in the dampness.

"So," said Aradia, speaking the language of the Upper Valley in a low and mocking tone, "there is justice after all."

She thought for a moment, of going over to strangle them, her hatred ran so deep. She could, she knew, put a spell on them which would make them unable to drink, no matter how thirsty they were. But what if they had had no choice but to loot and kill? She would be taking their lives without knowledge of the extent of their guilt. Being here on this ship, with these men making them slaves would be their repayment, no doubt. Aradia reached for her throat at the memory of how her friend Phesoj had been killed, his life's blood draining from his body as she stood helpless to do anything. The recall was so vivid that she buried her face in her hands trying to shut out the image. A low moan moved through her as her throat constricted, burning with memories of all the loss.

Shivering from the dampness, Aradia looked around for something to cover herself. In her searching, she found a metal cup. Tentatively picking it up, she felt the cool copper under her fingers, and recognized it as the design that was made only in her father's mine.

Besieged with grief, the memories of waving to her father and her two brothers as they went off to the mines on that fateful day confronted her. Needing to remember better times she thought of how proud her father had been of the family business. Upon inheriting it, he had asked his new wife to trust him and invest into the company, and she had. Her mother had a good head for business but she kept out of it and let her husband take care of the accounts while she tended to the children and sat back and watched as Aradia's father became one of the richest men in Etruria, who told everyone he was a rich man because his wife had faith in him. He then would laugh, patting his wife on the derriere and say, "Of course, it is good that I have strong sons to work the mine and gifted daughters to discourse with."

Her heart wrenched as she brought the cup to her face, the welcoming touch of the metal caressed her cheek. A tear mixed with the coolness of the copper, it slowly brought her to the present. No, she thought, I will not cry. I am stronger than that. I will not allow these men to see what they have done to me.

Jumping up, she banged the cup on the walls of the low ceiling, and cried out, "Acqua, acqua." Getting no response, she continued her onslaught until the trap door was finally opened and a bucket of brackish seawater was thrown down on her through the cage-like opening, drenching her. The men in the corner yelled at her to be quiet before worse would come down on all their heads.

But unable to keep still, she paced back and forth until, worn out, she fell, crumpling to the floor in an exhausted sleep.

Upon awakening bits and pieces of a dream from her fitful night began filtering through her mind, reminding her of the vision she'd had the other night. The message in the vision had been, 'watch your thoughts!' Yet how could she think of anything but anger. How could she not want to kill?

Focusing on her breathing, she realized she needed to feel warmth. Her body was chilled to the core, and the more she tightened up, the colder she became. Each breath helped her to relax and she pictured herself by a huge fire, basking in its warmth. She could taste the wine that was produced from the vines in her courtyard. She could hear the crackling of the logs as they splintered and broke apart creating iridescent colors and more heat. Yes, now she felt better.

The sound of creaking wood and a ray of light alerted her to the trap door being opened. A young man hesitantly came down the ladder with a jug of water and food in hand. "Ay 'tis food I be carrying," he said.

In the dim light, Aradia could see that his face was bruised, and his eye was blackened. As he bent over her, instinctively, she reached up to touch his face. Startled, he pulled away.

She said softly, "You are hurt, I am sorry. If you can go to where they store the food and herbs, I will tell you how to heal your cuts and take down the swelling."

The boy seemed hypnotized by her words, no doubt because he so rarely had a kind word spoken to him. Apparently unable to speak, his words catching in his throat, he gave her water.

Finally finding his voice, he said, "Drink slowly. When me deeds er' done I be down again. I be bringing ya food, real food, not this rot!" And when he threw it into a corner of the bulkhead, she realized to her horror that the hold was infested with rats. He gave her a quick nod and left.

Since Aradia knew from her earlier experience, that she must focus on pleasant thoughts to keep her body relaxed and her mind occupied, she began to daydream, thinking of travel, of seeing the world. Suddenly she began to laugh. It was hysterical laughter, but laughter nonetheless, and she considered the fact that here she was, traveling the world, and yet under what circumstances, in a filthy, dank hole with brutal men chained in the dark corner opposite her, watching, always watching.

Clutching a sack of food in one hand and a small lamp in the other, the cabin boy slipped down the ladder and lit the lamp. Aradia awoke from her daydream to the smell of bread. The cabin boy had also brought wine, and for the first time since being captured, she ate. She was in heaven as she observed an angel that had come to her rescue.

He was young…much too young to suffer such cruelty in his short life, so thin his shoulder blades jutted out from his back. Small, frail, and pale of skin, with blondish hair that fell to his shoulders in knotted strands, he looked as if a mother's tender hand had never touched him. A faint smile lit his face, as his eyes met Aradia's, and in the deep liquid blue eyes that held no bitterness, Aradia saw that this child had somehow been able to transcend the harshness of his life.

She boldly told this young man she was proud and thankful to share with him, but had no intentions of breaking bread with enemies! She asked him about his family and what his life had been like up to now. As he told her the sad tale, tears ran down her cheek for this boy, as she thought of how easy her life had been. He truly has never known a day's happiness, she thought. Yet he could smile and do her a good turn.

"What is your name?" asked Aradia, speaking the language of Greece very slowly, for she found he wasn't used to the refinement in which she spoke.

"Thaddeus it be. I carry ore' the name of me great-grandfather. He was a captain, went down with his ship."

Asking him where they were heading was hard for Aradia, as she instinctively knew she would not like the answer. But when she finally asked, he told her that they were to land at the great port of Athens.

"The Captain says you're worth your weight in gold, Miss," said the young boy. "We left port t' hurry right after they took you a board. I thought he meant your family was paying fer ya ransom, but the captain said they are all dead!"

Aradia flinched, changing the subject as she felt the bleakness of their loss rip through her; she clutched her stomach barely getting out the next words.

"Can you find out more without putting yourself in danger?" she asked him.

"I will fer you, mistress," the boy told her proudly. "I need ta feed the others now. It's a good thing they are that weak and chained or you might be in danger, me bringing you bread and all."

Hanging the light on the hook as he was leaving he looked at her with eyes that were wise beyond his years, eyes touched with pain and sadness, yet sparked with curiosity for the greater world. Watching him again, Aradia marveled at the fact that a part of him was untouched by the brutality and shame he carried. His plight touched her and filled her with compassion.

After Thaddeus left, she was engulfed in loneliness, in good part because he was about the age of her brother Megalita who had been twelve when he and Radarius, who was two years younger, had gone to the mine with their father. And now they would always be with him, just as Kouros, her baby brother, would be with her mother. At least none of them had been alone when they had died. Sinking into a cavernous pit of grief with every memory, she softly cried, "Oh, Sardiana, my sweet Sardiana...I left you alone!" A great heaving sigh escaped her. As she lay down to sleep, the meal, her first in many days weighed heavy on her stomach.

Aradia awoke to the ship rocking violently, and the gale blowing outside nearly deafened her. She had asked Thaddeus to get her something to read and he had brought her some maps and an old captain's log. Mesmerized by the information in the log she studied them until her eyes hurt from the poor light and the gale stopped blowing. She found the maps interesting but the log fascinating as it was a disclosure of huge slave markets in which the captain was taking more than his share from the man who owned the ship. Piracy was, she realized, a very lucrative business. Aradia did not know why, but she put the names in the log to memory using rhymes, as her grandmamma had taught her. She knew she had to put the lamp out, for if it spilled over it could cause a fire. Reluctantly, and in deep thought about what she had just learned, she got up to blow it out, and then she settled back down to try and sleep.

Chapter 7

Time lingered, as the long voyage continued. Aradia schooled her new-found friend in pronunciation and taught him some of the Etruscan language, finding that it helped to pass the long days and nights. He had a quick mind and a good memory. And when she asked him if he could find a way to secret her on deck, he said that there was one mate he could trust to do so and that when he was on watch, he would come for her.

"Oh Thad, this is glorious," whispered Aradia as they crept up on deck into the moonless night. The stars twinkling bright and low looked to her as if she could reach up and touch them. Thinking of the maps that he had brought her, and of the names of the constellations, she was awed at the knowledge she now possessed. She had learned from him that the constellations were how ships navigated at sea, the North Star being most important.

"The constellation that the North Star is in is called Ursa Minor," Thad had told her a few nights before. "It means Little Bear."

Looking towards the North Star, she shook her head as she realized all of the other stars danced around the North Star, as if hung by invisible strings, each star becoming part of a glittering canvas.

So I am seeing the world, she thought. Ships are not so bad. In fact, there was something mystical about being out here; the water seems infinite and immeasurable, silhouetted by the moonless night. She felt insignificant, yet at the same time, like the most important person in the world.

"T's lovely being topside, isn't it, mistress," the boy asked, remembering to speak properly as Aradia was working hard with him on his letters and his brusque way of speaking.

She laughed. "Yes, it is. Thank you for befriending me. It has meant a great deal to my sanity."

"I will be back, got duties to tend. Keep out of sight much as ye can," he cautioned as he left.

Aradia breathed in the fresh air. Thaddeus had given her a blanket which she spread out so she could lie down on the deck and take in the stars. She found the constellation Ursa Major, which looked like a pot for cooking, as well as Orion and amused herself by remembering the story she used to tell Sardiana of why Orion was placed in the sky.

Once upon a time, the lovely Goddess Diana, or Artemis as she is call in Greece, roamed the forest with her bow and her hound by her side. When her brother Apollo came upon her and challenged her to hit a leaf in a distant tree, she won, as she usually did, and he became jealous of her skill.

Then one day he came upon Orion swimming in the ocean and knew of his sister's love for the great hunter. So he challenged her to yet another target much farther away. "Do you see that little speck in the ocean? It is an apple and it is far too distant for even you to hit with your bow."

With pride and a bit of arrogance, she took aim, and of course she hit her mark. It was only after her sure aim that her brother confided in her that she had shot the man she loved, it left her howling in agony.

Jupiter, god of the sky, whom the Greeks called Zeus, came to see what was taking place. "Due to Orion's great skill as a hunter," he said, "I shall put him in the sky with his bow and arrows so that all can see and remember his greatness."

Aradia thought about the lesson the story held. Why was it that men were so jealous of women's skills, and why did some women become less of who they are to please men, and some women kill the very thing they love the most to prove...to prove what? There was something very important here which she must figure out.

A sense of longing for home washed over her, but it was not her home in Volsinii. It was her home in the sky. What a strange thought. Now she sounded like Grandmamma. But it was true that when she had told her of the royal blood being passed down from the warrior goddesses that came to the Earth in ships from the stars, Aradia had believed her. It was, she realized, only when children become older that they begin to question. When young they believe in themselves and trust in those that teach them. They see and feel things differently, and then they grow up.

When Sardiana was little, she had seen the colors around the other children. When, Megalita made fun of her, she stopped seeing the beauty and did not trust me to teach her about the fairies. Boys are not so open; it does not come natural to them. Perhaps… And then she felt someone trip over her.

"Blithering idiot, what in blazes…?"

Hastily sitting up, hugging the slim protection of the blanket, Aradia looked about for a way to escape, but only saw the rigger glaring down at her. Having been drinking deeply, he was in a foul mood. Crouching over her, he said, "Lookie what we have here. Oh, you're in for a treat, girl."

Slavering, he threw himself on top of her, one hand groping her breasts, the other undoing his breeches.

Aradia stopped struggling against him and willed her body to go limp. Breathing deeply she called on the elementals. Allowing herself no thought of screaming, she lay still, and heard, to her great relief, Thad's voice.

"Get off her!" the boy shouted, running to jump on the man's back and beginning to pummel him, all of which had the effect of a flea on a large dog. At first the man did not even notice. But when Thad tried to gouge his eyes out, he flung the boy roughly on the deck.

Stunned, as the most brutal man aboard the ship towered over him, Thaddeus trembled as the rigger moved to retrieve his knife.

Looking at the pockmarks of the leering face above him and smelling the foul breath from his rotting teeth, Thad curled into a fetal position as the man threatened to carve him up before killing him.

But as he bent over the boy, Aradia grabbed his arm and shouted, "Look over there!" And when the brute looked where she pointed, Aradia called on the elementals that came at once to do her bidding.

"Go to him, bring his worst fear
And as just that you will appear.
To injure himself he will be led.
And nothing more needs to be said!"

52

A wraith like figure stood just a few feet away, and holding a stick threateningly the ghost beckoned the brute with his other hand. Screaming "No, father, I didn't do anything wrong," the rigger began to run, tripping, falling and looking behind him, his face a mask of terror. Howling in fear, he ran to the rail and jumped overboard while Thad and Aradia scurried back to the hold.

"We won't speak of this," Aradia told him. "Not now or ever!"

The next morning bright and early, when Thaddeus came to bring her food, he told her that they were to reach port on the morrow. Aradia, noticing he was paler than usual, tenderly put her hands on his sweet face and placed a motherly kiss on his cheek. His blush was deep, and shyness overcame him for a moment. But then a glowing smile lit his face. Apparently that gesture from Aradia and the fact that they were near port and no one seemed to care what had happened to the rigger, helped ease his pain. He shared with her that he was very excited, because he loved to run around the city bragging to everyone that he was the cabin boy on the *Satarcia*. He loved to tell city dwellers that it was an African ship and the name meant, free as the wind.

The conversation took a more somber tone when Thaddeus let on that he felt uneasy about what was going to happen to Aradia. He had found out that the captain had been paid handsomely to bring back a beautiful young woman from Etruria, which was renowned for allowing their women to take part in scholarly pursuits. It was important, the captain had told them, that she know many languages, Greek among them. But Thad blushed again, when hanging his head he said that he could not imagine any man in Greece wanting a learned woman, though he knew men would pay much for a comely young maiden. Aradia, seeing his genuine concern told him not to worry, that she could take care of herself and that she had no intention of becoming anyone's slave.

That night in her dreams Aradia listened to the wisdom of the goddess again.

"So you embark on the next part of your journey?" Desimena spoke softly, her voice a musical balm to Aradia's soul.

"Yes... the ship docks tomorrow. I am apprehensive, yet glad to be done with this ship."

"Ahh yes, the unknown causes the most fear. Yet if you think of this part of your journey as an adventure, it will be easier for you. Remember the things we talked of before. It is important to watch your thoughts, for they open the doorway to the future."

Desimena's smile was softer than a spring shower. Resonating approval with a nod of her head, she slowly began to disappear from view.

❧

Remembering her dream from the night before, Aradia knew it was going to be very important to look at her life as an adventure and try not to think of herself as a martyr, or a casualty in this power- play of men. For when she did that, she noticed that she drew more suffering to herself. She could remember bits and pieces of her spirit guide talking to her last night, and the other times when she went into a trance. Yes, that is what she called herself, a spirit guide. Aradia realized that when she applied the positive thought process, she drew positive results into her life. Aradia breathed in deeply and said out loud, "This day is important to the rest of my life, and I will remember to feel powerful and positive."

❧

Sputtering and splashing, Aradia awoke in a deep, scented tub of water. Her senses were dazed, and time felt altered. She was only aware of the fact that she had been drugged when they carried her from the ship. Inhaling the aroma of perfumed oil, she observed a comely young maid scrubbing her feet. The maid chattered in a sing song rhythm. Looking around at the strange surroundings, Aradia tried desperately to get her bearings. Feeling the delight of warm water caressing her skin she wanted to relax, yet her senses were alerting her to *danger...*

Shoving the maids hand away from her, Aradia demanded to know what she was doing and was told that the girl had been paid to wash her and get her ready, although for what, she did not say.

"They'll be back soon," the girl said, eying Aradia's silken curves and the droplets forming between her breasts. "Hear you kin speak real fancy," she chuckled. "Bet you've got a lot of other talents, too."

Mortified, Aradia leapt out of the tub and ran to the door. Finding it locked, she demanded the key – and her clothes, only to be told that what was left of the robe she had been wearing had been burned.

Reluctantly, but knowing that she had no alternative, she slipped into the resplendent linen robe the girl provided before she begged for the key again.

"You must give it to me!" she cried. "They want to make me a slave! I must get away before they come back!" With a frightened look on her face, the girl explained that they were locked in and she was sure the door would be opened shortly.

Aradia began banging on the door. As she yelled and pounded louder and louder, her damp robe clung to her well-rounded figure, making the delicate cloth nearly transparent. Grabbing the pins the maid handed her, Aradia lifted her dripping locks away from her robe and hastily fastened her errant hair on top of her head. Furiously she resumed banging on the door. Suddenly, and to her great surprise, it opened.

"*Regina Bella,*" said a startled man who had heard the shouting and come to investigate.

The deeply resonant sound came forth from a finely chiseled face. Standing in the hallway holding open the door, stood a Greek God. For a long moment which seemed like eons they gazed at each other. Never before had Aradia felt as though she was losing herself in someone else's eyes, and it was only with great reluctance that she looked away, her thoughts tumbling over each other. What if he's the one who brought me here? What if it is he that wants to make me a slave...? What... Her thought hurtled to an end as he laid a strong gentle hand on shoulder, whereupon her arm tingled; waves of warm liquid traveled the length of her body, sending a flush to her porcelain cheek.

"*Regina Bella*....Beautiful Queen," his hand slid lightly over her arm.

Frightened of her own conflicting feelings, she suddenly pushed him out of her way. Leaving him felt wrong to her somehow, but she knew that she must be free. A long darkened hallway led to a narrow stairway. Taking the stairs two at a time she bound for the opened doorway that led into a bustling street lined with merchants, carts and boisterous people.

Soundlessly she darted in and out of the crowded thoroughfare. Sustaining a quick pace, her bare feet kicked up dust as she flew away from the hectic market area. Once away from the noisy avenue, she glanced back over her shoulder and was relieved that no one was following her. Heart pounding, she stopped to catch her breath. Bending forward to ease the sharp pain in her side, she murmured, "Blessed freedom."

Aradia wandered aimlessly for hours. She was glad to be free, but the original sense of exhilaration wore off as the sun began to slide behind the horizon. Following voices and strange scraping sounds she found herself in an overgrown courtyard where an old woman was sweeping the flags which constituted a walkway of sorts. The voices, which seemed to come from a room at the further side of the yard, were those of men who appeared to be drinking and cavorting in an unruly manner. Still, there was no way around it. She needed a place to stay the night.

As she began to address the old woman, who was staring at her with a look of amazement on her face, a pot-bellied man came bursting into the courtyard.

"So this is what they send me," he growled, looking at her lustfully. "I made a bargain for three of you. Where are the others? Does he think that because you have a certain beauty, one of you can service my customers?"

Aradia knew at once what he had mistaken her for, and began to protest, but the old woman suddenly roused herself. "This is the daughter of a distant cousin who is visiting from Corinth. There is not enough room for her at my nephew's house and she has been sent to stay here for a short time." Swearing loudly, the irate man reached for the small women, but she deftly ducked out of his way. "She can help me in the kitchen," said the frightened woman, "and – well - the courtyard needs attention. Do not fear. You will get much work out of her."

"I will pay," Aradia said, quickly following the old woman's lead, although she had no idea where she would find the coin. "And work… of course!"

Growling to himself, the man turned and plodded back across the courtyard, stopping now and then to send suspicious glances over his shoulder.

"I am Poletzia, the angry man is Giorgos," the old woman said. "Do not feel you must explain. I can see you are in trouble. Come. Follow me. Tomorrow you can speak upon your troubles, or not. That of course is up to you."

Looking about her new quarters, she mused that her cell-like room was smaller than the pantry they had had at home. She berated herself; I need to stop thinking like this. It is better here than the hole I have been in for the last few weeks. After all, here at least she could think, she could be free. Hesitantly moving to sit on the small straw mat that she assumed to be a bed, she breathed a sigh and settled in to her new room.

Poletzia came into the room quietly as Aradia slept. Startled awake, she was not in good humor. Looking forward to privacy once she got off the ship, Aradia told Poletzia harshly to knock the next time. The woman looked at her strangely. She handed her a plain robe and told her that she needed to wear it. "We start work at sun up," she said as she shuffled away.

The owner of the establishment greeted her as she sleepily walked out of her small quarters the next morning. Squinting, he feasted his eyes over her enticing body and rubbed himself as he licked his thick lips. His pot-belly bulged over his worn grayish robe, and his dullish brown hair lie on his head like a threadbare tapestry showing pink scalp beneath it. Stretching his short frame he made an attempt to assert power over Aradia saying, "I'll squash that saucy air of yours, and enjoy it!" he snarled, "What place are you from with your uppity manners? Never mind, it matters not. Here… what are you doing?"

"Looking to find a large pot," she answered, staring defiantly, "as we are going to thoroughly clean the courtyard, and not to waste any of the herbs for tea, we will boil them today."

He pointed down to where the pots were kept, and when she bent over to look at them he pinched her derriere. She was so startled, she at first thought it to be an accident.

"All women are whores," snorted Giorgos, as he pinched her bottom again, and then pulled her up close to his erection.

Aradia tried to move away, but he had her backed into a corner. Forcefully pressing himself against her, his strength surprising, he ran his rough hands over her breast. Reaching under his robe to expose himself, he rubbed his hardness on her leg.

In his ecstasy he lost his hold on her and she pushed hard, gaining just enough room between them to kick him with her knee in the groin. It was not a debilitating blow, as she was at a disadvantage and could not put a huge amount of strength behind it. Slapping her he grabbed for her hair. She slapped him back, but instead of moving out of his reach, she moved closer. Prepared now, she decided she would never get close to this man again without being ready for him.

Breathing deeply, she called upon the elementals. She leaned close to Giorgos's ear and said, "Bastido avere ne la pace e ne bene e rana cantare," placing a spell on him, "that he know no peace, and forever sound like a frog."

Aradia laughed, but the laughter was devoid of pleasure as she said to him, "You touch me again and I will squeeze the life out of your balls!" Brushing herself off, she noticed that her hair had escaped its pins. Sweeping it behind her shoulders, she said in a husky voice, "I will work hard in this place, from morn till dark to earn my keep, but you do not have privileges here," and she pointed to herself. "Are we understood?"

"Go to work, butana," he mocked her as she sauntered away.

A picture of her grandmother ran through her mind as she quickly moved away from him and out into the courtyard, gladly filling her lungs with the aroma of sweet basil. She would do well to be as strong as her, she thought; she was such an amazing woman. You either loved her or hated her. Aradia remembered the outrageous words her grandmother had said as they took her off to prison, "You are making a mistake young man, but I will tell you this about the women of Etruria… one little cunt hair is stronger than an entire army. So… putting me in prison does not make you a big man, huh?"

Her grandmother had gone to prison because she had been accused of poisoning two men through a spell. No matter that an enormous amount of women came forward to speak in her favor about the many mothers and children that she had saved with her talent as a mid-wife. Even men came to her aid speaking about her skill with herbs, declaring that it gave them more energy to do their work—a clever way of saying she put passion into their sex lives. But in the end, the accusers were believed. It was much easier to place the blame on a witch, than to think two high born women would poison their mates.

Aradia remembered how hard her father had worked to clear his mother's name, even after her death to set her free somehow. Aradia always felt that her grandmother did not need liberating; she just needed to be remembered for who she was. She had been a witch and she had been proud of it. She had never looked for excuses, nor had she asked for pardons.

Aradia remembered with a chuckle, that when her grandmother was being hanged, all of the prison guards had gotten sick and had kept disappearing to the outhouse. The judge hadn't been able to keep still long enough to read the crimes against her grandmother, busy as he had been scratching his red blotchy hives on his face and arms.

When it was finally over, Aradia's father had locked himself in his study for days. When he had come out, with his eyes swollen and his expression determined, he moved his mother's family coat-of-arms that had hung on his wall, from his study to the sitting room where it would be more visible. He had wanted the world to know he was not ashamed of her.

It suddenly came to her that she could make money working spells for women here in Athens. Her grandmother had always told her, "Never do a spell for others that they do not cross your palm with coin." Grandmother had indeed been wise.

Chapter 8

Dripping with sensuality, a deep male voice spoke in her ancient tongue. "Bella donna, siete venuti da dio la grazia di questo luogo desolato?" Aradia upon hearing, "Beautiful woman, have you come from the gods to grace this desolate place?" turned gracefully toward him. Struck by his rich smooth voice and mesmerized by his liquid eyes, she was tongue-tied. Here was a Greek god come to life.

He had come upon her in the courtyard, leaving the room where the men drank. He seemed so intent on her, that she found herself shivering. All day she had gathered the few herbs she could find in the courtyard and those which the old woman had brought her, and now she had been about to retreat to the whitewashed cell that was her bedroom.

Flickering in the glow from the lanterns hanging on the wall, his golden hair seemed bathed in stardust. He traced her shoulder caressingly, and warmth tingled through her arm and body. Standing perfectly still, her mouth slightly parted, her tongue seductively traced her full upper lip.

The pale velvet blue of his eyes pulled her into their depths, mesmerizing her with thoughts of an ocean on a sultry day. With sun bronzed skin, his shoulders broad and waist narrow, he glowed of vibrant health. His aquiline nose was the same as that of the drawings of statues of the Greek gods that she had seen, yet the statues that she had found so exotic had never troubled her in this manner.

"You do not desire to be with the men and…well the women?" she asked when she finally found her voice.

"Now that I have found you, Regina Bella," he told her, "no other company, no other laughter and no other woman will ever give me the pleasure that your presence is giving me at this moment. I have searched the streets since I had my first fleeting glimpse of you. I have questioned servants, slaves and noblemen alike, but no one knew where you had disappeared to. I have tossed and turned at night wondering when I will set my eyes upon you again. And so it is with the utmost restraint that I pull myself from your presence, for unfortunately I must leave, as the tide waits for no man. It is only the most pressing business that calls me away. But I will soon return, and then I will hear your musical voice as it speaks my name."

He took his leave so suddenly, wrenching himself away forcefully it seemed, that it left Aradia confused, as she realized that she did not even know his name. She knew that she wanted to hear her own name upon his lips; she wanted to breathe in his scent, and feel the aching warmth again that coursed through her when he was near.

Suddenly exhausted, she headed to her room and fell asleep at once, only to dream of the handsome stranger, dreams so bittersweet they caused tears on her pillow, yet they put lightness in her heart for she knew with certainty she was going to see him again.

Aradia's modest room had no window, but she knew the sun had already risen. Dressing hurriedly, she dashed out to greet the day. Coming out of her room, she nearly knocked Poletzia down. They laughed and walked out back into the courtyard together. It was the first time she had heard the old woman laugh. They sat down on a small bench.

Aradia whispered, "I have put a spell on the patrone. He is a miserable old man! Why do you work for him? Surely you could do better."

"I do not work for him. He is my husband," Poletzia acknowledged, hanging her head.

"*Pardone mea fallo,*" responded Aradia, so stunned that she used her own language.

Aradia had no idea what to say to this disclosure, so she repeated her words again, this time in Greek. "Pardon my fault. I do not know what to say. I thought you worked here. I cannot believe you are married to such a man. Will you tell him that I have put a spell on him?"

"What spell did you put upon him?" asked the woman with a curious glint in her eye.

Aradia dropped her head. Not wanting to lie, she quietly shared, "he will have no peace. You will notice he will not sleep well at night, and will sound like a frog when he is able to speak."

"May I ask why you spelled him?" said the old woman, more with curiosity than censure.

"He… you know, he …" Aradia did not want to put into words what had happened when Giorgos tried to forced himself upon her.

"Yes, I know, child. He has always been that way. Believe me, it will get worse. Then again… if you can do what you say, he may be in for more than he bargained. Heh, heh." Her laugh was a sad sound in the morning light. "Hmmm…I know of many women who could use your skills. What spells can you cast?"

"All manner of spells," Aradia told her. "But for that I need more herbs. Pray, could you show me the quickest way to a wooded area. I will not poison! For my Grandmamma hung for that crime. One infamous woman in the family would be enough!"

The old woman laughed again, and Aradia gladly joined in. When Giorgos came to the door and in a croaking voice ordered his wife to cook for him, it made them laugh all the more. Coming out of the door, his face contorted in anger, he picked up a switch and struck Poletzia with it.

When he raised it to Aradia, she wrenched it from his hands and yelled, "Bastido." Pulling herself up to her full five feet nine inches, and glaring down at him, she strode purposefully out of the small courtyard with the switch in her hand, tossing it aside angrily before entering the hallway leading to her room.

The patron came running after her. "This has nothing to do with you. It is not your affair! Where are you going?" he croaked, slight panic in his voice. "You cannot walk away from here. I will be disgraced if it were to be thought that I sent family away."

"I will stay, but you will not put your hand on me nor strike your wife in anger ever again! That is the only condition on which I will remain here." She folded her long slender arms across her breast. "What is your answer?"

"You misjudge me. My women expect me to be strong!"

"I go." She turned, and shrugging her slender shoulders, she moved down the hall and into her room.

He ran in behind her before she could close the door on him. Out of breath and holding his protruding belly, he croaked, "All right, all right, I agree!"

Aradia told him impatiently. "I am going into the woods to fetch herbs today. You will allow Poletzia to go with me."

As she left him, puffing behind her, she felt a sense of power, and though it felt good, she knew she should not gloat upon it. He made no further protest, due in part, Aradia knew, to the spell she had already put on him.

As with the night before, she hardly made it to her bed from the exhaustion. She slept fitfully and woke with the sun. Going out into the garden, she found two women in the courtyard awaiting her for spells. Aradia would have no peace in her mornings unless she spoke up. It had been like this every morning since she first did a spell for a friend of Poletzia. Grandmother said it was important to have quiet time in which to reflect, other- wise you would not be very good at your craft.

She made her decision and spoke firmly to the women waiting in the courtyard, "Go and come back at midday! Come bearing food, food cooked by your very own hands. Bring coin also, though the amount is up to you. Tell others wanting my service, to not disturb me so early. Come only at midday."

They said not a word, fearfully they nodded and left. She did not like to be so gruff, but knew she needed her quiet time. She wished she could go to spend time by the water. Hmm, she thought, I will make plans. I'll go to the Acropolis and see the sights of Greece which I have heard tell of, and then I will go and sit by the water.

Aradia's days were spent doing spells, and her nights watching from the shadows of the courtyard for the blue eyed man who looked so like Adonis. Surely he had meant what he said. She knew he had felt drawn to her, just as she had to him. But until he came, what was she to do but wait on fortune's tide? She knew the fate of those who were not citizens of Athens. If her identity were revealed, she would at once become a slave.

A moon had come and gone. The amount of business she was doing in the afternoons with the women of the city was keeping her busy. They were attentive, and brought her such delicacies as huge black olives and tender veal wrapped in grape leaves, but most of all she loved the baked honey and almonds in a flaky crust—so sweet. Aradia loved the food of Greece, though she could not say the same about most of the men.

Sitting in her tiny room counting coins and admiring the lovely pieces of jewelry the fine women of Athens had given her, she thought how sad it was that here in Athens, a great city state, scores of women were miserable.

Deciding to take a day for herself, Aradia begged the man who brought wine to the establishment to take her to see the city. He finally gave in, more because of her beguiling smile and the knowledge she displayed of the goddesses of old, than the money she had promised him. After all both of them knew that as a woman in Greece she was not allowed the freedom to go out without a male family member with her, and even then there were few reasons that women strayed beyond the home.

Aradia rose to her feet in the wagon as the driver rounded the corner and started ascending the limestone hill where the Acropolis rising high above the glory of the city with its marble shrines was located. The great citadel and the splendor of the buildings it encompassed were well known in Etruria, where art, beauty, and great accomplishments were often spoken of.

Aradia could not contain her excitement. Enthralled by Lycabettus Hill, with its unique molten hues standing out against the clouds and blue sky, she stood taller and peered upward until the driver begged her to be seated for her own safety as they negotiated their way up the rutted road of the foothills. As they came closer, she noticed how much larger the buildings were compared to those at home, though the structures were much the same. As always, picturesque scenery brought tears to her eyes.

"I would be delighted to accompany someone as lovely as you, miss," the driver told her with a huge, toothless grin as he stopped the wagon.

Having reached the level beyond which the rutty road would take them, he helped her to the ground.

"Let us begin, *Bella Donna*," he crooned as he offered Aradia his arm. He flattered her taking the time to speak a few words in her language. Their height the same, her eyes peered at dark brown eyes that reminded her of something in herself, something buried; something very painful. Shaking the feeling away she took his arm, and felt his lean and muscled strength. His short brown hair was graying at the temples, and his skin was leathered and deeply creased from the sun. She decided at day's end she would give him extra coin for being so courteous to her.

Nearing the entranceway, a mammoth white marble stone tinged with pink stood to the right, half her height and just as wide. Above it there was a statue dedicated to Demeter's daughter. Aradia was sure of this because the beautiful maiden was clutching a narcissus, the flower left behind by Persephone, when she was abducted.

"Here," the old man told her with grand ceremony, "is where the worshipers of the mysteries of Eleusis end their pilgrimage in honor of our mother goddess, Demeter."

Aradia carried flowers and food for offerings to the goddess and placed the food on the altar of Demeter, for are not all mothers concerned with nourishment Aradia pondered. As she knelt to pray to Demeter, she asked her to embrace the mother that she had lost and the sister she so loved. She treasured the story of Demeter searching the world over for her daughter, Persephone, who while picking wildflowers in a meadow was abducted by the god of the underworld. She imagined that the legend spoke poignantly of the lost innocence of women in general. At any event, her eyes were moist as she got unsteadily to her feet, and the wagon driver gently took her arm and guided her to the next path.

As they walked through a gate-like structure, she spotted an alluring sanctuary.

"Oh, this is lovely." The trees and bushes surrounding it were alive with all of the hues of the rainbow. The rose colored bench carved from stone, curved around the bushes in the shape of a crescent moon.

A statue of a partially naked young woman with a hound at her feet, carrying a bow and a pouch of arrows strung around one shoulder, caught her eye.

"Is this Artemis, Virgin Goddess of the Hunt?" asked Aradia, as she brought her hand to her mouth, her eyes widening with excitement!

"That is so," replied her companion as he folded his hands humbly in front of his heart. "Is she not beautiful?"

"Yes," observed Aradia, "in my country we call her Diana. She is connected with the moon, but then… I guess all women are."

"Yes," he said, "so true."

"Let us sit here and break our fast with bread, cheese and meat in honor of the goddess of the hunt. It is quiet and secluded and offers shade," Aradia spoke while not taking her eyes off the softly shimmering statue.

Untying the hemp that held the sack together, he made a show of placing the cloth and the food before Aradia. She felt honored at this display, and rewarded him with a brilliant smile.

After sharing the food, they continued their walk. Aradia sauntered down a worn path that led them through the center of the Acropolis. Laughter echoed off the walls as people strolled the grounds. Though the gaiety was lovely to hear she wished for silence, so she walked toward the deserted trail taking them to a quiet area.

"Pray, what is that grand temple?" asked Aradia, getting to the end of the path.

"It pays homage to Athena."

"*Minerva,*" she whispered to herself. The memory of the radiant face of this goddess on the gates of Volsinii came back to her. She could see it on that fateful day. Minerva's beauty destroyed, along with the city that honored her. It took Aradia's breath away. She clutched at her heart.

The gentleman paused, firmly holding onto her arm.

"No, I am all right. Minerva it is what Athena is now called in Etruria. It just made me yearn for my family, that is all," she stammered.

She could not yet speak of the atrocity, even to this kind man. She cleared her throat and pulled herself together saying, "Your Athena is a beautiful goddess. What does she signify for you?"

"In peace time, she is the Goddess of Wisdom," he told her. "In times of war, she instructs us to bear arms with strength and wisdom. She is a goddess that is fair and stands firm in her decisions. She will not begin a fight, but she knows how to win if one is opened to her. Knowing strategy, she teaches it well. But much of the old wisdom is lost," he added. "Many people try to make her just a warrior. We know better, you and me." And with a soft smile, he winked.

"Yes, it is so in my country as well," Aradia told him. "Minerva has much wisdom and strength. I see her with a golden sword beside her. It is the sword of truth. She uses the sword to remind us to speak with integrity. It is when you are not willing to speak your truth, that she raises her sword to your throat in warning. If you do not learn… then perhaps you will lose your head," she laughed. "It is just my own way of course, of understanding what she teaches. Do not mind my ramblings," she apologized.

Her companion became very somber. "Yes, yes, I like the picture it forms in my mind. I can see her like that too. People are not open with each other. The closer people get to someone they love, the less honest they tend to be. They begin to fear that they will hurt the other's feelings. They protect themselves by being dishonest. Small indiscretions, they think, what can it matter? But it eats away at the bond they have with the other person. Then soon it eats away at the relationship they have with themselves. My marriage died because of small untruths. I have come to honor truth above all."

Glancing at Aradia, the wagon driver hesitated. "It has been wonderful talking to you, and I don't even know your name."

"I am sorry, for you are correct. I have neglected to give it to you. It is Aradia. And yours?"

The simple gesture of taking his hand in friendship caused her to have a powerful vision. It was of a young woman lying on the floor of a diminutive but elegantly furnished home. There was blood around her heart and a great deal more spread on the floor around her legs. A man was standing over her with a look of anger, yet satisfaction on his face. Blood dripped from the knife in his hand. Aradia knew that the man standing over her was her mate, and this vision had something to do with the man in front of her. Yet she knew intuitively, that it was not he that killed the young woman.

"I have become much too familiar," he told her. "I have overstepped myself. Just call me Azarias. I will now go back to the wagon and give you time to yourself."

Aradia strode along, purposefully trying to shake the pain she had just touched into. She felt sad about the discomfort their conversation had brought up, and his reason for dismissing himself so quickly, though she enjoyed being alone.

After a while, the day became so alluring that she opened up to the sun and the feeling of healing that it brought into her body. She loved to look at the moon, in part because it made her certain that there were important things for her to do in the world. But the sun was very powerful too, she reflected.

Just then, Aradia spotted an outcropping of rock that beckoned her to lie down. Approaching it she touched its warmth and stretched out and began breathing deeply. In her mind she commenced chanting the names of the goddesses. She had done this many times before, to pray or to ask for visions. Relaxation filled her body as she paid attention to her breath.

Desimena appeared and sat down beside her.

"Yes, you are feeling the importance of the sun. The sun is a gift to all mankind. If only all people could understand that the moon represents the feminine and the sun represents the masculine, and both are necessary in life. One enhances the other. Many do not recognize that the moon shines in the day, just as the sun always shines. Both exist doing the thing they were put here to do; reflect one another. Is that not what relationships are about, Aradia?"

"I would not know. I have not had a relationship. The one I care about thinks I am a servant. If he wants me, it is probably for all the wrong reasons!" scowled Aradia. Folding her arms in front of her as if to say, how is it that you do not know the world is treating me poorly?

"It is not only a lover that is considered a relationship. You have relationships with everyone you bring into your life, even this short relationship here today with Azarias. You reflected something to him and him to you. Both of you are fighting it. He reminded you of your father, and you pushed it down because if you feel pain, you think you are weak. He, on the other hand, has pushed his pain so far as to believe it never happened. I am here today to ask you to be mindful of yourself and your reactions to others because they always have something to teach you."

Aradia pursed her lips to one side and looked away for a moment.

"When you began this day, you did not ask the wagon driver his name because you did not want to open the door to pain. You recognized a spark of friendship, but you were afraid to open the door to intimacy. For him it was the same. Being in the body is not about pushing down the pain; it is about experiencing it. Life is about experience of all kinds. The positive feminine principle allows you to feel the pain; the positive male principle picks you up and says 'All right, that hurt, but I have survived. Now what's next?' When you work with those things that are life affirming, this is the process."

Glaring at Desimena, Aradia put her hands on her hips and spoke in an explosive manner.

"I have survived, and I have been looking to what's next!" said Aradia, through gritted teeth. "How dare you preach to me? It is not you that has lost your family, been dragged to a foreign country and made to sleep in a cubical that should not be considered a room. Worst of all I have had to put up with a man that is mean, dirty and lustful! I was having a good day… and here you come to lecture me." Aradia turned away, but unfortunately she could still see Desimena in her mind's eye. "Oh, go away if you cannot tell me something pleasant!" Aradia spat at Desimena.

"Child… I love you more than you can know, and yes, you are picking yourself up and trying to survive. However, you have not experienced the pain. You have not talked about the deaths to anyone, or of what you have been through since their loss. You are building a new life on shifting sand. I am concerned. It is my job to help you with your life in the body, not to give you platitudes and empty words." Desimena's tone sounded more determined. "So then, I will go on with my teaching, seeing that the aggressive male part of you is present, and that is part of my lesson."

As she stared angrily at her teacher, Aradia leaned back, putting some slack in her stance, though she still held her hands on her thighs.

Desimena smiled reflectively and began teaching her errant student.

*"The **negative feminine** principle says 'I am in pain; I am a victim.' The negative feminine has two ways of dealing with the role of victim or martyr. The first says I will speak of my pain to everyone that will listen, and they will commiserate with me. They will know how I suffer; in that way the victim continues to be stuck.*

The second, the martyr, from a place of fear pushes the pain and anger so far down in the body that it becomes inner sadness. That is the quiet sufferer, but there is another way. The positive feminine principle allows you time to grieve, by expressing the pain and anger with someone whom you trust."

Desimena reached over to touch Aradia on the arm. "Listen well to that which I say now child, for it is very important." Desimena waited for a moment to see if there was any reaction from her charge but there was only stillness.

"If the pain is not experienced in the body in a positive way, the **negative male** *principle will become active. The negative male will become spiteful, aggressive or rude. Or the negative male will allow the anger to come out of the body in rage or in violence."*

Desimena realized she had been very long winded. "My job is not always easy, but I would have it no other way. You are worth the effort, and I will always be a part of you. No matter that I point out the things that test you in this life. I will always be the wings under your feet."

Aradia's spirit guide very slowly drifted off, hoping the words she had said would be taken to heart. Desimena wished that Aradia would let down her wall of protection, and let someone else be strong for her, just long enough so that she could learn the difference between strength and courage.

When she came back to the wagon, Aradia put her hand on the driver's shoulder in a warm gesture.

"Thank you for walking with me and acting as my guide, Azarias," she said. "It will be my pleasure to reward you well. The light of the day is fading. It is time to return."

"I have been rewarded well by sharing some time with you. I am sorry for the way I acted, but you remind me of my daughter. She died not so long ago, and my wife left me… I think because she could not speak of the pain. I realized that I too, had pushed the pain away and lived in a world that never housed my daughter. It was easier to think she never existed than to remember her death. The world is less because of her loss," Azarias spoke softly, as if testing the words. "Have you ever known anyone like that," he asked as he helped her into the wagon.

Aradia sat in quiet contemplation. She knew she was not yet ready to speak of the tragedy. But this kind man needed something to let him open to his pain. The words came hesitantly.

"Oh yes ... my sister Sardiana. She ... she died not long ago and the world is much less because of her. We were very close." A quiet tear slipped down Aradia's cheek. "You are the first person I have told. Thank you for listening. The world would be a better place if everyone was as kind as you have been to me today."

Seating herself in the wagon as it slowly began its trek back to Athens; she looked out over the Aegean Sea and felt a loneliness she could never have imagined. Talking of the tragedy today helped Azarias, she was sure, but remembering it now she gripped the wooden edge of the wagon. Fiercely squeezing the rough planks, causing rotting wood to splinter, she knew that her spirit guide was right. She needed to feel the pain-*but not now*! She was not yet ready. If she allowed her pain to surface, she feared she would splinter like the wood beneath her hands.

Chapter 9

Waking refreshed and ready for her day, Aradia vowed that next time she would spend more time at Piraeus, gazing the Aegean Sea. From all that she was told of the Athenian culture she was fearful that in order to get away she might have to take one of Giorgos whores, as women of that persuasion had freedoms that apparently she did not.

At noon, she met with a young woman in the courtyard and gave her some herbs.

"I want you to make a tea by mixing linden flower with raspberry leaf and then use just a bit of the herbs in this packet," Aradia told her. "Before and during your courses, you should drink a few cups a day. It will help with your pain."

Clutching the small packet to her chest the woman told Aradia she was to marry soon, and wanted a child more than anything. Aradia checked her wrist on her right hand. "Hmm," murmured Aradia, while tracing a line on the woman's hand.

"If you go to the temple to sanctify your marriage, the priests will not allow you to have the ceremony. Do you see this line?"

Aradia traced the top most line of the three that circled the back of the woman's wrist. Chain like, it curved up and into the lower portion of her palm.

"This would reveal to the priests that you cannot bear a child. I will give you a talisman and with much prayer and belief you shall indeed give birth."

Aradia took a small stone out of the pouch that lay beside her on the bench and pressed it into the woman's hands.

"This is a goddess stone. You see it has a hole in the middle. It represents your woman part and the sacredness of it. Pray to the goddess Demeter to help you conceive a child. Pray to the goddess Hera to help make you a good wife, but one that does not cower before her husband.

Hera never cowered before Zeus! His power did not dwarf hers, for she understood the royal line comes through the woman."

⚜

As she readied herself to help with the evening meal, she found her thoughts running to her handsome blue-eyed stranger. Aradia took extra care with her hair, pinched her cheeks, and entered the kitchen. It had indeed been a peaceful day. She felt good news would come to her soon.

Her pot-bellied host leered at her in his usual fashion and said, "So, your gentleman came last eve, put up a fuss when he thought you might be gone."

She flushed. It warmed her heart thinking that he had made a fuss, but not wanting Giorgos to see, she bent over to put away a pan in which she had heated her herbs. He rubbed her bottom then moved away quickly.

Throwing a flask at him, she said, "The next time it will be two of your best. You cannot win with me. Why do you try?"

"You try my patience!" he yelled, coming forward, and grabbing at her breasts.

She kicked him hard in the shin. "The next time it will be harder and higher!" Her words were hot and venomous, steeled with determination. "Do you understand me?"

"I've seen you making eyes at the blue-eyed devil," he told her. "He is too high-born for you! If he could, he would put you up in some room, and visit you when he chose to do so. A paid butana!" He began to croak miserably, and groaned in pain. "If you were my slave I would sell you to him!" he said with a hoarseness barely audible while cupping his throat to ease the pain.

A string of curses rang out of her mouth. He did not understand them. "You pig! You cannot sell what you do not own!" She picked up bowls and flasks and hurled them at him.

He lunged towards her. "Butana!" he croaked.

"I curse you for a fool," she said while she kicked and bit his arm, and then she spat at him.

"No! I take that back. There is no need to curse you with being a fool. You are one!" she said running to her room.

✦

"I cannot stay any longer," she told Poletzia later that night. "It is time I leave. I just wanted you to know."

"Please," begged Poletzia, "just a bit longer. I…it is important. I cannot yet tell you why. Will you stay? Besides if you leave here there is nowhere to go. You will become a slave!"

✦

Aradia stayed in her room that night although she wanted badly to know if the blue eyed stranger would come again. Giorgos tried to get in, but was unable to do so because she had pushed the bed against the door. He stood outside threatening her, his voice diminishing with every word. Finally he crawled off to bed.

Because she needed guidance, she sang to the gods and to the sweet goddesses. She put salt at the door and around her in a circle for protection. She asked to see her fate. The answer came.

"You are living your fate; it is time to carve out your destiny." This was repeated over and over. She did not sleep well, tossing and turning through the night.

Aradia arose from bed still tired and trudged off to the courtyard where two young girls were waiting and anxious for her help with matters of love. One of the girls reminded her of Sardiana. Normally, she would have sent them away, telling them to come back at noon, but today she listened to their stories patiently, gave them a love potion to satisfy their concerns, and sent them off.

But once she was alone, tears began to fall. Sitting on the oak bench in the courtyard with beauty and color and the scent of flowers all around her, she could not help but think of her beloved sister. It crushed her heart to see one that so closely resembled her. She knew only too well that she had not yet mourned the loss of her family. Aradia realized that seeing the young girl today was a catalyst. She let herself feel the loss, and began to cry. Heart-wrenching sobs tore at her as she pulled her hair, rocking back and forth, moaning words incomprehensible to any who would overhear. She was speaking the ancient Etruscan language that she had shared with her grandmamma when she was a child.

She cried for the life her brothers had not had a chance to live, and for the warmth of her sister's love, and grieved the fact that never again would her mother and father make love any longer, for she had heard them say that was what they would miss most when they left their bodies behind. Finally, she cried for herself, because she was in love with a man she did not know, and felt he believed her to be a servant.

How is it that he could be so blind? Had it been his intention simply to use her? She cried until her chest hurt, and the deep well of her tears dried up.

I will not let life push me down, she railed! I will take part in my fate. I will leave here soon and not be around the likes of the patron. He disgusts me! I will see what comes next. She then prayed out loud to the goddess Juno, goddess of love.

"Great goddess, hear my plea. Allow me to know what the blue-eyed stranger's intentions are for me. Goddess, I implore you. If he wants me not, then help me leave here. This place crushes my soul."

Later that night Poletzia crept into Aradia's room. "I have been getting coins from the ones who came to you for spells and I am saving to go to my sister's in Volos," said Poletzia in a whisper. "I am leaving my husband and the money is needed, for my younger sister is very poor. Please do not be angry with me. That is why I take a fee to bring these women to you. They are happy, you make a profit, and I free myself of the old bastido. The money I am earning will last the rest of my life if I spend carefully," Poletzia nodded, looking very proud of herself.

She continued speaking resolutely. "Aradia, I want you to know that though we have not been good friends, somehow I count you as one. That sounds strange, I know, but it is true. You have shut yourself off. I have tried to honor that, yet strength pours out from you. It gives me power right here in my gut. It makes me know that I am worth more than being a beating post for that brute of a man. I am sad for all I have missed in my life, yet I am determined in the same moment to grab what is left. I am an old woman, older than my years. But no matter what is left, it will be lived in peace with freedom to think for myself, and the laughter of my sister to soothe this old heart. Thank you for the gift you have given me. You need not say anything. I will go now."

Aradia sat up in bed, absorbing what had been said. It was true that she had not become friends with the old woman. She *had* cut herself off, judging Poletzia a fool for staying where she had been so little appreciated, in a place where whores came and went. But in this country she had had no choice. Yet she had a choice now and Aradia was glad she was taking it. As Poletzia was leaving the room, Aradia touched her shoulder. Poletzia hesitantly turned back and looked Aradia in the eyes.

Aradia smiled down at the old women, "I am very glad for you, but more than that I am proud to know you. You honor me in saying I helped you, but had it been my grandmother seeking refuge instead of me, you would have been out of here the night she met you. So by those standards, I failed. Yet it is my grandmother's very words that comfort me. If you try you can never fail."

⚜

When *he* entered the courtyard that night, Aradia felt his presence, but she did not look at him, fearful that she would be mistaken and not see love in his eyes. Then again she was more afraid that she would see his soul in his eyes, pouring forth a deep and abiding love, for such a love would surely frighten her more.

"*Regina Bella,*" he whispered. "When I opened the door to the bedroom at the inn where you had been taken when you first entered this country, apparently I rescued you from men who would have sold you into slavery."

Aradia stole a glance around her, at the shadows which might hide danger. She had known that being sold into slavery was her intended fate. And she had remained secluded here, for the most part, because she was aware of the laws of Athens. These stringent laws would have made her a slave in an instant, if it had been discovered that she was not one of Poletzia's relatives, but a foreigner. But suddenly she felt more vulnerable than she had ever felt in the past.

"These men are angry with me," he continued looking deep into her eyes, "They have followed me and questioned me to see if I know where you are." Taking her hand, he assured her. "No, they do not follow me now. I have been very careful. But what I have come to realize is that I put myself in harm's way so you can sell yourself into slavery here?" He motioned to her surroundings.

"Sir, there is more than one kind of slavery," she told him. "What better did you have in mind for me?"

"There is a large and exquisite villa on an island south of here. Dignitaries and reverenced academics are welcome there."

"Is this your villa, sir?" Aradia asked, hope stirring inside her.

"No, but for some time now, it has been my home when I come to Greece," he told her.

"I shall be leaving here soon," answered Aradia in a burst of defiance. "It will be my decision when and where I go, and only I will know!"

"On that you are wrong." said the handsome gentleman, turning her toward him. "I know your every move. I do not try to ensnare you, simply to see to it that you come to no harm." Aradia turned and began to walk away.

He touched her gently on the arm, and then turned her around to face him, saying softly, "*Tu'mea cour.*"

Silken words of love, so bold, so welcomed. She spoke them to herself, "You have my heart." She had never heard words verbalized that pulled at her heart as these three simple words. She knew that he meant them, and she experienced a timeless moment knowing that they have always loved each other and yet she felt she had never before made love to him. She wanted to experience that, loving him, making love to him, being loved by him-all of it! And yet, she was frightened. Would all of the emotions, the pain, the loss, the vision of her family lost to her and to the world come tumbling out if she opened her heart?

He spoke again, his honeyed voice bringing an image to her mind of molten lava caressing frozen tundra. "I have many words to say to you. I wish to know how you are called in your dialect. It means much to me."

"I am called Aradia. It means, bright orb like the moon or the sun," she said raising her chin and pulling herself up to her full height.

"Aradia...Your name fits you well. A-ray-de-a. I love the feel of it on my tongue. Please, I must speak to you in private. Come sit with me under the olive tree. There is a pleasant bench I see." His voice rich in timber yet smooth as silk, sent shivers through her body.

"*Regina delle strege,*" he said, as he knelt on the ground and took her hand, "*Regina della notte oscura della stelle e selle luna. L'amore che io te portata, vo per l'amore chi me porti e che io pure. Tu'mea cour, Colli votre luce sulle mea."*

The words flowed from his lips as he lovingly spoke her language, such precious words and sentiment said with enormous feeling. "Queen of all enchantresses. Queen of the dark of night and of the stars and of the moon. All the love I have felt of late, and by the love I feel, which I shall ever feel... until I die. You have my heart. Cast your light upon me."

Unprepared for such eloquence, she could not respond at first to this princely man kneeling at her feet. His words were very loving. But he thought her a slave or a servant at best, and could not be asking her hand in marriage. Was he then, asking her to be his mistress? Questions were colliding in her mind, collapsing her ever present need for independence.

Sitting there upon the bench, she experienced the same horrendous and helpless feeling that had come over her when she saw her friend, Phesoj being killed. Her energy drained and her body went limp, and she knew that her eyes were begging him to be gentle with her. Just for this moment... she wanted to lean on someone.

In a near-whisper, Aradia said, "I feel a great need to be held...but at this time take no liberties ... for I think my heart would break if you did."

He sat beside her and held her gently.

"I do not even know your name," she said.

"My name is Tomis," he told her, "and I will take you to the villa that I spoke of. It is owned by a man that has always made me welcomed. Many say he is unscrupulous in his business dealings, and that he has been a pirate in his day, but he has been nothing but kind to me. I am afraid it is quite a journey though, for his home resides on a little known island off the coast of Crete."

Aradia nodded her head and moving like one in a trance, she went to gathered a few things together. While placing them in a shawl and tying it tightly, Poletzia entered her room. She had decided to give her new found friend most of the coinage and all the jewelry she had been given by the towns-women. The jewelry had not held any appeal to her and the old women needed the coins far more than she did.

"Poletzia, I am leaving shortly," she said as she handed her the pouch. "Take this and leave here on the morrow. Promise me now, for I shall know if you speak the truth."

Nodding, the old woman gave her promise.

"Did you get a lock of hair from the patron as I asked?" said Aradia.

"Yes," she said, taking it out of her pocket, "and I have wrapped it as you requested."

Taking it, Aradia embraced her like the true friend she had become.

Rushing into the courtyard, she was relieved that he still waited for her. As they slipped away through the shadows, she saw Poletzia watching them, a smile on her toothless mouth.

But her reluctant host was waiting for them, just outside the courtyard in the narrow, rutted street.

"Have you stolen from me?" he demanded of Aradia. "Why, otherwise, are you creeping away in the night? Who is this man? What will I tell your relatives if they come searching for you. I took you in after all!"

Aradia could see that Tomis was about to push him away, but she interrupted him saying she wanted a word with the patron.

"Giorgos you are not sleeping well," she whispered menacingly in his ear, "and you can hardly speak. I have put a curse upon you. You have heard tales that I am a witch? Doubt it not. I will remove the curse when I hear your wife is safely away from you. I have given her the means to do such. If there is harm that comes to her, then I shall double the curse. I am sure that no one will care if you cannot speak, but I have been told that men die from lack of sleep. Heed me in this matter."

She took from her pocket the lock of hair that Poletzia had given to her. It was tied with black and red ribbon. He had no doubt from the color and coarseness of the hair that it was his.

"I hold the power in my hand," she hissed, and she knew from the frightened look in his eyes that he believed her. Aradia put it back in her pocket and with her fingers directed at him, made the sign of the evil eye.

Only then did she and Tomis step into the night, fog and darkness enshrouding them. Walking a short distance they came upon a small stable. The stable boy, giving Tomis a knowing glance, seemed ready and eagerly handed the reins of a deep russet colored destrier to him. Climbing up in front of him, allowing the rhythm of the horse to lull her and give her a sense of true peace for the first time in months, Aradia fell asleep in his arms.

Tomis did not know what he was going to do with this fascinating woman, but knew he could not lose her. He had never felt love before, but he was very aware this powerful feeling was far more than lust. Aradia rocking against him crazed him with desire, but the tender feelings welling up in his heart cautioned him to protect her and let her sleep. Those feelings won and always would, even though Tomis knew that to keep peace with his father, it was expected of him to marry for matters of state, and that this woman in his arms would never be a candidate for such a marriage.

Arriving in the dead of night at the Port at Piraeus, Tomis began to slow his steed. The dock was soundless. He knew of the many dangers that lurked in the shadows. His intent was to get Aradia aboard his waiting ship as soon as possible. The night was moonless as he peered out over the white-capped waves. He wondered if his beautiful queen was a good sailor. His intuition told him that the next few days on the open water would be intoxicating for a sea faring man, but challenging for a novice. He did not know exactly what devils followed Aradia, but he felt they would be safer once they boarded his ship.

Opening her eyes, Aradia turned toward Tomis and asked if he could see the ship they were to sail on. He assured her that he could, as he slid from the horse and held his hand up for her to dismount.

Finding a small rowing boat that was lacking one ore, Tomis smiled and said, "At least it seems to be minus any gaping holes." Climbing into the tiny craft they headed for the silent ship, anchored and misted in a foggy veil of darkness.

As Tomis rowed against the jagged white waves his mind drifted to the problems he had been trying not to think about. Soon he would be parted from her again, a thought so uncomfortable that he forced it away.

Tomis' mind raced back in time, before he met her... before he fell under Aradia's spell, he thought affectionately. A league of diplomats had left his homeland, the city of Tomi, a large sea port on the Black Sea, to create a marriage between him and a Scythian princess. Once he saw Aradia that first time, he knew that he could not go through with it, but he had been unsuccessful at putting a stop to it. He knew only that he did not want to marry anyone but this beguiling creature in his arms.

As a consequence, his fate was unknown to him, except for the sure knowledge that his father would most assuredly disinherit him for marrying a woman that he would find beneath his status. Thinking of the beauty that sat beside him as he rowed, he recognized that he had been barely able to eat or sleep of late. He shook his head with the unbidden thought, most men in his position had a mistress, but it was absurd to think that this headstrong, auburn haired beauty would content herself with being anyone's mistress.

As the sea was rough, Tomis had suggested that Aradia lie down until they reached the ship. Throwing her cloak over the damp wood she did just that, closing her eyes to the forceful stirring of the small boat.

"Ahoy...ahoy!" he called, as they approached the ship. Calling out again they heard scuffling above and soon saw faces peering over the rail. A rope ladder was thrown down to them and Tomis gave her instructions in how to climb in the windy condition that ensued.

Seeing the ladder swing violently in the wind, Tomis grabbed and held the bottom rung firmly with his weight. Aradia grasped it, her knuckles turning white as she struggled to get her foot securely on the ladder. His weight and hers did not stop it from slamming recklessly against the rocking ship. Slowly she climbed the unstable rope to the top. Tomis was right behind her, knowing that his weight served somewhat in stabilizing the precarious ladder.

Hearing an audible gasp Tomis looked up at the woman leaning over the rail who was holding her hand out toward the woman he loved.

Sovonya, his friend, had pushed the hardiest of his sailors out of the way, and she seemed to melt at the sight of Aradia.

"What hardship has this poor child endured?" she cried. "Oh dear, hurry follow me. Both of you are drenched, and the child is exhausted I see." Seeing that the cold and trembling young woman could hardly stand, Sovonya clucked at him to carry her, watching to see that he followed closely as she led him to the cabin she had made ready for her charge. She had seen fifty years but still had a fiery spirit and the remnants of blaze in her hair. Her golden eyes never missed a thing. Slim and with a pleasant figure, she was sharp yet tactful.

When Tomis laid Aradia upon the bed, she did not rouse.

"You are in good hands, Bella Donna," he whispered to her sleeping form. "I leave you with an old and powerful friend who is, like you, a sorceress. But she will teach you to keep your sorcery quiet, to keep you safe. It will do her good to have you for company. She quietly holds court over the villa we are headed to as if she owns it. You will love her as I do."

Placing a kiss on her forehead, he turned to leave. Aradia, sighing, turned over and moved more deeply into a sound sleep.

Sovonya stepped out into the hallway with him, concern turning her golden eyes to bronze.

"I need not ask what this lovely creature means to you," she told him. "I can see all that you feel in your eyes. Tell me nothing more at this time. As for the future, I know it will be hard for you, but you must keep your distance as much as possible, for she is indeed a temptation. You are betrothed, though word has not yet come that the princess has accepted. Well...perhaps she will turn you down, not wanting the scoundrel of Tomi after all," she teased. "We shall hope in that direction, it would make things easier I can see."

❦

In the next couple of days Tomis and Sovonya formulated a plan, whereby this young woman, Aradia, would become someone whose social acceptance would be dependent on the support which Sovonya would provide. She would see to it that the rumor was put abroad that she was being visited by a young relative from Corinth.

"They need know nothing more," Sovonya told Tomis. "She is here and she is beautiful. The important thing is that people become accustomed to her presence."

Sovonya was a romantic; she wanted to see Tomis have the woman of his dreams. Certainly, she did not want to see history repeat itself, for his father did not have the woman of his heart. She put the unbidden memories away. After all, what was she but an interfering old woman reminiscing about things that could never be? However, the thoughts were there, and could not be ignored. She pondered on them a moment before clearing her head, and then brushed them aside.

As Sovonya walked the deck the next morning, she realized that they were getting close to the island and she wondered how Rumaldea, when he returned from his latest voyage, would accept Aradia. He roared at times like a lion, and of course one of his ships bore that name, but he also helped many men find their way to fortune.

Trying to warm herself in the sun, Sovonya realized that when the word was out about her guest, the young men in her circle would be interested. But, she thought, she would try her best to protect Tomis' interests. Of all the young men who had come through the villa that most people called Lyons Gate, he was her favorite. Suddenly Tomis' voice interrupted the direction of her mind.

"Sovonya," Tomis said as he grasped her hands in a warm greeting. "The sea agrees with you. May I speak plainly? Perhaps share with you more on what we have already touched upon."

"You have always spoken plainly and with truth," she said, "after all we are friends you and me."

"I have spoken my heart to Aradia on the night I beckoned her to come away with me," Tomis said, "I know it was not proper. I cannot explain what came over me..."

He ran his hand through his golden mane, tossing it back. Thoughtfully he looked over the rail, but then shook his head from side to side in a manner of hopelessness.

"I did not ask for her hand in marriage, though I truly wanted to with all of my heart," he continued. "I dare not tell her of the betrothal, for I fear she has already been through so much. I am not sure the nature of what has transpired, and I know she is not yet ready to take me into her confidence." Tomis reached out to Sovonya, clasping her hands in his. "Please help me. What can I do?"

Tomis had spoken to Sovonya with such depth of emotion that it brought tears to the eyes of the great lady. But then she recomposed herself, for she knew she must keep her wits about her. Stepping back, she took her hands away from his.

"As for your marriage," she said, "you are right that it would not be proper for you to break your obligations in that matter. Your people are depending on your marriage to bring trade and peace between your lands. If you fail because the Scythian Princess declines, you will then be released from your obligation. But you know as well as I do, that your father will not take well to *your* declining. Please Tomis, have mercy on your father for he means well."

"You have always had a soft place in your heart for my father," he told her. "I was very surprised when you left Tomi, but even more surprised finding you at Lyons Gate. My father was very angry when his council made it clear that he could not marry you. His dalliances would have been a temporary matter, I am sure. He was not used to being told no, he…"

"This is not a conversation to have now," she interrupted. Desperately needing to change the subject she said, "It is time that we have some nourishment. I will see to that now." Walking away she peeked in on her charge and then went to the galley to see if she could find a cook to serve them.

When she first arrived on the ship, Aradia had slept for thirty hours. The last couple of days, Sovonya had kept her busy with sketches for new apparel and wild stories of Lyons Gate. Having explained that the villa was on an island and that though it was a polis of Greece, the people that lived there did not pay as much attention to convention and enjoyed a freer existence. Men and women enjoyed music in the court yards, and plays in the amphitheater and they even dined together on special occasions. A few… very feisty and talented ladies on the island were philosophers and mathematicians. And no, they weren't courtesans, she assured a stunned but happy Aradia. Then Sovonya teased her unmercifully as to just what she knew about courtesans.

"I have read about such things happening in Athens and personally I boil over at the thought that a courtesan can have such freedom simply because she gives sexual favor," simmered Aradia, "and a learned woman such as myself has to be cloistered away as if she has leprosy. Then again, it is not the fault of the courtesan. I have nothing but high regard for one who has the intelligence to get around the ridiculous laws of stupid men! But I would ask when will they, if ever, recognize the error of their ways and allow…there you see! Even I use the term. Why should it be men who get to *allow* anything! Why in my country I…we…"

Sovonya sat, playing with her most prized possession, her fan, given to her by a *client* from the orient when she was young and beautiful. The fan, as herself, was somewhat faded and worn but still had strength and character.

"You and I are much alike," said Sovonya. "But you are young and have not learned to pace yourself. Your beliefs are too true I am afraid, but you are a woman before her time. I shared with you that the land we are going to is more lax than Athens, but it is not an island in some future time- as in a story that we might tell the young ones. It none-the -less comes under the auspices of Greek men who honor money first, each other next, their family, and then possibly their wives-that is of course if she is a good little bird and never makes a peep."

"I need some air," Aradia claimed, and standing abruptly she discarded the sewing in her lap and rushed out of the cabin.

Tomis found her at the rail, looking pale as she watched the white-capped waves strike the side of the ship. As they conversed the sky darkened and the waves suddenly threatened to wash over the hull. He escorted her back to the cabin where she remained for the rest of the rough voyage.

Sitting on comfortable cushions, wrapped in blankets provided by Tomis, she and Sovonya bumped along in an old wagon, on a rutted road leading to the villa. Aradia was weak, and thrilled to be on land. Her heart embraced her excursion. But her stomach had protested the journey, nearly from the moment she boarded the ship.

Aradia's first view of Lyons Gate, a rare two story country house on a small hill overlooking the Aegean Sea, took her breath away. *Egyptian blue*, she murmured nearly hypnotized by the color of the bay, lying west and below the grand villa. Promptly she fell back to sleep, and was carried upstairs to her room by one of the slaves, as Tomis had put back to sea.

ᵕᵕ᪥ᵕᵕ

Aradia stood for hours never complaining, while the seamstress poked and prodded, turning her, this way and that, muttering now and again that she loved working with Aradia's proud stature. Everything the seamstress made looked stunning and she was able to charge double, as all the garments were needed quickly. Besides, as well she knew, when it was disclosed that it was she that had fashioned what Aradia wore there would never be a lack of business from that day forward. And she was to keep the sketches, she had been told. That alone was worth its weight in gold, as she could never draw such lovely things.

And when the sweet, willowy seamstress complimented Aradia for being able to stand so still, and asked her how she was able to do it, Aradia gave her an enigmatic smile while saying nothing and the seamstress, already enamored of her decided she was a goddess come to earth.

"The poor thing had nothing to wear when she arrived," she confided in the cook who was anxious to hear everything about the mysterious Aradia. "It makes you wonder where she came from." The cook, a large pleasant woman with a trusting face, nodded at the remark about Aradia's wonderful figure. She had her own plans to fatten her up; put some meat on her bones cause she's too thin, said the cook, who had been at the villa for thirty years. She thought everyone should put on a few pounds, and would have no trouble doing so if they ate the delicious meals she cooked.

The cherub faced cook loved it when Aradia came in to sit with her while she prepared the evening meal. They laughed together and she learned about herbs for healing. She thought herbs were better used to cook with, than to repeat some strange-sounding words while drinking them or spreading them around. Yet, hadn't she had already seen Aradia's magic heal the maids with coughs in their chest and fever in their blood?

Still, having heard the rumors about the mistress Sovonya, she was not surprised. Like were drawn to like, she often told herself. But how few were like these two women, old and young, and yet capable, she guessed, of so much more than anyone knew.

Chapter 10

Aradia marveled at the palatial gardens that were at her disposal. As she lounged with Sovonya in the courtyard she was aware that each of them was trying to move the conversation to a topic lying close to their hearts. Sovonya finally launched into what she felt was an essential discussion: the importance of decorum. Aradia listened closely, knowing that Greek customs were very different than those she had known and railed about that fact. Yet also she wanted to appreciate that she was out of Athens, where she was under the daily threat of being sold as a slave.

Perhaps, she thought, as Sovonya went on about the visit that was being made to their household soon by a legendary bard, almost as well known as Homer, she should confide in her about her family. But how would she start a conversation, she wondered, about being transported to Athens after your family had been butchered and would have been sold as a slave if not for a chance meeting with a sad and lonely woman. How, she thought, do you begin to tell a story such as she had lived through, and not elicit pity or questions about what she had suffered at the hand of the barbarians.

Aradia could not be certain how much Tomis had told her as to how he had happened to come into possession of her, or if he had stated his intentions, though since coming here, she had not seen him at all. He was away on business matters, Sovonya had explained.

"Perhaps I should tell you," Aradia began with great effort when Sovonya paused for a moment. But try as she may the words did not come.

"You have not found it within you to take me into your confidence," said Sovonya, "to share the tragedy that has befallen to you. But I know that it is grave. I have no intention of prying, and yet you came to us with no past, so I have invented one. Trust me on this matter, and you will have no regrets.

"The evening that the bard joins us," continued Sovonya, "you and I along with many of my friends, will be able to attend. An arbor has been set up for us. We will not be directly with the men, but we will be close enough that the men will have a clear view of the weaker sex. Well, I have a surprise for them! Rumors have spread of a beautiful young maiden staying here in the villa. Your dropping out of nowhere has set tongues to wagging."

With a touch of excitement, the normally regal Sovonya rose. Smoothing her gown she began pacing and speaking with animation. "Hearing of your beauty all of the town women are jealous, yet vying to come to see what will unfold. Well ... you, my dear, will unfold... so to speak.

"The women from the town want nothing more than to find that you have a tarnished reputation," she continued, "which would take you out of the running in their minds. However, the men hope you do have a scandalous past, so they will be in the running and into your bed. Of course that will not happen because you have more sense ... and I have more power than most."

Sitting down next to Aradia, she tapped her with her fan, and ceasing her excited manner began to talk in earnest. "The only one I am concerned with is my dear Tomis. He has caught your favor, but it would not be in your best interest to bed the man. Please, heed me as you would your mother, for I am not at liberty to explain."

Sovonya reached over to Aradia, and lightly grasped her hand while Aradia, in turn, sat very still and did not make eye contact, seemingly lost in her own world. Sovonya hesitated for a moment, and then with her free hand flipped her fan open.

"I do not want you to tell me of your past, save that you are a witch. That I do know and it must be hidden at all cost. It would in fact be best to tell the cook not to mention it. Talk with the maids, and swear them to their word they will not impart what you have shared with them. I will tell you something, my dear," she whispered. "I myself am a sorceress but do not try to tell anyone, for they will not believe you. Fine ladies and gentlemen on the island do not want to hear of these matters, so it is best left unsaid."

"I do not want to fool people, nor is there a need to do so," Aradia said, holding her head very high. I come from a very good family. I have my reasons for not speaking about it!"

"I do not think anyone would question that," spoke Sovonya lovingly, "Come, come my dear, there will be many handsome men that attend, and it is my guess that if we can keep the fact that you are not a citizen of Greece by birth quiet, you will have your pick. Keep an open mind and let all of the gentlemen seek your favor. Of course they will not present themselves directly. They will go through the proper channels. Tomis is my favorite, and I love him as my own; but I must caution you to be discriminating, as matters might not fall in your favor."

Aradia felt her breath cease. Her hand went instinctively to her heart. Sovonya was only thinking of her, she told herself, but her heart ached when she sounded as if there would never be a union between Tomis and herself.

Aradia, her breath still shallow, knew this fine woman, her friend, was waiting for her to speak. "You have gone to such immense trouble on my behalf. Please, do not find me lacking gratitude."

"There now," spoke Sovonya, "that is much better," and with a genuine smile, the great lady lightly tapped Aradia under the chin with her fan. "Wait until you see the garment I am having made for you. In fact, it is way past time for your fitting. I have kept you with my ramblings. Run along now. The seamstress is waiting for you in your room."

Sovonya thoughtfully watched Aradia walk away, and she wondered if her beautiful charge even understood herself the reason she was keeping her past hidden. She is being romantic like all young women. The great lady shook her head lovingly. Like so many of her age, she wants to see if Tomis will move heaven and earth to have her and yet, she takes such a chance , not so much with Tomis since the men in his family tend to fall in love only once... Ahh...who was being the romantic now?

Sovonya a sorceress? Imagine that, marveled Aradia. That was the most interesting thing that had happened since Tomis had gone down on one knee and called her his enchantress! Perhaps now that Lady

Sovonya has confided in her she can ask more about Tomis. She'd like to know why he left, and where he had gone. Though, tis true... up to now she had been very busy with fittings, and becoming accustomed to life here at the villa. And true, he does seem to have much business to attend. But still... entering her room all thoughts left her head as she beheld the soft emerald green folds of the dress she was to try on.

Aradia, hearing the music of the lute that the bard played with skill, could not contain herself. It had been so long since she had heard such sweet, lilting sounds that she could not keep still.

Iola, a demure, well -mannered lady's maid, was waiting for a particular piece of music to begin playing, before she would help Aradia with the finishing touches—an emerald necklace and a tiara set with emeralds, greener than the trees in mid-summer. Iola had been told to wait till the last minute to dress Aradia's hair, as it had a mind of its own, with tendrils forever escaping and curling around her face. A haunting melody began, and the maid excitedly told her it was time. Carefully she finished dressing Aradia's hair and gingerly aided her with the necklace. Aradia held the shiny copper plate so she could watch as Iola placed the gleaming tiara on her exquisite titian hair.

"My Lady, you look lovelier than a fairy princess!" exclaimed the maid, putting her hand to her mouth. "Oh, excuse me for being so bold, but I cannot help myself."

"Thank you, Iola. You have always been kind to me, and you mustn't think you are being too bold. Your compliments are a joy to me. Go, get some rest. Do not wait up for me. I will wake you when I need help to disrobe."

She had been dutifully instructed by Sovonya to speak only Greek. Though if people asked, she could say she was educated in Rome. A part of her cried out to put an end to this farce, but she was not yet ready to speak of her family, and how she had come to arrive in Greece.

Approaching the courtyard where people were already gathering, music wafted up and circled around her. Aradia had thoughts and images of her family and her life in Volsinii. Yearning to speak of her handsome father and loving mother, and of her siblings caused a throbbing pain in her heart. She wanted to exclaim that she had had a sister so sweet and wondrous, that she was love itself! But she did not know if she could, or if she would come apart at the seams like a poorly made robe, in her effort to speak of the brutalities and loss.

With difficulty she shook herself from her sad reverie. Sovonya was right. She must leave the past behind for her own good. If she were to share some of the story…all of the ugliness would come to the surface and perhaps she would be made to leave her new life, her friend…and… Tomis and she could not bear the thought of that. There is nothing to go back to; *just move forward!* she reprimanded herself.

Aradia automatically tilted her head in the manner of nobility, and cast her eyes on the throng of people at the opening to the courtyard. Trying to remember to be demure was difficult as she nearly floated in her garment of emerald green. It shimmered, embracing her every move. The emeralds that lightly draped her neck, accentuated the extraordinary color of her hair.

Aradia's sultry walk toward the women who were standing at the other side of the courtyard caught Tomis's eye. Watching him watch her, her heart stood still. Wearing a laurel wreath, his golden hair glistened in the fading sunlight. His robe, the color of the sea, brought forth his eyes, which were more dazzling than she remembered. It was thrown over one shoulder and open to the waist on the other side, showing off a broad expanse of muscle. Her attention was drawn to the indentation beneath his Adam's apple; she paused in her perusal to moisten her lips. Unbidden thoughts of kissing him in that spot filled her… and she noticed her womanhood clenching with a desire. She acknowledged him, her head bowing ever so lightly, and the bard, a bearded old man who sat with his lute in the center of the courtyard, began to sing of heroic deeds of old.

Aradia, who was now in the center of the group of scented ladies, heard them buzzing about her, and someone ran their hands over her hair.

"Pay them no heed," Sovonya told her. "Afterward, perhaps, we will satisfy their curiosity a bit. Or perhaps not," she said while displaying her fan, knowing that it always caused curiosity amongst the ladies. "Listen now. The entertainment has begun."

"Sing, O Goddess, the anger of Achilles, son of Peleus, that brought countless ills upon the Achaeans," the old man chanted. "Many a brave soul did it send hurrying down to Hades, and many a hero did it yield a prey to dogs and vultures, for so were the counsels of Jove fulfilled from the day on which the son of Atreus, king of men and the great Achilles, first fell out with one another."

The bard's singing was, Aradia found, hypnotic. Even in her own country, this tale was known, and sometimes told by traveling bards. But as she continued listening she realized she had never heard it sung so beautifully.

"For nine whole days he shot his arrows among the people," the rich baritone voice sang, "but upon the tenth day Achilles called them in assembly- moved thereto by Juno, who saw the Acheans in their death throes and had compassion upon them."

Aradia was aware that Tomis had moved a bit closer, and she knew that Sovonya was aware of it, too. She also knew that, at social occasions like this, if it were to take place in Athens she would have no chance to speak to him, for he would only stay with the men. Though here on the island there was some interaction between the sexes, normally it was only at rare dinner gatherings and times like this when young ladies were out in the open. But still, the attitude was look, but don't touch.

"The son of Peleus was furious," the bard sang, but Aradia realized that she was worn out from the foolishness of playing at being demure, her temples throbbed, and she needed to escape from the pretense.

At last, the old man paused and was offered wine. And in that moment, Aradia knew that she must be alone and quickly stepped into the adjoining courtyard which bordered on the kitchen garden where the gentry seldom strayed. She wanted to feel the earth under her feet. Sandals interfered with the calming effect that the earth had upon her. She slipped them off and released a deep sigh. She reached up to remove the tiara, as it was causing quite a headache. Removing it, her hair tumbled down around her face. She gazed up at the moon; it had just come out from behind a cloud.

"Now, that is the way I remember you," she said speaking up at the moon in a deep sultry voice.

Suddenly, Tomis appeared in front of her.

"Do you remember *me*?" he asked his voice intense from longing.

Startled, Aradia dropped the tiara, and stood motionless in the moonlight. Her heart pounding in her chest, she could not find breath or words.

"It is not like you to be speechless," teased Tomis as he admired the color and drape of her gown which hugged every curve and set her eyes sparkling like jewels. Verdant… was the word that came to mind. Green Goddess; temptress of mortal men, he thought. Now he was the one to be speechless.

"You seem to have a spell upon me," she said to him quietly, "for I have been affected such of late. I stand like a child with no words to say and my mouth agape."

"It is not I who casts spells," he replied in a low voice. "They say you are a witch."

"And who might *they* be?" she queried with a smile.

Tomis answered, his heart shining in his eyes. "All *those* who are not you and I. All *those* who have never seen you in the moonlight. And of course… *those* who do not know the difference between a witch and an enchantress."

"And you know the difference?" smiled Aradia.

"A witch spells you to love her, but an enchantress beckons you with her every move. She is a song that you can't wait to hear, she is the gentle current in a stream, and the rushing waterfall you cannot wait to bathe in. It is the enchantress that I have fallen in love with."

His words were a balm for her very soul, but needing a moment to get used to the thought, she queried, "and if I were a witch, would you run from me? Would you think I had put a spell upon you to love me?"

"Did you such?"

"I did *not*," said Aradia, managing to look offended and sensual at the same time. "But perhaps I would have! For my heart aches for you, my mind thinks of nothing else but you. If you did not return my love, then, yes, perhaps I would have been tempted to put a spell upon you. But I swear to you, if you turn from me, I shall not spell you to love me. You shall always have free will in that."

"If I turn from you, it is because of matters beyond my control, and it would break my heart. This I swear to you."

They moved towards each other. Slowly he encircled her in his arms. Holding him tight, and reaching to her full height, she nuzzled his neck.

"You smell of the ocean," whispered Aradia. "The ocean…when you are enveloped in it and can see, feel, or smell nothing but its mystery. It is most sensual. It mesmerizes me."

"Ah, and you smell of the Orient, a deep rich aroma that makes my body tremble and creates mind images of silk, just barely draped over your body." he told her, running his hands softly over her curves. "I want to sculpt you!" And then, his voice rising, he exclaimed, "Oh, yes! I must sculpt you!"

Her entire body tingled with warmth, and her womanhood cried out for him.

"Come, walk with me," he said, his voice husky from desire. "The moon is full. It will guide our path."

She put her arm in his as they walked deep into the garden. Pulling her into a gardening shed, he kissed her, softly biting her full lips. Returning his kiss tentatively at first, she reached up and touched his face, gently brushing her fingers across his cheeks and tracing his anxious lips.

"I have wanted to do that since the first day you walked into the courtyard in Athens," she told him. "You are exquisite. How can it be that you are so beautiful?"

"Men are not beautiful," he responded.

She closed her eyes as she outlined his high cheekbones with her fingers, and then traced his nose, his neck and on to the side of his shoulders.

Aradia slowly ran her hands down his partially exposed chest to his narrow hips. With a long low sigh she said, "Yes…you are very, very beautiful."

Quickly, he untied the clasp at the top of his robe and the garment dropped to the floor. His nakedness aroused her more. With the innocence of love and curiosity, she reached down and touched him; he moaned long and deep.

Slowly, Tomis undid the clasp between her breasts. As her gown slipped off, his breath stopped. There were no words; she would have to model for him. Only then could he show her the beauty he saw. With both hands he gently touched the outline of her shoulders and down to her back, over her hips and buttocks. She trembled in response to his sensual touch.

Spreading his robe out on the floor of the hut, he pulled her to him and she came willingly for she was ready. Kissing her neck, Tomis gently turned her around, his tongue tasting her sweetness all the way down to the small of her back. He marveled again at her curves, and teasing her, moved lower, then to the small of her back again. He lay gently on top of her, just barely touching her, and rubbed himself lightly against her buttocks. When he finally knew she could stand it no more, he turned her over.

Aradia begged for him, but instead his tongue traced her nipples and the fullness of her breasts. As he moved down to taste her, she tensed, not knowing what to expect at which he shifted his weight up over her, held her arms down gently and said, "Do you trust me?"

"My head wonders, but my heart and my body do not care," she told him. "Yes. Yes, I trust you." In fact, she felt as though she had been preparing for this moment her whole life.

Moving erotically down again to the light spray of hair protecting her femininity, he caressed her with his tongue. Achingly slow movements over her silky skin, teased her to shiver in pleasure. She moaned, as she moved against his tongue. She was so moist and hot, he did not know if he could hold out any longer.

Continuing to please her, Tomis found himself wondering if she had ever been with a man, though he wanted to believe she had not. Being gentle with her came so easy. He molded himself to her needs, hoping she would know how much he loved her.

Climaxing with deep intense moans, she realized that she had never known anything could evoke such pleasurable feelings. Entering her, he shattered her virginity and her sanity in the same moment, and together they climaxed as she wrapped her legs around him, holding him close.

Calling out to her as he climaxed, *Regina Bella! Regina Bella mea,"* in the words of her homeland enveloped her in a cocoon of safety and love. "Beautiful Queen, my beautiful Queen!"

Indeed, Aradia felt like his beautiful queen. She loved the sound of his voice and the depth of his words. The excitement drove her to climax again and again. She begged him with her body, with her words and her eyes. "Don't leave me, don't ever leave me."

After making love, Tomis held her close, realizing now, for certain, that she had been a virgin. Waves of guilt washed over him. He should have stayed away! It would have been the only way; he could not be near her and not ravish her. Lying there very still, he berated himself silently as a tear formed in the corner of his eye.

Aradia had not taken her gaze off him. She watched as the tear slid over his cheek and thought of her own tears when they were making love, tears of happiness. Reaching up, she kissed them away. "Tell me of your tears. And *perhaps* I will tell you of mine," she said softly.

Tomis hesitated, trying to form his words.

"I am not … I do not know what to say," he said finally. "You were a virgin. I am ashamed. I am ashamed because the thought even crossed my mind that you were not! I am ashamed, because had you told me before hand, I am not sure that I would have done any different. There are things I need to speak to you of, but I am not yet free to do so. Trust me and know *tu mea cour*. You have my heart. I speak those words in your language so that they will mean more to you. Say them often to yourself, for they will remind you where my heart is, when I am not with you."

"Will you be leaving?"

"Yes. But I shall not be gone long. When I return, will you allow me to sculpt you? I have wanted to do that since the first moment I saw you. Truth be known, I have already begun. I've needed to put my hands on your body even if it was only in my mind."

Aradia laughed and said, "But for now you have the real thing. Let us not waste time." She had thought of nothing but him for so long and now he is going away. But she would not allow herself to be sad while he was still here with her.

They made love again. Afterward, Tomis exclaimed, "We must go back to hear the bard. Hopefully no one will have missed us. If Sovonya has, no doubt she will make me pay the price."

It was only when they were gathering up their belongings that Aradia realized that she could not find her tiara.

"I dropped the tiara when you appeared in front of me," she told him ruefully. "Now we must find it or we will both be in discord with Sovonya."

"Are you sure it is not here," he asked, his face a mischievous grin. "We could look under the blankets or..."

"We are grown and acting like we have stolen bread from the windowsill, and Mama will scold us," her silken laughter lit the air.

"That is the first time I have heard you *really* laugh," he told her, "Before, something was missing."

She could tell from the longing in his eyes that he yearned for her to tell him something of herself. "Yes, she said, "It has been a long while since I have laughed. I was very lucky growing up. I was greatly loved. I know my laughter was filled with love because I was always surrounded with it. Well... no matter. You fill me with love now. From now on it is what you will always hear when you are with me. Always, I promise you, my love."

They hurried through the garden, and made their way back to the door from which she had made her exit. Two young children sat on the bench talking, near where Aradia had dropped the tiara.

Aradia hid and Tomis shooed the children away as he began looking for the tiara. It was nowhere to be found.

Finally Aradia got down on her hands and knees and frantically searched the area. Tomis, muttering to himself, moved the bushes aside and dutifully peeked underneath.

"Um-hmm!"

Tomis straightened up and Aradia, still on hands and knees, pushed the hair out of her eyes to see Sovonya standing there.

"Is *this* what you're looking for?" she said, attempting to hold a disapproving air as she waved the tiara.

"Why... yes. As a matter of fact..." Tomis stuttered while offering Aradia his hand, "I was helping Aradia. She took a spill and lost her footing... as you can well see."

"Her footing? Well, let us hope that is *all* she has lost! When I came upon the tiara a short while ago ....I, oh well... never mind." Sovonya said, shaking her head from side to side. "Do come and rejoin the entertainment. Tomis, why don't you go back first? I will help Aradia tidy...well... arrange herself!"

When Tomis moved off in the direction of the music, Aradia felt a cord of energy between them disconnect. She nearly cried out; she had to put her hand to her mouth to stifle the cry that tore at her throat.

Sovonya said nothing as she helped her charge straighten herself. Aradia felt there must be an unwritten law between women that no matter what the indiscrimination, when there was deep friendship one women's pain became the others.

Sitting with the other women listening to the bard meant nothing now. Aradia searched the crowd of men for Tomis, but knew in her heart that he had gone.

Aradia fell into bed as the sun came up, and slept the day through. Her dreams were vivid and sensual. She awoke with one hand around a pillow and the other clutching her femaleness. Stretching like a cat she purred, savoring thoughts of the night before and anticipating the next time she would see her lover.

Chapter 11

Sometimes Aradia felt that all she did was eat, urged on by Sovonya who said that she needed to put skin on her bones.

"I do not know what stripped the weight from you so, my child," she said, "and I do not want to know until you are ready to tell me, but you must do more than pick at grapes. Besides, cook will not be pleased if you send dishes back to her untouched."

Aradia looked down at her body and laughed. "I think you exaggerate, my lady. True, I was a bit thinner then, but no one can look at this body and call it skin and bones."

"Yes, yes," said Sovonya in a conspiratorial way. "Bodies like yours have been known to get ladies into trouble. Oh, to be young again with all the knowledge I have now and to be in a youthful body, but I guess I will have to wait till the next go-round. In the next life, I wish to be a courtesan aga..." Sovonya stopped abruptly. "Oh child, I am just muttering," Sovonya told her. "Pay no mind to this old woman."

"But yes," Aradia told her, blushing. "I can picture you as a courtesan to some great man. You would be the power behind great men like Pericles and Socrates, rulers and thinkers both, and you would have great fun at it!"

Aradia, no longer able to contain herself, laughed and eagerly grabbed her patroness's hand. "Thank you for taking me in and being so good to me. I have something I would like to share with you. I know it was a long time coming but I have not been able to speak of it to anyone until now. I...I am not sure even now. But I owe you such a debt."

Aradia's name was being called. A maid anxiously came toward them and shared that the seamstress had been waiting for quite some time for Aradia.

"Oh, it is time for my fitting. I so wanted to speak with you, but when we are together here in the garden, time moves with such speed."

Aradia hugged Sovonya, her eyes misting with love for her friend. "It is good. It will give me time to adjust…to speak on these things so long secreted."

"Run along, child, I will be all ears when we next meet," Lady Sovonya said with disappointment.

⚜

Aradia was sitting in front of her toiletries wondering why women needed such things when Iola came bounding through the door, all apologies for not attending her sooner.

"Iola," Aradia said with a smile. "I have not reprimanded you once, so why do you fret so? I am never bored, I am perfectly able to entertain, dress myself and even do my hair. It is you that thinks I cannot manage without you. However, please perform your magic, now that you are here. After all, you are the reason that so many gentlemen look my way of late." Iola, the dark haired maiden with sparkling eyes, laughed so hard she began to cough, which shook the bottles on the dressing table.

"No Ma'am, 'tis'ent what's here," she said, pointing to her head, "that keeps a man interested, but what's here." She pointed between her legs as she twittered and hid her mouth, happy that she had said something so outrageous. "Cook told me that this very day, and now I have shared it with you."

"Why, Iola!" Aradia cried, pretending to be shocked, "Did cook also share some of the wine she claims she puts in the food?"

The petite young woman blanched, the color draining from cheeks that were naturally rosy. Nervously she brushed back a brown curl that had escaped from her tightly braided hair. "You…you won't tell the mistress, will you?"

"Of course not, but next time when you are visiting with Cook drink less and talk more."

After her maid giggled herself out of the room, Aradia remembered earlier when Iola had been helping her into her night robe, they had both commented on how snug it had become. It was, she truly hoped, all the delicacies that Sovonya pressed on her.

Later, Aradia meandered through the garden on her way to join Sovonya, thinking how short a time it would be before the weather started to get cooler and the flowers and leaves would sleep. She had never liked the winter because it was so barren. At home, each year between first and final harvest of the season, when they celebrate the souls of the dead, she had always become sad thinking of the cold and stillness of the time ahead. Pondering on, she reminded herself all things have their season. If it were not for the dying of the flowers and trees there could be no new life.

Just as she joined Sovonya who was relaxing on a bench in one of the courtyards, she heard the sound of horse's hooves, and Tomis could be seen dismounting.

"*Cara mia*," he cried, running to her, his arms spread wide for her to fly inside. "It has been so long."

Sovonya, who had followed Aradia out to greet him said, "So good to see you, Tomis. So it is good news you have for us then?"

Aradia looked at her quizzically.

"No, no word on that matter yet, madam," replied Tomis, with a troubled look in his eye, as he disentangled himself from Aradia and embraced Sovonya, whispering something in her ear. Aradia only heard her response, to the effect that an envoy from his father was awaiting him.

Only when he had left them did Sovonya make any attempt at an explanation, one Aradia found unsatisfactory, at best.

"You may feel free with Tomis when the three of us are alone together," she cautioned. "But otherwise, decorum must prevail. These envoys are important personages. You do not want to set the wrong impression."

It was the next day before Aradia was able to see Tomis. He sent a note through Iola that she was to meet him at the gardener's shed. And because Aradia wanted to go to him undetected, she told the little maid to tell her mistress that she was unwell and she would remain abed for the day and skip the evening meal.

Aradia quietly locked the door to her room as soon as the maid left. She looked out of her window. Yes, she could do it, she thought. Opening the window she climbed out over the sill. The roof was cold on her bare feet. Feeling like a young girl again, when she would slip off to spend the day at the river, brought a smile to her radiant face. The last of it was a bit of a jump, but the ground was soft. Landing soundlessly she hurried into the garden.

Excitedly, she ran all the way to the shed and into his arms. They never said a word to each other in greeting, except for the moans of ecstasy and words of love whispered as they ravished each other's bodies.

Lying in his arms, feeling like a child that was being spoiled, Aradia shared with him, "I felt like a little girl again when I slipped out of my bedroom window," in response to which, Tomis laughed lovingly and embraced her tightly.

"I have thought," said Aradia with focused attention, "it is the child in us that makes love. Because when we make love, it is the same wild abandon that I felt as a child, hair flying, running in the wind and sneaking off to swim with the fish! Do you think me right?"

"I have been with other women," he began, measuring his words. "Most have never been children, not the kind you speak of, so they have no experience to draw upon. These women do not make love as you do. They do not think of lovemaking as pleasure and fun. I have once or twice been with ... what you would call a butana. These women enjoy themselves, but it is because they feel powerful with a man at their mercy, so to speak. They do not enjoy themselves as you do. It is because you enjoy yourself so much that you make love with such abandon; it gives me great pleasure. More than I have ever had in or out of bed. I have never laughed so much when I have bedded a woman before. It must be healthy for the soul, for I feel more connected to the gods and goddesses, and to the concepts of right and wrong that before I felt distant from."

Aradia was torn because there were so many subjects she wanted to speak on. But as a woman she asked the question that was nagging at her.

"So... you have been with many women, yet you find me pleasing?" she murmured, pressing herself closer against him. "That is good because they taught you what you liked and did not like. Perhaps though, you did not know that a woman is more a woman when she has the heart of a child. My grandmother taught me that. Though I did not know entirely what she meant at the time. She said it was a shame for a woman to outgrow her childhood completely. She was a passionate woman, my grandmother."

Aradia stretched slowly, erotically, her skin shimmering from their spirited loving making.

"I came to understand my grandmother's teachings about passion," said Aradia, "more when you and I made love for the first time. It was not as if she specifically spoke about making love, just passion. In fact, sometimes I think she talked about nothing else."

He again became quiet. After a few moments he said, "You make me think, *Cara mia*. I love that about you. You captivate me with your mind, your body, and your love."

Moving towards him again she wet her finger and with slow erotic circles traced his nipples, and seeing how quickly he was aroused, guessed that he had not even known how sensitive he was in that area. Slowly she wrapped her arms around him and nuzzled his neck, kissing him below his Adams apple. "I am wet. Here, feel what you do to me!" Tomis moaned, and pulled away from her, though he seemed reluctant to do so.

"No Cara mia, we have work to do." He tapped her lightly on the bottom. "Come over here, please." He moved her towards a chaise he had earlier put in the corner. "The light here is ideal," he told her. You are to pose. Today I sculpt you!"

"Oh!" She squealed like a child, throwing her arms up in the air in delightful abandon. But then, thinking of the pose she would hold she leisurely brought her arms down hugging herself, slowly tracing her body with her hands to feel the curves he would sculpt.

"Oh, this is so exciting!" She nearly purred as she held her arms out to him.

"You will not think it so exciting my little siren, when you have been in the same position for hours and still I tell you not to move."

Playfully smiling like a minx, she teased, "What will you give me if I make no complaint through the day?"

His eyebrow shot up. "You will pose for me all day and never complain? Humph," he said, "We shall see."

After positioning her on the chaise as he wanted her, he stepped over to the clay he had brought in earlier. Dipping his hands in water, he began to work with the clay. Excitedly he began to form the clay with an artist's eye. Looking over at her, he noticed that she had already moved from the position he had set her in, and was about to say something when he saw a rainbow of iridescent colors shimmering around her.

Closing her eyes, Aradia's voice a sensual song, she said, "This way I will not move."

Tomis watched, enchanted, as the rainbow of colors around her became stronger. Aradia remained motionless; her light breathing was the only movement that could be detected. She had a look of deep serenity that he wanted to capture, and he deftly began sculpting.

"Open your eyes for me," he murmured finally, and Aradia obediently opened them, a slight smile dusting her lips.

Aradia sat in the same position on the small lounging chair until daylight was fading, her robe thrown over one breast, one hand resting on her leg, her other arm by her side, and one foot curled behind the other. Tomis was well pleased with his work. Delighted with his progress, he had enjoyed every moment of the day. They had deep discussions on many matters, as well as soul-quaking silence. They had moments where their eyes locked and he was not certain how long he stood drinking in her depths.

At last, reluctantly, he took a wet cloth and placed it over his work.

"We are done for the day, *Cara'mea*. You were correct. That position was ever so much better than the other. Somehow it captured everything you are. But it is beyond me to understand how you can stay without moving for so long, and not complain."

Aradia noticed his eyes grow wide. A huge smiled crossed his lips and finally he spoke, a tinge of wonder in his voice.

"You are The Queen of the Fairies! I thought that after making love to you and then being lucky enough to listen to you discourse on political matters as well as philosophical ones, that there could be no other surprises. But yet, I was wrong!"

"You see them?" uttered Aradia in amazement!

"You have been told before that you have rainbow fairies that dance for you?" Tomis stared at her, his eyebrow arching in question.

"No…no one has ever been able to see them before, except my grandmother. But she had the sight."

"Tell me more," he requested, as he stood motionless, wanting to catch every move of the sparkling beings that lazily encircled her.

"I was told by my grandmother that my colors are like a rainbow. She also told me not everyone has the elementals with them. They…are different than fairies…they help you. But the day grows short; at this moment I want you here."

Beckoning for Tomis to come to her side, she made room for him on the tiny chaise.

His hands still wet and caked with clay, he dipped them in water and went to her, molding her curves as he had the clay. For Aradia, this was a most sensual experience; his hands felt like silk. He felt her purring vibration under his touch.

If the light were not failing, he thought, he would go back to his clay and work, instead he said, "It will be dark soon. We mustn't stay much longer. How will you enter the main house?"

"The same way I left," answered Aradia. "I see just as well at night as I do during the day. The moon is full, she will light my way."

He knelt in front of her, parted her legs gently and ran his tongue along the inside of her thigh. Throwing her head back in abandon, her back arched, she was his. He moved his tongue in circles. The feeling of her response excited him; she was present to his every move.

She began massaging his manhood with her foot and found that he was ready. She rose up off the small chaise taking his hand in hers and went back to the bed they had made of blankets. She knelt down on all fours and invited him by arching up to meet him when he came towards her.

He entered her from behind, moving his hand to her moist mound, touching her gently at first, arousing her with his finger. Finally, when his excitement rose to a peak, and he could not wait, he exploded, crying out, "Regina bella, mea Regina bella. Beautiful Queen, my beautiful Queen."

Feeling his hot seed fill her and hearing his words brought Aradia to climax again and again. Squeezing her womanhood around him to give him pleasure, she milked more seed from his shaft and he exploded once again calling out her name. Turning her over, he entered her again, gently pinning her down as he watched waves of pleasure washing over her radiant face.

Wrapping her legs around him, pushing herself ever closer to the brink, she cried out, "Don't ever leave me; don't ever leave me."

Climaxing for the last time, she sank deeper into the blankets and he collapsed on top of her and they slept as he shielded her from the chill of the night air.

It was early morning when Aradia finally pulled herself away from their house of love, as she silently called it. Running barefoot through the garden, she turned to look back, and saw that the sky beyond the row of Cyprus trees had a hint of color. Arriving at the back of the house she saw a rain barrel, and turning it over she moved it under a low portion of the roof, and then climbed on top. Stretching as much as she could to reach the low roof, she finally grabbed hold and pulled herself up. Quietly and lightly she tip toed across the roof and into her window.

Inside her room, she looked out over the horizon, excited that she would be able to watch the sunrise. Aradia had asked Iola to bring up a tray before she left to meet Tomis and knowing that she would have left it in the hallway so as not to disturb her, opened her door and took it inside, suddenly aware, seeing the grapes, apples, cheese and fresh bread, just how hungry she was. Sweet Iola, she must remember to reward her.

Aradia pulled a chair up to the window. Placing the tray of food on the windowsill she devoured every morsel, breathing in the brush of golden dawn that appeared in the horizon. Watching the clear glow of the slowly rising sun told her it would be a fine day. She would, she decided, pick a great bunch of anemones and so still feeling the powerful sensation of being a child, she crept out on the roof once again.

Dropping silently to the ground, she danced in the garden while picking bouquets of flowers. She felt drunk! Her dancing slowed and she found herself standing, just staring at the flowers. And then, suddenly, her mind's eye filled with visions of her sister, Sardiana. Sinking to the ground, she hugged the fragrant anemone to her heart, and found herself singing a sad little lullaby from her childhood. As the hushed lullaby came to her lips, one her grandmother had often sung to her and Sardiana, tears welled up from a deep dark place of despair, a place she believed she had locked away. Clinging to the flowers, which became a damp unrecognizable jumble of color cradled in her arms, she hummed the tune.

A light rain had begun to fall. Iola, looking for Aradia, peeked out through the window and seeing her mistress on the ground, clearly in distress, snatched up a shawl and ran down the stairs to join her.

"Why are you crying, Mistress" she pleaded, kneeling beside her. "Tell me what I can do."

"Sardiana?" Aradia asked, looking at Iola as if she didn't know her.

"No, it is me, Iola. Come, I must get you upstairs to a warm bed. Here let me take the flowers."

"No, I will keep the flowers," said Aradia determinedly, clearly recognizing her now. When Iola reached for them and tried to speak, Aradia gently placed a finger over Iola's lips. "Shush, I am alright. I *am* all right now. I know the flowers are crushed, but that is apropos. They are a reminder of how short a life can be... and perhaps a reminder to me - *to live life to the fullest?*"

Chapter 12

"What do you mean, he is gone? " Aradia cried. She had just received the news that Tomis was gone again when she joined Sovonya. "He would not leave without saying goodbye to me. I cannot believe it."

"Calm yourself, child," clucked her patroness. "He has left a note for you. I will bring it to you later on. The master of the house is back, and Tomis has been sent on a most urgent mission for him, after which he will go on to meet with his father. We have had free rein for more than two moons. Things are run differently when he is here. Thank the Gods that it is not too often, as I otherwise could not bear to be his wife!"

"Wife?" Aradia said, puzzled. "But I thought…"

"You thought, no doubt, that I hold a position here," said Sovonya, her face grim. "And, of course, I do. I am wife, although in name only. Otherwise, I would not be allowed the freedom I have. All Greek men need wives. It is the custom, even though they may, if they choose, never see them. Wives oversee the household slaves."

"Their slaves?" Aradia exclaimed once again.

"Where on earth do you come from, child?" Sovonya asked her. "Everyone who serves us is a slave. All city states are made up of free men and slaves."

"But what about women?"Aradia demanded. "Never mind…that I do know the answer to. Iola is a slave?"

"Yes, but as you see she is well taken care of."

"But Iola and the others are not free!" Aradia protested.

"That is true, as a woman within the limits of Greek society I have found a way to be free," Sovonya said, reaching over to clasp Aradia's hand, "it is what I am trying to accomplish for you."

"You said that the master has returned. How will that change things?"

"As you no doubt know on mainland Greece men and women never dine together," said Sovonya, "but the very nature of the master's business, shipping, has him visiting many cultures. That fact, and also his need for control, knowing exactly what is going on at all times, allows us some freedoms when it comes to dining. On his first evening home we receive those that see to the running of the villa when he is gone. Any guests, like yourself, are introduced to him, as you will be very shortly. Make no mistake that bending the Athenian ways, as we sometimes do here on the island, would not change the fact that the master is *Greek!*"

Rising abruptly, she told Aradia, "Go change for the evening meal." Sovonya took a deep breath before continuing, "It will be alright child. Remember my goal is to help you find freedom in a culture where women have no freedoms. Run along now, the dinner bell will alert you when it is time to meet the *lion*."

Upon entering the dining room later that evening, Sovonya introduced Aradia to the master, telling her to address him as Master Rumaldea.

Aradia had heard little about him, save what had been disclosed this very day and she could see why. As she took her seat he measured her with a penetrating glare. Aradia could understand why the servants and even Sovonya did not speak of him. Surely they could say nothing good, she mused.

She had been introduced as a cousin and she was amazed how false the story sounded as Sovonya stumbled through it. The man sitting to the left of Aradia was pleasant enough. He saw to the farming, milling and overseeing the slaves to work the land. The man sitting opposite Aradia next to Sovonya trained the horses. He kept his head down paying attention to the courses of the meal as they were being served, only to look up when being addressed by Rumaldea.

Aradia tried numerous times to converse with the men, only to be constantly interrupted by the lion, whom she felt was well named. He intimidated everyone at the table with his overbearing demeanor, even Aradia for a short time. This puzzled and amazed her, for up until this point in her life, no one could put her in such a position. So she set out to take his measure. Always study your enemies. Smile as you look them straight in the eye, her grandmother's words of wisdom nearly hummed in her ears.

Sitting up straight in her chair, and steeling herself for the intensity of his gaze, determined to use all of her training to hold her ground when he deemed it suitable for her to speak. She did however understand this was his house, and respect was in order. But to be spoken to with such disregard, as well as the condescending manner he used with his guests, went against her grain.

When Rumaldea finally addressed Aradia, she purposefully looked him directly in the eye; that did not seem to suit him. He was used to people averting their eyes, she thought, and bowing their heads when he spoke to them. Aradia's training and ingrained dislike for authority would not allow her to bow her head to anyone who would *think* themselves her superior.

Aradia noticed his long nose twitch in discomfort under her scrutiny. The pointed chin that was aimed toward her felt like a weapon; it made his hollow cheeks appear more prominent, and his narrow dark eyes vapid pools of burnt coal. For a moment she felt the chill of death pass over her body.

With determination she continued her perusal of him. As he turned to address one of the other guests she noticed his sparse brown hair pulled uncomfortably tight in a knot at the back of his neck. Turning back toward her, his thin lips drew a tight grimace, and Aradia decided with sadness it would probably cause him pain to smile.

She used the gifts her grandmother taught her to observe that he felt women were a necessary evil; he used them only to gratify his needs and felt dirty after cavorting with them. He probably scrubbed himself raw after an encounter, but she could not find it within her to feel sorry for him even when she intuitively knew he had been abused as a child. Making money and keeping large quantities of it hidden allowed him to feel safe. Helping men he felt were beneath him made him feel powerful, but there was little that helped him feel clean, as she had noticed that he constantly wiped his mouth and cleaned his eating utensils.

Gradually he grew tired of trying to intimidate her and he began to speak of his shipping line. He spouted off the large profits he made, and heaped praises on the good ship's captain, who would be coming to sup with them tomorrow eve. "Love the name of the ship, *Satarcia*. It means, free as the wind!"

Aradia choked on her food. "You ... cannot mean you own that ship...the captain he..." she blurted out before she could stop herself.

"What do you mean, woman? Speak up!" He thundered, half rising out of his chair. "The captain is a good friend of mine."

"I, ah...oh no, I am thinking of another ship, another captain to be sure." She had made a grave mistake. "Cook has outdone herself this evening." Aradia said, and beseeching Sovonya with her eyes, held out her wine goblet to be filled by one of the slaves. Her mind began to race, though she tried to put a look of serenity on her face. What would she do if the captain recognized her?

Lady Sovonya came to her rescue with a tasty morsel of gossip that had the guests laughing. Then with ease the great lady led the discussion to the huge amount of profit the farms were making.

"Timerus, wherever did you find that nice young man who has such knowledge about planting in the fields? You know the one who seems to magically know what days to plant, and when to cut. Why, he alone has increased the yield more than triple what has been produced on those fields in the past," said Sovonya, hoping his tale would be long and interesting. The conversation dwelling on his profits kept the lord engrossed and he soon lost interest in Aradia.

When Lady Sovonya had a quiet moment, Aradia leaned over and spoke into her ear.

Looking aghast at Aradia's request, Sovonya asked, "Why ever would you want to sit next to the Captain after your outburst this eve? I would think you would not want to be anywhere near him."

"It is most important that I not only sit next to him, but that I sit on his right side. That is his good ear. Do not ask me how I know. Please... it is a matter of life and death."

⁕

The next evening Aradia was not in attendance in the sitting room. Lady Sovonya impatiently looked for her, and made apologies to the other women.

The guests included a judge, and a councilman named Timerus. He was the brother of Timerus the younger, who was the land manager, and looked like his twin. His wife, a small mousy woman, very different from his brother's wife, perpetually cleared her throat, yet never said a word. The man who trained Rumaldea's horses was there again. He was lounging on the outskirts of the group, saying less than he had the night before.

The dinner bell rang and everyone amiably took their seats. Aradia waited until they were all seated, and then nodding her head to the master and mistress who were sitting at the opposite ends of the long table, she made her apologies and took her seat next to the captain of ship in which she had been a captive on.

The Captain of the Satarcia nodded his head in her direction, and with surprise looked again. "We've met before?" he queried.

"Yes... you know me, Captain Grisarius," she whispered into the captain's good ear. "You purchased me from the Capitan of a savage group of warriors that decimated my home and family. Your men brutally killed my friend in the seaport of Tarquinia and threw me in the hold of your ship. You had plans to sell me for quite a sum, for I speak many languages and have a way with numbers. It is because of that, when I was a *guest*...upon your ship, I found that you were cheating the owner."

The captain's expression changed, and he motioned the slave away that was serving him.

"You take your life in your hand, child," he murmured.

But Aradia would not be put off.

"While aboard, I had a look at the ship's log and I am aware of your stealing from the owner of the ship, who just happens to be master here," she told him. "If you think he would be happy over that, then go ahead and speak to him about it. But remember that I have proof of what I say and I know where you keep your personal log...In fact, why don't I tell him now! We'll see whom he believes!"

She had taken a grave chance, and well she knew it. He was frightened. She could see fear on his weather-beaten face.

"You must know that no one will believe you." He told her, though he stole a glance at the master of the house, "What do you want from me?" he muttered.

Heady with power, Aradia smiled.

"As for what will follow, let me think on it."

And with that, she turned her attention to the other guests.

Looking towards Lady Sovonya, The captain of the Satarcia, desperate to keep Aradia from speaking, smiled at his hostess saying, "I must owe ya' great favor for the pleasure of such delightful company such as this young lady. A man like me, out at sea fa' months at a time, with nothing this pretty ta' see…why I feel honored by her company."

Not a sound was heard. No one ate or breathed it seemed. Many had their mouths opened. He had been a guest before and everyone knew he had no interest in the ladies. Sovonya was pleasantly aghast at the fact that he could put a sentence together, never mind using proper etiquette. He spoke business to Rumaldea when they were ensconced in the library with their wine. Other than that, while at the table he ate and grunted at profound or sometimes drunken statements from the men, and openly sneered at any remark that she made. Sovonya was thoroughly enjoying the show! The captain was acting strangely, she thought, and she was absurdly amused! She did not know exactly what this awkward behavior was about, but it was better than the town's play she had attended last year.

⁓✥⁓

After dinner, as Aradia and Sovonya lounged in the garden, Sovonya blurted out, "It was sad to see the evening end. It was the best social evening I've had in quite some time. Will I be privy to your secret, or will I spend the rest of my life wondering what transpired as you whispered into the captain's *good ear?*"

Aradia inhaled deeply; then slowly letting it out exclaimed, "I have much to tell you." Hesitating, a wistful look etched in her eyes, she continued. "I am sorry that we have had no time of late. It is possible that soon, there will be more to tell. Then you shall be privy to more than you might want to know. I am sure that sounds mysterious but you have trusted me so far. Please… just a bit longer?"

"Has anyone ever turned you down when you have begged so?"

"I have been very lucky in my life. I have never had to beg," Aradia stated firmly as she got up to go. With a shrug of her slender shoulder she said, "And it is a good thing, for I have a grievous fault. I am too proud to beg."

"Oh my, I didn't mean…" stammered Sovonya. "Please forgive …"

Aradia bent over and kissed her patron on the forehead. "No. You mistook me. I have something weighing heavily on my mind. It is nothing you have said. I love you like a mother. I do not mean to be forward, but those words needed saying. Thank you for all you have done for me. You have been so kind. I will spend the evening in my room if that is all right. I feel poorly."

"Yes, of course my dear, I will have Iola check on you. You do look pale. Run along now," she added, clearing her throat. "Aradia… if it is any comfort, I likewise have great affection for you. If I had been blessed enough to have had a child, I would have been graced by the gods if it had been you."

Aradia could not speak because of the emotions that threatened to overwhelm her. Tears coursing down her cheeks, she ran to the house. She was so frightened of disappointing Sovonya, and she was concerned, thinking she would never see Tomis again. It had been nearly two moons since his hasty exit. And she knew she was with child. She had suspected for a while, but up until this moment she did not want to face it.

Aradia sat by her window, marveling at the last hues of daylight. She watched as the sun's golden orb melted into the earth, leaving behind multicolored rays pulsating in the backdrop of the now dimly lit sky. Deciding that she would tell Sovonya everything in the morning made her recognize it was easier being someone she was not. She could play the role and not face the fact that her whole family had been butchered. She could forget the horror of seeing her friend Phesoj killed, and push away the torture of being abducted. She could move through her day pretending all was well; only at night, when it was quiet, would she look at the truth of it. Yes, she would tell her in the morn. She slept fitfully that eve.

Startled awake, she could only recall one thing from her dream. Her spirit guide saying, *It takes strength to hide feelings, it takes courage to show them. It is possible you have waited too long.*

Turning over to stretch, playing the words of the dream over in her mind she was suddenly aware of a horrific sound rending the air. Sitting up quickly, she heard feet scurrying in the hallway, and Sovonya's maid, Stalena, poked her head through the door without knocking to tell her that she must come quickly, that her mistress had been taken ill.

Seeing Sovonya's pale face against the pillow, Aradia cried out against the unfairness of it all. "Noooo! Not you too? All those I love are taken away from me."

"It is her heart, erratic is what," declared the man who Aradia recognized as the one who tended the animals. "We'll just have to see," he said. "Bed rest is all that can be done."

Aradia stood there shaken. Well, she thought, there must be something else that can be done. Grim with determination, she headed toward the wing where the *lion* roomed. She was barred from entering by his slave.

"I must see the master," demanded Aradia pushing him aside, nearly knocking him over.

"He is having his morning meal. Whatever it is, it can wait," said the manservant, regaining his balance as he held her back.

"No! This cannot wait one moment. Mistress Sovonya is very ill." Aradia ducked under his arm, opened the outer door, quickly knocked and then rushed in.

"By Zeus, what are you doing here?" he demanded, half rising from the table. "Do you not know that only men are welcome here, you little barbarian?"

"There is something that needs to be addressed," Aradia told him, "Sovonya is quite ill, and she needs the best of care. A specialist from the city must be called for."

"Have you been appointed her post, or do you wish to appoint yourself my conscience?" asked the master, sneering at her. "Well, speak up, girl! What position do you wish?"

Aradia could not believe what she was hearing.

"Then you will do nothing!" she exclaimed.

"I have already done all that is needed," he told her, "and now I am going to have my meal. You will, I presume, find your way out?" The cool tone of his voice took on the quality of splintering ice. "And never attend to me like this again."

Aradia stomped out as he fastidiously arranged his tray paying her no mind. Head bent in sorrow, she returned to sit with Sovonya, about whom all the women of the household had gathered. Aradia was told that she had opened her eyes twice but that she was very weak and unable to speak. "Is she…will she die, Miss?" Stalena asked, tears streaming down her plump cheeks.

Aradia's stony gaze was fixed on her patroness. "I assured you that all is in hand. I will send for a physician.

The next morning she hunted down one of the stable boys and promised him coin to go into the town proper to fetch a man of medical knowledge. Giving him a small gold piece to make the ride, and many coins to give the physician, she hoped he was not a thief and would soon return.

Days went by with no change in Sovonya's health. Neither was there word from Tomis. Aradia spent all her time attending her friend and hoping that Rumaldea would leave. She had not seen him since the day she had barged in on him, and if she never saw him again, it would be too soon. He was a miserable old man. When he died, no one would mourn him, she thought. Unlike Sovonya, who was loved by many, he would not be missed. The medico never came and Aradia was left to wonder what had happened. When she tried to get another of the stable boys to go to the city, she was told that it was impossible.

One day, during one of Aradia's lengthy visits, Sovonya slowly opened her eyes and said weakly, "You must get in touch with Tomis, my dear. He is in his homeland. It is a great distance."

She then, painstakingly, told Aradia how to contact him before wearily closing her eyes. Aradia was excited about contacting Tomis. Sovonya had told her it was a complicated matter and would take a great deal of time for an answer, but it was a start simply to know where he was.

Sitting the next day she composed a letter to him and gave it to the maid along with the last of the coins she had tucked away from her time in Athens. Her instructions were to give the coins to the stable master, who would ride to the small port on the island and then make the appropriate arrangements with one of the ships that came to trade. In her letter she told Tomis of Sovonya's illness, and also asked to know how he was. She made mention how wonderful it was getting to know him and asked when his next visit might be, mentioning nothing of the child that she now knew was nestled in her womb.

"A moon yet passed and no change for the better," Stalena said dejectedly, as they sat beside the lady's bed. "Do you think she will ever get well, Miss?"

"I truly do not know," Aradia told her, "I had hoped for a physician but we are at the mercy of a tyrant."

She had attempted to send again for a third time when the other two attempts had brought no aid, but had been told that the master had ordered them not to interfere.

⚜

In order to enjoy the last remnants of sun upon her face, Aradia took a few moments in the garden, instinctively cupping her slightly rounded belly with one hand.

"The master wants your attendance," a slave announced, appearing with a suddenness that took her breath away. "Come with me."

Once in the men's quarters, she was hurried into the library, no doubt so that she would not be seen. It had been a long while since she had browsed tablets and parchments. She missed the smell of a library, the feel of writing tools and of the parchment upon which to write.

Caressing one of the scrolls lovingly, she heard the booming voice of Rumaldea. "Whose child is it? I'll have his name before you leave this room."

Holding the parchment scroll in front of her, she pulled herself up to her full five feet nine inches, and turned toward him. Glaring in open contempt she spoke with royal demeanor, not masking what she felt for him.

"You act as a deceived father. The role does not suit you. If that is why you called me here you are wasting your time. I am in attendance to your lady wife, sir. You may treat her like a servant, but that advantage does not extend to me. I have tended her duties during her illness and neglected nothing. The house runs smoothly. When she is well, I shall leave. I hear that you are off soon. I shall continue as I have been with your permission."

"This is the second time you have insulted me! There shall not be a third," Rumaldea spat in a rage.

Aradia marched regally past him. She was shaking, for indeed he could order her out of the villa and off the grounds. Her mind was racing. She did not want to leave Sovonya. If he ordered her away, she might never see Tomis again. Surely the letter had reached him by now and there would be one on its way back to her. Praying to the gods and goddesses, she realized she had been evoking them often as of late.

Aradia frantically paced the length of her room, reminiscing about the long and interesting talks she'd had with Sovonya before she took ill. How she wished that there was something more definitive that she could do. Aradia had taken it upon herself to not speak about her spell-making abilities to the servants, though she had made herbal remedies for some of them. She loved the servants and did not want to get them into any trouble with their master so she was very careful. It saddened her that she had not come upon an herb that would help Sovonya.

The day before last she had again gone to the woods seeking comfort and looking for an herb to heal her friend. The herbs in this country looked, tasted and smelled somewhat different. Aradia spent an enormous amount of time seeking answers while sitting at the bedside of her hostess, praying for knowledge of the right herb to use. Knowing she had to be careful in the administering of the herbs so as not to draw attention to her craft, she was being overly cautious. Besides, she thought, since she had fallen in love, she was aware that her power had diminished a bit, no doubt because her thoughts were so scattered. She was having a hard time controlling her breathing as a means to obtain vision. Grandmamma taught me well. How is it that when I need it the most I cannot seem to get answers?

That night, before she went to bed, she invoked the gods and goddesses of Greece. "All right," she spoke out loud, "I have begged my gods and goddesses to answer me and yet I have no answers. So I shall resort to call upon you Artemis, Goddess of the hunt and of the forests and woodlands. I beseech you, come to me with the answer to my prayers. I love Sovonya. Like my sister, the world is better off having her in it. You cannot take her. Show me the herbs!"

She sobbed the last few words and threw herself on her bed in exhaustion from her long day.

⌘

That night in her dream the Goddess Artemis was showing her a path out of the courtyard that led at great distance to a grotto-like area. The grotto had not been made by the hands of man, but was wrought from the hands of the Goddess. The word 'physis' the Greek word for nature had been repeated in her dream more than once. Then an odd-looking plant that was larger than life appeared in front of her. It was a stock with six leaves and tassel like appendages on each. The top of the plant was rounded with what appeared to be a fluffy substance. The plant grew smaller and floated down the path, nestling itself under the shade of a large jagged rock.

"Ah, my sweet child," said her own spirit guide, "you seek to help one you love. Your heart is in the right place but you are very tired. It is important to take care of yourself for the sake of the child. Take your dream to heart. Go and seek the herb. It is called Silphium. It cures many things in this strange country you find yourself in."

Desimena watched her charge sleep. Then she repeated the words again, inserting them firmly into Aradia's dream, hoping to reach her with the vital information.

Early the next morning, Aradia hurried out of the courtyard through the villa's compound and to the hill lined with groves that she had seen in her dreams, excited and certain that she could find the herb of which she had dreamt. Great was her joy when she found that the dream had been correct. Finding it exactly where Artemis had shown her, she hurriedly went back to the villa to prepare it, knowing in her heart that it would heal Sovonya.

Stalena hesitantly entered Sovonya's room, her cheeks stained and tearing. Wiping her eyes on her apron, her skin grew even paler and her hands shook as she nervously approached Aradia and told her, hesitantly, that she was wanted outside, that the master's slave was waiting to take her to him.

Aradia had been sitting next to Sovonya, affectionately holding her hand and gently feeding her the third dose of tea she had made from the information in her dream. Aradia felt encouraged and thought the unique brew was helping. Sovonya had smiled at her and it appeared that she was a little stronger, and it had only been two days.

"Thank you, I shall come down in a moment." Aradia was not looking forward to this. She had heard that the master had canceled his plans to leave for business and that he was in a frightful state of mind.

Aradia was led to the library by the slave; there was no one there when she arrived. She stood at the fireplace to draw a bit of heat. The weather was turning cold as winter fast approached. She had never liked this desperately bleak time of year. Looking out of the window at the desolate coffee colored landscape did nothing to shorten the minutes that she waited. She tried to quell the dark uneasiness with thoughts of warm summer days in the sun.

Three men entered the room. Behind them strode the master. For a moment Aradia felt like a caged animal; a feeling of helplessness swept over her and her knees felt weak. She was not used to feeling this way, and became angry with herself for cowardice. Throwing off her fear, she faced the men, reminding herself of what her grandmother would say to her in such a situation. If you are not moving forward, then you are going backward.

The smallest of the three men said, "You have been accused of crimes against this household. You will be tried on the morrow, as is the custom. You will be escorted to your room and the door will be bolted. Food will be brought to you."

"That is better than you deserve!" the master shouted, turning red and pounding his fist upon his desk.

Aradia paid him no attention. She looked at the man who had made the statement. "And who might you be?"

"I am the magistrate. I tend to any crimes against the master's holdings. We will not hear you now, but on the morrow as I explained. You will be taken to your room."

The two men standing quietly by took one of her arms, and suddenly Aradia remembered the men that had taken her prisoner after killing Phesoj. It felt as though these same brutes were taking her prisoner once again. Fiercely she pushed the men away, as powerful feelings of being thrown into the ship's hold washed over her. And when they came at her again, she pushed them away with all her strength, and began to run. But both men were quick and strong. Before she had taken a few steps, they twisted her arms behind her back and forcefully removed her from the library.

The pain was so excruciating that she felt as though her shoulder would come out of its socket. Renewing her fight, she protested vehemently, ordering the men not to touch her. As they reached her bedroom door, a strong desire to call on the elementals engulfed her, but her remembered promise to Sovonya kept her from doing so.

The men pushed her roughly through the door and towards the bed. Grabbing a tray of food on the stand beside the bed, she flung it at them. The startled men could not dodge it fast enough. Milk compote, cheese, bread, and a pitcher of water hit the frame of the door, splattering both men. The last thing she saw and heard were their startled faces as the door closed and the horrifying sound of the latch click into place.

Sitting on the bed in confusion, Aradia tried unsuccessfully to calm herself. What a sight that must have been, she thought, them dragging me kicking and screaming through the household. But that was beside the point now. What she needed to do at this moment was to decide how to proceed. What would grandmother do, she wondered? And what of the precious child she and Tomis had created?

Opening the window she gingerly began to climb out, but the chill in the air reminded her of her boots and a blanket. Going over to get them she noticed the bread and cheese on the floor. I must eat, she thought, for the child. She stored the remnants of food in her shawl. Remembering the jewels Sovonya had leant her the night of the gala, she peeked into the ornately carved trunk at the end of her bed. I have used the last of the coins, she reminded herself. I will need something to make a fresh start for the sake of the child. Hesitating, she rummaged through the trunk. She thought, Sovonya will understand.

Again she went to the window, this time over the sill and onto the tiles. It was different with boots on. It was slippery so she moved at a snail's pace. Approaching the end of the roof, she looked down and saw the rain barrel. "Oh, Minerva, goddess of war," she spoke out loud, "please come to my aid. And Demeter," she begged, "Please…protect my child."

Letting go of the roof edge, she put all her weight on the barrel. It tipped over and she landed hard on her left side and shoulder. Lying there very still, she thought she felt the child kick. Placing her hand over her belly in an attempt to soothe and comfort the child within, she whispered softly, "It will be all right, mea bambino. I will take good care of you."

Aradia moved quickly but quietly towards the stable. She did not know how to bridle a mount. She was surprised to see the stable boy that she had paid to go to fetch a medico. He had never returned, or so she had been led to believe.

"Would you bridle her for me?" she asked, pointing to one of the horses.

He nodded and moved to do her bidding without a word, his eyes downcast. He led the horse out of the stall, put a blanket and bridle on her, and handed the reins to Aradia. The stable boy helped Aradia onto the horse and she slowly left the stable area. Her heart was racing with anxiety but she knew she had to hide her feelings for fear the stable hand would detect something amiss. Not wanting him to become curious she rode away from the stable area as casually as possible, holding her breath, her thoughts raced.

Picking up speed, the bouncing began to feel uncomfortable. She could stand it, but could the child? Looking over her shoulder, she saw two men on horseback galloping toward her. Spurring the horse to move faster, she hoped to outrun them.

Suddenly, and without warning, one of the men was beside her and was reaching over to grab her reins. Trying to block him from doing so slowed them down enough for the second man to catch up. Realizing it was useless she gave up the struggle. Putting her hand over her belly, she said silently, I will protect you. I do not know how, but I will protect you.

Without speaking the men led her back to the villa. When they reached the steps to the main entrance, one man dismounted while the other held the reins of Aradia's mount. Once inside her room, one of the men gruffly asked, "What have you in the wrap?"

Nervously, she spoke. "It is just some bread and cheese."

The other, a thin grim faced man, picked up the bag and roughly opened it, un-wrapping the food the jewels fell on the floor.

Saying not a word to her, the men left, taking both the food and the jewels. The door was closed and locked again. The sound offended her ears. Aradia went to the window and looked out. There she saw a guard sitting on a tree stump.

The same two stern and disapproving men came for her in the morning. Feeling their eyes bore through her, she knew what thoughts were filling their heads. Sitting on the side of the bed in her best garment, she was ready! She knew she looked attractive. Her skin glowed and her breasts were full mounds. Her hair was swept up, with small curls escaping the pins.

Indicating that she would not try to escape, she followed the men out of her room and down the stairway. Keeping her head high with a regal tilt, her eyes sought out the many servants that peaked out from nooks and corners. As they made their way past the library they headed for one of the meeting rooms. Cook, Iola and Stalena, standing by the kitchen door, openly cried and sought her eye, trying to give comfort as she passed.

Six men, all formally dressed in elaborate togas with gold patterned stitching down the front, sat behind a large oblong table. Some of the men were visibly awkward and fidgeted in their chairs, but all showed varying degrees of discomfort. Many men who Aradia guessed were from the master's holdings sat off to the side, looking as though they were there just to observe. Some sought her eye in compassion, others in curiosity, but most simply looked uncomfortable. She was told to sit at the smaller table in front of the six men.

The master of the house was seated in a huge cushioned chair, alone and off to the left of the larger table. Aradia, the panel of six men, and the entire proceedings were in his view. A small ornately carved desk with writing tools and a gavel sat in front of him. Beside him was another table holding an object that was wrapped in hemp.

Two of the six men at the large table were unfamiliar to her. She nodded to the magistrate from yesterday, and then to the councilman and judge she had met at dinner when Rumaldea had first returned to the villa. Then noticing Timerus, she gave a slight nod. She had expected Captain Grisarius might be one of her judges, perhaps even strangely hoped, as in his case he had much to lose by condemning her, but he was not in evidence.

The magistrate who yesterday had told Aradia she had committed crimes against the holdings, stood up, and clearing his throat, looked down at the parchment he held and began to enumerate her crimes by number."You are accused of the following," he said somberly.

1. "The crime of being a witch and of using that witchcraft to gain entrance into this household.
2. The crime of seducing Tomis, of the land of Tomi, with your witchcraft to extract secrets from him to use against this household.
3. The crime of being with child and not stating whom is the father, therefore creating a liability on these holdings.
4. The crime of theft, as in your possession we found jewels belonging to the mistress of the house, wherein you erred against the Master.
5. The crime of using your spells and witchcraft to poison your mistress."

Hearing the last charge, Aradia gasped, nearly crying out. But cleared her throat instead, bringing her emotions under control. She would present a brave front, no matter what it cost her.

With a grim face, the magistrate uttered, "What have you to say?"

Aradia tried to keep the list of accusations straight, going over them in her mind. Pushing her chair back, she stood tall and slowly looked at each man on the board, and then looked the magistrate in the eye.

"As to the **first**, yes, I am a 'strega,' a witch, as you say. It is not a crime to be a witch in Etruria, my country of birth. It has been passed down in my family since the beginning of time. As to the **second**, I used no witchcraft upon Tomis, nor have I any interest in secrets or intrigue."

Taking a deep breath, she looked over at the master and addressed her answer directly to him.

"As to the **third**, I have inherited a fortune from my father. When I can prove that I am alive to receive this fortune, there shall be no drain upon this man's holdings."

She could not help showing her disdain and disgust with him as she continued, openly challenging him with her eyes.

"It would then be no matter who the father was, for I am not asking the master of this house to take care of what is my responsibility."

Reluctantly bringing her eyes back to the judges sitting at the large table, and then to the magistrate, she continued. "As to the **fourth** accusation, the mistress lent me the jewels. I am not guilty of the crime of stealing."

Aradia stood even taller. Closing her eyes for a moment, she tried to remember the last accusation but could not bring it to mind.

"As to the **fifth**… could you state the fifth again?" she requested firmly, looking deeply at the magistrate.

Becoming unsettled under the steadiness of her gaze, the magistrate looked down at the parchment in front of him.

"Ah hum … the … poisoning of…of the mistress of this house."

"As to the **fifth**, who accuses me of that?"

"We are asking the questions here and *you* are answering them," the master roared. Hatred of Aradia and her impudent behavior toward him blazed in his eyes. He had wanted to put her in her place ever since she first looked at him with those bold cat green eyes. She should be trembling in fear, he thought, yet she is brazen and unrepentant. Clenching and unclenching his hands, his voice rang out sharply as he attempted to regain his position as master of the proceedings. "Answer the charge!" he shouted.

Staring at him with quiet venom, she finally answered, "As to the **fifth**..." And then, becoming tired of the game and with the sad recognition of the outcome her shoulders dropped as she said, "All of my answers at this proceeding have been totally honest and completely sincere. I swear this in sacred honor of my beloved family. My answer to the *second accusation* answers this one also. "I have performed no witchcraft in this house..."

She faltered for a moment remembering the special tonic she had made with such love for her friend Sovonya. "I have at no time, *ever*... used poison in my craft."

"You have been seen giving my wife something evil. It was poison meant to kill her," the master roared, his face contorted with rage.

Aradia ignored him and looked at the magistrate. She sat down, her knees shaking but her face composed. Sitting quietly and perfectly still, she waited for the panel of six men to judge her.

The master of the house stood up from his seat, accusingly pointing a finger at her and bellowed, "You are guilty of seducing a man, or men, with your womanly wiles. You have been impudent and rash in your behavior. You have caused injury to me and to my reputation. It is now time to admit your loose nature, and thieving ways. Admit to your outrageous behavior. Admit it!" he screamed at her, still pointing his finger and waving it madly. "Crawling out of windows at every opportunity and..."

Picking up the object covered in hemp which had been resting on the table beside him, he tore off the wrapping and disclosed the statue Tomis had molded. "This is indeed witchcraft!" he roared, as his face became an unhealthy reddish hue.

Aradia thought of the statues she had seen of the gods and goddesses, naked and glorious in their delightful and sometimes erotic poses. Her hands clenched in her lap, she took a deep breath and in turn looked each of her accusers in the eye. She began to breathe the deep green of the earth up through her feet. When she felt the earthy essence, she allowed a deep red light to embrace her womanhood. Letting the profound red of passion flow up and through her, she imbued her aura with sultry vibrations.

It was then, rising to her feet again, her head high and her shoulders thrown back, she knew she had nothing to lose. In a husky voice dripping with sensuality, thoughts of her lover foremost in her mind, she declared, "I am guilty of making love to a man…I am guilty of giving him pleasure and of enjoying him to the fullest… I am guilty of thinking of him and desiring him and holding him unto my heart…"

Aradia ran her tongue seductively over her top lip, and recalling their lovemaking, she closed her eyes for a moment before opening them in all their misty sea-green glory.

"I am guilty of enjoying my nakedness and posing for a statue of beauty," she said in her melodious voice. "I am guilty… of romping as a child, from the very act of making love to running in the garden."

She placed her hands on the table in front of her and leaned forward, invitingly displaying her sensuous feminine attributes, speaking softly so that they would have to lean in to hear her words.

"Yes…I am guilty of climbing out of a window to meet my lover. *And…* there is not one of you here that is not inflamed by the thought of a woman wanting you so badly… that she would leap from a rooftop to fly into your arms! So hang me if you will. But you'll not get the name of my lover!"

Aradia pointedly looked at each man on the panel as she slowly spoke, "And you'll forever wish," she said with a haughty, seductive smile, "… that it was you … I ran to."

She sat down, for she was shaking inside and her legs could no longer hold her. She knew she had put her head in a noose but at the moment she did not care.

The panel, lust in the eyes of some, compassion in the eyes of others, whispered among themselves for a long while. The lion kept shaking his head 'no' his gaze threatening and overbearing, seemingly in disagreement with all of them, he continued to badger them unmercifully. Finally, with eyes downcast the magistrate stood to make the announcement.

"It has been decided," he said sadly, clearing his throat, "that you are guilty and you will be put to death. Punishment will take place after… after the child is born. May the gods be with you."

Victoriously Rumaldea stood up and proclaimed, "I have only one thing to add. It was Tomis, to whom we have opened our home, that accused you of seducing him with your witchcraft, and it is because of our commitment to his father and their homeland that we take firm action in this matter."

Moving aside the writing tools from the desk in front of him, he carefully unfolded a note. "I have it here in his own hand. He refers to you as *Regina Bella*." He scowled at her, ice in his eyes. "She is guilty," he said while showing the letter to the other men. "She is guilty, I tell you."

Inquisitively each man looked at the letter as it was passed around.

"It is not in our language," noted one of the judges.

"I have had it translated. Worry not! I am aware of what is in the letter."

Aradia, upon hearing this, became numb. The fire and passion that she had displayed earlier drained from her body. With every ounce of effort she could muster she held her head up as two guards led her from the room.

Frozen, heavy with dread, the long excruciating walk through the villa to the west side, ended all too briefly as the guards opened the oaken door. The end of her freedom and the beginning of her forced imprisonment lay before. Leaving the room, one of the guards turned and callously exclaimed. "You will remain there until your death!"

Aradia listened as the huge wooden door closed. The harsh and insensitive sound of the heavy bolt left her with nothing but stark reality.

Chapter 14

Sitting dejectedly on a raised platform with hard matting that served as a bed, Aradia, as if in a dream, observed a young woman she had never seen before enter her prison like room carrying a chamber pot and some water. With deep set eyes and lined pinched mouth, the small bird-like woman spoke. At first Aradia could not focus on the gritting sounds as they echoed through the nearly empty room. The maid's dull eyes scanned Aradia with wariness. Having heard rumors that she was a witch, she scowled at Aradia, and squawked in clipped tones.

"Food will be twice a day," she told her. "If you try anything ta hurt me or ta escape, they say they will not wait till the child is born. Seems cruel," she said with a shrug, "but I'm just doing my work is all. If any of the slaves from this household help you in any way, they will be put to death, as well as their families! If ya try and enlist them to your plight, you're handing them a death sentence! There'll be a guard posted, and they have taken an oath on their family to not speak; good day ta ya."

The screeching sound of the bolt on the door as the maid left reverberated through every part of Aradia's body and her eyes filled with tears as she brought her hand to her stomach.

Yes, she thought. Any day that someone was sentenced to die must be a good day for the populace. It is something to put spice in their lives no doubt, as they are such a dour lot! Those were the precise words her grandmother had spoken to her as she was taken off to prison.

Perusing the inhospitable room, her eyes sought comfort. But there was none in the old worn desk and stone like chair or the cold hard bed with its austere table that held a lonely candle. She felt her fate wrap around her like an ugly cavernous tomb. Moving toward the barren fireplace in anticipation, actually wondering if she could climb up through the chimney, she laughed scornfully at herself when she saw how narrow it was. However, she did look again, to see if there were any footholds to use in case she decided to try. Resigned to her fate, her eyes lit upon a small chair tucked away in the corner. "Oh Goddess thank you," she sighed. And sitting in the small chair she gently rocked her body to and fro, as she sang a lullaby to her babe.

Later, having asked for writing tools, she sat each day and wrote until the light was gone. Never was there a fire to warm her. It was bitter cold and the dampness went deep into her bones. She lay at night waiting for the light of day so that she could sit and write again.

Aradia was hardly eating, and the maid remarked, "T'is not my concern miss, but you'll not live long enough for the babe to come into the world."

Aradia had no hunger. The morsels she ate were for the sake of the child. She would hold on to her belly and rock back and forth in her chair and repeat over and over. "I will protect you, I will protect you."

On occasion she sang the song of the sirens who roamed the sea, and sometimes harsh laughter would follow. "I am no mermaid! It is a shame for if I could, I would lure a few men to their deaths with my song. Just like the stories of sirens and sailors, so sweet….so deadly!"

The maid overheard her as she entered with the evening meal.

"If you'll be doing spells and curses you'll be put to death afore your child comes. Tis only because they see no evidence of your witchcraft that you are still alive," she told her. "Well no matter ta me, ya foods here."

Aradia sat on the bed and rocked. Nodding her head to the maid, she made no move towards the food.

The cold had set in her bones until she was stiff, and she shuffled when she walked. The two months she had been imprisoned seemed like an eternity. She had tried early on to make friends with the maid repeatedly asking her what would happen to her baby. She also begged her to make contact with the city of Volsinii in Etruria, wanting her child to be brought up in her homeland. And when she asked after Sovonya, she was always told that there was no news.

One day, out of the blue, Sovonya's maid appeared to tell her that the herbal medicine that Aradia had been giving the older woman had just been found and it was their last hope to cure her. The maid begged that Aradia disclose how to prepare it.

Relenting with a sigh, Aradia said, "Yes, you boil half this pouch in this much water till it turns dark. It will not take too long. Give her this much just twice a day and, pray to Artemis to bless the herb, for she showed me where to find it."

Aradia slowly turned away and went to her desk, dismissing the maid with her indifference. Once the door closed she wept to think that the woman who had succored her was now so close to death. She could only hope that the herbs were not too late.

⚜

As the days turned into months Aradia's only solace was her writing. One evening, having fallen asleep exhausted, as she had many a day at her desk, she awoke to stabbing back pains and a commotion outside the door behind her. Hearing it burst open, but too exhausted to turn around, she was startled when she felt a hand on her shoulder and heard a familiar voice telling her not to turn around.

"I cannot bear to look into your eyes," she heard Tomis say, as he placed his hands firmly on her shoulders the shock of his voice glued her to her chair. "I need to say what is on my mind," he continued. "I have not understood why you did not answer my letters or why you might not want to see me. I was angry at first and very confused."

He took a deep breath while Aradia seemed to struggle to grasp his words, to fully comprehend that he was here at last. Aradia listened although she was unable to rouse herself completely from her trance-like state.

"I have heard such abominable things. But I needed to see for myself. I have been told you have chosen to become a whore rather than be mine. Our love...I cannot fathom it."

The words were torn from his heart. It was difficult for him to speak.

"I have come to see if the rumors are true," he went on. "I cannot believe that you have been here all along, and chosen not to answer my letters! And the men! The Master wrote me of all the men that you have taken to your bed."

A sob escaped his throat.

"I...I have come to tell you of my arranged marriage. I am going to meet her, for the first time, but I needed to see you first. To understand what went wrong. For months I have tried to stop this marriage. When everything failed, I decided to tell her in person, to tell her that a marriage between us is not possible. But everything took so much longer than I expected. This is what I could not share with you earlier. This marriage was planned before you and I met. It is a matter of state, not a matter of the heart. When I thought I had your love, though I knew I would be exiled from my family and country, I was willing to give it all up. Tell me all that I have heard is wrong, talk to me…"

Slowly, achingly, Aradia rose. All the anger, pain, indignities and abuse that she had experienced since the death of her family came to the surface when she heard the word "marriage" and she realized he was talking of another woman. She hated him in that moment, as much as she had loved him.

Facing him she asked, "You bother to come now? You bother to tell me of your marriage?" Moving into the dim light, she cried, "You call *me* a whore?"

Tomis was so shocked at what he saw, that he was incapable of speaking. Aradia's once magnificent hair hung limply around her thin pale face. The loathing that he saw in her eyes terrified him. Her robe, dirty and tattered with wear, barely covered the fact that she was a skeleton except for the protruding stomach.

"Who – whose child do you carry?" he gasped, and then seeing the look in her eyes, "Do you mean that it is my child? Our child! Oh, God, that it should be so and I not know!"

For the first time since she had set foot in the villa to which Tomis had brought her, Aradia summoned the elements.

"From the east I call to you, Paralda, bring your Sylphs to me
From the south I call to you, Djin, bring your Vulcani to me
From the west I call to you, Necksa, bring your Undini to me
From the north I call to you, Gob, bring your Gnomes to me."

Out from the lining of her robe she pulled a lock of Tomis's hair, a golden lock he had given her in love, to keep under her pillow when he was gone. Now she would use it against him.

"I cast a circle, a circle of fire, come do my bidding. I order it so!"

She raised her right hand over her head and made a circle pointing to the east and ending in the north. She pointed again to the east.

"They are here," she said in a menacing voice, glaring at him.

Tomis was rooted to the spot as the room seemed to take on heat. An eerie glowing light formed around Aradia.

"I call out to those who have the power, the wine he drinks wilt be sour.
I call out to those who grant the fire, he's no longer apt to sire.
I call out to you who quench; his heart for eons will be wrenched.
I call out to you who provide the grain; all that he eats will cause him pain.

"I curse you such, and yours of yours,
Unto the seventh generation
You will suffer for what you've caused!

The wheat of the field you cannot eat.
The seed of your loins it will not seat,
And always... I will know of your defeat!"

"Be gone!" she shouted to the elementals, "for I have called you out for the last time. It is set. It is done. So be it!"

Staring at Tomis with hatred in her eyes, she collapsed on the floor.

He turned pale when he saw water and blood where she had been standing. Shouting for help, he knelt by her side, softly whispering, *"Regina Bella, mea Regina Bella."*

Sovonya, who had just risen from her sick bed, arrived in time to see Tomis carry Aradia's limp body toward the small cot. He ordered a fire to be lit and told the maid to send someone for the midwife. When he was told there was none available, the bird-like maid said that she had tended a birth or two.

The master of the house was not far behind them. Roaring like an enraged lion, he burst through the door and was about to order everyone out when he saw Tomis.

"What in heaven's name are you doing here?" he shouted.

"I might ask what Aradia is doing in this dungeon of a room, cold and damp, in her condition? What were you thinking? Why was I not informed that she was with child?"

Tomis turned from him in disgust as the little maid prepared for the birth, and Aradia groaned piteously.

"Sovonya, I order you to leave!" the master said, "All of you leave immediately, except the one to help with the child. I am told it is on the way."

"You have ordered me for the last time sir," Sovonya waved her cane towards him in a threatening fashion, declaring adamantly; "I am staying to help with this birth!"

"If you stay, it might be the last thing you do!" he warned her.

"I think you have done enough injury," Tomis said to the master of the house, standing protectively in front of Sovonya. "Leave now!"

The master found himself being propelled towards the door by a furious Tomis, who barely able to contain his murderous feelings, was shouting, "Allow the women to do their work!"

"Go!" Sovonya cried in agreement. "I am given to understand that Aradia nursed me for more than two moons before this hideous situation befell her. It was Aradia's herbs that finally roused me from my illness. Be gone, before I turn you into a toad! The sight of you sickens me!"

And leaning heavily on her stick, she sank into a chair close by the bed on which Aradia lay groaning. "The staff has told me he took the letters you wrote to her," she told Tomis. "He used them against her. She never saw or read them. He did not let the letters she wrote to you leave this house."

Tomis knelt down and lovingly gathered up the parchment that Aradia, in her distress, had left scattered on the floor.

"Is there anything I can do now?" he asked the older woman.

"No, it is up to her now," Sovonya said, "We need to see if she will rouse herself from this faint. But you should be here. It is your child."

"Yes," he said, tears unashamedly spilled from his eyes. His face contorted, showing deep seated pain. "Rumaldea kept news of the babe from me. He lied to me. Why?" But finding that Sovonya was murmuring words of comfort to Aradia, he unrolled the parchment and carried it to the fire where he began to read the story of Aradia's life. He read about her grandmamma guiding her, teaching her *la vecchia religion*, the old religion. He learned of her enormous love for her family, and her close tie with her sister Sardiana. He was aghast at how *they* were butchered along with nearly everyone in the town…everyone she had written so glowingly about. He openly cried, his tears blotting the ink as he read of how she was taken captive, beaten and forced by her protective instincts to kill. His breath caught in his throat as he read that she was thrown in the hold of a boat like an animal and brought to Athens to be sold as a slave.

With drooping shoulders, hunched close to the fire in order to read every word, Tomis ran the gauntlet from ice cold anger to fiery rage as he felt her pain. Slowly, as he read he began to understand the depth of the lies told to him by Rumaldea, and worse…the poisonous lies told to taunt and hurt Aradia. In the name of what, he riled? What excuse, what useless emotion could ever make this despicable treatment anything but inhumane?

The lines on the parchment tore at his heart as he read of the deep feelings she had for him. Looking over at her as she writhed on the bed, he wept, the tears streaming down his cheeks, dampening his robe. With a pang, he remembered when she kissed away his tears.

Sovonya's heart was breaking for this child…a child having a child. And she was bearing the threat of being hanged, as well. She swore to herself that she would prevent that no matter what she had to do. If Aradia lived! Oh, if only she lived! Don't let it be that I have come too late, she begged the gods. "I came as soon as I could," she cried now, hoping against hope that Aradia could hear her. "Oh child, do not leave us," she prayed aloud. "Here, hold my hand, squeeze, it will help. Push! It is time to push again."

With Sovonya's encouragement, Aradia roused herself and pushed, crying out as she did so, "Do not let the master have this child! He is a monster! Please take my babe back to my homeland. I have told the maid, given her instructions. Please, I'm so sorry I disappointed you… that I did not take you into my confidence. I … I'm sorry I took the jewels. I would have repaid you."

"Hush, hush child," Sovonya said, assuring Aradia she would see to it that the child was brought back to her homeland. She would do it herself, if need be.

"I will protect you," Aradia kept repeating to her child, as she lovingly held her belly, trying desperately to bear the waves of pain.

Tomis was shaking severely as he continued to read Aradia's diary. Reading of the trial, and of the words she had spoken to the judges… words that were to protect him wrenched at his heart. With each new sentence he connected with her pain! The master had told her that he, Tomis, had accused her of seducing him with witchcraft. Outraged that the man he had once trusted had produced a letter supposedly written by him, he realized that he could kill him with his bare hands, knowing the damage that those words must have caused her. And now he was witnessing the outcome of the lies.

A fierce primal roar came from Tomis as he read the last words, the words of a woman only living to bring forth her child as the desperate cold, the deep loneliness, and his abandonment of her had finally won. She had nothing to live for.

Leaping from his chair by the fire, he ran to Aradia's bedside and knelt on the floor. *"Aradia, tu mea cour!"* he cried. "I never accused you! Never!" Crying out against the injustice of what was happening, he implored, "Please, please don't leave me, Regina Bella, *tu mea cour."*

When the head of the baby crowned, Sovonya whispered, "Push, push," and with her very last breath, Aradia propelled her child into the world.

"I never accused you, never," Tomis wept as he clutched her lifeless hand and begged her not to leave him, at the same time that Sovonya sobbed, "She is gone, Tomis. She is gone!"

Chapter 15

Aradia, floating above the bed, heard Tomis say that he had never accused her.

And when Desimena, her spirit guide, appeared beside her, Aradia grabbed her arm and shook her as she cried, "He was not the one to accuse me. I must speak to him!"

But no matter how she tried to get his attention, Tomis could not see her. Sobbing, he sat on the bed caressing a slender white hand.

"He cannot hear you, Aradia. You are not of that world anymore. You have left your body behind, and you have left much karma to deal with. What goes out must come back. When you know of these things as you do, then they return threefold."

Desimena's face was awash with understanding, but she shook her head in sadness at the outcome of Aradia's life.

"I am not chastising you child, but you spewed forth such hate, and its residue will be felt for a long time to come...no doubt, for many incarnations. Come, child, it is time for us to leave. You have much preparation, for it is possible that you are to be born again very shortly. Those who take their own lives usually return very quickly."

"I did not take my own life!" Aradia declared in utter astonishment. "I died. Beside what of my child?"

"You allowed your body to waste away. You wanted to cheat them of killing you! You pushed away parts of your soul with your distrust of Tomis and the growing hate you harbored. One of your redeeming factors was that you sang to your child, and ate just enough to bring him forth into the world. He shall be a great man, mayhap a king in his time. Yes, you took your own life for you were determined it would not be taken from you."

"I needed to be strong ... I needed..." faltered Aradia.

"There is a fine line between pride and humility. If you are too humble, you lose yourself in meekness. If you have too much pride, it becomes

arrogance. And in arrogance you lose yourself just as surely as you do in humility that serves no purpose."

Aradia looked puzzled.

Desimena shook her head. "No, child, I will not explain it to you. It is one of the lessons you must learn for yourself."

"What should I have done, thrown myself on the mercy of the master? He is a monster! I could not lower myself to rummage in the dirt with him. I am no coward!"

In frustration, Aradia turned away from Desimena. Flashes of the spell she had cast filtered through her mind. It was true. She knew better. It was not as if she had not been warned. Her grandmother had certainly told her; never do a spell in anger. And her spirit guide had gently and lovingly tried to keep her on the right path.

"Will I be punished?" Her words came in a rush.

"There are many roads that can be taken on life's excursion and all of them eventually lead to learning. Life is a journey, not a destination. Life is eternal; therefore your passage means liberation, not punishment. ... Let us go child, for there are many waiting to greet you."

Desimena took the hand of her beloved student and charge. As they entered a great bluish-white tunnel Aradia heard the voice of her sister. She looked to Desimena with excitement.

"Yes, she is waiting for you," Desimena assured her.

Sardiana was at the end of the tunnel waving and laughing, and motioning for Aradia to hurry. Aradia ran to meet her sister. They hugged and hugged and as their tears of happiness mingled, Aradia was pulled more firmly into the spirit realm.

"Welcome home!" laughed Sardiana, and then, taking Aradia's hand proclaimed,

"I wanted to be the one to meet you."

Aradia watched as a familiar gate appeared before them. Her breath stopped as she recognized where Sardiana was leading her. Wiping the tear that trickled down her cheek, she cried out in joy, "Oh, Sardiana!" And arm in arm they walked through the gates of the city of Volsinii.

Looking around in amazement and taking it all in, Aradia asked, "How can this be, Sardiana? How can Volsinii be here in the spirit realm? It is more beautiful even than I remember it."

"Let us spend time with the family. They are waiting in anticipation to see you. In a few days we will talk of this marvel, and how it comes to be."

Sardiana spoke as if she were the older sister taking Aradia under her wing. An elfin smile crossed her face, baiting Aradia to ask more questions.

Aradia, deciding to take her counsel, smiled at her sister. "Well sister, you have beaten me! You have come to be here first, and now you can teach me for a change!" Aradia gave a quick laugh then became instantly serious. "Oh! I will get to see Grandmother. Why did she not meet me?"

Sardiana, biting her lip, confessed that Grandmother had reincarnated. "You know that she was never one to sit still long!" she added.

"I am glad she has reincarnated. Nothing much ever held her back, but it does not make me miss her less."

"Hmm ...yes, and I'll bet in your journey on earth, you will encounter her once again. Remember, Desimena told us that families tend to reincarnate together."

"If this is true, why are you not getting ready to go back to earth?" asked Aradia.

Sardiana, with just a touch of humor in her voice said, "Because you're the one that is always in such a hurry, and as you just learned that holds true on this side of the veil as well as on earth."

"Desimena said it was because I committed suicide." Aradia's shoulders sagged as she added, "Well, she did not use that word exactly, but the reference was there."

❧

Sardiana and Aradia lay in a grassy field atop a glittering mountain in the Apennines overlooking the Tiber River. They had been together constantly since Aradia had arrived, and they enjoyed every moment of the laughter filled days. They watched as the river meandered on its way toward the Tyrrhenian Sea.

"I will now answer your question of how this comes to be." Sardiana swept her arm out over the vast beauty of their surroundings. She turned over on her stomach and put her hand under her chin as if in thought.

"On this side of the veil ... as well as on earth and every other planetary system, everything happens because of thought," she said, measuring her words. "But in the realm of spirit it is instantaneous.

"You think of a place you love and it manifests right in front of your eyes. Enough people love Volsinii and all of Rome, to hold the manifestation in perfect order here on the other side of the veil. Let me show you. Think of a place you love. Picture it, taste it and smell it. Picture me there with you. ...Go ahead, try, Sister."

Aradia brought to mind the tree she used to sit under on the 'Tiger River,' as she had loved to call it. She pictured herself putting coins in her coffer box in her secret place. She could feel the box and smell the river, and a slight breeze wafted the tendrils of hair gently caressing her face. She dutifully pictured Sardiana beside her; she then opened her eyes. She was sitting in her favorite spot, under the tree on the river with her special box in her hands, and Sardiana sat beside her. Then the memory of the fateful day, the horror of all that took place moved through her mind, and all of it disappeared.

Sardiana, looking impishly arrogant, said, "You must have not held onto the pleasant thoughts or we would still be there. Well, no matter, you get the idea. I will continue. This is fun being your teacher.

Earth is a very low frequency planet; therefore thought manifestation takes time. Though I have learned that, when you are on the earth, quiet time in meditation and prayers facilitate matters. Oh ... and also positive thought, can raise the vibration of the body, allowing thought to produce more quickly.

"Unfortunately..." said Sardiana, hesitating as she searched for the right words, "angry thoughts, because they are so powerful, can also produce quick results that will boomerang back to the person who thought them."

Sardiana had been lying on her stomach with her chin propped up by her hand. Stretching she turned over onto her back, and sat up putting her hand on her sister's arm to get her attention.

"Oh, my wild and beautiful sister, I never thought to be having this conversation here, in this world, with you. Remember on earth how I worried so often about your using your magic? I worried that it would come back to hurt you. Well, I have learned about karma and that is what Desimena wants to talk to you about this morning. She is going to begin *your lessons. She will teach you about ... oh, so many things that your head will be spinning when she finishes. Desimena will..."*

"Wait a minute, wait just... one... minute," said Aradia pointedly. "You have been so busy teaching me, my little sister that I think you have forgotten one thing. The very basis for all of this is preparation for the next life."

Getting to her feet, with a satisfied smile, Aradia swept her arm in an arc, taking in all of the resplendent land before them. "And the talk Desimena is to have with me this morning is about the karma you create that follows you into your next life. Therefore I was right all along! You always pushed away any thought of more than one lifetime."

Gleefully, Aradia put her hands on her hips. "So it is I teaching you little one, just as I did on earth! Well?"

Sardiana stood facing Aradia, and copied her stance. "Yes. But I was here first, and if you don't mind your manners I'll not take you to visit the Hall of Records, and assist you in picking your next life!"

She looked every bit as smug as Aradia, as they stood there glaring at each other.

Aradia then began to howl, her laughter causing everything around her to shimmer, her sister joining in and they hugged and began to dance in a circle. As their joy poured forth, a nearby tree began to bud and then flower right before their eyes. As they recognized their eternal love, their tears of joy mingled and created such purity it radiated out in luminous waves, creating rainbows that danced in their midst.

⌘

Desimena had given Aradia time to be with the family she had lost. But now they would begin in earnest to prepare for Aradia's next life. When Aradia and Desimena finally met for the lessons, it was in a lush and fertile walled garden, the atmosphere pleasant but never a distraction. The pastel colors of the delicate flowers, and the faint aromas emanating from them had the subtle effect of calming her body while invigorating her mind. A large willow tree, its branches low and gracefully bending down to embrace the ground, stood behind the white marble bench where Desimena motioned Aradia to sit.

"Why is it that when most everyone goes to earth, they forget their past lives and when they come here are able to remember them?" queried Aradia in an attempt to keep her teacher from speaking about karma.

"No one that I have spoken to on any of the dimensions that I have visited seems to have a better answer than what I am going to tell you. It is easier on the human body to have brief glimpses, than full memory of past lives. First of all, the mind would run rampant with all the past memories, never mind the future ones." Desimena held up her hand. "No child, I will not explain future memories now. It is for another time."

"Meditation and contemplation are two ways of retrieving past life information," continued Desimena. "Also, another reason most don't remember their past lives is that they would glory in them, or hide themselves in a closet because of shame. Humans would begin to take their merit by the lives they lived as a king, or they would constantly hang their heads in apology because of the monsters they had been in their last life. This is a good system; for the most part it works. Most souls that have incarnated have had anywhere from several hundred to seventeen thousand past lives, on many planets and galaxies throughout the universe. But now it is time to speak of the karma you created in your last life."

Desimena paused, knowing one of the harder huddles they would encounter was concerning Tomis, and getting Aradia to accept what came after she left the earth. So she decided to change tactics. "What are your limitations?"

Aradia, caught off guard by the question, looked around at her surroundings and thought of all that she had learned. "I…don't feel limited. You have taught me of the limitless abundance that encompasses us here and on earth. You have expounded upon it…"

"Yes," interrupted Desimena, "but I inquire for a very important reason. In the very beginning, when you asked about Tomis and your son, I assured you that they were alright, and I told you that Sovonya had taken your son to live in Tomi, Tomis's homeland where he has placed his son to be next in line as ruler. He is called Knyaz Artyom."

"Ahr-TYOM?" Aradia pronounced her son's name as she had heard it."

"Yes, Prince Artyom. Tomis named him before he and Sovonya took him to meet his grandfather."

Desimena looked intently at her student before reaching over and lifting Aradia's chin with a graceful hand, her words soft and loving. "Tomis felt he had to clear your name. He went back to Greece and insisted that the master recant the story he had told about you, and own up to the lies he had concocted about him. What a coward the man was in the end. He picked another man to fight in his stead. It was decided that if his man lost the match, the master himself would have to come forward and clear your name. At the end of the battle Tomis was left standing, but the master was underhanded and sent men to kill him.

"You mean that Tomis"---

"Yes, Tomis has come and gone. It was best for both of you that you did not meet on this side of the veil. It might have delayed him from doing what was necessary."

"You mean going back to earth?" *Aradia asked with a forlorn look.*

"Precisely," *said Desimena as she nodded in sympathy.*

"Would you like to peek in on your son?"

"Can we do that?" *asked Aradia with a hopeful note in her voice.*

"We can. Would you like to go now?" *asked Desimena with a glint in her eye.*

"Oh yes, I would love to but, what did you mean earlier when you asked what my limitations were?" *queried Aradia, as they began through the etheric realm on their journey to earth.*

"Well…two things really. Many beings on this side of the veil become frustrated when they visit earth and their loved ones do not seem to know they are there. There is limitlessness to the All as you have been taught; yet when you move between the realms the frequencies are different."

"So if I visit they might not be aware of me?"

"Not in the way you might hope for, but they **will hear you** on some level, if you speak to them lovingly."

"You said two things?"

"Yes, I did. I did at that." *said Desimena thoughtfully. After you died, Tomis learned just how much the master had deceived you both. His rage clouded his vision. He needed to reach you on a* **spiritual level** *to tell you how much he loved you, but his humanness and his fury only allowed him to feel* **limited**. *So he went about clearing your name, in the only way that seemed open to him. He fought for you; it is what men do. What he* realized too late was that he had become angry, and his anger had taken over his life.

The most important thing is that Tomis understood what it was like to be on both sides of rage. He realized that rage limits your mind and spirit. He knew that as soon as he could, he was going to try and reach you though his prayers and invocations. He had begun to heal the rage, and was making peace in his heart. He was anxious to get back to his son, when he died."

"Well you have asked many questions on our journey through the etheric. But we are here," said Desimena, looking proud of herself as they stood in a huge room bathed in sunlight coming from a high window to the east. The sun had risen a few hours ago and was pouring through the opening. Rays of light gently played over a huge bed. A cherubic smile occupied the lips of a curly headed young man as he stretched and reached out his hand to touch the beams of light.

A knock at the door disturbed his reverie and he called, "Come in," laughingly adding "though you best have food as an enticement for my getting out of bed!"

"Well, well!" said a familiar voice, "It is nearly mid-day. It is time you joined us. You cannot use the excuse of your birthday. You celebrated that long into the night I hear."

"Oh Vonie, you celebrated along with me! Glad to be rid of me, no doubt! What will you do with your time now that I will travel and no longer be at my studies each day?"

"Don't you sass me young man. I'll always be wiser than you-it comes with age they tell me!" Sovonya said while putting her hands on her hips.

Aradia was pleasantly stunned as she watched the interplay between her son and her former protector. There was an easy peace between them and love that comes from a bond built over many years.

"How handsome he is, so like his father. How many years does he have?" asked Aradia.

"Eighteen years have passed here on earth."

"But…"

"Yes, there is no time in the etheric world. We spoke about that concept when you first traveled through the astral world, before you entered the earth realm."

Desimena knew that Aradia was avoiding the subject of Tomis, and what had transpired after her death and how her son had come to live in Tomi rather than **her** homeland.

"But I was told that I would be returning soon to the earth, because I committed su...well, you know. Eighteen years is a long time." said Aradia raising her eyebrow in question.

"Yes, when you first came we thought you might be going back immediately, but things changed and it was decided otherwise. You were content to visit with your sister and your family and come to classes. Of course it was easier to keep your mind occupied, once you started teaching classes about your life on the Moon and speaking to those who had yet to go to earth. But...I can tell you that you will be going back very soon."

Desimena waited for Aradia's normal impatience, but today she was circumspect.

"Let's observe your son and Sovonya as they go through their day. I will give you more information about how all of this came about. When you are ready you can speak to him."

Aradia said nothing so Desimena continued. "Sovonya sent messages to Volsinii to ask after your son's inheritance of the metal works and the land. The metal works had fallen to disrepair and poachers had come in to take the land. There seemed nothing she could do, and nowhere she could turn. In the end, however, Tomis took Sovonya and the child to his homeland and told his father that he must accept the babe as the heir and prince, or he would disappear with the child and his father would never see them again. As it worked out when Sovonya walked in to present the child to his grandfather, the grandfather at first was not able to take his eyes off her, the only woman he ever loved. When he broke his gaze to observe the child, he fell in love again, and there was never any question of the parentage.

I asked you earlier about limitations. Tomis felt limited in how he could show his love for you, after you left the earth. On a much deeper level, he had lessons to learn about limitations. In many ways Tomis lived in a black and white world. Limitations were something to accept or to find a slow and plodding way around. He simply never walked through the boundary, thereby never breaking open old belief patterns. He was limited in his humanness, he could not physically hold you, comfort you, or whisper words of love, so he sought other ways to prove his love to you as well as to himself. As men often do, and women don't understand, he showed you in the ways open to him at the time. He fought for your name, he abdicated his reign and he named his son Artyom which was in honor of you."

"How so?" asked Aradia.

"The name Artyom in Tomi is Artemisios in Greek and"---

"Oh Artemis! Tomis gave our son his country's male version of Artemis? An amazingly strong and wise being! I told him many stories of her"---

"Yes," interrupted Desimena, "and you also prayed to Artemis to help heal Sovonya and the goddess showed you where to find the herbs." Desimena leaned into Aradia and whispered, "I want you to know that it also has a deeper meaning; your son will forever be connected to you and your goddess mother through his name. Artemis is the Greek name for **Diana.**"

Aradia nodded her approval. She was watching her son as he ate a hardy meal while sitting in the garden. He was breaking his fast and excitedly talking to Sovonya about his plans for riding later in the day.

"I believe that stallion needs to be gelded; he is wild!" Aradia's former patron told him, her gaze following her husband as he made his way through the garden.

"Do not be talking about gelding in my presence," he commented as he joined them. "I will think you are complaining about my attention to you," he chided laughing.

"Oh, do not say such things in the presence of innocent ears!" said Sovonya as she cooled herself with her ever present fan.

Aradia had never seen Sovonya blush. And though she hid it with the fan, her color was high and she looked at the king with such love that Aradia hungered for her own lost love. Shaking her head to clear such thoughts she went closer to her son and whispered to him.

"You are the product of great love, in your conception, in my heart and in the home that you have come to have. I wish you the greatest of all things. I wish you to always know that you are loved."

Artyom stopped and listened, "Did you say something Sovonya? I heard a woman's voice."

Aradia turned to Sovonya then. "You have the sight," she said to her. "I want you to see me now, to know that I am here! I want you to tell my son of my love for him."

Desimena asked, "Aradia do you know what you are doing?"

"Yes, she has the gift; she has the ability to see me. I want her to know I am here. She will not be frightened. It will be alright."

Aradia closed her eyes and pictured her energy becoming larger. She went within and she began to flow pleasing thoughts toward her old friend as she continued to change her frequency.

Sovonya looked up and directly into Aradia's eyes. She did not seem startled. Her husband brushed her on the cheek with a kiss and firmly placed his hand on his grandson's shoulder and bid them to have a good morning as he walked off.

Sovonya looked over Artyom's shoulder and into Aradia's eyes again, and said to her charge, "Have I ever told you the story of the day your mother put the kitchen in an uproar, bustling around cooking special treats to offer to the 'goddess.' It delayed the meal and the master expecting his meal on time turned red and shrieked at the staff."

"No Vonie, you have never told me that one. Tell me please. I love to hear of my mother."

"She loved you very much! I heard tell from the staff that she sang to you every day as she sat waiting for your arrival."

As Sovonya continued with her story, Aradia smiled and nodded to her, and softly she and Desimena moved into the ethereal realm.

Chapter 16

Aradia worked to comprehend the hatred and distrust that had pervaded her last days on Earth. She was reminded that what she would learn on this side of the veil would just assist her in understanding the karma she had built up on Earth, not erase it. Karma needs to be worked out in the physical where it is created, she had been told.

"You were sent on a mission by your mother, the Goddess Diana," Desimena said to Aradia, while they shared tea in the garden. "Before you left the Moon, you were taught spells and the use of herbs to better the lives of all women upon earth. You were instructed to help them to be strong and to find their 'heart's desire.' When you prepared for your earth life you chose a family in which your craft could be used for good or ill. The choice was yours.

"You chose well. You used your gifts to help women throughout the years of your young life. It was not only your gift of spells and healing herbs that helped them, but also your wisdom in helping women find out what it was that they really wanted out of life.

I observed you one morning when two young girls came to you for assistance. As you touched one of the girls on the shoulder, you had a vision, and realized that she had a great voice. You encouraged her to study at the temple. She did, and it was truly her 'heart's desire.'

"When you looked at the other girl, you told her that there was a grand love on the way. You spoke to her telling her that there would be some sorrow, but that she must be strong so that she would find the 'love within the love' and she trusted you. Had you told her that she would marry and that he would die young, while she was heavy with his child, she would have become very depressed and that may have pushed her in another direction. Having a child was her 'heart's desire.' If you had said more or less she would not have accepted your words. As it was, she opened her heart to the child and has indeed had the grand love of motherhood.

"Another time, when I observed you, you were speaking to the cook when you stayed at the villa. You felt there was a man she was interested in. She believed she was too heavy and he would not be interested in her, so she chose not to tell you about him. When you hugged her on the way out of the kitchen, you had a vision of the man and saw how much he loved to eat. You encouraged her to cook special foods for him when he came to deliver the grain. They have had many happy years together. There is no question you helped her fulfill her greatest wish.

"You also encouraged and helped Poletzia to go to her sister. It was indeed her 'heart's desire,' to be amongst her loving family. There is so much more, but you can see how you have followed through on your mission. These things are good karma that will come back to you in another life.

"On the other side of that," said Desimena, shaking her head, "you ultimately used your magic against one who served only to love you."

Aradia, hoping to keep the talk away from the negative karma she had created for herself, put a beguiling smile on her face and asked a question about star seeds. She had heard Desimena use that phrase, and she loved the sound of it.

*"Yes," said Desimena with a huge smile, "your star seed would be considered the Moon." As they walked, Desimena continued with the lesson. "As pure consciousness, you were first drawn to the luminosity of the Moon, for like draws like. Those that are drawn as star seeds to her brilliance will eventually have to learn of their own vulnerability. For the Moon also has a dark side. It is not negativity that I speak of. The dark side represents the need to **hide** what one **feels** is an inadequacy.*

"The Moon is feminine in its nature," said her spirit guide, "yet... its strength moves the tides across the land. It is a quality of the Goddess. Her femininity is never in question...and her strength is always in evidence.

"Strength is the ability to shine," Desimena said, looking deeply at Aradia. "Courage is accepting the dark and deep emotional nature that can and does surrender. It takes strength to stand guard on your emotions; it takes courage to let down that guard, to fall, to make a mistake, and to ultimately learn."

Desimena took Aradia's hands in hers, thoughtfully considering her next words.

"When looking up from the Earth, the Moon shines as a beacon. Those that first make their home on the Moon tend to shine when they go to Earth.

Strength is never something they are short on. It is courage they go to earth to learn."

Aradia stood very still. "I have had a hard time with that," she admitted. "Will I remember it this time when I go to earth?"

"If you remembered everything, I would be out of a job," Desimena said with a grin.

"You made a joke," said Aradia laughingly. "There's hope for you after all!"

Desimena, smiling fondly at her student, put her arm through Aradia's as they walked along the winding path out of the walled garden. With a knowing smile and nod of her head, Aradia acknowledged her teacher's wisdom.

❧

After many such sessions, Aradia became impatient and began to ask when she was going to go to earth. So… early one morning Desimena smiled at her and said, "It is time!"

"Oh no!" exclaimed Aradia, managing to look frightened and excited at the same time.

Desimena understood that a huge part of Aradia's lesson was patience. She knew that no amount of wisdom on this side of the veil would prevail! And so, with an ephemeral smile and a loving heart, Desimena nodded her head and declared, "Beautiful child, you have begun on a course. The sail is set and you cannot turn back now."

Aradia could hear Desimena's soft melodious voice in the background. "Choose your name carefully. Your name, like everything else, is a specific vibration that sets the tone for learning, therefore it is very important."

Aradia's eyes searched for Desimena. The bright mist that was enveloping her had a luminescent otherworldly hue, beginning to obscure the goddess from view.

"I will miss you." said Aradia, noticing that her voice seemed to resound in the void.

"I am always with you, my child. Hold on to the memory of me. The veil is heavy between the worlds and the mind/body connection seems to eradicate most of the memories of the spirit world.

"Remember to pick your name carefully."

And with that, Desimena faded from view.

Aradia saw a woman lying on the floor of a hut. It was the dead of night, and the woman was with child. The sky was alit with lightning and thunder rolled across the hut, hiding any sounds from within. All of a sudden, Aradia realized that this was her new mother and that she was about to be born.

"Hold on to the name," she repeated to herself. "It's so dark …oh… I am in the womb.

Oh …

What is the name? Yes! Now I remember."
Hands reached in, turning her, gently drawing her into the world …
And Eurynome was born.

Book Two
The Golden Shield

How much has to be explored and discarded
before reaching the naked flesh of feeling.
~Claude Debussy~

**Our story begins approximately two thousand and three hundred
years ago, in the rich woodlands surrounding the ancient city of
Eregli. To the north shimmers the Black Sea, and to the north
east the coveted city of Hattusus, home of the Goddess Cybele.**

~Aradia has been reborn, and she has taken the name Eurynome,
which means ~ Earth's Moon. ~

Chapter 1

Darkness invaded a cluster of small huts huddled in a clearing, shadowed by ancient oaks. A small bent figure paced back and forth, illuminated only by the dim flickering glow of coals from the now abandoned fire pit. Her eyes searched darkly knotted trees for a glimpse of anything that moved, while her ears strained to catch a whisper from the forest. It seemed like hours had passed before she was rewarded with the sight of a gracefully moving figure striding confidently through the darkness. Tension left the shoulders of the old woman as the shadowy form emerged from the trees and moved effortlessly to her side.

"I've been worried!" the old woman exclaimed. "The sun has been down for a great while. Where have you been?"

"Grandmother," declared Eurynome rolling her eyes to the heavens. "I find my way by moonlight just as well, if not better than by the light of the sun. It is my birth right. Besides, I went to seek a vision, and I have been assured that I am going on the pilgrimage."

"Child, we have been over this before. There will be no pilgrimage for us! I will not speak on the subject!"

The smoky walls of the small dwelling welcomed them as Eurynome bent to open the flap on their thatched hut.

In an effort to calm her grandmother, she quickly made a fire and shook out a faded wool blanket, worn and soft from years of use. Smoothing it down, she placed it in front of the fire. Lovingly, and with great respect, she addressed the woman that had raised her.

"Come Mamma. Tell me again of my birth and the strange happenings of that night. Let us sit by the fire and share the berries I have gathered while you tell me the story."

"You have heard it over and over my child. I am weary. Let me rest."

Sighing, the old woman eased her slender body on to the blanket by the fire. Her bones were feeling stiff from the chilled air, making her keenly aware of her years. As she brushed a wisp of long chestnut hair from her face, her dark brown eyes closed. When she opened them again, Eurynome was sitting next to her on the blanket, with an expectant brightness in her eyes.

In the end, the story was told, for when Eurynome called her Grandmother Mam ma, her heart went out to this motherless child.

As Eurynome's grandmother sat by the fire gathering her thoughts, she looked intently at the curious mixture of child and women before her, who carried the powers of old. The royal blood had been passed down from mother to daughter, it shined through her worn clothing and unshorn hair. She was a rare beauty, thought Theba, taking in every detail of her tall and lithe grand-daughter, who was well muscled from her training with Jontue. Her hair always amazed her. Its rich russet color shimmered in the sunlight as the streaks of auburn glistened and formed a halo around her head. A deep sigh escaped grandmother's lips. But it was when Eurynome pinned and wound it around her head in a way that highlighted her high cheek bones and piercing golden eyes that she looked most like a queen. As she often did, the old woman wondered who had fathered this extraordinary child.

With resignation, and the hint of a smile, her grandmother began the story with the very same words that she always used.

"Once, a very long time ago, at the first hint that I might be with child, a goddess appeared in my dream. She told me her name was Desimena. I'll never forget the sight of her. Her dark olive skin and deep rich raven hair was not anything I had ever seen in this world. The golden sparks of her sable brown eyes held my attention and her lips formed a perfect bow, as she assured me I would have a beautiful daughter. I could feel her garment brush me, as she came closer as if to tell me more. Her blue-green robe, the color of the Aegean Sea, had golden writing on the flowing cuffs; they caressed my face as she leaned forward and whispered a special message in my ear."

"Tell me! Tell me exactly what she whispered, please, just this once Mamma!"

"All in good time my child."

The old women chewed the berries slowly until, finally wiping the juices from her mouth with the back of her hand, she continued her story.

"I never knew my daughter was with child until the night you were born. It was an ominous night, filled with screeching owls and the howling of the wolves. There were many clouds in the sky and your mother and I were piling fir-wood branches in the openings of our hut so that our belongings would not be damaged. It was certain there would be a cloud burst and a blowing, for we had had an omen earlier in the day. A blackbird had entered our hut, which of course means death. But then he called out three times, which portended a birth. I tried to engage your mother in a conversation about the confusing message, but she had become very quiet, and chose to work on this very blanket that we are sitting on."

Grandmother lovingly stroked the soft wool, a mist forming before her eyes as she continued.

"I gathered up my herbs, thinking it would be Theta, your mother's friend, giving birth. She was 'near her time' you see. I called out to your mother to gather the straw matting and cloth, in case we were called, but she did not answer me and I found her at the door of our hut, curled up and moaning. Blood swirled around her and mixed with the new falling rain. When I reached for her, my hand fell upon her belly and a jolt of energy ran up my arm, and with it a vision of a young woman leading other women in a revolt against…I know not what! They were burning a village, sparing the women and children, yet killing the men. I pushed the vision away, for I knew I was losing my daughter with every moment that I delayed. Pulling her into the hut, I raised her legs and lowered her back in an attempt to stem the flow of blood. I knew that I would have to bring out the child soon or both would die. I bathed my hands in fennel water and quickly returned to her."

She paused for a moment to look lovingly at Eurynome.

"I reached in. I turned you gently, and pulled you forth," she went on, "and in that split second a loud clap of thunder shook the hut and a flash of lightning filled the room. Though the door was by then sealed to the weather, we were surrounded with golden light as the fir branches fell from the opening and I could see the full of the moon. I christened you as your mother clutched my hand. She never spoke, though she smiled when I placed you to her breast. She died peacefully with you in her arms.

I never knew the man who fathered you. But I did know what to name you, as that is what the goddess whispered when her apparition appeared in the luminescent light. She told me that my daughter had something very special to do. She was to birth *Earth's moon*, and when she accomplished that her mission here on earth would be done. So as I looked at the radiance of the Moon and holding your mother's hand, I named you Eurynome. The storm suddenly ceased and feathery moonbeams caressed your face. As I lifted you from her breast, I could swear that you reached your tiny hand out to play with the wispy light of the Moon. I have not had a vision or a dream since that time."

Eurynome reached out and hugged her grandmother. "It's all right Mamma. I am here. I love you very much."

"I know, child, but my heart aches that I did not know your mother's pain and that we could not talk of your birth and plan for you. I now know that she gave her life gladly to bring you into the world, because there is greatness lying ahead for you. I want you to know that you have been enormous comfort to me in my aging."

She stroked Eurynome's head with gentleness and care, feeling deep love for her daughter's child. She missed her daughter, though they had never been as close as she and Eurynome had become. Indeed they were opposites. Her daughter was trying always to please everyone, whereas Eurynome seemed not to care what people thought about her, though she seemed to always study people and their intentions.

"Grandmother, is this why you worry so when I am gone long in the woods? Do you think my mother was raped by one from a marauding band, or one of the gods known to stalk the woods looking for virgin prey? My mother could not deny a god her virginity, yet she would feel ashamed that she was dishonored. It will not happen to me! I will cut the heart out of any man or god that takes me against my will! I have my knife." She pulled it from its hiding place in a flash.

"Yes child, I can see that you are well armed, but rape can be of the mind as well as the body."

Eurynome looked at her grandmother and huffed, "No man will trick me! I am prepared. I have come to *make war on men*."

"Yes child, I have heard you say that, but what does it mean? Never will you take a husband? Do you have such disdain for men that you will never mate?"

Eurynome grew quiet and withdrawn, and her grandmother knew she would get no answers on this particular night. Her thoughts ran back over the last many winters snuggled by the fire listening to Eurynome's fantastic tales.

She would speak of a battle she would win, all the while carving a weapon she called a labry, a double sided hatchet, from a special piece of wood called Laurel Oak. She would tell her grandmother Theba, "One day I will have a real labry, made from a very special piece of iron ore that fell from the sky. When it is ready I will ride out into the night to my destiny. I have seen it in a vision."

Theba shivered, as chills ran up and down her body, and she remembered the vision from the night of Eurynome's birth. It came back in a flood and it brought tears to her eyes. She had never told Eurynome the end of the vision and did not want to think of it now.

"Grandmother, what is wrong? Are you feeling ill?"

"No. No child, just a chill. Come let us make for our beds as the sun will not wait on us on the morrow."

Chapter 2

Eurynome watched as the red tailed hawk circled in the sky. His agility thrilled her and his attention to his prey was mesmerizing. She knew he had spotted his morning meal as she watched the circles grow smaller, and he flew closer to the clearing on the other side of the stream. She also knew he would land high up on the gnarled branches of the sacred oak by the water to enjoy his treat. He was keeping a steady eye on her, and would fly off if her gaze became too intrusive. When he wasn't hunting, he would sit close to her in contentment, as many of the animals did.

Most would not have heard Jontue's stealthy approach, but he had trained Eurynome well. Turning, she cautioned him to be still and motioned with her head to the hawk now sitting on the tree with his meal. Jontue stopped for a moment before moving toward her in absolute silence and joined her, sitting on a fallen tree by the stream. Both of them knew not to be too curious of the hawk and his prey, though both stole fleeting glances in fascination of the hunter.

The hawk, finishing his meal, flew in an enormous circle, silently tipping his wing as if to thank his friend for her respect.

"So we prepare you for your pilgrimage?" Jontue said, turning to Eurynome. The dimple that accompanied the smile made it clear that he had something exciting to share. "The blacksmith is done with your labry, and says it is a fine weapon. He also made something special for me, something very special. He thinks, as many do, that I am going on the journey with the women. But I had it made as a gift for you. You have not told anyone that …well…that I cannot go?"

"No," she told him. "If it would help you feel better, then I will stay. There is always next year. You know that, don't you?"

"Yes, Nomie, I know that you would stay if I needed you, but I also know that you want to go on this pilgrimage more than life itself."

Eurynome peered at the swelling on his forearm; the wound was red and jagged. Thinking of his valor protecting the fortress at Hattusus, she realized yet again, just how proud she was to know him.

"Jontue, how are you sure that the arrow that nicked you was prepared with a slow poison? Couldn't it just be the same sickness that comes upon you when you stay in the village too long?"

"I have only been back from Hattusas less than three days. I see all the signs of the blue death. No one has been able to find a cure for what some call the slow death. I am certain, I'm afraid, that it was indeed a poison arrow. The fact that it only grazed me will make its effects slower than usual. You know that my health was failing anyway. This is just a quicker way to join the Goddess in the heavens."

He smiled at her lovingly and added, "I have taught you that there is no death, and to be afraid of death creates an imbalance in the birth, life, and death process. I will be fine. But you need a bit more instruction and now you will have a wonderful new weapon. Come. Walk me back to my village."

"You act as though you are going on a journey, like the pilgrimage I am to go on! Who will I talk to, who will understand the memories and the questions and....well, all of it?"

"I am not going anywhere. I cannot die because I will be ever present in your heart. You will still be able to talk to me. You'll just have to listen differently."

As they walked back to his village, Eurynome questioned him intensely about what the blacksmith had made, but he would not relent and give her the information she cunningly sought. Instead, he questioned her on her knowledge of animal tracks and the sounds that animals make when hunting, when in distress or the unusual sounds they sometimes make to fool their prey into thinking they are harmless.

On the little used path, small branches and leaves snapped under their feet. Gnarled branches hanging over the trail were pushed aside or subdued by Jontue's sturdy blade. Eurynome's golden eyes held concern as she stole an occasional glance at Jontue to see if he was out of breath or if she could detect a blue tone to his skin. When he breathed a sigh of relief as they crested the top of the hill, Eurynome stopped.

"It amazes me that as close as we are we cannot see your village from here," she said.

Being out of breath but not wanting her to know, Jontue did not comment. He gratefully stood by her side, taking a moment to rest. He signaled her with a nod that he was ready to continue and they walked carefully down the winding path that led to the embankment of his camp.

Once on solid ground, Eurynome glanced at Jontue as if looking at him for the first time. Though he was ill, his countenance glowed. The proud chiseled lines and high cheek bones of his face accented the softness within his eyes. They were mesmerizing and had a depth of love and kindness she had seen in no other. How was it, she wondered now, that she had never noticed that his countenance spoke of strength and his eyes held peace and solace?

Arriving at his village, he was greeted warmly by the few men that made up the small band of warriors. The men ranged in ages from eleven years to that of forty-nine, which as a warrior was an age to be proud of. Their village was stark, with very little shelter and hardly any sound except the blacksmith hard at work fixing or replacing the weapons that they had used in their last skirmish.

Eurynome was the only woman who had ever been inside their village. When she first arrived as a curious little girl on the shoulders of Jontue, the inhabitants had all steered clear of her and she of them, as she trusted no man except Jontue. She very seldom ventured into their sanctuary and when she did, they just nodded in her direction and made themselves scarce. It was in deference to Jontue's stature as scout, as well as knowing that he would bring no one into their safe haven unless they were to be trusted, that they allowed it at all. Most of them had a price on their head, or would be run to ground till dead if they could be found. So they guarded their privacy at all cost. Everyone in Eurynome's village knew of them, but no one except her could ever find their refuge.

"Palion!" shouted Jontue over the racket. "Palion, I am here to retrieve the labry I had you make for Eurynome."

Palion was a giant of a man with the roar of a lion. In fact, he was sometimes called Lion and Eurynome, seeing him now from so close, could see why. His hair was red and seemed to stand up around his head in all directions. His beard covered most of his face, and only his red cheeks seemed prominent as his eyes had the lazy look of being half closed. But she knew that to ever think that this man did not see everything that went on around him would be a grave mistake. Perhaps the lazy eye look fools his enemies, pondered Eurynome. But it doesn't fool me.

He roared a greeting to Jontue, and unenthusiastically nodded in her direction as he reached for the labry that he had made for her, although she recognized his reluctance since he never made anything for a woman. She also knew instinctively that they had been enemies in a past life.

Quietly standing her ground and ignoring the way he was glaring at her, she respectfully asked him if she could take a closer look at the weapon he had crafted. His pride for his work then came to the surface, and he began telling her how he had forged the labry from the special metal rock that Jontue had brought him. At the edges, each blade was as thin as a piece of grass and there could be no question by its look of its sharpness. Taking it in her hand, she felt how the handle fit comfortably, and the doubled blade shone black-blue like that of a raven's wing.

"You made this from my crude drawing?" questioned Eurynome.

"No," he sneered in disdain, his natural suspicion of her returning.

"Palion, tell Eurynome how you came to know of this fine weapon," Jontue prompted.

Hesitantly, he turned back to her, shrugging his large shoulders as he spoke.

"When we've been in battle beside the women from the Euxine Sea, it was this weapon that they carried. So when you drew it I knew what you were referring to. With the knowledge of its use, it can be a fine weapon."

Palion's condescending look told her he thought it would be wasted in her hands. "How did *you* know about it?" he demanded.

Eurynome's eyes darted to Jontue, as he was aware that she had seen it in a dream.

"I told her about the unusual weapon the women carried, and she thought to have one of her own," Jontue retorted quickly, saving Eurynome from the need to explain.

They said their goodbyes and moved toward Jontue's small lean-to, where he stored his weapons and a supply of dried fruit and meat. He had learned a while back, that eating the grain that was cultivated by one of the men in the group and enjoyed by all seemed to disagree with him, creating weakness, and cramps. However, he did find it difficult keeping away from the porridge made from the grain. It was a quick and easy meal in the early morn, and was almost irresistible when mixed with honey from the bees that some of the men in his tribe kept.

Pulling a large well wrapped package out from his lean-to, he said, "Come. Before you open it, let us go and sit by the brook. But when Eurynome reached for it, he kept it tight to his chest, and said in a cautionary tone, "Remember, no one knows that I am not going on the pilgrimage. Palion thinks this was made for me, so you must wait a bit longer to see my surprise."

When they were seated at the brook he handed it to her. Holding her breath, she gingerly un-wrapped the leather cloth surrounding her surprise. A *golden shield* glistened in the morning light, intricately designed with fire breathing dragons, the rising and setting sun and the moon in all her phases, remarkable for its workmanship. Eurynome just stared, unable to comment on its beauty. "He…he….Palion did this?" she questioned, stunned by its splendor.

"He made the shield," Jontue told her, "When he was finished, it was my turn. I carved the symbols and designs especially for you. The dragon is to remind you of your courage. The rising and setting suns represent the warrior's journey, for there is always a beginning and an end to the physical warrior. But the moons phases indicate that the soul is ever growing and moving forward in its evolution, if we assist it with courage and valor.

"The shield is to protect you in battle, but the symbols on it are to remind you that no matter what the outcome if the warrior is brave the battle will always be won."

Eurynome put the shield aside and hugged Jontue. She had not hugged him since she was a little girl. She felt the warmth of his heart, though his skin was cold and his ribs much too evident in her embrace.

"Ah Nomie, it is time for you to go now." She began to say something else, but he put his finger to her lips.

"No… there is nothing left unsaid," he told her. "I will be leaving for Hattusas in a few days. I wish to sit again at the feet of the goddess, to work with her on any obstructions that might be in the way of my final journey. She will look deep into the soul; nothing can be hidden when you are able to look at the records that are kept there."

Seeing the worry in her eyes, Jontue moved his finger from her lips to her cheek.

"Go," he said with finality. "And remember… there is no death."

Chapter 3

"Come child, what is all the fuss? It is a new day and already you wish to argue with me. We have much to do. Can you not mind what I say? All of the women in the village come to me for wisdom yet you push aside my knowledge as if you were the elder!"

Eurynome's grandmother knew that look. Her grandchild was determined to discuss the pilgrimage many of the women of the village were planning. There was constant chatter and excitement about the Goddess Cybele. In fact, it was nearly all that the women could talk about. Though there is little known about Cybele's heritage, what was whispered was that the ancient God Zeus had ejaculated on the ground and from it had sprung a hermaphrodite. The other gods were jealous of any being that could procreate without a partner, so they castrated the male appendage and Cybele, 'Mother of all,' was born. It was rumored that she married a mortal and her children carry the royal blood.

Jontue had told her and Eurynome that he had looked into those born of the line of Cybele and although Theba and Eurynome were poor cousins so to speak, their blood carried the mark of royalty. This was why a brother will many times marry his sister, to carry on the royal line, because there is a special portion of the female's blood that carries the immortal mark of the Goddess. A mother could give it to her son, but he could never transfer that portion to *his* child. Only a daughter could carry on the royal line, Jontue had claimed with certainty.

Grandmother could see that all too familiar determined look in her eye.

"I know what you are thinking child!" she said. "But you know we are too poor to make the pilgrimage to the Great Hall of Hattusas."

"Poor is in the mind," came Eurynome's quick retort. "You have told me that many times. I *must* go! If I meet with the Goddess, I will ask her for blessings on my life of service and if…well nothing else matters but that I go. It is predestined!"

As Grandmother watched Eurynome do her chores she was not amused by the fact that this headstrong child would go with or without her permission. The gathering that was taking place this evening was to pray for strength for the village women who were to make the journey. Some would also pray that their offerings would allow their daughters to stay at the temple to study to become a priestess. Only the most beautiful and intelligent young girls were chosen for this honor. Grandmother, looking at Eurynome with enormous pride, knew there were few girls more beautiful and more intelligent than her granddaughter. But she could not afford the gifts it would take for Eurynome to be accepted as a novitiate. Grandmother smiled, shaking her head as she thought, even if for a moment the child could behave like a lady, rather than one of the wild animals she incessantly talked with in the woods!

As Eurynome gathered dead branches and small logs for the communal cook fire, Marta came out of her hut, and at first it looked as though she would avoid Eurynome. They had been friends as children, but none in the village befriended Eurynome now since most were afraid of her visions. Marta was secretly jealous that Eurynome had the 'knowing;' feeling cursed that she had none. The few men that were in the village hated Eurynome because she spoke her mind and sometimes knew the future. They said she was evil and kept their women and children away from her. Marta didn't have that problem because her father had left as soon as he had found out her mother had been pregnant. He told her he was going to the next village to barter for sheep, but he never came back. It was sad Marta thought with a wry smile, that so many of the women of the village told one another stories about how their men would return some day.

"Eur, are you almost done?" she asked Eurynome hesitantly. "I…I thought you might tell me what you know about Hattusas. My mother and I are going on the pilgrimage. I could help you with the gathering, then…"

"I'm done," Eurynome claimed as she threw the last of her gatherings onto the wood pile. "Let's sit under the oak tree near the path to the woods. I can't go further as I need to speak to Grandmother when she is done with her chores."

When they sat, Eurynome closed her eyes and focused her attention inward, to her heart, where the stories that Jontue had told her could be found. Her face became an ethereal reflection, as she swam through the silky sea of memories that came from inner visions, as well as what Jontue had lovingly shared. Opening her golden eyes, she gazed up at the tree, and reaching out her arm felt its leaves beneath her hand. She searched for an acorn, and finding one, began her story.

"Long before you approach the Great Hall in Hattusas, there are two enormous stone appendages gracing either side of the road that, it is rumored, were fashioned by the gods themselves, to protect the dwellers of Hattusas. Some say that if you do not have good intentions you should not journey toward the city, because you would be struck dead before you could move beyond the stones. It is important to place small offerings for the gods there at the opening, and to walk through with your head bowed and reverence in your heart."

Eurynome turned the acorn, holding it up to the sun, mesmerized by its significance and knowing that Marta, who was sitting on her hands to contain her excitement, did not quite understand. Eurynome's voice had taken on a deep compelling quality that seemed to open the mysteries of life. She knew the power of her gift, and made Marta wait as she looked intently at the acorn. When she knew that Marta could not handle any more silence, she began again.

"If you make it beyond the entrance, you are met by a colossal statue of Cybele," she continued. "Her face bears strength *and* beauty, a combination that is prominent with most goddesses. Adorning her is a mighty acorn headdress and her hand is resting protectively on one of the two small children beside her. The acorn, coming from the most sacred of trees, represents the fertility that Cybele brings to the land and the small figures beside her bear that out. Her other hand is placed on her heart. I truly believe that if you listen you will hear the words that mother goddesses have chanted throughout the ages. *I bid you welcome, and grant you fertility of the heart, mind and body.*"

Eurynome looked at the treasure in her hand with respect.

"So it is that Cybele's vast wisdom is enclosed within this acorn," she said, tenderly handing it to Marta, "that from this tiny acorn is born an enormous tree such as this."

With reverence her arm swept above her towards a gently sloping oak branch, just as a raven swooped in to perch.

"The oak is a sacred tree," she continued. "It conceals the doorway between the world of the seen and unseen. Ravens see things many do not. They teach us this, by the fact that they feast upon the eyes of their prey. In essence they are telling us, use your eyes to see, or we shall come for them. Brother Raven came today to teach you that many are ignorant and superstitious; they claim evil where it is not. It is up to you to know the difference between good and evil. You wish to have the sight. Raven came to extend that gift to you. But you must ask that the gift be yours, not envy that it is not."

Marta found herself staring at the acorn and when she looked up Eurynome was gone. Marta did not know whether to be angry or appreciative that Eurynome had spent the time with her.

Grandmother busied herself with her chores, trying in vain to ignore the attention her mind kept giving to the subject of the pilgrimage. The sun's glare was so harsh that it was necessary for her to shield her eyes when she looked at Eurynome. Her granddaughter, she thought, could one such as she be groomed as a priestess? Imagine her constantly being told what to do and not to do, ha! She had it in her head that the Goddess Cybele would recognize her in some way, and bless her! Madness!

As Eurynome approached, Grandmother, with frustration in her voice, said, "This trip is impossible! What good will come of dwelling on it, child?" But then the events of the night Eurynome was born flashed into her vision. With a shrug of resignation she thought, mayhap I should consider making the trip if…

Eurynome, impatient with the silence that had followed her grandmother's last remark, said, "We have Two Door. He'll gladly make the trip with us. I'm sure if I explain to him the great honor of being accepted as an offering for my audience with Cybele, he would be proud to do it."

Grandmother was aghast at the impudence of her granddaughter.

"You mustn't take the name of the great goddess so lightly," she scolded her. "Acting as if it is your right to have an audience with her could bring torture on you and any that you will beget."

Eurynome's head snapped up.

"Never!" she vehemently mouthed the word. "I will beget no child until I cleanse the world of men who grind women under their feet, taking their pleasure and tossing the woman and child aside as if they were something foul when they are finished! Men sack temples and put their gods above the goddesses. You know the only reason Hattusas is still intact is because of the female warriors vigilantly protecting the great hall. The thickness of the walls and all its great towers would do very little good if not for the proud women that protect it.

"I will be such a warrior!" Eurynome, her face pinched in an expression of disgust, jabbed her finger toward her heart. "But I will not wait till the men come in the night with their stealthy ways. I will find out where such men are and kill them! I will be swift and give no mercy for they have given none."

Eurynome herself was surprised at her own vehement outburst, instinctively knowing, as she did, that some of this hate and distrust came from another lifetime. She wished she could understand more. Her mind seemed constantly to be searching for answers that seemed to be just out of reach. Her grandmother's words interrupted her musings.

"Oh child, I am fearful of the ideas you entertain."

Yet, at that moment, Grandmother knew clearly that the child would become a woman on the pilgrimage, and she knew it was her destiny to see that Eurynome would make this journey. And yes, she sighed, with a peculiar smile, thinking, the pig Two Door, aptly named because he could not fit into the shelter unless they opened up both doors, would make a good offering. He was supposed to be their meat for the next winter, yet this trip could change many things. What was the good of looking so far ahead when life was so uncertain, she thought as she exhaled noisily? Yes, the only way was to make the journey. Her decision was not an easy one, yet really the only one she could make, knowing somehow that it would be just a short while before the time would come to part with her granddaughter. All this hesitation was just putting off the inevitable. What greatness lay ahead for this child... and what sorrow? pondered Theba.

The next month went by quickly. Grandmother noticed great changes were taking place for Eurynome in body as well as mind. She had become much quieter now and closely observed everything, even the tiniest insect and the color change of the leaves on the trees. She spent less time in the woods, yet she was never really separate from nature and its workings. Eurynome would sometimes take an apple, slice it through the middle, and just sit and stare at the seeds in the center.

Just as Grandmother was thinking of this strange behavior she observed the child, or could she even think of her as a child any longer, take the apple she was holding and place it in the crook of a large branch. Then, backing up a distance, she threw her hatchet, halving the apple, and calmly took half of it to ponder under the shade of the tree. Grandmother knew she missed her teacher Jontue who had gone to Hattusas.

Eurynome indeed was remembering his teachings, as she stared intently at the half apple she held in her hand. "The core of an apple is shaped like the womb of a woman," he had told her, "The seeds in the middle are to remind you every time you eat of the fruit that the goddess is central to all life." Jontue had told her to ponder the apple as her journey to womanhood unfolded. Eurynome found her development fascinating, yet still was getting used to the seemingly enormous breasts that got in her way as she threw her labry, her double bladed hatchet. Also, when she used the bow and arrow, she needed to adjust to her new growth.

"It is time we spoke of the journey." said Grandmother with a big sigh as she lowered herself to the ground next to her granddaughter.

"What is left to speak on?" asked Eurynome with a shrug. "We have all of our food prepared. I have spoken to Two Door and he is quite content with his fate. I am clever with my blade and labry. I have decided I will move ahead of the party and see to their safety. What more will we discuss?"

Grandmother's voice tightened as she said, "Now see here, how is it that you have taken it upon yourself to be the asculter? Jontue is to be the one to scout for us. I know he is sick, but he has always been the one to lead pilgrimages. He will not allow this!"

Eurynome looked directly into her grandmother's eyes and in a dry monotone voice said, "He is dead. It is better that it is over now. He has prepared me for this," spoke Eurynome with finality. "He and I knew he would not make it to Hattusas with us."

"There has been no signal of a death!" Grandmother spoke sharply. "The men with him are few, and care not for us. But they would have alerted us if Jontue had died!"

In the same emotionless manner, Eurynome answered, "Make no mistake about it. The spirit of death has come and gone." There was a deep sadness about her, and yet a strong resolution as she looked toward the northern sky. In the twilight, a ribbon of smoke softly played against the hills. It was a funeral pyre from the other village.

Spotting the smoke rising from the distant hills, yet again Grandmother realized that this frustrating child had insights that could not be denied. So she picked herself up from the ground with resignation and made peace with the fact that Eurynome would lead and keep them safe on their journey to the Great Goddess. I pity the Goddess Cybele, she thought, as she will have to deal with this willful and headstrong child. And she reminded herself that she should no longer think of her as a child.

Chapter 9

Motionless as a statue carved from marble, her breath smooth and easy just as Jontue had taught her, Eurynome stood beside the remnants of Jontue's funeral pyre. The men from his village had all gone and she was glad to be alone.

Memories of times with Jontue came flooding back to her. He had told her glorious stories of ancient goddesses, and had spoken of the grand statues at Hattusas, bringing them alive for her. He was the only man she had ever trusted, perhaps because of his age; he had already become a man when she was born. Warmth flowed through her as she remembered how she had recognized his voice, even as a child. Upon hearing it for the first time, she had flown out from behind Grandmother's robe straight into his arms. As she grew older, she knew his was a voice she had loved throughout time, yet intuitively, she also knew she had disappointed him in their last life together.

She had tried to speak with him of their past-life, but when she did, he would just shake his head and tell her it was not important. Only the moment was important. "Live in this moment," he had said many times. He had great inner strength, but since she had been born, it seemed the food he ate disagreed with him and sometimes weakened his body. Then he would go off into the forest, eat berries, and drink the pure water, and his health would return. As soon as he would come back to the village and eat the grains that were offered, his body would fail him again. It was a mystery, one that he had told her not to ponder, as some things need not be known.

He had taught her how to be still and also how to move as fast as a mountain cat. Everything that he had learned as a warrior of the Goddess Cybele, he had shared with her. They had spoken of the complicated thought process of the human and the uncomplicated thoughts of the animals and he had told her, "When you are in battle you must know how the human enemy thinks, but you will out maneuver them every time if you listen, smell, and move like an animal."

Jontue had always treated her with love. Even when she would rail against men and their corrupt ways, he would laugh and agree that men sought power, whether through war or lust.

"It has been so since the beginning of time," he had always said. How she missed his deep, resonant voice.

Eurynome was startled when she felt a tear in the corner of her eye, for she never cried. In the act of disclaiming her weakness, she began to angrily wipe her eyes, but then collapsed on the ground with great anguished sobs, and reaching for his ashes rubbed them on her arms and legs. Memories of all that they had shared made her body tremble despite the warmth of the day. Intoning an old familiar chant, she slipped into a light trance and Jontue appeared to her, looking healthy and vibrant.

❧

"Jontue, don't go!" she said, reaching out her hand to him. "I know you said that you taught me everything that I need to know, but you did not tell me how my heart would feel when you left. You did not tell me of the missing piece, and of the tears that would come. You never told me that I would lie on the ground covered in your ashes, and feel no purpose in living any longer."

Their surroundings began to slowly shift and around them there appeared a magnificent garden, the trees laden with copper leaves. Jontue, she remembered, always liked fall when the leaves changed and the weather became cooler.

"Ah, Nomie," he said, motioning to a fallen tree trunk, "come sit by me."

Eurynome hesitated. She felt deep within her heart that if she complied, he would tell her goodbye. As she felt herself fighting that thought, the vision started to fade.

"Yes, yes. I'll come and sit by you if you tell me a story."

"I will, and with the one story, every story I have ever told you will be embedded in your mind so that you may entertain the women on the pilgrimage. I know… I know you think to protect them, not entertain them.

However, a good leader knows how to settle in the warriors at day's end. So I will tell you the story of Aradia. She was of noble birth, just as you are."

"You've teased me with the fact that I am of noble birth before," Eurynome said, shrugging as she settled down to listen. *"I won't give you the satisfaction of asking you to explain as you are more stubborn than me"*

Jontue smiled, and began.

*"There once was a Moon Goddess named Aradia. She was a weaver of magic spells and had a remarkable talent with herbs. She was revered upon the Moon, loved and honored by all. Her life was one of ease and veneration. She had no challenges, you see. Her mother, the Goddess Diana, Goddess of the Moon, realized that in order for her daughter to be immortalized in the heavens **and** on earth, she would first need to become mortal and take up the challenges of earth. Earth life would teach her the distinction between strength and courage. It would allow her to garner wisdom from all of the knowledge that she had learned on the Moon, and most of all, she would learn compassion and humility. Diana knew that her daughter would succeed in her challenges, but she did not know how difficult it would be to ask her to take up the mantle of a human body, nor did she know how exhausting it would be to see her daughter suffer.*

"In the end, Aradia did come to earth. In her first life, through anger, she misused her powers. Then because of arrogance that she believed was pride, she succeeded in taking her own life."

"You mean she killed herself?" sputtered Eurynome in disbelief. "What would bring her to that? You said she was strong and filled with knowledge. This is much different than the stories you usually tell me. The hero is always strong and even if they waver, they are never cowards!"

"Ah Nomie… life brings us many twists and turns. Aradia's strength and beliefs worked against her. All that she had been, and learned on the moon, did not serve her here. At least it did not in her first life."

Jontue looked very sad, and he spoke hesitantly.

*"Nomie… what if I told you that **you** were Aradia, and that the mission you go on now, what you do, how you handle yourself will serve to erase some of the choices you made in your first lifetime? It…"*

Eurynome vehemently interrupted. "That could not be!"

"No child, listen and then tell me what you think. As Aradia, during the last of your life, you were angry, angry especially at men! Can you not look at your life and see that you came back into this new life with that

ugliness clinging to you? When you leave life in the manner you did, you start the very next lifetime in very similar conditions and with all of the emotions, hates, loves and fears in place. In the lifetime you are now living you need to learn to trust one person completely and to find some good in men."

"But are you not a man?" asked Eurynome as if that resolved her of any past sins. "I've put up with you haven't I?"

Jontue chuckled. "Yes… you've done an admirable job putting up with me…"

"Well…you know what I mean. I've listened and learned everything you've taught me, I've…"

Jontue interrupted, "Yes, and you've ignored the fact that I am a man very well indeed! Though tis true, I never approached you in that way."

There was a long pregnant pause as they looked longingly at one another.

"It is time," Jontue said finally, "I must go. Prepare yourself, for in our next lifetime you will feel all the love I carry for you, and you will know what it is to be loved… and to love."

As his image started to fade, Eurynome stood abruptly, and stamping her foot, declared, "I don't believe it! That is just a story. You cannot expect me to believe that I am the great Goddess Aradia, and that I made such terrible mistakes. What kind of story is that?"

Jontue's voice reverberated from a great distance, and with a chilling sense of loss, Eurynome heard this final words.

"There is always truth in the stories of old, and many times there are lies in the stories you are living."

Chapter 5

"Caw, caw, caw!" A mutinous call broke the tranquil dawn. The dusky morning sky faded from view, as a massive flock of crows hummed low over the heads of the pilgrims as they began their journey. The birds' black swath veered to the left, leaving only deafening sound in their exodus. Some women reached for their children. Eurynome caught her grandmother's eye, and shook her head as if to say, I know the crow's direction is a warning to postpone the journey, but our destiny awaits... say nothing!

The motley group of women, young girls and animals headed northeast over the mountains to Hattusas. Some were herding sheep. The group moved slowly, yet in a very determined fashion toward their destination. There was a collective excitement that began to build in all of them as they sang hymns to the Goddess Cybele. Chanting the name of the Goddess, they prayed for good weather and strength for the journey.

Eurynome moved methodically ahead of the others, keeping the sun to her right, taking her role as a guide very seriously. Noting landmarks that her teacher had told her about, she paid attention to the thickness of the bark on the trees and the side the rock's moss was growing on, so that she would know that they were heading northeast at all times.

Jontue had taught her well and if truth be told, it seemed that some of the knowledge came from memories of a different lifetime, a lifetime that did not take place on earth, in which she lived by the law of the land, intricately connected with nature, and navigated by the stars and shared her food and bedding with the wild animals.

❧

Night arrived softly, as food was put away and cooking utensils cleaned. Wearily the women prepared their bedding, and fell quickly in to a deep slumber. Eurynome awoke early, all of her senses sharp and alert. Dawn had not yet arrived. Quietly, she left the sleeping area, and sat down beneath a large oak a short distance away.

Long gnarled limbs were bent low, as if to give her shelter. As her mind cleared, she sent a silent prayer of gratitude to the Goddess. She did not know how it could be, but she knew that she would play a pivotal role in the outcome of this journey, and in the women's lives that were even now sleeping soundly nearby.

"Dear Goddess, help me get them safely to Hattusas," she murmured. She lay down beneath the tree, feeling a quiet peace for her part in the journey. She let her eyes slowly close, knowing she would awaken again before the others.

On this first morning of the journey, it seemed even the Sun was having a hard time getting up. Eurynome, with a firm foot, nudged the women who found the foggy morning a good excuse not to get up. She then proceeded to leave camp. The early risers were cleaning the cookware with leaves and storing the barley bread for their second day of travel. As they finished up, they began to follow the trail marked by Eurynome. Marta and her mother Theta were done before the others and headed out in good humor. Thiscara, grandmother's friend, called out, "Mamma, we are off. Are you nearly ready?"

Some of the clan called Eurynome's grandmother Mamma in reference to her elder status. The name, an endearment, also came from a place of love as she had brought many of them into the world or touched their lives through healing herbs.

As the second day closed, a tired group gladly huddled around the cook fire while Eurynome told stories of the goddesses in their varying degrees of splendor, wisdom, and even irreverence. Then, hesitantly, she spoke of a Goddess named Aradia. Having never heard of her, many of the group encouraged her to continue the story. Enthralling them with things she had seen in her dreams or visions, she attributed it all to the Goddess Aradia. As she spoke, her aura took on a golden hue. Grandmother noticed, and looked around to see if others in the group had seen the shimmering energy as it took on the shape of a goddess with a golden shield and sword. Eurynome slowly stood, her face etched in reverence and pain, her eyes misted over.

"The rest of Aradia must be left for another time."

The women moaned in unison, begging her to continue.

"Perhaps Aradia's story is yet unfinished," Eurynome said, as she emptied her cup on the ground. Pouring it slowly, watching the fluid seep into the soil, her face softened and she heard Jontue's voice say, 'There is no death.' As she turned to leave, there was a murmur of regret from the circle.

The third morning broke quickly and clearly, resonating birdsong carrying through the trees. The first group was out of sight and as the second group headed into a pass bordered by granite rock, laughter and song intermingled with the hum of the awakening day. Suddenly a loud piercing sound tore through the hills, followed by the bleeps of an injured sheep. There was enormous confusion and some of the group headed toward the sounds of the wailing animals. A few of the women scattered, going in different directions, but a cry for Eurynome arose from them all, hanging in the air with the haunting echoes of the sheep.

Within moments of their cries, Eurynome appeared at the top of a granite cliff wearing a breastplate and carrying a golden shield that glistened in the morning light. Holding a spear in one hand, with a double sided axe tucked in her belt, she emanated all the qualities of a golden goddess, unsullied and unafraid. As the sun filtered through her burnished hair, creating a dappled halo of rainbow flashes, Grandmother was captivated by the breathtaking sight. For a moment she wondered why Eurynome was heading toward the echo, rather than in the direction the terrifying sounds seemed to be coming from, but then intuitively she knew that this is what her granddaughter had been trained for. Clearing her head she instinctively grabbed the woman closest to her and began to issue orders.

"Find something to use as a weapon and head for cover," she cried. "There! Toward that cave!"

Recognizing the danger for the young girls, Theba physically moved them into a darkened crevice and told them to be very quiet. Some of the women who had been in chaos, seeing grandmother's calm deliberate manner, began to respond to their own maternal instincts to protect their young. In unison the strong supple ones began to pick up rocks as weapons and searched through their packs for knives used to slaughter the animals.

Now, from the direction of the sounds of tumult, Eurynome's shouts could be heard, mingled with deep voices barking commands. And then, suddenly, screams of terror rent the air, to be followed by a silence even more alarming. After a moment, Eurynome appeared at the opening of the cave, blood dripping from her spear and oozing from wounds on her head and arm.

Grandmother, recognizing the ritualistic marks of the first kill, was more frightened at first by the blood painted on her granddaughter's cheeks and across her nose and forehead, than the wounds she could see on her arms.

Approaching the cave, the girl knelt and ransacked through the stores until she found some sea salt and cloth. Reaching under her short skirt, Eurynome, removing the small knife that was strapped to her thigh, placed the leather wrapped hilt of the knife into her mouth and applied the salt to the gushing wound on her arm.

Concern grew among the women, as they gathered closer to Eurynome who, taking a few deep breaths, assumed an expression of pride as she looked at the women who had armed themselves.

"We fight or die on this hill," she told them. "We are up against a small band of renegades looking for quick plunder and rape. They will not think anything of killing the old ones and they will take your daughters for slaves. I see that some of you have armed yourselves. Will you fight beside me?"

Eurynome could see fear and doubt in the ashen faces of a few of the women, and knew that they must be convinced to follow her.

"We are many, and out-number them," she said. "If we surprise them by attacking, many of us will live. They have surrounded Theta's group and believe they have won. Right now, they are celebrating. Do you not hear their cries of victory and shouts of joy? By now their weapons are discarded, for they are raping your sisters! Do you hear me?" Eurynome continued, and she felt their apprehension turn to outrage.

"It will take two or three women to attack each man," she cried. "You can do it! Are you with me?"

One by one, courage replaced fear as they raised their weapons high in the air. As the women moved single file out of the cave, Eurynome indicated for three groups to form. Quickly telling them what they would need to do, she had one group take the trail; another she motioned towards the ravine. The strong sure -footed ones followed her up and around the rocks above the area where the renegade band had surrounded Theta's group.

Motioning for the women to stop, Eurynome posed atop a crag from which she could see two men beat and rape her friend Marta. With deadly aim, she threw her spear and saw it penetrate the back of one of the rapists.

With a loud war cry, she jumped on top of the other man, knocking him to the ground. Taking the hatchet from her belt, she dealt him a fatal blow. The others followed her lead; hissing, scratching and using rocks and make-do weapons, they surprised the band and killed or injured all but two, who chose to run away.

While the attack was taking place, Grandmother, after checking to see that everyone was safe, quietly moved toward the area where Eurynome had first appeared covered with blood. Grandmother was not sure what she would encounter, but was glad to meet three women on the trail that she thought might have been killed. Speaking all at once, they told her that when the shouting and cries came from the ravine, Eurynome came out of nowhere and moved like a panther toward the strange echoing sounds. After she had disappeared, they heard shouts and war cries, and becoming frightened, stayed hidden until now.

Tattered and worn the small band of women followed Eurynome, making their way to the others waiting in the cave. The women cheered when they saw the returning group although Eurynome did her best to stifle their sounds, trying to alert them to the danger that could still be lurking. She knew it was important not to let the renegades know where they were hiding. But the adrenaline of victory was so sweet the women could not contain themselves. They hugged, cried and softly chattered amongst themselves.

Just as Eurynome looked around for her grandmother, another joyous cheer went up as Mamma and the small weary group she had encountered joined the women in the cave. They all turned toward Eurynome to honor her, but the distant and somber look in her eyes stopped them.

The events of the day had aged Eurynome's voice, adding sadness and anger to its natural depth. Standing at the entrance to the cave, she looked toward the Sun. It was not even noon; her heart ached for man's inhumanity and worse, for women's willingness to allow it. A voice rife with grief, fury, rage and sorrow echoed softly through the cave.

"We must bury our dead."

The austere cave that had offered solace became desolate and uninviting, as everyone looked around to see who was missing. The women realized that in their relief they had not taken into account the dead and the fact that two mothers were grieving because their daughters had been taken. With eyes downcast, they went out to gather their dead and began to prepare themselves for the burial rites.

Chapter 6

"My heart is heavy," Eurynome said, as she stood unflinchingly in the middle of a circle of saddened and disheartened women, few of whom bothered to look her way. The funeral rites had been extremely emotional. Many of the customs and rituals they would normally perform could not be undertaken, for it was not safe to have a fire. Looking around sadly at the group, she took a deep breath and decided with resignation she must continue.

"What I am to say is not easy, but it must be said!" she declared.

Grandmother looked on in astonishment as the child she had known became a warrior and leader, right before her eyes.

"Eurynome," Marta cried accusingly, "you knew this would happen! Look at you in your breastplate and fancy shield, wielding weapons we have never before seen! You are flaunting your prowess! I saw you, blood painted on your face and war-cry's on your lips. You were eager to fight. You are no longer my friend. You are evil!"

Continuing to stand firm, Eurynome faced her attacker. Her golden eyes did not hold animosity, yet they held no pity. Instead she searched for the strength that she knew was inside of her friend.

"You…you," Marta tried to continue, but in her weakness her voice failed her. She sobbed openly as she nursed her arm that had been broken in the attack. It's your fault!" she went on. "All of it!"

Theta looked at her daughter and stopped herself from weeping. She wanted to gather her in her arms the way she used to when Marta was just a tiny babe, but intuitively knew that this was not the time. Instead, slowly, she found her voice.

"I for one value my life and yours, my daughter," she looked pointedly at Marta. "I know you are in pain. But if not for Eurynome, you would be dead, or tethered to a lead following one of the renegades back to his village. Eurynome did not make us come on this pilgrimage; we were determined against all odds. Again… if not for her intervention, you'd be dead!"

"I wish I was dead," Marta sobbed, "I wish I was dead! It's her fault, all those evil visions, the stories…"

Her tirade stopped abruptly as her mother came up behind her and tenderly placed her hand on her head, lovingly beginning to stroke her hair, hoping against hope that she would have the courage to continue. But so many of the girls and women about her were standing stock still, and wearing expressions of distress and fear. She thought of all the mistreatment Eurynome had endured for being different, being independent and having an opinion. Her deep sable eyes sought and held those of Eurynome across the circle, and a thread of consciousness bridged between them. As she addressed the group her voice pulsed with truth and awareness.

"How does it matter that Eurynome knew in advance of this event?" she demanded. "Would we have listened to her had she forewarned us? No my friends….Sadly, we would not have. Some of us have loved her, some feared her, but all of us believed her tales and vision madness. I say we listen to her words. Can you not feel the weight upon her? Let us listen not only with our ears but with our hearts to this goddess among us. Let us not be jealous or fearful for sometimes the only difference in greatness and madness… is the outcome."

Eurynome felt all eyes upon her. The weight of these women's lives and the lives of the children that were yet to be born weighed upon her. They could return to the village and tell the men that the children had been stolen. The men would shrug and say, "We can always have more children." The women would shrivel up in self-pity, and lead ineffectual, hopeless lives. She prayed, Goddess, give me strength to say the right words, to do the right thing.

"Do you know why my heart is heavy?" she asked as she moved gracefully around the circle, affectionately touching each woman as she passed. With a strong firm hand she raised a chin here and there, as she moved and looked deeply into their eyes or stroked their hair and touched a shoulder until she had stood bravely in front of each and every one of them.

"Thirty and one was how we started out. Now there is twenty and four."

Slowly, she continued to walk among them, hoping to imbibe them with the courage to follow her to the village of the renegade band that had killed or maimed their friends and stolen their children.

"My heart is heavy, not only for what has happened yesterday as the sun rose, but what will happen on the morrow if we do not act. Let us go back in time. I want you to remember the actions and words of your sons and mates upon learning of your pilgrimage. How did they support you? They suggested Jontue be the guide, even knowing his sickness was worse than ever. They also made the grand offer of two youths, brothers, to accompany us, who have had no benefit of male influence to teach them anything about scouting!"

A huge sigh passed Eurynome's lips as she continued.

"In the end it was at my prompting that we say nothing about Jontue's death. The men would not have offered any other help, but they would have tried to stop you from coming. For some of you, traveling to the great city of Hattusas is the opportunity of a lifetime to see a world thought to be by some, a figment of women's imagination. For others, your daughters, this journey opens doors that are only dreamed about. To train as a priestess at the beloved feet of Cybele in her sacred temple."

The sun, flashing over Eurynome's left shoulder, burnished her copper hair with fire. Fearlessly, though she saw doubt in the eyes of some, she proceeded.

"Those of you that have a mate found you could not speak of the pilgrimage or your man would become quarrelsome. All of the men were laughing about the Goddess. Joking about Queen Cybele losing her power because she had taken a lover and how he would now take over and rule in her stead"

Anger coursed through her for a moment. "I think most men forget it is the female blood that carries the royal line. Or if they know it to be true, they wish to forget it! Many of you thought, over the years, that I talked to myself, muttered as you call it, in the woods. No, I talked to all those who have gone before me. I dream the dreams of forewarning because I esteem my ancestry. I hold that each one of you has intrinsic knowledge that you refuse to honor. Each one of you has abilities that lie hidden deep within, and *it is because it frightens your man* that you refuse to use your powers."

Eurynome knew there was no turning back now. A few of the women moved forward and Eurynome could tell they were listening with their hearts. And so she spoke clearly and resolutely to them, prying open their courage with her own.

"You are strong and courageous but you have become weak and dependent on, or fearful of men. Look and see what is happening before your very eyes. Men are fearful of the Goddess and wish to destroy all that she stands for. It is why they rape, to belittle the inherent power of women. Have you not noticed when there is a child, especially a female child, the men found a reason to move on? How many of you wait? It hardens my heart to see you spend your youth talking of when your mate returns.... as if it were something real. It is ludicrous! I could not bear to be around it, so I retreated to the woods!"

Eurynome concentrated her attention on each upturned face, and as she slowly moved in a clockwise motion, her mood lightened as she identified attentiveness and sad recognition in the eyes looking vigilantly in her direction.

"I see you are now ready to hear truth," Eurynome asserted, nodding her head.

A loud wailing vibrated through the gathering as Marta called upon the Goddess to curse her father for deserting her. Next she cursed all of the men in their village for being too cowardly to take her as a mate.

"How dare they look down upon me simply because my mother does not have a proper offering," she wailed and stamped her foot. But her sorrow opened the door to understanding.

Each of the women in turn began crying or shouting at the disrespect they had received at the hands of men. Between bursts of anger, there was a deep lament of longing and loss. They were slowly beginning to see that their deepest anger was at themselves for pretending to be weak when they were strong and fearful when there was courage to be had.

When the wailing ceased, Eurynome said, "Your tears are good. *The Goddess tells us that tears are the well-spring of power.* Their salty taste is to remind us that the same power that moves the tides resides within each of us."

Gathering momentum, Eurynome persisted. "Some of you have not seen the sea, but all have heard tell of it. If you choose to go on with this journey you will know the greatness of the land and the loving power and strength of the Goddess. Our journey leads us first to the Black Sea and then to Hattusas, the greatest fortress ever built."

When the women cheered in unison, Eurynome took courage from their trust in her and spoke with a level and clear voice.

"If we are to gather power and feel the Goddess flow through us, we must locate the village where our sisters have been taken. We must find those responsible for taking three of your daughters and butchering four of your sisters. Let us rest and then we will talk some more."

Listening intently, the women gathered around the circle in a tight knot. Eurynome looked carefully at the mothers of the girls that had been taken.

"The men that ran off with your daughters will head back to their village," she told them. "I can follow in their footsteps, even when they believe they leave none. It will be a big surprise to them! They will not expect a group of women to be able to follow or find them, but find them we will! You will have your daughters back very soon, that I assure you. The men attacked by first sun, for the Sun represents all that is male, but we will attack on the night of the full moon. The Moon Goddess will light our way. She will help us find our sisters and bring them home."

Thiscara and Theta knew that Eurynome was trying to bring hope to what seemed to be a desperate situation. The sight of the two young mothers reminded all of them of how important hope was, and they embraced the two in motherly love, as they listened intently to what Eurynome had to say.

Eurynome found a smooth oasis on a boulder that jutted out from the rocky mound near the cavern. Letting out a soft sigh, she sat, leaning her back against the cool granite, feeling the taut muscles in her shoulders begin to relax. Deep in thought, she wondered how best for them to follow through on the raid, and looked down, her features drawn in concentration on the clan below; she did not want to lose one more life. The group would be surprised to know how much she cared. But she did not care for the lack of independence they displayed, or the fact that some of them were starting to believe there was something wrong with female rule. Ignoring that fact, she decided she *only* cared for the greatness that was hiding deep within each one of them. Her long, lithe body slowly unwound itself from its comfortable position.

"Jutia!" Eurynome exclaimed as a heavy booted figure approached her. And then, with a spark of merriment in her golden eyes, she asked, "Have you ever heard of an elephant?"

Surprised, Jutia stopped abruptly.

"I ...ah... no! I came to tell you that a few more nights are too long to wait," she complained, drawing her thick brows together in a frown. Her dark wavy hair was cropped boyishly short since, years ago, she had decided that long hair just got in the way of what was important to her, and that was being a mighty warrior.

"Yes, and we will put that time to good use," said Eurynome, "I will show you how to wield a knife, how to disable an opponent very quickly, and how to protect yourself when someone attacks you."

"I know very well how to protect myself from anyone!" Pride and anger rang in Jutia's voice.

"Then I will tell you about elephants, and show you how they walk," said Eurynome, smiling now, "I will also tell you about their gentle yet protective ways, and the fact that they never forget kindness."

Leaving Jutia's simmering anger behind, Eurynome reached toward the pack that she had prepared earlier. As she began her reconnaissance, she thought of Jutia and her discontent at not becoming their leader, because that was where her anger stemmed from.

Eurynome knew that Jutia had strength, courage and a good mind. She also knew that she lost patience easily. As she gave thought of how to handle Jutia and the situation that she knew was brewing, she found what she had been looking for. The men had traveled alongside of the river, occasionally moving into the shallow water just in case they were being followed. Once she was sure of their direction, she headed back to camp. She had so much she wanted to teach the women, because the night of the full moon was fast approaching.

⌘

After a morning filled with practicing knife throwing, and learning how to fall without being hurt, a tired group of women moved stiffly, following the trail left for them by Eurynome. Even Marta, whose injury was still causing her a lot of pain, tried to emulate the quiet

189

moves Eurynome had shown her. Marta's arm was hurting less because, earlier in the day, Eurynome had located a mulberry tree, and caringly provided her with mistletoe to provide relief from her discomfort.

Marta had given quite a bit of thought about their friendship when they were younger, before all the children made fun of Eurynome and she, too, had pulled away. After her friend's gentle care, she couldn't help but remember the time that Eurynome had given her a butterfly, its delicate wings still wet, fresh from its cocoon, telling her to safeguard it, till it could fly on its own. She said it would make a very long journey in its lifetime, flying many, many miles. She then told her something that Marta would never forget. "We are like this butterfly, Marta. Someday we will fly free, just as this one will. We will go on a long journey together, and that journey will change us forever."

Loving the experience of the woods as always, Eurynome was deep into her exploration of the area when she spotted a clump of linden flowers. While absorbed with gathering some to brew a tea to help with the monthly pain some of the women suffered, she heard the rustling of bushes, and noticed that the animals had gone suddenly silent. Eurynome froze as four men passed by her on the trail, nearly stepping on her as she blended soundlessly with the trees, the wild flowers and the tones of earth. And when the danger passed, she moved slowly into the deepest part of the woods, away from the rough honed trail.

Appearing out of nowhere, Eurynome rushed into camp and motioned for the women to stop and be very still and quiet. All became motionless.

"They are very close," she whispered, holding up four fingers, and pointing to the North. Motioning the women to take cover, she pulled out her knife and indicated that they should do the same. Without a sound, she crept forward in the direction that the men had been coming from only to find that the danger was over. The men had moved to the east away from the river; the women's camp site was safe for the time.

There was no fire at their camp that night. Eurynome had cautioned everyone to keep their voices to a whisper because of the danger of sound traveling. There were mixed feelings about the raid. Some of the women were very frightened, and the two mothers were anxious for their daughters, because of what they might be going through.

In these last few days, Eurynome could feel the power of their excitement. Teaching them to fight and wield their knives had been a powerful experience for them, although more time was necessary to make them proficient. Thinking of Jontue, and how many hours, days, months, and even years he had prepared her for this moment, she felt a weight of responsibility to these brave women, knowing that they placed their trust in her, and vowed not to let them down.

The sound of raised voices and scuffling distracted Eurynome from her reverie. Silently, she leapt toward the offenders and gave quiet but stern orders to hold their tongues.

"I am getting impatient! Why must we wait one more night?" argued Jutia.

"It is for the full of the moon we wait," answered Eurynome, indicating that Jutia should keep her voice down.

Jutia was much older than Eurynome, and perhaps because her family openly boasted about royal lineage, seemed to be the only one having difficulty taking orders. Taller than most, and muscular, with large bones, she angered easily and had a fierceness which intimidated many of the young women, although she had never showed her temper in front of Eurynome. Now, the inner core of Eurynome's body tingled with awareness; it was time. The events of the last few days brought out the pure animal instinct of a natural leader. Eurynome wanted to shake Jutia, like a lion shakes her cub, telling her to behave. But she knew chastisement would not work. Jutia was too proud.

"The Moon's waxing! It's nearly full. It matters not that we wait one more night!" Jutia nearly growled at Eurynome. "We are wasting time, don't you agree?" Her voice was a loud gravelly whisper as she spoke to the others.

There was a low mumbling sound as the group deliberated amongst themselves. Jutia decided to take this for accord and shouted, "Then it is agreed we go tonight." At which the mumbling rose to a roar.

Eurynome put out her hand to quiet the group. When she had their attention she declared, "I have had a vision. The raid takes place on the full of the Moon. If we go hither this night all will be lost." With that she calmly turned her back on her angry sister, knowing full well that Jutia had her knife drawn and hidden behind her back.

When Jutia lunged, Eurynome pivoted on her left leg and kicking the knife out of Jutia's hand with her right continued the spin until she once again faced her. With raised elbows aimed for her opponent's neck, Eurynome knocked Jutia over and pinned her to the ground. Many of the women barely had a chance to blink before it was over.

"You have done well my sister" Eurynome said, raising her opponent up and clapping her on the back, "though we can all do with more practice. We have learned a great deal on this journey!"

Jutia stood, dazed and astonished, as Eurynome spoke to her with approval in her voice.

Eurynome turned to the group and said, "When you are a natural leader, as is Jutia, it is hard to follow. Your sister is anxious, as are all of you. But we will soon allow the Goddess to lead us to victory!"

With her heart in her eyes, trusting that Jutia would do the right thing, Eurynome turned and hugged her. The women held their breath, and watched.

Stunned for a brief moment, Jutia did not know what to do. Eurynome had caught her off guard by not attacking, and now this… the praise… saying she was a natural leader. It gave her pause, her face becoming a theatrical mask of confusion, her arms hanging limply at her sides.

And then, suddenly, Jutia, smiling, was lifting Eurynome off the ground in a bear hug. The group quietly raised their arms in praise of the Goddess Cybele.

As Theba sat watching the scene, she wondered how this child had come to learn the talents she so easily displayed on this journey. Yes, it was true, she thought, it was all because of Jontue. Jontue who was loyal to the goddess, and taught about the womb and the mysteries of life and of the black goddess who brings the mysteries of death, it was she who destroys so that new and stronger growth can take place. Her thoughts, she knew, were rambling, but it was indeed a good day to reach into the past so that she could understand the future.

Grandmother moved her stiff back against the ancient oak she had found until she was more comfortable. Glad of the relief, she continued to ruminate.

How was it, she wondered, that we had become fearful of speaking of our greatness? Surely no man could be accused of being so timid. Shaking her head, she recalled how some men taught their sons how to fight and hunt and boast of strength, sometimes hurting each other to show off. But they belittled their daughters, if they allowed them to live at all. She could remember how, during many cold winters, the women gave no challenge to the men who, little by little, found excuses to keep the women home and away from the special days that honored the goddess. Yes, she could now see the insidious ways men had found to denigrate all that was female. All but Jontue, for he was loyal to the goddess, and to the olden ways. He had taught Eurynome, and passed on to her all that he knew, for she was the only one willing to listen to 'the ravings of a sick and unusual man.' Grandmother began drifting off to sleep as these thoughts, like ribbons, tied the past and the future together.

"Mamma, come… lie back and let me cover you against the night," Eurynome said, bending over her and stroking her hair. "There is a slight chill, and it is to be a mead moon on the morrow. I have saved the fermented honey and we'll add berries to the brew and we will celebrate with the goddess on her night."

Murmuring endearments, she began to settle the old woman for the night.

"I will tell you the story of Selene and Endymion." Eurynome said as she snuggled next to her grandmother. "Selene was a beautiful and seductive goddess of the full moon who always rode across the lunar heavens in a silver chariot drawn by two white horses. One night she saw Endymion sleeping amongst his sheep in the mountain forest. Ravished by his beauty, the heart of the goddess burning within her, she seduced him by putting a spell on him so that he would sleep in a deep cavern, except on the full of the moon when he would come to her and they would join their bodies together in love. And it is said that together they produced fifty daughters, all of whom are moon-maidens who light the way for young lovers."

As her grandmother fell asleep, Eurynome rose from her side and went to wrap herself in her own blanket. How would she keep her here tomorrow out of harm's way? She realized she yet had so much to learn from the generous spirit of her grandmother, which had always lit her path, gently leading her to see others from the heart. As Eurynome fell asleep, her spirit guide whispered to her,

"Yes... you have often veered away from her guidance, in search of strength. Strength serves to protect the heart, yet does not necessarily open it. True courage comes from an open heart."

Chapter 8

The sun hung suspended on the horizon as the group shared dry tasteless pork that had been cooked two days earlier. Quietly regaling them with stories to keep their minds off the meager fare, Eurynome spoke eagerly about the fortress of Hattusus, sharing all that Jontue had taught her, painting word pictures for them just as he had done for her with the result that the women, mesmerized, sat taller focusing on the inner strength that they were recapturing.

Getting up to leave camp, Eurynome reminded them to eat lightly in order to prepare them for their evening's raid. Their mood, as they sat around their fireless camp, was as varied as a rushing brook finding its way into a still pond. Before she left camp, Eurynome decided to lead the group in a prayer to all of the warrior priestesses that had fought for the preservation of the goddess. The prayer helped to reminded them of the reason they were on the journey.

Watching the sun's precarious balance between the backdrop of golden sky and the unknown deep cavernous pit that swallowed it each evening, some wished it would never submerge. The few who were anxious to rescue the young girls or to engage in combat were silently cheering the sun's quick journey.

On the way back to camp after scouting, Eurynome walked purposefully, knowing it was time to speak of the raid that would take place in just a few hours. As the group gathered, she reviewed what she must tell them, the direction they would attack from, what signals they would use, and which women would move toward the huts to find the girls that had been taken. When they were gathered, she began with no preamble.

"It is significant," said Eurynome, "that those of you whose kin we plan to rescue are not involved in the raid."

"But..." interjected one the mothers that had a daughter missing.

"No, there is no room for error, and you both are too emotional and would only get someone killed if you participate!"

The mother that had two daughters stolen sat in stony uncomfortable silence, with a look of near mutiny on her face.

The compassionate, story-telling young woman was gone, and since there was a no-nonsense expression in Eurynome's eyes, both women acquiesced without further questioning.

"During the raid it will be most import to always go forth in pairs," she said, looking from one face to another. "If there is a fallen sister, take her to the cave we have agreed upon. The rock cave I have shown you is nearly impossible to find, therefore safe, but you must keep a good ear for the sound of the wolf. I have taught Grandmother to make the sound. If you should lose your way, this will lead you to the cave. But remember that it can attract others of our four footed friends. So have your clubs and the vial of wolverine scent ready to use if it is needed."

Eurynome could see concern written on the faces of the women. There was so much to learn, and so little time. Inhaling deeply, she felt her profound connection to the forest and wished she could infuse within the women the love and nurturing that she received each time she breathed the scent of pine, heard the cry of a wolf, or watched an osprey dive for its prey. She understood how gifted she was to have Jontue, and realized he lived still in the teachings in this circle.

"Most animals will not attack the wolverine," she told them. "Even a bear will not challenge it. Be careful with the vial I have given you. Put only a few drops on a strip of cloth and tie it to your belt if you feel an animal might be tracking you. Hopefully we will not have to retreat to the cave. Besides," she laughed, "you'll not be welcome there if you by hap' spill it upon yourselves."

The mellow tone of Eurynome's laughter, so seldom heard, did Grandmother's heart good as she listened in earnest along with the rest of the group.

"It is now time to leave. When I give the signal for the raid to begin, take the balm I have given you, mix it with dirt and cover your face and body. It will darken your skin so that you become nearly invisible."

Eurynome had spoken to her grandmother earlier, knowing how useless she must feel, telling her that she was counting on her to take the younger girls to the cave. She was pleased to see that Grandmother, wanting to do as much as she could for this courageous group of women, gathered herbs along the way, healing herbs that might be useful after the raid.

The group followed Eurynome silently, walking single file and keeping close, hardly breathing. It felt like a long walk to some, but to others, every halt was a delay that made them impatient. Dread, apprehension and trepidation reared their ugly heads now that they had arrived at their destination, and many wondered if in battle, they could accomplish the same things they had in practice. Eurynome came up beside each one and whispered last minute instructions and gave encouragement before moving to the next. The most important advice she gave them was, "It will go well because it is blessed by the goddess."

Constantly throwing back her head to stare at the Moon, Eurynome went over the plan again and again. Once positioned, there would be three groups; two women from each would crouch at the edge of the small village, listening for the signal, as well as two to the north and two to the west. It was a good plan. Still, a sense of foreboding lingered, undermining the victory she knew was theirs. Had she planned for every possible outcome? Could she have missed something?

Jontue's story of Aradia and the mistakes that she had made occupied her mind.

"What if I told you, you are Aradia..." he had said. Striving to remember his words, for they seemed to be vastly important to her now, she thought, what if she made a mistake? So many lives would be on her conscience if these women were to die. She reached deeper within to retrieve his words, and felt him, Jontue, so close to her. Then she heard his words clearly.

"Remember that the mission you go on now, what you do, how you handle yourself and the women, will serve to erase some of the choices you made in your last lifetime."

Then came a moment when she knew. A moment split in time, an insight... clear and deep, 'I am Aradia!'

❧

Eurynome headed for the east end of the village which was bordered on one side by the river. On the two nights she investigated the village, she noted that usually one of the men guarded the small boats. Tonight, she hoped this one was asleep. It would make her work easier. She speculated again on why they had not taken the boats down river, and froze when suddenly, seeing how protectively the guard hovered over the boat, it all became perfectly clear. These boats belong to visitors! Why hadn't she realized that before?

Silently cursing her blunder, and with mounting alarm, she understood the peril this posed to her band. There were more men in the village than she had previously thought. At that moment, she heard muffled screams coming from the huts and her first thought was something had gone wrong. Hearing the 'all is well signal' from the other two groups, she felt imminent relief, but it did nothing for the fact they were facing something altogether different than planned.

Loud laughter came from one of the huts located in the same direction that the screams had come from. Now it all made sense to Eurynome. They were probably selling the girls to these visitors and they were raping them now. Instantly, she was overcome with rage, even though she knew that she must not let angry thoughts cloud her mind

Now, however, she realized they could not wait until the village was asleep as they had planned. If she was right and these visitors were the men Jontue had once told her about, they would brutalize the girls and then take them when they left. She tried to remember what Jontue had said about the vicious warriors that used the river at night. What few memories there were, made her realize she had rather not encounter these men, although that might not be an option?

She could not see the design on the boat to assure herself that these men were not the *night travelers*. So, as she was trained to do, she would have to assume they were the evil men who traveled through the night attacking unsuspecting villages and taking young girls to rape, trade and barter. Jontue had told her that if captured by them, it would be easier for a girl to kill herself than to be subjected to their sexual torture. Bile rose to Eurynome's throat, but she swallowed, willing it away.

Knowing that the men were probably drunk, which would make them easier prey, she waited until one of them stumbled out of one of the huts, shouting something over his shoulder. She saw that he was heading down toward the river. Eurynome knew what she had to do, and motioning to Jutia, whispered into her ear.

"Go like a ghost to the ash tree, and do as I have shown you. Become part of the tree," she said with quiet determination. "And then, when he walks by, aim sure! Come. We are ready!"

They both moved silently toward the path, and Jutia took up her place next to the tree. The intoxicated man stumbled many times, calling out complaints that he was being sent to relieve a lowly guard.

Jutia held still until he walked right beside her, then with a quick motion, she swung her club, stunning him. Eurynome jumped on his broad back and slit his throat in absolute silence. And although he was a large burly man, both women saw to it that his body did not make a noise as he fell, and they dragged him off the path. Then, they headed for the man guarding the boats.

Having taken the garment off the man they had just killed, Jutia covered herself and with her short hair could easily pass for a man. Beckoning wildly to the guard by the boat, she cried out to him in a deep, heavy voice, slurring the words so that he could not understand. Then, as he came closer, Eurynome jumped on his back and plunged the knife in his neck swiftly and silently, just as Jontue had shown her and he fell easily to the ground.

Eurynome sighed, realizing it was easier to know how to kill than it was to kill. Knowing that there was no choice that they must get to the girls, she clasped Jutia's strong shoulder and whispered again in her ear.

"We work well together. You are a great warrior."

Then, motioning for the other five of their group to join them, she sent out the signal for the attack to begin.

Running toward the village, two women stopped at the edge as had been planned while the others from the group kept going. Eurynome headed first for the hut where the screams had come from earlier. The light peeking out from under its thatched door was the only illumination, other than that of the cook fire in the center of the village that was now becoming soundless embers.

Eurynome stopped a few feet from the hut, grabbed Jutia, and told the others to wait, indicating that if the men gave chase the women that remained outside should be ready.

When they entered the hut, the four men inside were so surprised that two were on the floor moaning before the others knew they were being attacked. When she and Jutia backed up close to the doorway, the men grabbed their weapons to follow only to be clubbed into unconsciousness and tied up by the women outside.

Women from the group as planned went to the young girls that were lying on the floor. They were bleeding and bruised; one was tied to a large post, and the other two had their hands tied together and did not look like they recognized their rescuers. In their fear, the girls began to scream, and within seconds, the village had come alive with shrieks and sounds of terror.

Eurynome and Jutia, once sure the girls were being tended to, went outside, and seeing men rush from their huts with weapons they headed for the largest man. Jutia circled around as they had practiced, and came up behind him. Eurynome fell to all fours in front of him and Jutia pushed him towards Eurynome so that he lost his footing. Jutia then jumped on top of him and plunged the knife into his neck.

Feeling a hard kick to her side, Jutia looked up and a man was standing above her wielding a club. Helpless to move, she protected her head as he began to swing his club. In the next moment, he fell forward, completely limp, nearly crushing her. With effort, she pushed his foul smelling body off and rolled to her feet.

Looking toward Eurynome, she saw that she was removing her knife from the man's throat. Jutia noticed that her leader halted for just an instant, a deep look of pain crossing her face before she moved back into the fray.

Despite the confusion and pandemonium the group worked well together; it was obvious their plan was falling into place. The men were surprised and could not see well as they piled out of their huts, running into each other with drunken perplexity. The women of the village were busy protecting their children, and did not seem the least bit interested in helping the men.

"She is their leader. Kill her!" roared one of the men as three of them headed for Eurynome. Surprising them, she ran toward them and came off the ground with both feet squarely hitting the first man in the chest, knocking him down. She landed, rolled and crouched before throwing a dagger which caught one of her attackers between the eyes. A third man, larger than any human she had ever seen, grabbed her as she was rising and pushed her back on the ground. His knife glancing off her armor seemed to enrage him. Fury, reverberating like thunder, shook the ground under her.

"Whore, whore!" he shouted. "I will gut you, and as you slowly die, I shall have my pleasure!"

Discarding his knife, he fumbled with his crotch, giving Eurynome the opportunity to reach for the sharp weapon. He foiled her attempt, and clutching it by its hilt, he plunged it into her armpit, going deep into her flesh. A searing pain tore through her body before everything went black. As she slumped forward, he removed the knife to strike again, but Jutia was quick to grab a club and beat him till his mountainous body lay helpless on the ground.

Eurynome rose up slowly, helped by Jutia. Blackness chased her consciousness, as she made a show of dusting herself off. The noise, clamor and shrieking had subsided and there were no men left fighting. They were either dead, wounded, or running toward the boats.

Eurynome noticed Jutia and her daughter Ageianna were chasing one of the men who was heading for the river, and realized that if he were able to get away, the pilgrimage would not be safe.

But Jutia's feet were swift. Coming up behind him, she vaulted through the air, knocking him into the water. Anger radiated from him as he emerged, spitting mud and cursing.

"You will die for this!" he shouted, raising his fist. "Do you know who I am?"

As mother and daughter attacked him, he fought ferociously! Hitting Jutia with a closed fist on the side of her face, he knocked her under the water, leaped on her and held her down. Ageianna grabbed a rock as he was choking her mother, and hit him again and again, though the force of the first blow was sufficient to render him unconscious. Jutia, sputtering and coughing, reached out to her daughter, and they fell into each other's arms, overwhelmed with relief to be alive.

"Yes, I know who you are!" Jutia cried, raising his lifeless body to the surface by his hair. "You are dead! Dead! Do you hear me?""

Both mother and daughter crawled from the muddy water, looked around at their victory and began to dance, crying, hugging and calling out praise to the Goddess. The raid was over, and they had rescued the girls, and looking around it seemed that all of the women of their clan had survived.

Chapter 9

Jutia and Ageianna joined the circle that was forming in the center of the village. Linking their arms, their voices raised in a haunting and somber melody in praise of the Goddess.

"Hail Cybele ma belle. See us shine for thee.
Hail mother hold us, hold us at your knee.
Hail sister who is mine. The Goddess, she does see.
Hail Goddess, Mother, Sister… I am all that I can be."

The band of women, now warriors, began to move rhythmically in a circle, their arms still linked, their voices merged as one. The spiraling energy which rose from the circle transcended the savagery and the suffering of the last hours, bringing forth a palpable sensation of awe and gratitude that the Goddess had so blessed them on this day.

The dead men and their male visitors had counted twenty and three, but there were scores of women and children. As the dazed and bewildered women and children watched the strangers who had appeared from out of nowhere, they moved closer, drawn by the exultant power of the women before them until, creating a circle around them, they joined in the singing.

Many were openly sobbing. The two mothers and their three daughters that had been rescued were sitting in the middle, laughing, crying and absorbing the healing that came from the voices encircling them. It was then that Eurynome realized that all of the women and children in the village had been captured, tortured and made slaves by these brutal men. And now they were now free.

～❦～

Tears flooded Eurynome's eyes, blurring her vision. Wiping them away with the back of her arm she noticed dampness on her left side. Her eyes burned and blackness threatened for a moment, but she shook off the weakness. Taking one of the women by the arm she said, "I see you have healing abilities. Will you assist my grandmother with the wounded when she arrives?"

With gnarled hands the woman reached up to touch Eurynome's face. She did not seem surprised at Eurynome's knowing of her art. "You remind me of my daughter," she said. "These men – well, she was beautiful. They used her too often and her body gave out."

Nodding at the old woman, Eurynome clutched her hand, taking strength from the resilience she saw before her. Looking around, Eurynome watched, her golden eyes filling up again at the sight of strength in the way the women held themselves. They're glowing, she thought, as she watched the fear leaving their faces.

Eurynome lovingly halted the voices, telling the women there was much time for celebrating after they took care of the injured, and gave orders for two of the women to go for her grandmother and the children who had safely been left behind in the cave.

Then, unable to stand without help, she attempted a casual air, as she ambled slowly to lean on a tree. Thiscara, Marta, Jutia and Ageianna moved toward her asking what they could do, and once instructed, hurried off to attend to the injured and the prisoners. In her weakened state, a powerful vision encompassed her. She saw herself with Jontue; he looked very different but she knew it was he.

They were seated in a garden of flowers; music pulsated from every direction, filling them with a harmony that went much deeper than the music alone could bring. She felt for him a forever love, that was deep and sensual, yet it vibrated with a purity of heart that once felt was never forgotten.

It stunned her to feel the sensual feelings in her body as she viewed the vision. Yet, the feelings belonged- like smooth rocks lining a river bed, like leaves gracing a tree and like water in a bubbling brook. The feelings belonged!

༄

"All of the bodies of the men that have been killed are to go into those huts at the end of the village," Eurynome told them. "The huts and the dead men will be burned, and then you will take the boats and go up stream."

Eurynome was clicking off orders and checking on some of the wounded as they entered the hut behind her that had been set up to care for the women that had been wounded. The village was buzzing with activity.

"There are not enough boats for all of you. Jutia will lead a party to take the boats upstream," she said, and then she made her way to the slight figure of the shy young girl that she knew as Miyah.

"You have been very quiet on this journey, Miyah," she told her, "but I think your time has come. You will go with Jutia to watch the children, for with your injured leg you will be no good along the path. But your love of children will help to keep them occupied while they learn a new way to travel. Tell me, how is your leg?"

Miyah, seeing the pain that Eurynome was in, quickly assured her she was all right, and added that she would be proud and happy to help with the children traveling by water.

"Ageianna will lead the party on foot," Eurynome informed them. "And Neya, you are fearless and have astounded me on this journey. I noticed you have a natural instinct for the trees and animals. Your understanding of how the sun travels across the sky will lead you to the sacred city of Hattusus. And so you will scout for the party that will go by land."

"But, you…I do not understand…" Ageianna began, "You must lead…"

Eurynome interrupted with a knowing grin. "You have pure instinct when danger lurks. Your instinct saved your mother. I noticed that you follow what feels right from here in your center. And when there is a problem between the women, you go with what is right from your heart." Ageianna's eyes filled with tears; she reached out instinctively, letting Eurynome lean on her as she continued speaking.

"Jutia, I signal you out to lead the party by boat; there is no doubt in anyone's mind why. Hap I say, you are courageous, quick and strong, and a fierce fighter."

She looked at Jutia with her arm around her daughter. "Look at the proud love in your daughter's eyes."

Eurynome's voice failed her. She cleared her throat, forcing herself to go on.

"Look around you, every woman in the group gives you enormous praise for the outcome of this raid."

There was a loud din of approval from the women in praise of Jutia. But seeing the concern in her eyes as she focused on their leader, they turned to Eurynome. Weakly she held up her arms to stop the clamoring.

Grandmother, upon arriving from the cave, let out a loud shriek and clutched her heart in pain. Some of the women went to their knees when they noticed the immense amount of blood under Eurynome's arm. The stain went to her hip and continued down her leggings. They rushed toward her and she tried to wave them off, but was too weak.

"Get her into that hut!" her grandmother cried, but Eurynome would not hear of it. Instead, she ordered them to take her to a large oak tree down by the water even though, when they tried to support her under the arm, it made the wound bleed profusely. They were forced to construct a litter out of branches to support her. As they laid her under the tree, full daylight was breaking over the mountains; it was going to be a clear and beautiful day.

Grandmother wanted to examine the wound and many of the women gathered around, hoping to help. With immense effort, Eurynome spoke in a slightly weakened voice.

"I am still your leader... Th...there is much to do and there has been no sleep. Jutia, Ageianna, have some of the women sleep, and the others can make ready for leaving. There is no time to fuss on those that don't need it."

Jutia hesitated and was met with a determined stare. She moved off and began calling orders.

"Mamma, stay with me" Eurynome murmured. "Come let us sleep for a while. I am so tired."

Grandmother took Eurynome's head in her lap and said, "Child why did you not tell someone of your injury?"

"You know why. You have always known."

And exhausted, both she and the old women fell asleep. Grandmother was awakened by a hand lightly touching her arm. Eurynome also awoke.

"Are you all ready to leave?" she asked Jutia who was bending over them.

"We are prepared," she replied. "Let us help you into the boat."

"I go not," said Eurynome, her eyes glazed with pain. "It would be madness for me to take up room in one of the boats. No. This tree is my resting place. We are happy together. Do you hear the birds singing for me? When you go, many animals will come and welcome me to their hearts. We will become one. It is as it should be."

"There has been a huge loss of blood," Thiscara said sadly. You know not what you say."

"No… I know what I say, and Grandmother knows also. Let us tell them of the night of my birth, tell them of your vision…. tell me."

"I have told you before." Grandmother said weakly.

"You have not told me the end of your vision."

"Child please…Do not do this," Grandmother sobbed.

Eurynome reached up lovingly, caressing her grandmother's face. She touched the tears running over the lined beauty of the woman that raised her, and brought them, a salty reminder of the Goddess, to her lips.

"Remember what I told you about the sea and our tears. It is the Goddesses' way of showing you your strength, your beginnings."

With effort and to relieve some of her pain, Eurynome adjusted her body against the tree before she began again.

"Goddess teaches there is no death! I know this for I have lived before, as all of you have done. Search your minds for things that are familiar, things or places or people that you know instinctively. Watch Jutia as she maneuvers the boats, as if she has done it many times before."

Eurynome struggled for a breath. "Acknowledge Ageianna as she leads you. She was born with vast ability; she will have no trouble keeping you safe." Cocking her head at her old friend, she said, "Marta has inner knowledge of herbs; she is dreaming the dreams of healing with the gift of fore-knowing from the Goddess.

Marta jumped, lightly holding her arm, startled that Eurynome knew her secret.

"Yes it is true... My arm is better because I have learned on this pilgrimage that I am a healer. I seem to know the right herbs to use because I see it in my dream the night before. I see myself picking the herb and sharing it, and it leads me to know what to do for all of you. I am excited about this new knowledge."

"Once I stopped feeling sorry for myself," said Marta, "this knowledge became very strong." She looked miserably at Eurynome, feeling inadequate to help her. "I am so sorry. Please forgive me?" Her tears became a flood and her mother, Theta, took her in her arms, and both sobbed holding on to the other for strength.

Eurynome's skin was shining from perspiration. Her hair hung in ringlets, framing her beauty. Her face was a canvas, as she looked into the eyes of each woman. The pain she was feeling was replaced with respect, pride, honor, wonder and love.

"Ahh..." she said. "That is what shines in your faces. Passion! Passion for life, and for the Goddess of creation, that it stems from. How can men hold that their gods are all powerful? How can you have life without the mother? She creates! Without her there is nothing!" Eurynome's breath was coming with great effort.

"The...the last thing I want to teach you is this. To have power is to not fear death." She weakly drew a circle on the ground with her knife. "This is life. May 'hap one of you can show me where is the beginning, and where is the end?"

"You cannot leave. You have not finished the story of Aradia!" Marta brought her hand to her mouth to stifle the anguish she felt over all the sharing she had missed and the friendship she would never get to enjoy with Eurynome.

"That is true... about Aradia. It is not that I have held out on you; it is just that I do not yet know the ending."

"Child, don't leave me!" Grandmother beseeched, sobbing, trying to ward off the inevitable.

Eurynome smiled at her and said "I shall be back." Her eyes fluttered and her body slowly became limp.

Chapter 10

Hovering above her body, Eurynome looked down on her beloved grandmother as the old woman held her limp body and sobbed away her grief. Then, looking, off in the distance, she saw a radiant light glowing with a blue-white luminescence which formed a cone-like tunnel from which a familiar voice emerged to tell her that her work on earth was done and that now it was time for her to leave.

The light was so peaceful. It reminded her of the times she'd spent at the pond in the forest where the serene atmosphere had always lulled her to fall into a deep sleep from which she would awake with memories of a lush and magnificent garden. But more importantly, she vaguely recalled an ethereal goddess that sat with her there. The goddess had so many answers. Answers to questions Eurynome had not even known she wanted to ask.

Now, although she was drawn toward the light, she was torn by the knowledge that her grandmother needed her, that she would be so alone without her.

At that moment, however, a beautiful being, clad in a diaphanous robe of sea foam green, reached out her hand.

"You cannot help her as you are, for you dwell not in the earth, nor yet in the heavens. You must come with me," she said. "The in-between world serves no one."

A halo of golden light glowed around the being and her voice was melodious. "Take my hand," she said. "You will be safe. We have awaited you. I promise your grandmother is not in danger, and that she will honor you by being strong."

With that, Eurynome reached out her hand and moved through the tunnel with the radiant and enchanted being.

When Eurynome opened her eyes, an exquisite goddess stood before her. A spray of glitter ran across her high cheekbones splashing stars in her loosely coiled raven hair. Her musical voice was a respite of calm and comfort.

"You have slept for a great long while," she said as Eurynome looked about in confusion. "The sleep of the dead, we laughingly call it. Ah, but I see that you are not amused"

Looking around, Eurynome realized she was on a velvety blue curved sofa. Soft colorful pillows were scattered about, and off to the side there was a crystal waterfall, above which hung a mural of a castle with its turrets piercing the clouds. The ethereal goddess stood in front of an intricately designed window with curtains so sheer, light, and airy that they hardly existed at all. Beyond, stretched a majestic garden such as she had never seen before. Or had she?

"What is this place?" Eurynome demanded. "And who are you?"

"All in good time," answered the translucent goddess. "First I must say you take your mission very seriously."

"Mission...what mission?"

"The mission you were given before you went to reside upon the earth. Tell me, does the name Aradia mean anything to you?"

"It sounds familiar...Something Jontue might have mentioned," Eurynome admitted.

"Hmm...It is sometimes ourselves we know the least." The goddess paused a moment, seeming to considered her next words carefully and then she murmured,

"I am told that going through the womb when entering the earth is an interesting experience. Most times it creates a veil of forgetfulness," the goddess continued. "Coming here seems to have that same effect...but only at first..."

"Coming here?" Eurynome interrupted her impatiently, "If this is not earth...then where? And who is Aradia?"

The extraordinary being said affectionately, "Where you are... you will understand before long." And after another lengthy pause... "As to Aradia...why, that is you!"

*Looking puzzled, Eurynome shook her head in disbelief, and with more than a touch of irritation, questioned, **"I am Aradia**? Then who are you?"*

"My name is Desimena," the goddess told her. And you are the great Aradia, daughter of Diana, Goddess of the Moon. My name means teacher of many. I am your spirit guide when you are in the body, and I tend to you and others here on this side of the veil. I see that you are impatient and I understand. But believe me when I tell you that all will come in good time, and that is something we have a great deal of. We use the word time, though time does not exist here, only because it is a concept you have become used to on earth. It seems we are stuck with the word. It is murmured often by students such as you."

"And what kind of students would that be?" Eurynome questioned, raising an eyebrow.

"Those that are in a hurry and those that are very curious. Let us begin with the basics. First, I will be calling you Aradia, for that is the name your mother Diana gave you."

As Aradia settled in, Desimena began her lesson.

"All things are male and female, and all things are being created in the moment. I say "being created," for it is an ever moving, ever merging energy that is never still. If you could look upon the face of Source, in the next instant it would change. For Source itself, as well as an individual soul like you, is an evolving process. It continues on...

Desimena stopped abruptly as she watched Eurynome's expressive face light up. "You have come upon an understanding?" Desimena asked with a wide smile.

"Yes, no... I... I am sorry. I was listening! But I just realized something."

"Well please be kind enough to share it so we both can have the look of pleasure you are wearing."

"It is ongoing, this learning. I was educated by a very wise and kind man when I was on the earth. In turn, I taught the women, and now you're teaching me. I did not mean to interrupt the lesson, but I remember Jontue, my scholarly teacher on earth, saying that learning never stops. Is that true?"

Desimena looked thoughtful. "Well, let me put it this way. The lessons are ongoing and they seem to come in cycles like this." She pointed to the wall above the waterfall, and magically circles appeared. "The lessons are inter-linked." As she declared that, the circles joined and formed a ladder moving higher and higher. "But learning can stop for some who are not interested in growing. These beings become stagnant and they move from one lifetime to the next repeating old cycles."

"How many lives have I lived?" asked Aradia.

"Many people on earth and other cosmic systems have lived hundreds of thousands of lives!"

"Hundreds and...?"

Desimena raised her hand. "Well...suffice it to say you are but a child in this process. Your journey began when you were drawn to a matriarchal society on the Moon and..."

"Diana! Oh I remember!" Aradia cried. "I can see her in my mind's eye, an exquisite goddess, sitting on a window bench dressed in emerald green and around her neck there is a tear shaped necklace and a crown on her head with emeralds that look like stars. I can see it, and I feel it too!"

Aradia covered her heart with her hand and a tear formed in the corner of her eye.

"I see her addressing me with love, but there is great sadness in her heart. She is sending me away! Oh, I remember now, she sent me to earth! I can't remember the rest. I am awfully weary."

Desimena's eyes reflected love and pride as she said, "Soon we will speak more of what you have learned on your journey to earth, but now it is time to rest."

Chapter 11

Aradia arched and stretched her sleek body as she awoke from a deep slumber. Dreamily pushing back her full rich hair, she found herself unable to remember where she was. In a rush, all that had been happening in the last few days came back. Or... could she think of it as days, for there seemed to be no night. She reached out her hand as if to touch the luminous quality of the light that always shone.

Desimena approached, her tall, lithe body glowing with positive energy.

"You are well rested," she said. "That is good. Come, take my hand. We are going on a very special journey. We are going to visit your grandmother."

"But she will not know I am there," Aradia protested. "I..."

"Perhaps you underestimate her," said Desimena, her eyes sparkling.

❦

Aradia's grandmother was in a place that Aradia did not recognize. The bed had numerous blankets and looked soft and comfortable. The hut was spacious and sturdy. There was a small table covered with potions and herbs, and the sweet smell of jasmine wafted through the night air.

Aradia crouched down by the bed and spoke quietly, stroking her grandmother's hair, eliciting no response. But still she kept whispering. She had so much to thank her grandmother for that she poured her heart out and just when she thought she was not being heard, saw a tear forming in the corner of the old woman's eye.

"Eurynome," she murmured. "I feel you. I hear words in my head that only you would say. I miss you. I knew you'd come. Stay with me a while."

The tears slipped down parched and weathered skin, and her hand reached up as her granddaughter stroked her forehead, and in a while she slept, a deep and peaceful rest.

213

꧁꧂

"You did well when you visited your grandmother," Desimena told her, beaming with satisfaction. "You can visit her again. I will teach you how to go by yourself. But now we are going to learn more about the soul, this time on a personal level."

Aradia had learned that this palatial setting was called the Temple of Knowledge. They were in their usual 'classroom' that overlooked a floral garden teeming with color and wildlife.

When Desimena moved toward the wall and waved her hand, a light shone and a circle appeared.

"We will suppose this is the whole of creation, though it cannot be contained," she explained. "Show me your soul."

"I can't," Aradia told her. "There are no smaller circles."

Desimena tilted her chiseled face in a questioning manner, the splash of stars that ran across her cheekbones glittering in the luminous light.

"Here, follow me," she said after a long pause. "Let us take a stroll down to the ocean." Moving gracefully, she began to walk out of the room and into the mysterious wide corridor that opened to the anteroom.

Aradia looked about her in awe, as slowly the otherworldly magnificence of this extraordinary sanctuary of wisdom unfolded before her eyes.

"Ah, yes child," Desimena murmured. "We have been so busy with our lessons that I have forgotten to show you its splendor."

The enormous building was bathed in delicate radiance which came from openings in the gracefully slanted high ceiling. Aradia followed, forgetting her thoughts of an ocean as the corridors and rooms before her came alive with shadowed robed figures moving with slow deliberate intent in the hushed atmosphere.

The temple hummed with excitement though very few words were exchanged. Rather there was an aloofness of total concentration that emitted from each person.

Aradia beckoned quietly to Desimena to pause, so that she could peek into one of the rooms. Seeing the shelves lined with gold embossed volumes, and many huge maps sprawled on an array of tables that were dotted with small intricate tools, left Aradia awestruck. Watching hooded figures bending over charts and diagrams, she exclaimed, "I must know what they are doing! I want to understand!"

"Of course you do! But one thing at a time!"

Taking Aradia's hand, Desimena led her outside through an oversized entrance hall where two mammoth golden pillars graced the doorway and opened to a tiled terrace of muted shades of sand. A curved stairway led down into stepping-stone paths bordered with flowers and shrubs.

*Aradia, taking it all in, moved slowly, her face and eyes shimmering with questions. Over the doorway they had just come through, she saw the words '***Thine own self thou must know.***'*

Walking the path closest to the temple, they rounded the corner and there before her was water as far as the eye could see. Foam and seaweed washed up on shore in white-sea capped waves.

"The ocean at last!" Aradia cried. "I made it to the ocean!"

Desimena watched adoringly as the young woman played in the waves like a child. It was, she thought, easy to see why Aradia was interested in the mission of bringing sorcery to women. There's passion running through her veins. She has a thirst for knowledge, a lust for life, the heart of a child, and the mind of a warrior. A most interesting combination!

Desimena made a cup with her hands and motioned for Aradia to bring her some water.

Draped with seaweed, she responded to Desimena's call by emerging from the waves laughingly and with a small amount of water in her hands. Desimena touched one of her fingers to the water. A drop clung tenaciously to her delicate finger.

"All that is can exist in this one drop," Desimena told her. Then, taking Aradia's hands, she slowly opened them. The glistening water slipped from her hands and disappeared back into the gently rolling waves.

"And yet all that is cannot be contained in this ocean, this world, the earth, the sky or anything known. For Source, God/Goddess is unknowable." Desimena scooped up a handful of water and said, "This is your soul... how is it different from the ocean?"

Aradia stood in quiet wonder, feeling every word that her teacher spoke.

"When I hold this water, it becomes individual, yet it contains the essence of the ocean." Desimena spun around, creating a sparkling aura of color, her words reverberating over the waves and misty shore.

"All that you see... and all that is unseen is consciousness," she continued. "When you first decided to live in a body, you emerged from non-physical

consciousness and became physical consciousness. You were having an experience in a body.

"Your soul is the bridge that keeps you connected to pure consciousness from one lifetime to the next. Your soul stays in contact with you at all times through your emotions. If you are happy your soul expands. If you feel the discomfort of angry, resentment, judgment or vindictiveness your soul begins to contract, because these emotions are the opposite of love, and the simple truth is…that love expands and hate contracts!"

Later in the day they walked pensively along the ocean, each with deep churning emotions. Aradia's earlier happiness had allowed the timelessness that was part of the etheric realm to weave and bend, to play like drops of rain on a rainbow and shatter the endless hour-glass of time. Yet each knew that on earth time existed, and soon Aradia would re-incarnate.

"Now comes the hard part!" Desimena declared on their next meeting. "Now that you remember, you must participate in a life review. You must look at your judgments and harsh feelings toward men. As you view your lives on earth, do it with no reserve."

"Am I to go back soon?" Aradia asked.

"Oh yes…yes, of course you are," came the laughing reply.

In the viewing room, Aradia quietly observed the day her mother Diana, Goddess of the Moon, had sent her on the mission of teaching herbs and sorcery to women on earth. Dispatched from her comfortable position as teacher and beloved daughter on the moon, she was to assist women on earth to understand their personal power. Unfortunately, she thought, she had abused her own!

Next, the short lives she lived as Aradia and Eurynome played out on the screen. She made mental notes of questions she wished to ask. Recognizing her anger in the last days of Aradia and how it carried over to Eurynome, she winced. How had she become so cynical in so few years on earth she wondered?

"What do you think?" Desimena asked, seeing Aradia's contemplative demeanor.

"I am definitely learning the hard way," Aradia told her. "Making war on men is warring with half of me! I like being free and independent, but

it does not have to come at the expense of hating or distrusting men. If I get it right in this lifetime, perhaps I won't have to come back....I"

Desimena interrupted, her face was a mask, unreadable except for the slightest hint of a raised eyebrow.

"Well...let us think of life as a play, with numerous acts. In act-one you placed a curse on your lover that would last into seven generations. Did you think you could be an observer in the play? No. You might take on different roles, but in the end 'the play must go on,' and you are to have a starring role." Desimena became very still, allowing Aradia to absorb all that she had just said.

As Aradia nodded yes, her titian hair framed her exquisite face, and slowly her eyes began to show complete acceptance and greater understanding.

"Yes, well....that being so, you said that I will have a mate in this lifetime. How will I learn to accept my personal power if that is the case?"

"So... even here on this side of the veil, you as a woman believe you can't have a mate and still hold onto your individuality," Desimena said reflectively. "You still believe you cannot be powerful in your own right, make your own decisions and have an opinion, if there is a man in your life.

"I shall answer your question this way. You have taken my counsel, and chosen to work on the Sacred Rays in sequence. During your first life you explored the Red Ray. As Eurynome, you delved deeply, and with great results, into the Orange Ray and now you will be working on the Yellow Ray. Perhaps you can turn it into gold! I guess we will just have to see."

"Remind me of the lessons offered by the Yellow Ray," asked Aradia.

*"Of course," said Desimena, seeming glad that her student had thought to ask. "The **Yellow Ray is referred to as Sacred Action and Intelligence.** The Goddess of this Ray is called, **Enchantress of Records**. It is the objective of this Ray to give articulation to Divine Intelligence. This ray provides the underlying intelligence of nature. It is the force that animates human thought. Its purpose is to reveal the Mind of God/ Goddess within the consciousness of humans. This is the ray most associated with karma, for it holds the memory of all that has ever been, what was, and what is to be. Entities born under this Ray have the ability to be leaders, and through their intelligence and their enthusiastic nature they can inspire others.*

*"**The lessons** that will be offered to your soul as you become enveloped in the Sacred Yellow Ray will be to form self-esteem and personal honor,*

to develop integrity, to learn the difference between strength and courage and to recognize life as a precious gift. **On earth,** *when a soul refuses the lessons offered by this Ray – it negates honor and chooses mistrust over trust— dishonesty over truth- limitation over self-awakening. The key words would be,* **honor oneself.**"

Aradia shivered with dread and exhilaration at the prospect of learning to honor herself while discovering how to trust and honor a mate.

"Our time together here in the astral realm is coming to a close," Desimena said to Aradia with a mixture of sadness and pride. "But as you know, our journey together is not over."

Aradia's eyes filled with curiosity as a small band of goddesses filed into the room. "Perhaps you remember the Karmic Board," said Desimena. "As you know, they will help you pick a name that will match your purpose in this next lifetime. And of course they will help you to choose the exact moment of birth, for as you remember, it is very important that all the stars and planets in your chart be in line with your purpose."

Desimena's deep smile reassured Aradia, and as she turned to go, the intriguing group encircled her student, excitedly sharing with her their thoughts on how she could garner the most from this next, and very important lifetime.

⋙⋘

Coming softly up behind Aradia and resting her silky hand lightly on her shoulders, Desimena said, "You know that it is time. Remember to call upon me, for I will always be near. You will do well in this next lifetime. You will find love."

Aradia knew that Desimena's words should have cheered her, but instead she felt a restrained sadness.

"I…I'm not ready yet," she began. "I have a question…."

Desimena moved to stand in front of Aradia. Tilting her head to the side so that the glittering stars at her temple caught the light, she said, "You know that all of your questions will be answered at some point. Come child… take my hand."

As Aradia followed Desimena out of the astral realm and toward earth, the very last thing she heard was the goddess's voice saying, "Hold on to the name you have picked. The strength and conviction you have in your choice is what allows your parent to **hear** your name!"

❧

Aradia floated in a dark moist chamber, feeling safe and warm. She wanted to hold on to all that she had learned and most importantly, she wanted to make sure she held on to the name she had picked.

Then she felt herself outside of the womb. The jolt of leaving the secure environment created confusion which only lifted when she concentrated on the name, as she had been told to do, repeating it over and over again. She rejoiced in the fact that soon she would be witness to her own birth.

During the process of labor she moved in and out of her mother's body, feeling the pleasure and pain of birth. Then, in the moment she had been advised of, the moment that the head of the child crested, she knew she must make a decision.

And yet she hesitated… for she also knew that it was possible when she took up the raiment of a body, that the sleep of forgetfulness would come again.

*All that she had learned on the astral realm filtered through her mind. A colorful kaleidoscope of consciousness and knowledge collided, and then, remembering that **he** was waiting for her, she made her decision.*

Her soul moved into the tiny body…a loud cry pierced the room… and Czarinaea was born.

Book Three
The Warrior Queen

"Just beyond the fall of grace, behold that ever shining place"
~ From the movie - Far From Heaven.

Our story takes place approximately two
thousand and two hundred years ago
on the still and shallow Sea of Azov. The regal
Rypaie Mountains stand guard
as the Tanais River flows abundantly into
the sea, creating a backdrop
for the great Scythian tribes that inhabit the wetlands of Mæotis.

It is here that Aradia has been reborn, and she has chosen the name
Czarinaea. Her name means - Empress of the Land
and giver of good counsel.

Chapter 1

Myrina beamed with excitement as she stood outside the make-shift arena her sister had constructed. Hidden underneath the pleasure of watching Czarinaea perform cartwheels on the back of her flying steed, was a glint of uneasiness. Certainly not just with the task in front of them, but rather a nagging feeling that something mysteriously profound was about to happen.

Shifting her weight from foot to foot, she wondered what could be more important than Czarinaea doing well in her test today. After all, according to clan tradition this heralded the move from young girl to woman. Czarinaea would pass, and when she did, she was going to approach their mother again and ask to go to the temple to train as a priestess. Yet… there was that feeling again.

Rejecting her sense of unease, Myrina placed her hands on her hips preparing to deal with the matter at hand. Waiting patiently as Czarinaea danced toward her, wearing that all too familiar, somewhat smug look, Myrina withheld the smile she felt in her heart in hope that her words would have an impact on her reckless sister.

"Are you mad?" she demanded. "Mother has ordered you not to do that type of stunt! She has also told us both that it is important when practicing that we have someone with us. You sneak away, even from Lotzar, your very best friend, because you are afraid someone will get wind of your activities. I love watching you, but it is so dangerous out here in your hide-away. What if you fell and no one was here to help you?"

Having run out of breath, Myrina looked at her sister with pleading concern.

"And here I thought you were watching to learn something," Czarinaea said with a playful grin. "Have you come to chastise me instead?"

Utter defeat was etched on Myrina's face as she shrugged in exasperation.

"And what good would that do?" she asked. "No! I've come to tell you it is time to go to the hippo-dome. I am nervous for my part in the mounted pick up," she admitted, "and I don't want you to fail because of me."

"No one ever fails in life because of another," said Czarinaea. "At least that's what Natila tells us, and she is the wisest woman in our clan."

"Czarinaea, what will you do if mother does not let you go to the temple?"

"Ah, sweet sister, you truly love me, but then it is your nature to love. Somehow I think I need to learn what my little sister already knows."

Reaching the ring at the hippo-dome, they watched in awe as their mother Antilene took flight, her long dark hair flying in the wind. Boldly, she stood atop two horses running side by side. Becoming part of the wild beasts, with one foot firmly planted on each of the horse's backs, she circled the arena. Then, in a lightning move, Antilene went to her knees and quickly mounted one horse. Circling around the arena once more, she came to a hair-raising stop in front of the girls, her mount pawing the air.

"I am ready," Antilene said, not the least bit out of breath from her effort. "Show me what you have learned girls."

Czarinaea eagerly mounted and rode out to the appointed distance, before beginning her gallop toward Myrina, veering away at the very last minute because her sister had turned to the left, a common mistake that could have led to disaster. Antilene praised Czarinaea and chastised Myrina.

"I want you to do the pick-up with me," Antilene shouted, motioning to Czarinaea.

"You are too heavy!" her daughter protested, concerned that her mother would pull her from her animal on purpose, something she had seen her do many times to other girls because she felt they were not ready. "I will not be able to lift you!"

Her mother sat waiting, not going to any lengths to hide her impatience.

Tossing her head of jet black curls, Czarinaea turned up her strong chin and rode off to the appointed distance. Then, racing toward her mother in a hard gallop and reaching out one arm, she tightened her legs on her mount, and leaned to the left, at which time her mother smoothly landed behind Czarinaea and hugged her with affection.

"So," said her mother. "You are ready! It is not strength as I have told you before. It is skill."

It was an exciting moment for Czarinaea, and as she began to walk away from the arena she look forward to her sister joining her at the bathing pool where they usually met for their mid-day meal. Czarinaea was hoping Natila, the ancient one, would join them and continue her story of Artemis the forest nymph.

"Rina," called her mother as she walked her mount, stroking her neck lovingly. "I want to see you. Meet me at the stable. I have something important to tell you."

Czarinaea cringed, for her mother only called her Rina when the news would not be to her liking. The last time she called her Rina it was to tell her that the horse she had chosen was not the correct choice. It had been many hours of contemplation before she had remembered that a horse with four stockings was not a good mount, for the animal could be temperamental or bring ill luck. Czarinaea had taken many things into account, the animal's height, the spread of the nostrils, and the dip in the back, but yes… she had missed the stockings.

Alarmed by what her mother might have to say, she lingered at the hippo-dome as long as she reasonably could, only to find herself slammed into a wall of words as soon as she reached the stables.

"A match with a great Scythian leader has been set for you," Antilene said, throwing her shoulders back and taking a quick breath. "There will be much jealousy amongst the other girls, for he has *chosen* you. I am to announce it this very night, and want you to know that this is predestined, for though I have just had this news brought to me, the elders have whispered of just such a thing for a great long while now. You will be Queen to a legendary tribe. You…"

Seeing her daughter grow pale, Antilene's words froze on her lips.

Czarinaea's hands rose in a gesture resembling hopelessness as she reached for words, words that would allow her a life, words that would free her of the destiny her mother thought to be hers.

225

"Emetchi," she said softly, using the sacred term that meant great horsewoman. "I beg you do not do this! I want only to be a priestess, to study at the Temple at Ephesus. Mother, please reconsider," she pleaded, holding her breath.

Czarinaea waited, hoping …and then letting out her breath in a burst of energy she roared, "I will work harder! I will become the best, the very best rider! I will work each day with my bow. I will do anything." Czarinaea paused, her shoulders slumping as the life she had planned disappeared with a sense of longing. A last plea left her lips, as her voice cracked with tension and her heart constricted. "I want not a mate, the thought frightens me! You have none. Why must I?"

"This is not a punishment, but a great honor," Antilene told her. "It is because you are the best horsewoman and the most beautiful that you have been chosen I am sure!"

She had known that her daughter would balk at this arrangement, but she had also known that unless this bargain was sealed, a vast number of her clan would be killed. She had always been aware that Czarinaea was meant for great things since it had been predicted before her birth, and she had prayed to Goddess that she would do the right thing for her daughter. At this moment she was praying for patience, as she had no tolerance for disrespect.

"He is paying for me! That is it!" Czarinaea stood tall and looked with resolve into her mother's eyes, knowing it showed a lack of respect to look thus into the eyes of a warrior. Too late, she caught herself.

"You challenge me!" frustrated her mother shouted. "You dare to challenge me!"

Czarinaea stood tall for a moment longer, and then she bowed her head in surrender. "I will do as you bid," she murmured. "But I will die a little each day, for you have reached into my heart and squeezed out its life. You have put me in a cage and you want me to feel honored?"

Czarinaea waited to see if her mother would soften, but instead saw a determined look in her mother's eye.

"When I become esteemed," she said with cold rage washing over her, "and doubt not that it will happen, they will bow to me and say, 'I bring word of your mother' and I will tell them I have no mother! She died mid-day in the month of the long sun and I mourn her not!"

The hard, firm set of Czarinaea's jaw hid the fact that her heart was aching. She knew her mother could have her punished, even killed for her disrespect. She was aware also, that there was nothing else her mother could have asked that would have received such a response. For as long as she could remember she had wanted to study at the temple to become a priestess. Tears streamed down her cheeks as she turned and walked toward the river. She knew her mother was calling after her to attend the meeting at which the news would be announced that she was to mate with... she then realized she did not even know his name. What would it matter? She was dead inside. He would get an empty shell, a body, a warrior, not a mate... never a mate.

It came to her then that she would be expected to have children, and with the realization came the unbidden thought that if she had a daughter who treated her as she had just treated her mother...But no! She would never force a daughter of hers to mate, particularly as her own mother was doing now, to elicit payment in the form of gold or more horses. Yes, horses! Mother would stop at nothing to possess a valiant steed.

Czarinaea's stride slowed as she came to the end of the path. Dejectedly she sat down on a large stone. The water glistened in the afternoon sun, sending golden ripples of light toward the horizon. It was one of the most beautiful parts of the river, but today she did not notice. Instead, she found her eyes straying to the spot where she and Myrina had placed stones around the sides of a small inlet so it would not be muddy. They had worked hard stepping the stones to create a cascade of clean water which made a perfect bathing area. Suddenly, she felt a need to cleanse herself, to scrub herself of the deep feeling of betrayal that permeated every part of her being.

Taking off her tunic and short skirt, she picked up one of the stones that they used to rub themselves clean. When she gazed into the water, however, her reflection startled her. It had been some time since she noticed her looks. She remembered two summers ago when her kin Fiona had said they would get her into trouble. Now, she looked hard and long at the reflection of her light silky skin. Dark curls softly moved in the slight breeze, setting off her high cheek bones. Deep dark eyes with golden highlights that others always said sparkled when she laughed, were now looking back at her with grief.

Her tears created ripples in the clear water. As the pond once more became a mirror a beautiful goddess appeared behind her, the same goddess that appeared in her dreams. She had told Czarinaea once that she was her spirit guide and she had helped her many times by showing her future events.

"You have no business here!" Czarinaea cried. "You could have warned me. You could have helped me." And then, through gritted teeth, "Go away, and don't come back, ever!"

Great sobbing sounds penetrated the air and the water beneath her feet. She had sent away the only one who came to comfort her and there was no one to hear the heartbreak as it echoed off the stones, and vibrated through the trees.

Walking away from the bathing area, the look of a child was gone. In its place was a new found aloofness and poise that some spend a lifetime to acquire.

⚜

The next year went by exceptionally fast. She was to wed Marmareus on the feast of Ma-Cybele, the great Goddess of life and she had yet to meet him, though he had seen her a year past and been so smitten that he had offered fifty horses for her. To be fair to her mother, Czarinaea knew that this marriage was to keep peace between their tribes; she wanted that, it was *most* important to her… but it came at such a high price.

The wedding day was fast approaching. Czarinaea's friend Lotzar gave her a big hug and headed for the door, knowing that the sisters needed to spend time together because they would soon be parting.

Czarinaea broke the silence that invaded the room when the door closed behind her loving and boisterous friend.

"He is a goat," she said to Myrina, sounding worldly "and an old goat at that! I will be bored and repulsed by him," Czarinaea said, giving an involuntary shudder.

"He has become famous for his bravery and wealth," Myrina pouted. "If I were fair like you and had the world offered to me I would not be so brazen and foolish to repeat such words aloud. I dream on each full moon that a warrior such as he comes for me. It is so romantic," she sighed. "He has no other wives, your king, though it is his right. You must have made quite an impression!" declared Myrina, making a face at Czarinaea.

"Watch that you do not get what you dream!" Czarinaea warned her. "I know for certain that 'my king' is no bargain. Mind you what Natila teaches comes from the Temple. She told us that when our dreams of the day become dreams of the night we cast a circle in which our dreams take on life and come back to us." Czarinaea closed her eyes as if she was trying to remember something.

"I have an idea," she cried. "I shall cast a circle and bring a lover to me. He will worship me and bow at my feet. He will change my life so that I will be free, but I will have a choice and I will choose the Temple. He will ne're love again and he will die for he cannot have me." Czarinaea turned, beginning to cast her sacred circle.

"Oh no!" said her sister in horror. "Natila warns us against wishes such as that. You heard only half of what she said. She has been clear that if we wish harshness on others, so comes it back. My ears tell me that you are willing to give one misery for another. But my heart tells me you must recant those thoughts and give over your service as warrior and mate to Marmareus."

"I give over my shield unto his battles," Czarinaea grumbled, "I have been trained well. It is not within me to give my heart to him. If it were my way, all men would be taking care of the house duties and the children. They will never match the Hippodules in battle, for females are born to horses the way a man could never be."

She stood up to go. "Come," she said. "It is time to see the garment I will wear in the ceremony. Someone needs to be excited, this way you can get more seeding for your dreams. I will tell you thus," she added, tossing her head, "I have seen you riding a magnificent mount by the side of a king. So wish not for a man like mine. Wish instead for one who is gentle and kind."

"You have had a vision!" squealed Myrina, overjoyed that her sister could have envisioned something about her that was so grand.

Czarinaea pointed to her forehead in between the eyes. "Three nights past I saw it clear. Besides, you know that I have had numerous visions. Most seem to happen in my dreams now, particularly since I told my spirit guide to never visit me again."

"You didn't!" Myrina exclaimed. "Why would you do that?" And then, seeing Czarinaea's frozen stare she said instead, "Your visions have helped many of the girls make the right decisions regarding their futures. Oh Rin, I am so sorry that you are leaving. I do know it is hard to see the happy fates of others when you are so miserable."

"Yes, I have always asked that the goddess give me visions to help the women of our clan know their purpose. Though, when I ask for my purpose, I am told to await my destiny!" Czarinaea's eyes crinkled at the corners as she pondered this seeming unfairness.

"I know how upset you are and I know that you didn't mean to wish harm. Please take it back so that I won't worry about you," Myrina pleaded.

"It is too late; it was a night dream. You reminded me when you spoke of yours. Now that I have put it to words in the day, it will come full circle. It has already begun. Pray to Goddess Cybele to light my way." Head held high she walked proudly toward the door.

"I have changed my mind, you go look at the dress. I am going to my arena," she said. "I need to be alone."

"Rin, do you ever go to the waterfall in the forest? You know, where you first saw the beautiful goddess?"

"No, I never go there anymore! What good is learning about magical things from my spirit guide if I cannot go to the temple? I will not need magic with my husband, but I am sure I will need a strong stomach!"

Chapter 2

Calm, quiet and poised, Czarinaea sat at the window overlooking the harshly cut road winding through the misty marshland, watching as the great Scythian tribe rode into their encampment.

"Rin, you must find the gift I have hidden," Myrina said with a broad smile. "It is bad luck if you do not find it before the wedding today, therefore you know I have not hidden it well."

Czarinaea glanced fondly at her sister knowing that she might never see her again. As she looked within her eyes she saw an in-dwelling truth residing there. She thought her beautiful, and kind. She was, Czarinaea knew, a feeler, a lover, and a dreamer, not fit for the valor that was expected from all in their clan. Myrina wished only be a wife and dreamt of the marriage bed as something precious. Well... it might be for her, after all in her visions Czarinaea had seen her sister riding in a precession, proudly looking at a man who seemed to be a king...

"Do not make excuses," Myrina said, interrupting her reverie impatiently, "for you are not busy. You've done nothing but sit at that window and gaze. What is it you seek?"

"Perhaps I seek the man who will change my destiny," Czarinaea told her. "I speak not of my husband-to-be, as you well know. The one I seek will be young and handsome and have passion coursing through his veins."

"How do you know this is not the case put before you? You have never met Marmareus and do not know his age."

"Because I have had a vision and I know that when I meet this man, I will be wed to another," startled from her poise, as the powerful vision invaded her consciousness again, Czarinaea declared, "Oh! He is in a battle *against* us," she muttered. "He is not one of my husband's warriors."

With slow purpose in her movement, Czarinaea rose from the window-seat, her voice desolate of emotion and said, "There is no use waiting to catch a glimpse of him for twill not be today I catch his eye."

Myrina, shrugging dejectedly, went to the hiding place under the matting on her bed.

"Here," Myrina said sadly, holding up a small carved horse hanging on a thin piece of hemp. "Let me put it around your neck. Perhaps it will protect you." But even as she said the words, Myrina wondered if anything could protect Czarinaea from her anger and her disappointment in life.

Lotzar poked her head around the door and told them the ceremony was beginning. Czarinaea's robe was a light coffee color and around her slim waist she wore her golden Amazon girdle which, like an un-scalable wall, represented her virgin status as a warrior.

The ceremony took place under a laurel oak. And when she met her bridegroom, nothing about Marmareus's bulk, long unkempt hair and beard startled her, nor did his gruff unctuous personality and grating voice. Endless nights of distressing visions had prepared her for his crusty manner. Observing the scars above his eyebrows, she was sure they were well deserved.

When Mareus, the head councilman of the abhorrent man standing beside her, came forward with knife drawn, Czarinaea and Marmareus put forth their hands. Mareus lightly ran his sharp knife over their palms until their blood flowed freely. He then held their hands, pressed together above their heads for all to see, indicating that the marriage was now official. It was the custom to remove the girdle at this part of the ceremony, as this bespoke honor and obedience to the new mate.

Her hands visibly trembling, Czarinaea removed the belt and handed it to her mother who raised it high, sealing her daughter's fate. The crowd cheered, and music came out of nowhere while their guests danced and waved their hats in the air, Czarinaea, seeking silence, climbed the oak tree and watched from her perch as if to distance herself from the inevitable.

As a bride of only one day, she vowed to count the nights that she did not have to pay her wifely duties as rainbows in an otherwise dark dismal sky. Those nights would be something to look forward to, just as had the reprieve she enjoyed last night. Neither the bride nor the groom was in good humor after the long celebration following the marriage. He blessedly had passed out, and Czarinaea, desperate to be alone and having had a bit too much mead, stumbled through the woods and ended up spending her night sitting under a large oak, staring at the stars wishing she could will herself to become one with them.

Czarinaea had known she was going to be required to take off her Amazon girdle when it was announced that she had become his queen, but head held high, put it back on just before she and her husband left for their journey to the Scythian camp. Czarinaea did not look back as they rode away from her childhood home. The gloom of the cloudy sunless day echoed the depth of emptiness in her heart.

Husband and wife had little conversation on their journey. When they had ridden nearly a full day Marmareus told her that the capital city of the Scythians was called Tanais, and it was located on the mouth of the Sea of Azov. He then said, sounding cocky and sure of himself, that she reminded him of the Azov from the moment he had first seen her. Like the sea she was still and calm on the surface, but he knew that underneath was tumultuous and powerful, and he vowed that day to own her.

Czarinaea had not looked at him fully until that moment.

"No one can own a sea for it belongs to itself, just as no one can own me!" she declared, looking him straight in the eyes, waiting for him to rebuff her words.

A low rumble accompanied the predacious words she had expected.

"There is nothing that I have wanted that I have not come to own," he told her, "and that includes you!"

There was a queenly tilt to Czarinaea's head as she ignored her husband's words and sat taller on the Arabian mount she rode. Seventeen hands tall, he had bragged as he insisted she ride it, hoping no doubt, to make her uncomfortable riding a steed that was unpredictable and hard to handle. However, the opposite had proved to be true, as she easily rose to the challenge of the head-strong animal.

Marmareus had attempted to get the upper hand by complaining about the fact that she insisted on continuing to wear the girdle that represented her status as an unmarried woman. Making it quite clear that she would not remain a virgin long, he began discussing children. When she stated that the child belongs to the woman as it has always been and that the royal blood passes from mother to child, he practically unseated her from her mount.

"You will honor me in all things!" He shouted loudly enough for his entourage of men to hear. "It is by my good graces that your village still stands. I could have sacked it a year ago, taken what I wanted and left ashes. I have instead given horses and left an open invitation to the Emetchi to come and take part in our war games."

"You say the word!" she spat at him, "but you do not understand it!"

"What word do you speak of, my dear?" He mocked her, clearly delighted that this banter should enrage her.

"Emetchi! You are not worthy to utter this sacred word. Emetchi means honored horsewoman. It carries with it an understanding that a woman is strong, independent, and sacred! You think women are part of your rule and treat them like slaves!"

"That is untrue since, as you can plainly see, the slaves are walking, the warriors are riding. You, my lovely, are riding; therefore you are considered a warrior and my wife, not a slave. Twill be changes if you are not of the nature of minding your manners."

"You see, that is just what I am speaking of. If I do not behave I am punished!"

His voice was thunderous as he cut her off. "I punish my warriors if they needs be, and any continuance of this insolence will bring the lash upon your back."

He lunged, swinging his powerful arm at her back, nearly unseating her again, but only managing to hurt her pride as his unmerciful laughter caught the attention of his men. Leering at her they shouted praises for their leader.

When Czarinaea pulled on the reins, the Arabian balked. Leaning down to pet the animal she whisper in his ear, and was able to easily pull him out of line and with head held high went back to ride beside the slave guard. I will not be bullied! she thought. The next time he tries to unseat me I shall be ready for him!

Reaching for Myrina's gift, which had been such a blessing during the chaos of these last few days, she rubbed her thumb over the small wooden horse hanging on a piece of hemp which she wore around her neck, reminding herself that it was made of ash, one of the sacred trees of the goddess. "Preserve me as you preserve all those who seek comfort in your limbs," she prayed as she felt the wood heat under her fingers. It was three days journey to their destination and she thanked the goddess for the reprieve of her wifely duties.

The Scythian city was teeming with life. Small wooden carts and horses were everywhere and street vendors were hawking their wares. Fish mongers called out, "Buy fish, dry fish or have a harsh and hungry winter."

There was time yet before winter, Czarinaea thought, glad of the reprieve from the cold. Taking a closer look at the large amount of food being stored, she spoke to the man riding beside her.

"Apparently there is a war brewing?"

"Yes, but then there is always a war brewing," he said nodding towards the overflowing grain shack at the end of the lane.

Czarinaea intuitively began to pick up his discontent, his worry about his family and the love he had for his children. Then she felt his shame at taking orders from a man such as Marmareus. As she wondered why he would be a slave guard, the realization came to her that he was, no doubt, their only hope since he alone treated them as human beings. And he shared her contempt for her husband. She was certain of it.

Czarinaea reminded herself that the Scythians would not take lightly to her feelings and visions. She had thought that she had put that part of herself away. But the visions, though not as often, had continued, although thankfully her spirit guide had been absent. Seeing her was a painful reminder of just how little control she had over her own life.

When Marmareus rode up beside her, her companion, casting him a scornful look, took his leave, taking her brief insights with him, and leaving her to the grandiosity of the man whom she had married, a man who was interested only in pointing out the greatness of his holdings.

Loathing the fact that the trip had ended, she decided she would settle in this city and await her fate. Hesitantly she dismounted and noticed that their home was spacious compared to the huts and make-do shelter that many of the warriors called home. She was also surprised that some of the warriors had patches of grain growing alongside their small abodes. A few of the huts had millet and corn growing, as well as numerous grazing goats. She had heard that some grew it to sell and trade. The Scythians were known as a nomad tribe, but she could see that there was stability to this village. It seemed that many were putting down roots.

Her new home must have taken a great deal of time and men to build. Bones that came from the mammoths of ages past had been used to interlace the structure with strength. These bones displayed carvings depicting the Scythian warriors on horseback with their short bows defending themselves in battle. The shapely women in the etchings were adorned with golden jewelry, lounging on what seemed to be comfortable beds. Well that sums it up, Czarinaea mused. She had now joined the ranks of the amply endowed, well taken care of, healthily fed and completely bored Scythian women.

Marmareus gloated as he showed her around the five rooms that they would call home. Forcefully he pushed and shoved his servant-slaves out of his way, and proudly pointed out that there was a fire-pit in each room in worship of Tabiti, the goddess of the hearth. Czarinaea, stunned that the Scythians worshipped a goddess, was just about to ask about it when Marmareus pointed out that two of the rooms had ovens. All thoughts of his goddess worship left her head as she stood thinking, "I hope he doesn't expect me to cook!"

Later that evening when Marmareus came to her bed, cooking was the least of her worries. He raped her repeatedly, reminding her when she struggled that the safety of her clan resided only in his good graces.

When he finally fell asleep, Czarinaea inched her way out from underneath the vast bulk of her husband, every part of her body aching from his abuse. Though she felt the marriage bed was something she would have to endure, even in her wildest dreams she could never have thought any man could be so cruel.

Her fingers edged to her throat, thinking by her touch she could relieve some of the pain. Continuing to move slowly toward the edge of the bed, she lifted his arm gingerly. Just as she thought she had achieved freedom, she heard a low and menacing growl, and a hand snaked its way to her throat.

"If I send you back for not being a wife to me, then you'll go back stone cold," he told her. "Your funeral pyre will ignite the night sky, and your family, friends and beloved horses will burn at the altar of your shame."

Each word was accentuated by his lethal pressure on her neck. He moved, slowly controlling her with his weight and his legs on her thighs as he entered her swollen womanhood again, clearly relishing her discomfort. He took his time, telling her in detail what he did to the slave-women as he made their husbands watch. He also gloated about the wives of his men, and how they welcomed him to their homes and beds as he made his rounds.

More than two years had passed. Marmareus was gone much of the time. Czarinaea was able to achieve a small amount of happiness when he was absent and did not care that he populated the surrounding villages with children.

Their clan had fought in a few small skirmishes, and had won, which added to the size of their holdings and brought new warriors to their tribe or slaves for the menial tasks.

Their marriage was a battle ground in which Marmareus constantly fought to hold the upper hand. Czarinaea patiently waited, and watched him slowly lose the respect of his people through his callous treatment of her, his abusive nature with his slaves and his disgusting dishonor with his house servants.

Czarinaea spent her days training the warriors in the methods of battle taught to her by her mother. The Scythian warriors in turn taught her how to use the short bow that their tribe was famous for. Most of the warriors became her friends. They never talked to her about the scratches and bruises that she did not acquire in the mock battles they fought with her, but they spoke of it among themselves. They knew from their interactions with her that no man could get the better of her unless she allowed it, and spoke among themselves of her enormous love for her clan and great respect for her mother, though she refused to talk about her. Many had asked her to tell stories about the conquests of the tribe that most men called the Amazons. She regaled them with details of battles and amazing stunts on horseback but never referred to the leader as her mother, only Antilene. When asked if Antilene was her mother, a desolate quiet sadness tinged her solemn words, *"I have no mother."*

⁓⁂⁓

Marmareus was on one of his excursions, and had been gone just long enough to allow Czarinaea time to relax into his absence, when he stormed through the door yelling at the top of his voice.

"You have made a fool out of me for the last time! Come, show yourself and be made aware you've gone too far!"

Czarinaea heard him but chose to ignore his shouts of anger since she was being fitted for a new breast-plate and helmet preparing for the battle that was sure to come.

Finding her in the sleeping quarters, half undressed, with a man tugging at her belt and talking under his breath, he realized that she was being fitted for armor. His anger was replaced with lust, which, Czarinaea knew, was also fueled by rage, because of the fact that she so often vexed him.

"You called for me?" asked Czarinaea, showing little interest. "As you can see I am not dressed to greet you."

His anger rose again, for she never greeted him. It was always he who had to search her out.

"You have injured one of my men and you have made a fool out of me for the last time!"

"We were just sparring," Czarinaea said, as if speaking to a child, "just having a bit of fun, when the others circled around us. He changed his approach and came at me with full strength. T'was only in protection of myself that I threw him and that he landed hard on his arm. He knows better than it, for he's been trained by the best."

Marmareus, no doubt thinking that she referred to him, preened and softened for the moment.

"I've schooled them all in how to fall." Czarinaea continued. "It's not like he does not know. It's just that he's not remembering. How can you put the blame upon me?"

Her words enraged him and he came at her. As the fitter ducked and flew out of the room, she dodged his outstretched arms, and moving behind him, kicked at the back of his knee. When he fell, hitting his head on the wooden frame of their pallet, she was on top of him before he could move, pinning his arms to the floor with her legs, in a vice-like grip. Taking her knife, she reached under his neck with one hand and placed the flat of her knife to his throat with the other. She could have easily slit his throat and she knew that although he was dazed he was very aware of this fact.

"There you see!" she cried, pushing herself off quickly and jumping away, "You see my talents. Why should I be punished for something that is such a benefit to you?" Moving towards the hallway, she shouted back over her shoulder. "I am a great asset to you in battle! I am fine proof of how your wife supports you and rides by your side."

Leaving the house quickly, fully aware that this time she had gone too far, she thought to give him time to cool down.

"I will serve you if only you will tell me what needs doing," gasped one of the house servants, running along behind her. "Is it a horse you need, Emetchi? I'll be quick about it... but we are going the wrong way if I may say so."

Czarinaea stopped and looked thoughtfully at the old man. He was stooped and somewhat slow; remnants of vigor were just a spark in his eye. She thought with longing about her mother and how servant-slaves were always chasing after her with remarkable reverence. She had, she realized, never acknowledged how like her mother she was. But did she have her capacity to love? And though she was still angry with her, she had to admit that she had come to miss her mother's strong affectionate nature.

Noise and confusion roared through the roadway where they stood. She looked down the dirt street and saw a Gewgaw tradesman hacking his wares. All manner of items were displayed, many were on a blanket, but some special items were on a small roughly built table.

"Come," she said to the old man as they approached one of the street stalls where tradesmen were hawking their wares. "I want to buy a talisman for good luck in the battle to come."

Her thoughts were heavy. She fingered the wooden horse hanging around her neck with leather and thought how much she missed her sister, her family. Touching her belly and remembering the fear of being with child two moons past, made her shiver. Fortunately, she now had herbs that would avert any such problem in the future. She knew Marmareus would kill her if he knew, but she had no intention of having his child.

The hawker bowed low in deference to her station as the wife of the King.

"I am looking for a talisman that will bring me good luck with this conflict that is leading us to battle," she said firmly.

"Yes, yes, this one would be just the thing. It will keep you safe." The one that the tradesman pointed to did not entice her, so she looked over the selection that was being offered. A gold covered quiver appealed to her, and she picked it up to inspect it further, but decided against it. Gold jewelry was abundant but she had no thought to adorn herself with it, which would indicate she was the property of a Scythian man. A cold chill ran through her again, but she gave herself solace with the knowledge that she was not his pawn in the matter of children.

Czarinaea's breath caught as she spotted an emerald that was shaped like a tear. It was set in a semicircle of gold; it was a perfect crescent moon.

"It is this!" she said picking it up. "I must have it."

The tradesman was horrified. "No…No! This has a curse! Please," he said reaching for it. "It is meant for a woman who would steal a man from another woman. It would not bring you happiness."

But although he pointed to an array of mammoth bone bracelets and amulets with intricate woven designs which were indeed handsome, Czarinaea knew it was the crescent moon she had to have. Picking it up again and placing it in the palm of her hand, she moved it to catch the last glint of fading sunlight. Mesmerized by its feel, she turned again to the hawker.

"Shush… do you really believe in such things?" she demanded, and seeing the tradesman's face turn ashen, could see that to purchase the talisman would mean rumors flying to the ears of the King.

"You are quite right. It is the first one I need," said Czarinaea, respectfully placing the amulet down on the table. "You are right, of course." She looked toward the servant who was still trying to catch his breath. "Pay him please and we'll be off, for the sun is setting and it is time to sup."

As she and the servant slowly walked back to the house, she was hoping that Marmareus' temper had cooled. Her thoughts went back to the grudging respect that the tradesman had shown her. But that thought made her realize that the slaves and servants that had come to know her and many of the warriors also now treated her with something close to admiration. There had been quite a change since she first came to the clan. She realized that she liked the challenge of earning the respect of these proud and arrogant men.

Czarinaea moved even slower as they began walking on the wide horse path that led to her door. The servant, who looked tired, no doubt anxious to return to his quarters and hoping to avoid the king's anger, also slowed his walk and asked if there was anything else she needed.

Taking a deep breath as she entered the house, Czarinaea told herself that tomorrow she would send her faithful friend Lotzar to the hawker, and that the charm would soon be hers, and no one, not even her husband, would be the wiser. Oh, she could already see it in her mind's eye. The crescent moon hanging from a piece of leather, lying in the soft hollow of her neck, sitting elegantly high above her armor, and glistening in the bright morning sun as she rode into battle.

Chapter 3

"Well, do not keep me waiting. I want to put it on!" Czarinaea scolded impatiently. "I must see how it feels."

Lotzar twirled around, showing quite a bit of leg as she imitated her flirtatious manner with the tradesman.

"I must tell you the story first," she said, affecting a respectful bow. "Surely you can wait a quick moment my queen."

They both fell on the bed laughing at Lotzar's attempt to act like a servant. The only child of their housemaid, she and Czarinaea, being the same age, had become the best of friends. They had learned to ride together, though when it came to hunting, Lotzar said she would rather cook and clean, even if no one had ever seen her do either. It seemed she was good at telling stories that entertained, and at flirting with the male servants, which in turn, got her anything she wanted.

"You begged to come with me, to be a servant, therefore you should be submissive and hand over the necklace." Czarinaea laughed until she finally had to hold her side at the sight of her friend bowing to her 'queen' and talking as a servant would.

"Lotzar, do you even know how to be a servant?"

With a sparkle in her eye Lotzar said, "I know much about being a friend! The rest I can acquire."

Czarinaea's renewed laughter brought tears as she realized that she was friendless except for this incredible girl. Lotzar had such integrity, she thought, and would zealously protect her in any situation. Had her mother not sent her to me, she reminded herself, she would be alone in this bedlam of men while they preen themselves and war at the drop of a hat. Then again I've heard of tribes of women that are just as bloodthirsty, but the Emetchi only fight to protect themselves or others that are being taken advantage of. Unbidden thoughts of her mother emerged like a bolt of lightning winding its way through a dark murky sky. She reached for her friend and cried in her arms. There was no need to say a word.

Lotzar recognized the pain, for she also carried a deep longing for her mother and their homeland. Then, taking Czarinaea's hand, she lovingly placed the necklace in her palm.

Pushing her raven curls off her face and wiping her tears, Czarinaea stood and put the amulet gingerly around her neck. Composing herself she remembered the last time she had cried; it was at the bathing pool. She was very aware that crying marked periods of great change in her life. Reaching for the talisman, she painfully realized that the crescent moon that harbored a tear shaped emerald was hanging in the very spot from whence came the warrior's cry.

She touched her finger to her bottom lip and felt a slight quiver. A soft, sad "hippa, hippa," the cry that female warriors make when entering the battle field, involuntarily passed through her lips. She knew that for her, all of this was a battle and she must not weaken. Her dream of going to the temple would never come to pass, but she was to serve in another way. Her visions told her that she was to lead men and women alike, and that her name would linger long after she was dead and buried. She would be known as a woman that was fair and brave. She was not sure how she felt about the visions, but she was aware that they always proved themselves to be true.

Both women, sisters of the blood, walked out into the herb garden and gazed up at the moon. It was waxing... a golden crescent that looked exactly like the amulet that Czarinaea wore. They both knew it was an omen.

Marmareus woke her from slumber, roughly shaking her shoulder.

"The Medes are riding north. We can intercept them," he told her. "The surprise will leave them at our mercy. Come! It is time to ride."

Because he had been telling her for days to be at the ready, her tunic and belt were at her bedside. Lifting her breastplate and her new shield, untouched as yet by battle, she suddenly envisioned a scene in which she *was sitting beside a man who she knew to be her teacher. He was lovingly handing her a shimmering golden shield that had been intricately designed by him.*

Stunned by the premonition, she stared at the protective shield in her hand. Today she was going to meet the man that had fashioned for her a shield in another life. Panic rose, yet her heart pounded. Slipping excitedly into the armor, she moved quickly and steadily behind Marmareus. The knowing smile that passed her lips seemed to heighten the importance of the premonition, as it dangled intrigue before her.

The horse handlers stood outside the gate, the scouts already in the saddle anxiously awaiting the king with news of the enemies' position. The king was excited. This would lead to the eventual fall of Media, a prized city. He would kill and take the heads of the leaders, and plunder their goods. He could taste victory. It was his. On entering the open countryside they were joined by more than a thousand Scythian warriors.

They rode steadily all day, and when it was time to make camp Czarinaea rode off in the direction the scout had taken earlier in the day, knowing full well that Marmareus would doubtless fall into a rage and send someone after her. But if he did, the man did not find her and when at last she returned and crawled into the space where her mate was feigning sleep, he pointedly ignored her.

"They have changed direction." said Czarinaea matter-of-factly. "They come toward us. Our fires are out so they will not spot us this night. On the morrow we will meet them on the field of battle."

He did not move nor ask her how she knew this, and she knew that, no doubt, he was ruing the day he had seen her by the river and that he was damming her as a brazen hussy, no doubt because he knew she was right, and hated her for it. His scouts had fallen for the misleading clues that the Medes had left.

Czarinaea was up before the sun crested the horizon to tell the men to be very quiet and to eat dried food. There would be no fire. Small groups of them were being told of the new development and it passed to all the warriors. They now knew that there was no way to surprise the Medes. The call was given and they rode out forty abreast in the direction she had indicated.

The scout came toward them, shame in his eyes, and turned to retrace his path. Marmareus, Czarinaea and a small party followed him to the top of a precipice where they stopped and took in the scene below. Seeing perhaps five hundred well armed men galloping toward them,

Marmareus told the small gathering to ride back and have the troops split and ride around the small hill they stood on. They would take the enemy from the east and westerly flank.

"East first. Let them think that is all we have. We outnumber them. Keep this in mind!" he shouted to the party as they rode off.

King Marmareus was known for his battlefield strategy. Many times he had surprised his enemy. This time the tide was turned, however, and he was not pleased.

"Shall we ride together or should I take the west group and ---"

He cut her off. "We ride together, my queen by my side. Is that not what you have told me, dear queen?"

Brazenly the enemy came from the east, battle cries and the beat of war drums filling the air. King and Queen rode neck and neck, spurring their horses on, keeping a keen eye on everything happening around them. The sound of metal on metal wrenched the air as armor was struck by arrows and swords. Horses cried out as they careened into each other and the heavy sounds of bodies hitting the ground rent the early morning dew.

Czarinaea moved through the throng of horse flesh, deftly defying many who sought to bring her down simply because she rode beside the King. Her maneuvers took her to the middle of the battle, where she attacked the most mighty of the warriors, swiftly unhorsing him just before a sharp blow to her head from behind stunned her. She fell forward as her horse reared up from a brutal injury to his neck.

Momentarily dazed, her world threatening to go black, she swayed and felt something sharp enter her side above her belt. Looking down she saw that a dagger had penetrated in an upward thrust just under her armor. Weak as she was, she tried to focus on pulling it out. Knowing that she was not going to be able to stay astride much longer she pulled the reins hard to move away from the middle of the battlefield. Her horse in pain, reared up again, pawing the air.

She fell hard, and although she tried to roll to her feet, horses and men seemed to be taking every inch of ground. Then, suddenly, Czarinaea felt herself being pulled out of the mayhem. As the battle continued she went limp, giving in to the weakness that had threatened and to the safety she felt in the arms that surrounded her. A face appeared before her, and a voice, seemingly from a distance, asked where she was hurt. Gentle hands knowingly prodded her body for injuries.

I've seen those eyes in a vision, she thought. But everything in her world was hazy. Those eyes! Why couldn't she remember where she had seen them before? She struggled to remain conscious, but little by little the scene before her became a distant play, the sounds lost their shrill tones and then complete blackness engulfed her.

During the next few days Czarinaea was semi-conscious for small periods of time, only half aware of the people around her. The smells were different and the small bits of food that she was fed seemed spicier than the normal fare. She did not feel frightened, for the dreams she was having were so delightful. She had over-heard the remark more than once that she was out of her head, but if that was what this was, it was glorious.

She immersed herself in the enticing inner vision she was having. The sights and sounds and colors were more vivid than anything she had ever encountered. Out from the brilliant hues rode a superbly handsome man, who was racing beside her, and both were laughing at the fact that she had won.

Not wanting the vision to end, she squeezed her eyes shut to deny the outer world and willed it to continue. Moving in a haze of vibrant colors, she saw herself and the handsome man diving under sparkling azure water, playing like children. When they emerged from the water they were naked and he was throwing colorful flowers at her feet. Drawn to his mesmerizing eyes, she recognized that this was the man who had taken her from the battle field. Oh those eyes! Had she brought him to her with her foolish magic? She recalled her sister's warning.

"No, no!" she cried, beginning to struggle violently until, sitting bolt upright, she attempted to leave the pallet where she was lying only to be gently forced down again. Those strong arms, she realized, belonged to the one that had been in her visions all along. Desperately she tried to erase her youthful folly.

Her forehead was being bathed with cold water and the voice that spoke lulled her to sleep again, a voice like the sounds of a gentle river on a still day.

In her dreams, she heard herself say, "I cannot do this! I am queen and I will lead the people. They depend on me. I must be strong. No man can hold my heart for it would bind me. I have not come into this life to serve a man. I've come to free women from oppression and cruelty and to stop the destruction of the sacred shrines of the Goddess."

But even as she said the words, she knew that she hadn't been doing as she had promised. But who was it that she had promised? A goddess! The name on her lips was Diana.

"I've promised…I've promised. She sent me on a mission," As her dreams, her visions and her waking time seemed to run together, she began to worry that she was out of her head.

But far worse than the fears of being delusional were the moments of absolute certainty that she was awake and everyone that came and went from her room had halos around them. The man, the beautiful man with soulful eyes had bright gold around his head and rich verdant green around his body. It was startling to see how strong the colors in his aura were when compared to others that she saw. But see them she did and it was frightening. Yet there was awareness on a deeper level that it meant something. She searched for answers and finding none she wondered if her spirit guide would help … and *then* she realized she wasn't speaking to her. She felt desolate and alone and thrashed about on the pallet seeking forgiveness, even though she had no knowledge of whom or what she was asking forgiveness of.

Czarinaea felt strong arms around her, but did not know if it was a dream or if he was really holding her. It was so extraordinarily comforting that she did not want it to end. She cried out, "Goddess you want too much of me. I cannot do this thing you ask, truly I cannot! Do not ask, do not…"

Her voice drifted off as she slowly slipped into a deep healing sleep.

⛤

Holding her, Stryangaeus called out to one of the house boys to come and help him.

"Gaylor, bring a new pallet and follow me." He lifted her gently and carried her outside.

The teachings of the Goddess say the light of the Sun is healing he thought to himself, as he walked toward the river remembering his mother's words, "a clean pallet and lots of water and mashed berries from the Golden Rod tree will hasten healing." He had given the cook the precise instructions for creating the potion.

When Gaylor laid the pallet where his master had instructed, Stryangaeus tenderly laid her down. Holding a pouch of coriander seeds he wet them in the river and put them on her wound. This was his favorite spot on the river. He would keep her here till the setting of the sun. Perhaps when she woke, she would not be so frightened.

Gaylor, fascinated by his master's concern for his enemy, stood staring, his blond hair sticking up like hay and his freckled face red from his exertion of bringing the bed. Stryangaeus knew this young man cared for him. He recognized the fear and confusion in his eyes and he soothingly put his hand out and ruffled the young man's head.

"It's alright Gaylor. Go to the cook hall and see if the medicinal tea is ready, and if so bring it to me. After that perhaps you could fish for our supper. Would you like that?"

⁓⁂⁓

For three days, having carried her outside into the sun, Stryangaeus sat by her side at the river, as he sang the lullabies that he had heard his mother sing to the babes that were born after him. Remembering with his mother hardly cold in her grave, his father had been busy with the house servant. The only justice was that she had died in childbirth too. He remembered that he and his sister attended her, for none of the midwives hurried to her side. Some even claimed that his father's wench had given poison to his mother to get her out of the way.

Yes t'was father's way to charm the ladies, Stryangaeus mused, as he glanced down at the beautiful woman lying by his side. His olive skin and light hair glistening in the sunlight was a stark contrast to her pale skin and deep blue/black curls wet from his efforts to wash away the blood. He gently placed his hand on her shoulder, trying to move himself away from the direction of his thoughts. But they still plagued him.

What on earth was he doing here with this woman? How was it that she had won his heart as no one else had been able to do, and yet she had not even spoken his name? What was to come of this? He was wed, and she belonged to another.

Stretching seductively like a sleek mountain cat, her muscled body rippling under her light clothing, Czarinaea stirred from her long slumber, her whispered breathe a deep purr of contentment.

She had inspired his heart, and now the sight of her awakening tore through his body. Passion came like thunder out of a darkness he did not know he possessed. She is weak in body and spirit, he thought, I can' nor slake my passion upon her....

Chapter 9

Golden embers danced in the dark depths of Czarinaea's eyes as she looked deep into those of the man she had seen in her visions. Running her tongue over her lips she opened her mouth as if to speak, but found she could not.

When Stryangaeus took his index finger and traced her full lips, she did not move, nor did she turn away from him when he wetted his middle finger in his mouth, even though the moisture from his finger on her lips created hot wet heat in her woman-hood. Instinctively she reached for him, and they melted together. Their hearts recognized ancient flames of desire, dancing in a circle of forever. It was the perfect merging of one body, one essence and one heart. When he entered her, she cried tears of such deep sadness, tears of longing that she had only dreamed of, tears of release, of coming home in some way that she could not fathom.

Czarinaea felt herself lifting from her body. Above, in spirit she watched the bodies below. Observing the tenderness and in awe of the passion that raged through her, she recognized she was observing and feeling the heat of the union all in the same moment. She did not want the moment to end, for if it did, she was not sure it would be possible to make sense of what was happening to her.

When the lovers, sated, lay side by side with hands entwined, Czarinaea finally spoke.

"I was once betrothed to a man whose name I did not know," she told him. "And now I am besotted by a man who has not shared his name, but somehow has given me an understanding of the depths of who he is and the measure of the man he has always been. My good sense tells me that if we part now our lives would be easier. My heart tells me I must know everything about you, even before you tell me your name. Do this for me. Tell me of your life. Tell me every bit of it, all that you can remember."

Stryangaeus said, "I will if only you do the same, for I want to know your life, to hold its essence in my hands and feel every nuance. Just as I have felt the immeasurable spirit of your body, I must feel the boundless spirit of your life."

And so they talked for hours, lying side by side. She told him of every vision she had had, including the ones in which she had seen him. Czarinaea hesitantly told him about seeing an aura around some people when she was a child. But now the colors were brilliant and she could see them around everyone, which only happened since the injury on the battle field. She asked him if he thought there was something wrong with her eyes.

"No, quite the contrary," he assured her. "My mother saw color around everything, trees, flowers and people alike. She said that it gave her secret information about plants for making herbs and important information about people, whether they were good or bad."

Then he happily shared with her how his mother had taught him of the culture of the goddess and always let him know that prophecy was a sacred and holy event.

"Did your mother have lots of visions? Did she have a spirit guide? Did your father believe in, well...you know?"

"Have you always felt you could not speak of these things to a man? I'm sorry for it if you have, but now you know that you can talk to me of these things."

Stryangaeus stroked her face tenderly, enamored of the golden sparks in her eyes.

"To answer your questions, yes, mother had lots of visions. I don't know what a spirit guide is, so I suppose my mother didn't have one. And no, my father only believed in himself, and in gold, which was very sad. He missed out in life, because he never knew what love was, though my mother loved him well."

They spoke about their childhoods, their beliefs and their friends. At one point, he ordered a meal and Gaylor came and merrily laid it out for them, all the while stealing covet looks at his master's prisoner, and giving her a shy smile when she asked his name, but he seemed reluctant to speak.

"This is Gaylor," Stryangaeus said proudly putting his hand on the young boy's shoulder. "He is going to bring us fresh fish for supper. I happen to know he is a great fisherman as I taught him myself."

Gaylor started to bow to her, but then uncertain if he should bow or not, to a captive, he ran off in search of friendly fish.

Shielding her eyes from the sun, Czarinaea watched until the young boy was out of sight before she covered Stryangaeus with her hungry body saying, "I want you again. I need you." Pulling off her light tunic she purred in his ear. "Then you may tell me your name and why I am here. But not until I have had my fill of you."

Her lips lightly brushed over his high cheek bones and moved to kiss his ear. Her breath hot and sweet sent shivers down his spine. Her husky whispers made his manhood ache as if he had not made love in a great while.

"My queen, my queen!" he cried out as his passion rose to a fevered pitch. "Never leave me."

When they lay side by side again, feeling the comfort that familiar lovers do, Czarinaea asked, "Why do you call me your queen when you wear the tunic of a Median soldier?"

Stryangaeus paused for a long moment, composing his thoughts, knowing that he must tell her of his position as prince of the Medes, and of his wife, and his willingness to betray all of it because of his love for her.

"You are queen to me," he finally said. "You represent all that I have ever wanted or needed in a friend, a lover and in a wife. Your sensual beauty, your regal bearing, your courage and strength all call out to me to be more than I have ever been before. I would strive to be king for you, or give away all I have worked for until now, in the name of love. I would fight a battle to the death if you were to be my prize. I would lie, cheat and steal for you, yet I would die if you thought I was immoral, for until now it has not been a part of my life."

Rising, he reached for her hand.

"I call you queen, for it befits you. Come let us walk for a while."

His heartfelt words made it very difficult for each of them to speak of the reality of the situation. Stryangaeus was ready to lie to the Scythians. He was willing to say she had been killed in battle, but they both knew that custom dictated that he would have to produce her dead body. After all, she was a queen!

Czarinaea knew it was hard for him to understand, that, though she despised her mate, she needed to go back. With a huge sigh, she finally spoke.

"The Goddess dictates that I lead the Scythians. I do not know how this will come about, but I will be their leader and they will become my people. I cannot shirk this duty nor do I want to. Let me stay for a bit with you. Then...well...then you must send me back. We will meet again, trust me. I have shared my visions with you, and I have seen us together in the future."

"Yes. It was because of your visions that you welcomed me unto your body," he replied. "I know I must have faith. Does your vision say that we will be lovers again?"

"Oh, yes. A short time hence we shall again be lovers," Czarinaea said, closing her eyes as she ran her fingers down his face, allowing the visions to mesh with reality.

"Will you then release me back to the Scythians?" she added sadly.

Stryangaeus hung his head when she said this. He was so proud and beautiful that she hated to see him in this pose. She could feel the passion that was his nature slipping away. When he looked at her his eyes were filled with pain.

"I shall release you to your people," he told her, "but there is something I want you to take back with you."

He gingerly pulled a small earthen bottle out from the confines of his robe, tears misting his eyes. "Here is a gift," he murmured, "one that speaks of all that you mean to me."

Czarinaea took the stopper out of the bottle and the scent of roses wafted through the air.

"The rose is the most regal flower on the earth," he told her. "My mother always said it was gifted from beings that came from stars to remind us of our light. You are a light, and others will always follow you. The Attar of Roses is to remind you of your destiny, and to allow you to know that my love is as eternal as the stars."

Clutching the earthen bottle to her heart, she turned from him to hide the deep sorrow that was etched across her face at the anguished thought of leaving him.

The few days that they had together were filled with laughter, tears, passion and tenderness. Their hearts brimmed with fullness for all things that have ever been or will ever be. They slept very little. Instead, they rode, swam and ate. Everything they did was full of passion, yet their eyes shone with gentleness for each other and anyone they encountered.

A truce was set up so that the Medes could hand over the queen to the Scythians. A promise was given on both sides that no lives would be lost during, or on the day of the exchange.

Stryangaeus knew the ego of Marmareus was going to have a hard time dealing with his wife being nursed back to health by his enemy, especially after there was no clear cut winner in the battle they had just fought. Also he knew that Marmareus had many more men than the Medes and that must be a thorn in his side. Stryangaeus had indeed outwitted the cagey Scythian.

The villagers surrounding the camp of the Scythians started to bake acorn bread for the occasion. Gossip and songs arose about the effect of their queen on the Mede warriors.

The Medes, it seemed, had become quite enamored of her and were caught up in the festivity of the truce, preparing fruit and vegetables to share with their former enemies. They were even singing songs that hailed a warrior queen.

Of the songs that were sung in the countryside, one detailed a woman of great beauty that was neither Scythian nor a Mede, but an Emetchi. She was born with inner knowledge of horses, the heart of a loving woman, and the mind of a warrior, so the tunes proclaimed. One song in particular mentioned that a strong and kind warrior prince had fallen in love with a woman called Czarahippa, which means, 'She who Reigns over Horses.'

When the appointed day arrived, Marmareus was in a foul mood. The festivities had enraged him. He could not stop all the furious thoughts in his head. All this fuss about that brazen hussy! He wondered how she had convinced them to release her and his incense at her talents boiled over in his mind. A contest of skill with the best they had to offer, no doubt! They are not warriors, not a decent one among them, he thought. It's time he put her in her place!

The songs he had heard enraged him. She was his property. He could not allow his mind to give credence to the gossip. He wondered why she was still not with child, and pledged that he would see that when she was returned to him, he would not let her leave his bed until she was. A few good beatings and she would bend to his will. And with a child in her belly, she would not be so quick to reproach him. He pushed from his mind again the songs he had heard of the Prince and Czarinaea being enamored of each other, telling himself that was impossible! But the Mede's seeming respect for her had him confused and fuming!

Majestic hills stood in the background of the deep green valley where two warriors came forward carrying banners with each clan's crest of honor blowing in the breeze. The white scarves just below the banners belonged to King Marmareus and Prince Stryangaeus, indicating a temporary truce and if one life was lost the person that erred would lose his head. It was an ancient custom and all knew it would be followed.

The warriors exchanged scarves and turned their horses so that they were facing their units. Their backs to the enemy showed trust to the other side and honor for the ones to come onto the battle-field to surrender, and to receive the queen. The king rode forward and at the same time Stryangaeus broke formation and rode with Czarinaea toward her husband. Marmareus glared at the queen and stole glances at the one beside her.

Ha! The great son-in-law of the Mede dynasty, he thought with disgust. He will pay for this! He will pay with his life. The strength and anger that gripped him as he reached for his lance was enough to make his horse rear up. This brought him to his senses for the moment, and he vowed to take vengeance on Prince Stryangaeus in the next battle, or *before* if he could manage it.

Stryangaeus dared not look at Czarinaea for he knew that if he did, he might weaken and ride off with her. He looked only forward and did not see the hate in the eyes of Marmareus.

As the reins were ceremoniously handed over to the king, a great cheer from both sides went up. This seemed to anger Marmareus even more, and he galloped off towards his men. When Czarinaea reached for the reins, he kept them from her and lashed his horse harder bringing both horses to a full gallop.

⚜

Marmareus' court was in an uproar. Looking down from the sleeping quarters where she had been imprisoned for nearly one moon, Czarinaea knew the din below was about her. The people were not happy with the way Marmareus treated her. They felt she was to be worshipped as a Goddess, for had she not enchanted the enemy?

There had been one more small battle between the Medes and the Scythians, and then peace reigned. Talk of a marriage contract to seal the peace started between one of the Scythian warriors and a well-respected lady of the Mede's court. The king let the talk continue, allowing time for his devious plan to unfold. On a moonlit night he set out to surprise the Medes in their beds.

The journey took five days, for Marmareus had misled his troops until the very last minute when they arrived at their destination in the middle of the night, just as the king had planned.

Though his men were exhausted, he ordered them to cover their bodies in mud and move stealthily into the quarters of the king, the prince and princess. Many were disgruntled, some fearful. Most were angry at the reckless tactics of their king. Though they were confused, they grudgingly went about the attack. But the men were not privy to the fact that Marmareus wanted to take Stryangaeus as a captive to regain his ego and take revenge on the man that had imprisoned his wife and set tongues to wagging. Marmareus had been able to think of nothing more. He had allowed the talk of peace so that the Medes would be caught off guard.

It could not be called a battle; it was a slaughter. Stryangaeus was captured. He was brutally beaten and taken in his night clothes. His wife was with her father in their home on the Black Sea. King Marmareus had not counted on that. Getting into the quarters had been easy. Marmareus preened himself on his prowess until he realized why there were hardly any guards posted. He took it out on Stryangaeus, watching his men nearly beat him to death.

He had hoped to rape and kill the princess in front of her father, the king, before killing him. He felt a man who was foolish enough to let a warrior marry his daughter and then allow the people to treat him as, and call him their prince was too weak to live. And of course he ached to let Stryangaeus live just long enough to completely degrade him. The Scythian king made Stryangaeus run along behind him for the three day journey back to Tanais, delighting in his revenge, even though his captive remained silent throughout.

Stryangaeus assumed this meant that Czarinaea was still alive for he realized that he was being taken back to be put to death in front of her. His eyes misted over as he remembered how it felt to have her arms around him and her lips on his. He was not sorry for what had happened, only that their love had caused her grief. And he was fearful for her life. He wondered how Marmareus had found out, but if one were to listen, the songs that moved through the countryside told the story.

He was treated like an animal by Marmareus, but he did not utter a sound, holding fast to the hope that somehow he would see Czarinaea again. Then he would sing her the songs he had heard the peasantry sing of her and make love to her over and over again.

Before Marmareus had left on his secret mission to slaughter the royal family, he had left word that the queen was to not to be fed until his return. But he had not counted on her friend Lotzar bribing her way past the guard at the door with the promises of sexual favors. Lotzar had made nightly visits with her friend bringing sweet prunes, acorn bread and ale, and when the queen fell asleep, she would venture out to the guard and fully enjoy the promise she had made earlier in the evening. Falling into her bed exhausted, she felt powerful from having been so bold in the face of danger.

On the eighth night of Marmareus' absence, Lotzar entered the queen's room with the food she had smuggled in. Soon she ordered that water was to be heated and a tub brought up after reminding the attendants that there had been no order that she not bathe, just that she did not eat! Soon the walls rang with laughter as Lotzar taught Czarinaea the rowdy songs of the peasantry.

Lotzar then began to imitate one of the king's councilmen. Both fell into peals of laughter as Lotzar rolled her eyes with the mannerism of the staid man's dismay at the fact that Marmareus had secretly left camp. He was a funny little man and she mimed him perfectly.

Czarinaea sobered for a moment, said, "I have had another vision but I daren't tell you. You could be killed for knowing it! But I can tell you this, I will see him again. We will be together.

"Have you ever loved, Lotzar? Really loved?"Czarinaea asked, shaking inside as she recognized her enormous discomfort as fear. Memories of the few times in her life she had experienced fear came to her mind, along with a memory of her spirit guide telling her that when she encountered fear she should ask for its name.

The sober moment turned to one of deep self-reflection. Czarinaea stopped and sat on the side of the bed talking under her breath. Stryangaeus had taught her to feel and to *trust in love. Trust takes* you away from *oppression.* So, the name of this fear that gripped her must be *oppression.*

Looking at Lotzar, she said the words aloud. "So the name of my fear is *oppression.*"

Lotzar, who had been in the midst of answering at length Czarinaea's question about love, ceased speaking, and stood there astounded.

"Who can oppress me if I choose it not?"Czarinaea said with great conviction.

Watching as Lotzar's eyes widened in fear, she thought, she knows I am about to change the direction of my life, and though she does not quite understand, she will stand by me no matter what.

Lotzar went to sit on the bed next to her friend and took her hand.

"My husband can brutalize me but he cannot oppress my spirit unless I let him," said Czarinaea, her eyes golden with fresh understanding.

"I've worn my pride like armor, but it has not always served me! It is our pride that tells us that we must behave in a certain manner, like not wanting to look weak in the eyes of someone you feel is less than, or more than you."

Czarinaea hung her head, and a tear slipped down her cheek and fell on to their entwined hands.

"I've worn my pride like a mantle," she continued. "I've preened myself with it and I've come to trip over it."

Czarinaea's face lit up and looking into her friend's eyes, she knew what she must do. "Lotzar, bring me some jewels and the garment from the east that Marmareus presented me on my wedding day," she said. "I must greet my husband in style."

Surmising just what her friend had in mind, Lotzar acted quickly to abide by her friend's decision.

Czarinaea was dressed and ready none too soon. She knew that she must act weak, for her husband needed to be convinced she had not eaten for days. She must look as though she had thought things through, and it would help if she could even act a bit afraid of him. That would be the hardest, but nothing else would work in this instance. If her vision was right Stryangaeus would be with him and....

A loud clamoring was heard from below. Stiffening her spine she went to peer out of the window and her heart caught in her throat upon seeing the condition of her lover. She forced herself to look at her husband, to smile and wave. The men raised their shields towards her and cheered. Many were glad to see her, for they knew Marmareus had imprisoned her when he left.

Lotzar scurried out of the door and Czarinaea politely asked the guard if he would accompany her down to greet her husband. He seemed unsure, but Lotzar smiled and flirted with him.

"Well," he hesitated, "it was not specified that you should not greet him on his arrival home. Let us make our way to him and welcome him back."

Chapter 5

As the guard opened the door for the queen, Marmareus could be heard barking orders to his council who were standing in the entrance hall. Czarinaea's raven hair was piled high atop her head and loose curls framed her captivating face. Chin held high, she fairly floated down the hallway toward her husband's booming voice. Lotzar, in an effort to not miss anything, was not far behind. The guard made a quick exit as Czarinaea bowed gracefully to Marmareus and nodded to each councilman.

"Welcome my husband," she said in the hush that followed her appearance. "Your arrival gives my heart joy." She smiled at each quiet face behind him. "I shall have sup set for you and your leadsman also, if you would like. Then you may tell me all about your conquest."

The men in the entrance way did not want to leave, so eager were they to have the pleasure of her company. Yet all of them wanted to be out of the unpredictable path of the king.

Stunningly beautiful, the silk clung to her finely chiseled body, her hair swept off of her face defined her high cheekbones and her eyes sparkled yellow-gold from the wine she had drunk in hope that it might make her more amiable.

Czarinaea was a sight to be remembered and there was no doubt in the minds of all who watched that her splendor would be on the lips of the peasantry and in their songs for many years to come. When the king glared at the members of his council, they scurried away, taking one last coveted look their resplendent and sensuous queen.

"Lotzar, alert the baker and the kitchen lass. Have them prepare a feast for my husband," Czarinaea commanded. "Tell them to bring jasmine oil to rest his bones."

And then, having said all this, she slumped a bit forward, allowing her husband to catch her in his arms.

Sighing, she asked, "Pardon sir, I am just a bit weak. Perhaps I could sup with you?"

Marmareus, caught off guard and exhausted by his journey, and spellbound by the beauty of his wife, gladly accepted her suggestion, thinking she had finally come to her senses.

Mareus, the lead councilman, the only one that had not scurried off, looked in admiration at Czarinaea as he bowed to take his leave. Catching her eye, Czarinaea could tell that he was aware that she had not conceded anything, but perhaps he was uncertain of what she might be up to.

During the meal Czarinaea was delightfully attentive, listening to every word and bowing her head often. Marmareus gladly took this for respect just as she had hoped. In truth, there were times she thought she could not pull it off. She knew that if the emotion she was really feeling showed in her eyes it would be a weapon her mate could use against her.

She talked pleasantly about the celebration they should have because of his conquest, the types of food and music they would present. It was with a great effort that she retained her sensual appeal, especially when her husband spoke of his mockery of Stryangaeus and she was forced to turn her eyes away lest he saw the hatred in them.

The sadness she felt as she listened and compared the two men was overwhelming. She could not picture her lover being so cruel toward his enemy. She knew that if he were to execute someone it would be quick and clean, leaving the man and his family dignity. She had no respect for the man sitting across from her and it was hard not to let that show.

Having had Lotzar put a sleeping solution in the king's drink, just enough so that after a long day's ride that he should fall deeply into a hard and restful sleep, she led him to the sleeping chamber, attended his needs, helped him undress and disappeared conveniently until he was sound asleep.

Finding one of the young guards outside of the entranceway to the house enjoying Lotzar's outrageous flirting, Czarinaea asked that he accompany her to check on the prisoner for the king, and followed as he led the way to the high walled area that contained the huts used for housing enemies and horse thieves. Calling out to the guard to let them inside, he proudly stationed himself at the entrance,

Boldly encountering the unkempt and impassive prison guard, Czarinaea spoke with authority.

"I will attend the king's questions of the Mede leader alone," she told him, "as he has entrusted me with this duty."

Once the door to Stryangaeus' cell was opened, she paused and whispered to the guard, "As I have shared with you, I need to ask questions of the prisoner, questions that are important to the well-being of the Scythians. But first I must gain his confidence. Have Coleus bring me water, lye, and soap. Also bring some gruel to feed him with, and a pallet for me so that I may be in comfort while attending these matters." After the guard had reluctantly left them alone together, Czarinaea walked toward her lover, her back straight, her face a mask.

"Say nothing," she said in a firm tone, then noticing his weaken state, softened her voice, "I am here to tend your wounds. I will not go into your arms until you listen to my plan. I intend to speak to the King's councilmen of a truce between our people. Talk of such has long been bantered about, but the king's ego has been in the way. I will tell the council that you have shared with me that the Medes are willing to pay an enormous dowry to our distinguished warrior Benoeus, for a royal marriage to your wife's cousin Lycea. This union has much merit and will bring peace to our great tribes."

When her lover held out his arms to her, she backed away and cautioned him by raising her hand.

"Not until you agree to my plan. I realize that to offer the king gold for your release will not work, but this will," she continued in a low voice. "He will of course recognize that it would be prudent to keep you alive to bring this marriage about, as it will bring much gold to Scythians and to *him* personally. The council will make him see the benefit of this plan, but it must look as if the plan came from him."

At that point Coleus appeared with the things she had sent for.

"I thank you, Coleus," she told him, knowing that her past kindnesses to him would guarantee his loyalty. Often she had sat by the fire and listened to the men as they told their stories of the battle, instilling in them confidence and respect, knowing that they often spoke, when thinking themselves alone of the fact that she was a jewel in their king's bed.

"Please close the door and station yourself outside to ensure my safety. You are a loyal soldier."

Inside the prison room Czarinaea worked slowly to clean and tend the wounds of her lover. She had brought with her salve from the Golden Rod tree and seed extract from the yellow fruit that took out infection. Stryangaeus tried to speak, but placing her hand over his lips, she pleaded with her eyes for his silence, knowing his words would break her heart. He was weak from infection and loss of blood from many deep wounds; it seemed that he did not have the strength to argue. Not allowing the knowledge of his pain to interfere with what she needed to do, she deftly tended his wounds.

His feet and legs were the worst, for small pebbles were imbedded under the skin and huge lacerations had peeled away so much of the skin that she wondered how it would ever heal. At one point she called for Coleus to bring more light, which he patiently held as she worked through the night. As dawn approached, Czarinaea quickly finished and left reluctantly to hurry back into the king's bed before he awakened.

Czarinaea quietly slipped under the coverlet of their bed, and lay very still, aware that she must not fall asleep for it would be hard for her to awaken after such an arduous night.

Awakening, the king turned toward her, and roughly turning her on her face, took her over and over again with raw heated passion until finally, his lust abated, he fell into a fitful sleep.

When Czarinaea arose, she felt more battered than she had on the night he left on his secret mission. That night he had caught her off guard by pinning her under the covers. Then he had tied her hands and secured them above her head. And although she had struggled violently, he had been able to tie her strong legs down as well. Then, ripping off her night clothes, he beat and raped her, snarling crude and ugly words in her ear.

"You will bow to me," he told her. "I am your king, your husband! You are no more than dirt under my feet unless I say that you are more. Say it! Tell me you will bow to me. Say it. Say it!"

Remembering that night she thought of all the other times he had mistreated her. In the beginning she had fought back, but when she would best him, he would become devious and sadistically brutal, and with every opportunity would injure her in any way that he could. When she talked of going back to her people he had said, "If you choose that path, I will burn your village to the ground!"

Finally Czarinaea fell into a restless sleep, haunted by the face of her lover. As exhausted as she was, inner knowing awoke her just as Marmareus was waking up. Like lightning she jumped out of bed, saying she would see to the morning meal.

Everything was to the king's liking, yet at the meal he spoke to the cook and the kitchen lass in hushed tones, constantly asking to be assured that only they would prepare the food and serve it to him. Though he was enjoying his wife's new found submissiveness, it was clear to Czarinaea that he suspected her motives.

"Prince Stryangaeus is to be executed this afternoon," he said at last when he had cleaned his plate several times over. "There is no reason for delay, and afterward we shall have the celebration you spoke of."

Calmly she said, "Oh, so soon. I would like more preparation time for the celebration. Could we say three days hence?"

Startled, he sat for a moment, rubbing his chin and then declared, "Well, why not? We will have more time for the excitement of it."

As soon as he left their dwelling, she sent for Lotzar and had her hurry to the councilmen that she knew could be trusted, to ask them to meet the queen in the garden for the noon meal.

Czarinaea knew that the king usually spent the first day back from a battle of any kind visiting his many women throughout the providence, women with whom he created bastard children just to prove that he can sire sons.

When the councilmen arrived, Czarinaea stood, nearly naked in a sheer tunic and leggings that were a little more than a puff of material, and greeted them warmly. Today, her hair was also swept off her face with a comb of gold and jewels holding it in place. Her skin was shining and her eyes glistened, for she felt the need for a bit of wine to loosen her tongue.

Asking them to be seated, she immediately placed goblets in their hands and began by asking them how their families were. Charming the council with her genuine warmth, she told them how much she trusted their judgment. She also pointed out specific circumstances in which they had shown good leadership. Keeping their wine glasses filled and plying them with sweet delicacies, she then spoke of how their families would thrive if there were to be a peace treaty with the Medes.

Czarinaea skillfully worked the conversation so that she was not the one to recommend the marriage that had been briefly discussed earlier between the Medes and Scythians. The match had been originally suggested after each side had lost many men in the last battle. When she referred to the king, she was careful to say that if it increased his larder he would be amenable. Before long, it was unanimous that they free the prisoner so that he could be the go-between for the marriage. They even spoke of a tempting dowry price that would be acceptable and to the king's liking.

They left happy and excited, declaring they would call a meeting on the morrow, all of them in agreement that it was in the king's best interest that he not *think* that they were going behind his back. The councilmen filed out shaking their heads at their own wisdom while making plans for the next day.

Mareus lingered behind as the rest left, asking for a moment with her. She respected this kind man and gladly accepted his company for one last drink of mead.

"I think you've pulled it off!" Mareus said as he raised his glass in a toast to her.

"What do you mean?" Czarinaea asked, pretending insouciance. Realizing it was probably more difficult to fool a good man as opposed to fooling a brute, she said. "To be frank, I think perhaps I have. I do have my reasons, but I would not do it if I did not think it was the best move for the clan."

"I agree," he told her, narrow-eyed, "so let us drink to peace over our long enmity with the Medes… and I think I would like to also drink to peace in your heart," and with a smile nodded to her as he took his leave.

Czarinaea collapsed heavily on the sofa when he left.

"Are you all right my lady?" Lotzar cried, rushing to her, but the queen burst out laughing at the serious expression on her friend's face.

"This ruse with Marmareus, and then the council, is harder than any battle that I've ever fought," she told her friend. "But to have Mareus look through me, knowing that I was leading them, twisting them to my needs, to have him look through me like that…And *yet* he agrees!

I am astounded! But I vow after this is over I shall never take this road again!"

"But you are a warrior," Lotzar reminded her. "You command men as well as women. You do not need to resort to such dalliances. I have no choice in the matter. I am a servant and because of great luck I am healthy to look at," said Lotzar proudly.

"What you say may be true," Czarinaea agreed. "Hopefully, someday I will command and do it with great respect. In the case before us, however, it was being a woman that ignited this situation. I thought I would use being a woman to ignite flames in a different direction so that we may have peace."

The depth of sadness in Czarinaea eyes was so apparent that Lotzar averted her eyes.

"Yes, and most importantly, so that your lover can live," Lotzar said, sitting down beside her friend and taking her hand. "T'is nothing wrong in that. But I am hoping that your flames do not bring the world down around your head. May the Goddess have mercy on you, for there's fear in my bones about the lot of it. Can you tell me of your vision? Perhaps now it would help to talk of it?"

"No, I daren't speak it. Just sit with me for a time," Czarinaea said, as the vision of her sitting at the head of the council, *as their leader*, surfaced again. Always, just as a warrior stood and accused her of treason, the vision would abruptly end. Clearing her head, she realized that her friend was speaking again.

"How did you know to address them so?" asked Lotzar.

"I learned from the best," Czarinaea said with a quick smile. "Oh, I have watched you flirt freely with the men. Invariably you get your wants taken care of and many times extra to boot! So I mimicked your manner, and well…the dress or lack of it certainly helped!"

Lotzar smiled back broadly, "So I have taught you something. Of that I am glad, for you have given me much my friend."

"Stay with me. I need to rest," said Czarinaea, and putting her head in her friend's lap, she fell into a deep and undisturbed sleep.

Chapter 6

Much later, when Marmareus returned, Czarinaea feigned sleep. After servicing his women, he was weary enough not to disturb her and he slept late into the morning, leaving her free to creep out of bed. Relieved to start her day without her husband, and happy to be in the fresh morning air, she used the quiet time to think of how to set things right.

When Marmareus entered the dining area ready to break his fast, the serving girl announced that the councilmen had been waiting through the morn to speak with him. He asked that his food be brought outdoors so that he could join the men and watch while Czarinaea broke one of the horses that had been giving the men a problem. In fact one man had been killed and one injured in an attempt to make a riding horse out of this one. And, tempting her with the possibility that once broken in, the guerdon would be hers, he had set about to wait until it was time for him to claim it for himself.

Watching as the animal tried over and over again to throw his wife and fail, he told himself that the animal was a great prize, just as she was, and began to feel passion rising in him, only to find himself playing unwilling host to his councilmen who, with the greatest care, approached the subject that had brought them to him.

The King was feeling very satisfied with himself. Yesterday had done much for his ego. With Czarinaea acting as she had, he decided that she was jealous of his outings, and hadn't she waved and smiled at him fondly just now. The committee spoke at great length, being very careful to concede to his ravings. Being well aware of the signs of the king's stubbornness, Mareus deftly led the conversation constantly toward financial gain, mentioning again the amount of gold that would be added to *his* personal treasure box until the king's greed finally overcame his mulish rampage.

"Perhaps I have come up with a good plan," he told them smugly, as Mareus, behind his back, winked at his colleagues. "I know Stryangaeus. He will die too well. I am glad I have realized that a much better use of my capture of him should be made. It will please me to no end to make him look like a fool! Ha! Doing the bidding of a marriage in return for his life will show him as a weakling!"

That evening the king was in a jovial mood at sup and teased Czarinaea to guess what incredible feat he pulled off during the council meeting. Playing his game, she spoke of the many feats that he had taken on since their marriage. Heady with wine, he puffed out his chest and recounted the plans for release of the prisoner.

"I suppose something must be done then to announce the marriage treaty, and mayhap we will be announcing the birth of our first child at the same time. Should I start making plans now sire?"

Knocking his chair over, he picked her up and swung her around. For a moment Czarinaea was almost caught up in his overwhelming joy, but then remembered her fear that he might realize that the child was not his. Before the thought progressed any further, he surprised her.

"My lovely fruitful one," he announced, "I will sleep in the smaller sleeping quarters and leave you the large bed, so you will deliver me a healthy son!"

Czarinaea caught her breath with relief as, carrying her into their bed chamber; he placed her down gently and departed.

As she lay on the bed, Czarinaea, scarcely able to believe her good fortune, could only thank Goddess that he had not suspected the truth. And when Lotzar entered the room, it was clear she was bemused.

"I've come to help you undress, to put you abed and to see that you take your rest," she told her mistress sternly. "I've orders that you are not to ride! He is calling a meeting to replace your service as a warrior. Is the house burning down around us now… or is this just the torch that will eventually set the kingdom aflame?"

Czarinaea motioned to Lotzar to come closer, and then whispered in her ear, "Shush, he believes the child his, for the sake of the child we must see that he continues to believe that."

"But… Yes, I see. Of course it's his!"

Czarinaea felt like a prisoner in their bedroom. Her heart ached to see Stryangaeus. Quietly going to the bedroom door in the middle of the night, she found that there were guards placed on either side. Smiling and nodding their heads at her in a conspiring way, they acted as if they had been privy to a wonderful secret. So she began to devise a plan. If her lover was still imprisoned this night hence, she would visit him.

The day was busy, but she was all too well aware that she was constantly being watched. As long as she was seated, Marmareus allowed her to see as many people as she wanted to. Throughout the day, she went about making plans for an assemblage and proper entertainment for the announcement of the two great events. So as not to give thought to either her lover or the child, for both were so intertwined and both gave her great pleasure and great sadness, she kept herself occupied. Yet waves of fear for her child and her lover gripped her if she let her thoughts go any further than the present moment.

Sitting alone, Czarinaea counted the days again of her last menses. She must, she knew, be honest with herself. She did not want Marmareus' child, and had taken great measures to see to it. Yet could she be absolutely sure? To have a child and constantly search his face for recognition... or to see there what she wished not to see... She could not bear it. She would not hold on to her senses. Putting her hand on her stomach brought her a mixture of love and fear. She *knew* this to be Stryangaeus child, and yet when the fear gripped her she lost her inner knowledge and the truth eluded her.

Going in search of Lotzar, she pulled her down the hallway and into the bedroom. Flinging herself into her friend's arms, she cried, "What can I do?" The two friends wept together. Finally the long sobs subsided and Czarinaea pulled herself together.

"I must see Stryangaeus" she said, cupping her stomach. "He is still imprisoned, as he has not yet agreed to be the go-between for the marriage. I must convince him."

Lotzar asked, "Do you have a plan?"

"Yes," Czarinaea replied. "We will exchange garments. I will pull the hood of your robe over my head and leave this room as if I am you. Then I will go to him."

"You must not risk it!" Lotzar cried, alarmed. "I am not speaking of this night! I mean the child, Marmareus will know. You must seriously look at this situation and do something about it!" Wringing her hands, she paced nervously.

"Don't worry. I am doing something! I am keeping my wits and moving ahead. This is what mother has always said to do in a battle."

"This is not a battle" said Lotzar pleadingly "this is..."

"Oh yes... It is a battle and there will be death, for I have seen it! Though I know not who will die," said Czarinaea with a sad distant look in her eye. "Yet there will be no winner. But still I must ask. Do this for me. I must see him. Marmareus is away. I will be quick about it. I have to do this. Please," pleaded Czarinaea.

❧

Staging an argument, the two friends raised their voices in feigned anger. Czarinaea burst from the room, throwing a tirade of curses over her shoulder, startling the guards. Drawing the hood over her face, she raced down the hall. The guards shrugged and exchanged a knowing look, as if to say, "Women!"

When she arrived where Stryangaeus was imprisoned, she bowed her head and said her mistress wanted her to see to the needs of the prisoner. One of the guards recognized her garment and thinking it was Lotzar grabbed her and said. "Perhaps you will have some time for me afterwards, heh?"

Czarinaea slapped his hand away and, lowering her voice and coughing, said, "Can't you tell I'm feeling ill?"

When she entered the small room Stryangaeus did not even look up, thinking it was one of the king's servants.

"Go away. I am fine," he said in a cold still voice. "I wish no bother about my wounds. They will heal in good time. Or is it that now there is thought of profit, they wish to keep me alive? Truly I would rather death, for such degrading mistreatment as I received from your king is abhorrent."

But when she uttered his name, the stillness in the room spoke of ageless recognition. "Czarinaea..."

Pressing her fingers gently to his lips she said, "There is worse than to be dragged by a horse and beaten in front of the warriors of your enemy. There is worse even, than to be imprisoned and to play at politics in exchange for your life. You balk at this, as though it matters not if you live or die…" Her words became heavy like molten lead running the course of a dry riverbed, and he shuddered at the sound of her pain.

"There is worse."…She hesitated drawing a long deep breath. "To be queen, to have the trust and love of your people, yet betray it. To love a man, a prince, who is an enemy of your people… a man who is not free to love you… and worse still… to carry his child. Within this there is nowhere to turn. Even my death will not erase the mark on the child if it is allowed to live. And so this queen begs you to take the offer of your life… to leave from here as soon as can be arranged and to never turn back."

Her breath stopped in her chest as she waited for his answer.

He knelt at her feet. "My queen, my queen," he begged, "do not ask this of me. My love for you can move mountains. I will find a way."

Hugging her legs he buried his head in the softness of her belly and his tears dampened her garment. She bent and caressed his head, his beautiful hair. A silent tear ran down her cheek and mixed with his. Her fingers touching his skin set her on fire and she moved down and melted into his arms.

He pulled away for just a moment and said, "I do nor want to hurt you."

"The hurting is not in the loving," she told him. "It is in the losing, for surely this cannot happen oft, this kind of love? Surely it is meant for us to be together… in some other lifetime mayhap…?"

Her words trailed off as the pain of losing him tore through her heart. Holding him closer, she beseeched the universe to take pity on her and assure her somehow, somewhere in time, he would be hers.

As before, they melded together and their spirits rose above their bodies and their souls entwined. She saw them making love and felt it at the same time, being part of it yet becoming part of all there is. There was a deep knowing in her heart that she belonged to this person, that she was more because of him and somehow she was diminished to think of a life without him. Yet she felt strength through his love, to do what had to be done.

A small shaft of light fell on his face as she guided him inside of her again. His ecstasy flowed through his eyes, allowing her to be part of his adoration of her, giving her an overpowering feeling of control and abandon, of strength and weakness, and of height and depth that took her to the edge instantly.

He lost himself in pleasure and agony. As he climaxed, he felt his hot seed spilling inside of her, and in her passion her nails opened his wounds creating a stream of warm blood on his back which made him rejoice since the pain allowed him to know this was not a dream, for he had dreamed of nothing but her since they met. Physical pain was no match for the emotional pain of not being with her.

Soon enough I will be queen, she thought, but for now I am a woman. I will enjoy him while I can for there will never be another to take his place. As they reached yet one more peak together, they looked into each other's eyes. Love, admiration, and respect mirrored between them, firing anew their passion. Over and over they climaxed wanting only more, until their salty tears unified their bodies, blending their hearts for all time.

The tears moved him to cradle her, and as he did she felt waves of tenderness wafting from him as if he were comforting a new babe; and then he began to sing a tune from his childhood as he rocked her to sleep in his arms.

Oh…. the sound of his voice… One more thing to lose, she thought as she drifted off. No, I will think of it on the morrow for now I am in his arms.

Meanwhile, Lotzar, afraid that Marmareus would come home and find her in the bedroom instead of Czarinaea, spoke through the door sounding like the queen.

"Fetch me my maid," she demanded. "She is with the prisoner. Knock first before you enter, for I have told her to keep him happy this night."

It was important that word got back to Marmareus about the night long tryst with Lotzar on orders of the queen. It would further the doubts that he was having about anything between his wife and the prince. If her child was to have any chance at all she must move suspicion away from herself and Stryangaeus.

Czarinaea had just settled under the blankets when Marmareus' booming voice shook her bed and she sat bolt upright. He entered and threw a warm wrap her way telling her that she much rise and see what her plan had accomplished. She could not tell from his manner whether he was pleased or not. Then again, she thought if it was not his idea, no matter what the outcome he might not be pleased.

He ushered her to the enclosure just in time to see the prince escorted out of the prison, and brought to the center of the town where prisoners were tortured or sometimes beheaded. It took every ounce of her will to not cry out as she turned toward her husband.

"You have had me awaken for this! I shall go back to bed now for I am feeling a bit weak."

Her knees buckled, and for the second time in two days he caught her, from the look on his face she could tell it made him feel strong and needed.

"Being with child has taken the sassiness out of your manner," he boastfully told her, "I shall have to keep you in this state!"

Feigning interest in what he was saying to her, she listened instead to what her lover was saying to the councilman, amazed and relieved at the strength in his voice as he spoke of marriage plans and peace. Her eyes filled with tears of happiness, but she knew she must not allow her emotions their sway.

"Oh," she said, "he has moved beyond his stubbornness I see."

"Yes, my dear," he said, putting his arm around her, "thanks to your generous gift of last eve."

Her heart skipped a beat as he continued, his voice tinged with lust.

"Lotzar must be very talented. Your strategy in politics is as good as your ability with horses."

Czarinaea flinched. She had not realized that if the plan worked he would place a lustful eye on Lotzar. She felt a heavy burden for placing her friend in such a light. What had she done? What cost this love to all of those who know of its existence? She felt as if her heart was being crushed, and her thoughts moved to the wife of Stryangaeus. This child should be hers. She had not only taken her husband's love, but his seed. And now she, Czarinaea, must right all that has been put wrong.

His release was first and most important. Czarinaea continued to act as if it meant nothing to her. But her every thought and prayer was on his safe return to his land. I will pray to Artemis to help me bring this to pass. She has known what it means to lose her lover, yet she found the strength to go on. In the back of her mind was the story she had heard of Artemis shooting her lover by accident to prove she was a better shot than her brother, but she tried desperately to think instead of the merry stories she had heard about Artemis and her wood nymphs, and her adventuresome spirit.

"Artemis, great Goddess," she prayed. "Give me your strength. I need the courage to send away my lover for his safety, and also because it is the right thing to do. He will rule his clan and have a kingship because of his marriage. I have heard she is a wonderful blend of child/woman with a quiet nature, and many say she is an endearing spirit. Mayhap if I had known this in the beginning... But, no it would be foolish to think anything could have kept me from his arms. Still, so much harm has been done. I must be brave... Artemis, please help me!' she implored.

With empty eyes she looked up to see her husband standing with a group of his warriors, watching as four guards rode with Stryangaeus, taking him back to his people.

Lotzar came to her side. "My friend," she said. "Let me help you to bed."

"No... there is much to do, I must..."

"I did not say my queen. I said my friend!" Lotzar interrupted her. "And as such I have the right to tell you that you do not look well. I must, if not for the sake of you, then, for the sake of your child, do what is best."

And knowing that her friend was right, Czarinaea went to her bedroom where she slept for two days, with Lotzar standing vigil.

Chapter 7

In a fortnight, a rider came from the court of the Medes with greetings to the king and queen and a list of suggested dates for the wedding and a roster of those who would attend. It was hinted that the ceremony be on neutral ground, and that an emissary would be coming with the dowry. This pleased the king who turned to Mareus and said, "As soon as the emissary arrives I want all of you in attendance to count and inventory the gold and jewels. You Mareus are responsible for it till it is hidden and safe."

⚜

Riding atop a magnificent Arabian stallion with a golden bridle, Prince Stryangaeus boldly entered the city of Tanais. A slight breeze blew his sun bronzed hair away from his compelling face, his light emerald eyes taking in every nuance of movement around him. His garment was made of the finest skins and he wore no armor.

The arrival of the prince set all of the peasants bustling. His entrance was quite a different one this time. Reining in his horse at the prison, he rode by it very slowly, and then came to a stop at the entrance of the great hall. Many Scythians had gathered in curiosity and excitement. When a councilman approached and asked if he could help him dismount, Prince Stryangaeus said,

"I shall await your king. I was here by his... shall we say invitation before, and I would like to see that I am here by his invitation this day as well."

Most of the councilmen looked stunned, but one of them hurried off to fetch the king.

There was no need to go far, for King Marmareus had been watching. His anger showed by the high color in his face, but his greed pushed him forward.

"Prince Stryangaeus," he said, trying to affect a leisurely walk toward the prince, "Welcome! Our city embraces you and the good fortune you bring to us as emissary of your people. Come, take mead with us. It is made from the finest honey and malt. Then mayhap you would wish to rest from your journey."

Peasants and warriors alike cheered, throwing their hats in the air and clapping each other on the shoulders, and some cried, for their kin that had died in battle with the Medes. "Now the killing can stop. Many lives will be spared," they cried in unison.

"It is an auspicious day," said one of the councilmen. "Our children will bless us if we can keep peace between us."

Czarinaea watched from the bedroom window with Lotzar, both of them expressionless. Each was worried about the other, and Czarinaea was already planning how she would be able to see her lover. It was so easy to feel the conviction of her choice when he was in his homeland. But to see him, the beauty of him…to have him this close… She could not make pleasant talk to him when they dined, she told herself. It would be torture to be so close to him and not be in his arms. And he had been fool-hearty to come. What had possessed him to insult the king on his arrival? She admired his courage which, albeit brazen, was indisputably right. By his action he made it known that there is more to the situation than him buying his life. This is not the action of a man who cowardly begged for his life as the king would have the populace believe.

Czarinaea's mind wandered once again. The king clearly had such mixed feelings about Lotzar since the night he thought she'd bedded the prince. It is evident he desires her, yet he seems to hate her at the same time. He begrudged her new garments, and at their last outing had made unbecoming remarks toward her. He was used to women falling at his feet, and the Emetchi bowed to no man.

Lotzar treated him like a brother, Czarinaea thought amused. One to be weary of no doubt, but as an equal none the less. She showed respect for his office in front of the council. However she did not act like a servant. The king made subtle advances and Lotzar acted as though she did not notice. Czarinaea was fearful he would next order Lotzar to submit, and then there would be trouble.

Holding one another's hands tight, they looked into each other's eyes, and knew that life from this point forward would never be the same again. With unspoken commitment to each other, they tidied up each other's garments and hair and made way, silently, to the dining hall where the king's council and the prince had already been seated, both women held themselves straight and tall, Czarinaea felt they were walking into a lion's den.

With that thought Czarinaea had a brief flash of a vile and evil man ordering everyone out of a dark cold room. Seeing herself lying on a small pallet she was aware of the pangs of childbirth and that she had been imprisoned by him... he was called 'the lion.'

Shivering, it became clear that in the past life she had just seen, her husband Marmareus was the lion.

Knowing she dare not show fear, she went through the entrance and said. "The Goddess shines upon us this day. Do you bring your good wife, Prince Stryangaeus?"

"She did not feel well enough for the journey, but she sends her... her thoughts. Yes and warm wishes for the success of our business."

"Her absence will be felt," said Czarinaea. "But I am sure the business of the court is well attended."

She took her seat next to the king, and Lotzar moved toward the prince, sitting in the empty seat to one side of him. Czarinaea could feel the king stiffen, noticeably upset when Lotzar flashed the prince a smile. At the same moment, she felt a sudden movement in her belly. Surely it could not be the child, she thought. No, it was much too soon for that.

A meal of sweet fruit, cheese and mead was being served, but to the queen it tasted like dirt from a fallowed field, and the queen could only sip the mead. The women sat straight with subtle ears turned to any word that might set things off.

All went very well until the prince asked, barely able to hide his sarcasm, "Shall I have the same quarters as last time?"

"Lotzar will show you to your quarters." Czarinaea put in rather quickly. "We hope you find them to your liking."

"But first, my dear, the prince and I have some business to attend," the king said brusquely. "If you will follow me," he said to Stryangaeus, "we will get the matters of court out of the way so that you may enjoy your stay. Give instructions to Ludeaus here," he said, pointing to one of the councilmen. "As to your desires for entertainment, riding, hunting, or any other sport, you need only let him know."

It took all of the king's control to be civil. He will not get Lotzar if that is his desire, thought the king. Perhaps I will find him one with the wasting sickness. Ha! Or...

The king glanced at the aides that followed the prince. They were weighed down by the amount of coin and jewels they carried. This stilled any further thought of him lashing out. Half of the dowry was his. The rest went to the council to be divided how they saw fit, and one tenth went to the groom. The groom, however, would have a chance to speak to the council of needs he might have above the amount he would receive. Perhaps if he was a really good speaker or dazzled them with a sweet song, he would receive another ten percent of the original amount. It was all part of the festivities before the wedding.

❧

The king was developing an obsession with Lotzar. Though his wife was by far more beautiful and raised his lust much quicker, it was up to him not to jeopardize the delivery of a healthy son. Many women flung themselves at him but that took the sport out of it. He liked the challenge of what he could not have. Wanting to learn every detail of Lotzar's movements, he set men and women in the court to spy on her, and especially to report what the two women might secretly devise. The servants were given strict orders to let him know immediately if Lotzar went to Stryangaeus.

"My lord, two nights hence she is to go to his room," stuttered one of his lackeys the very next day. "It was organized so... for you will be on your rounds visiting your...the outlying clan."

"But why keep it a secret?" Marmareus demanded. "Why would she care? She has done it before in the open?"

"I did not know 'bout the before, me Lord," the small wizened figure shriveled all the more into himself. "I am sorry. I am sorry to be so bold, but she is your wife, would... would not the fear be of that?"

"My wife? *My wife*! What is it you're about man? How is it you accuse my wife?" shouted the king.

"No, no, milord, I daren't accuse your good wife," said the peon while crushing his hat in his hand, and slowly backing away. "No accusation, just repeating what has taken place in the time since the sun came up this morn. I'll be on my way now. Please... there is no reward for doing this work, happy to be of service to my king."

Marmareus' anger rose in waves. All that he had suspected when Czarinaea had been captured came back to him. The king's face turned brilliant red and his body began to shake violently as he let out a howl like that of a wounded animal.

ᚷᚥᚷ

Hearing a bellowing roar from the front of the house, Czarinaea came up out of her chair. Next to her, Lotzar covered her mouth to stifle a scream. Instinctively Czarinaea touched her knife that rested in a specially made pouch at the small of her back.

"He knows," both women said in unison, both terrified, one because she knew what he was capable of, and the other because she did not know. Czarinaea felt fear for her lover and her unborn child, but relief that she did not have to live a lie any longer.

The king rounded the doorway with club in hand and reached for his knife. "I will kill you," he told Czarinaea. "As sure as I married you, I will kill you. I will not only kill you, I will gut you, for that is not my child! Speak woman, for it will be the last chance you have to do so."

Czarinaea stood her ground and said nothing, while slowly taking her knife from its sheath. Lotzar was so frightened for her friend that she cried out, and for the first time the king noticed her.

"Aha! It is two strumpets I corner like rats. How convenient for me. I do not have to look under Prince Stryangaeus to find one of you, and the other doing her bidding! The choice is difficult. Which one do I kill first?"

As Lotzar shot out of her chair to protect her friend, he caught her roughly and slit her throat, flinging her body at Czarinaea.

"Your servant!" he said viciously, savaging the air with his dagger. "Indeed your friend, pity that! You'll have no one to scheme with. Well, no time anyway. Do you not want to pray to your Goddess? Your lover does not have a chance. I will challenge him to fight me and then I will see to it that the toast before the match is laced with poison. I want to see his eyes when he realizes what I've done. Then he will know he is not the only one that can be devious."

Marmareus lurched dangerously close to Czarinaea, and noticing the knife she held, shifted his weight from side to side, sizing her up.

"So you see the lot of you will be dead and I will cheer and dance around your funeral pyre," he shouted. "I will piss on your mound and bring all my bastard children to do the same. I will tell them how I cut out your child and watched you slowly die."

They were circling, knocking furniture out of the way slowly edging closer to each other. Czarinaea noticed a lantern hanging above her that she knew would hold her weight. "Keep your wits and move forward," she heard her mother's words in her mind. Slowly and steadily she placed her knife back in its pouch, confusing Marmareus, who hesitantly took another step forward. But in his uncertainty, his weight shifted and it was all she needed.

Jumping for the lantern, she swung toward him, kicking the knife out of his hand with her right foot and hitting him squarely with her left, splintering the bones in his face. Continuing to use the lantern for leverage, she pushed herself off his body, and then slammed back into him, wrapping her muscular legs around his neck. When she let go of the lantern, they both fell heavily to the floor. Her weight atop him and her legs in a strangle hold served to weaken him. Blindly swinging the club, the king lanced a blow on the side of her head and slamming his knee into her rib cage, knocked the wind out of her. Czarinaea knew that if she did not do something quickly he would have the advantage. Grabbing her dagger in her right hand, and clutching the hair of his head with her left, she plunged the knife into his jugular vein, holding his head fast till it was over. Trembling, she rose to her feet. The blood drenched knife dropped from her hand to the floor as she stood transfixed.

A vision of him in a past life blurred her sight. 'The Lion,' they called him. He had been an ugly, mean spirited man who hated women. Falsely imprisoning her, he had ordered that she be hanged? Hate that she had felt for him in the other lifetime boiled up and out of her, and as she looked at the blood on her hands she said, "It is done! So be it!"

Hearing movement at the door, she struck a warrior's pose ready for attack, but it was the shield maker, and the old servant that she had befriended. Both bowed low to the floor and cried,

"Victory to the queen! Long live the queen!"

And then, going to Lotzar, they turned her body over, tears pouring from their eyes.

"She will be sorely missed," the old man said.

The shield maker who was very liked and respected in the city put his hand on Czarinaea's arm in a loving way and said, "I saw the king going mad. He has always been unpredictable. My word will hold great meaning. It is a shame he drove you to that. But there is great love for you here. The people will be glad to have such a brave queen, let us..."

He broke off as Czarinaea clutched her belly. Her face turned ashen and she swayed, nearly losing her balance, blood pooling beneath her.

"Queen Czarinaea," they yelled in unison, "you are hurt."

"Get the midwife," she gasped. "My child is coming. Hurry!"

The shield maker ran out in search of the midwife, and the old man helped Czarinaea to her room. Both thought it was too late for the babe, but the old man prayed that they would not lose their queen.

"My queen, when the shield maker comes back with Diana, the midwife, I will go along to the head councilman. His feelings for you are..." He hesitated for he could not insult her by saying the councilman was enamored of her.

Czarinaea said, "Yes, Mareus will be the best one, and then he can break the news to the rest. I will close my eyes for a bit now."

Seeing how weak she was, he closed his eyes and beseeched the Goddess Tabitha, of hearth and home. "This is a good woman and she will lead us well. Take her not, for our people need a strong and just leader."

When Diana entered, bustling and calling out orders, she rushed to the queen's side. Alarmed at the ashen skin of her charge and the unnatural amount of blood, she hastened into action. Opening her tattered bag of herbs, she prayed to Tabitha to save the queen, as it was obvious it was too late for the child.

When the shield maker returned again, he brought with him a party of men that could be trusted, men that were very much in favor of the queen. All were happy to know that she was still alive. One of the men went to call out the graves-man who would see to the body of Lotzar and prepare her for burial. The council of course would need to make the elaborate plans for the king.

After examining the room where the killings had taken place, and talking with the shield maker and the old servant, the councilmen concluded that, despite Czarinaea's beauty, the king had been determined to have Lotzar, and she had flown into a temper to protect herself. But the king would not take no for an answer, and he killed her in a fit of anger.

When confronted by his wife, his anger turned to blind rage and the queen had to kill him in self-defense. They were also aware that there was a faction that would not care and would want Queen Czarinaea's head, but luckily they were few.

The councilmen decided to put the word out that the queen was under strict orders of the midwife, whom they could easily bribe if necessary, to stay abed else the babe might be lost, knowing that if it were put about that she was still with child, no member of the clan would kill her.

Once the crisis was over, Diana went to the bedroom door and asked, "Who is in charge?" to which there was such a universal response from the councilmen that she murmured, "Whenever a bit of power is at stake, insanity is to be expected.

"Well you'll nor enter till one decides who's in charge," Diana said, crossing her arms in front of her ample chest, "for the lot of you is far too many for her now. So we be in want of some kind of vote, or perhaps I could send the house boy to the barn for straw, so that the lot of you could draw for a turn!"

Hearing this, Mareus stepped up to her and said, "Of course it will be me as head councilman, but my brother Vareus has just arrived. He has a sharp mind for tactics. I need him at my side. We need to protect the queen!"

"If that is what you're up to, enter!" Diana said, knowing that the queen could use the least bit of friendship. "For, in truth, she has lost the one closest to her, then her babe in the bargain."

"We must speak to you about that, please," Mareus said. He was joined by two others who explained that it was not time yet to speak of the queen losing the child. It was for her protection.

The mid-wife nodded in agreement. "Tis no problem bout my speaking," she told them, "since most think I'm off of it anyway, and the rest think I will put a curse on them. Others care not what I do, as long as I attend their wives when the babe comes. There is something to be said in getting old and having many secrets. Take my word on it."

Unlike most of the other servants, she brazenly looked them all in the eye as she barked out her orders for the queen she was possessively tending.

"Now as to my charge," she announced, "the queen is not to be disturbed! I have stemmed the flow of blood, but she need stay in the position I have set her in for a time yet. You may talk but do nor fret her, for she is still very weak. You must take the burden from her mantel if you want her to survive. A feeling of protection must come from the lot of you. Only then she may indeed get well. She is filled with honor and integrity and her will is like iron, but right now she is in need of the care that only I can give her."

And not content to leave it there, she stepped into the hallway, and looking every man in the eye, declared, "She may be full of moral integrity, but I am not. See to it that she comes to no harm or you shall know why the townsfolk refer to me as a witch."

Chapter 8

Stryangaeus unable to visit with Czarinaea, and finding himself bored, had gone on a two day hunting trip. Upon his returned he found the Scythian Court in an uproar, and although no one would satisfy his questions as to what happened, he knew for certain there had been a death, since on his way back into the city, he had seen a huge burial mound beyond the gate. Furthermore, he had heard some lackeys talking. "He attacked both of them he did," one of them had said, "and I don't know as you could blame him. She was his and he didn't want her showing her wares elsewhere. Ta'shame though, she was a pretty piece."

Concerned by what he'd heard, Prince Stryangaeus jumped down from his horse and ran quickly toward the entrance of the king's manor. His heart was pounding and he could not keep himself from calling out Czarinaea's name. Finally when a serving girl appeared, he grabbed her and said, "Is she dead? Just tell me is she dead?"

"Why yes Sir, sorry Sir, she is." She told him. And not knowing that she spoke of Lotzar, the prince's eyes clouded over, his shoulders dropped, and he moved woodenly to his room where, sitting on a hard stool near the window, he watched for hours as the dusky day turned into a strange and dismal sunset.

Only when the maid came to ask if he would sup alone, did he rouse himself. Seeing tears running down her cheeks, he asked why she wept.

"What will happen to me now, with my master dead and gone," she cried?

It took a moment for him to hear what she had said. "Did you say master? Do you mean the king?"

"Yes milord, I thought you knew. Everyone knows the king is dead." And with that she started openly bawling. Stryangaeus knew he had to soothe her to hear more of what had transpired. But as she began to speak her tale meandered about. Finally becoming very impatient, he interrupted the young maid. "Tell me of the queen!" he demanded.

"Don't know milord," she told him. "They be keeping us out, like we would be in the way. The mid-wife is with her is all I know."

"Show me, show me her room!" he demanded.

"No, no I daren't go there," she sniffled. "There are men watching and councilmen in and out and the mid-wife's a fearsome sort!"

"I will protect you," he told her. ""Just tell me where she is! I must go to see about matters of Court."

Stryangaeus stood tall as he approached the two guards standing on either side of her door.

"I see you're in charge here," he said boldly. "Call out one of the councilmen so that we may discuss the matters of royal significance."

"None but the mid-wife attends her now," one guard replied.

"And that is as it should be," the prince replied. "However, I wish to offer my services to your good queen and my condolences as to the king."

With that the guard knocked firmly upon the door, and Diana, stepping out into the hall, indicated that he should follow her so that they could speak in private.

"T'is time you showed your face," she chided him. "She has been asking for you all day.

I could not bring you here without bringing undue attention to a bad situation, so I have been waiting."

"My dear, blessed lady, I was under the impression since mid-day that the queen was dead. Please assure me again this is not so. It is so good to hear it, for today seemed an eternity. Since the sun rose and set this day it seemed as if all life ceased. I must know how this situation came about and most of all how she is. Please take pity on me and tell all that you know."

"T'is sure the queen would want you to know the truth," she said. "Poor lady. She frets and is frightened so for your life. There are a couple of warriors that would kill you just with the thought that you stole a glance at the queen, for they are loyal to the king and his death only makes them more so. Come, let us have a seat here by the window and I will inform you as to the queen's wishes."

"I must see her," the prince said when he had heard all. "How can we arrange this? I am not concerned for my safety but I wish nor to put her in harm's way."

"It will not be easy right now," she told him. "I will think upon it and speak to the queen. We will put our heads together and come upon a way to bring this about. I know that just an audience with her will not bring about the healing that is required. Time is needed for two hearts to speak to each other."

He bowed deeply to her. "Blessed lady, I thank you."

"I easily observe what the queen sees in you," she told him, blushing. "Make it your business to have no one else know of your feelings for the queen, because it could mean death for the both of you. I believe in a short time that will change, but for now it is best!"

As he walked away, he contemplated death, seeming right now, so much the easier way than to face a life without her love. How has this come about? he pondered. He believed that it was true, as some said, that there is only one time you truly give your heart, one person that fills you so completely on the joining, that all others seem like empty vessels. Some never find it, and they search hundreds of faces and beds looking for this love. But then again love is just a word, for when he and she were together there was no need to speak of it. It was so profound, it was in every look and every move and every smile.

Finding himself back in his room, he succumbed to the lure of sleep and lay, wrapped in skins, for many hours, after which he spent three long days pacing his room. He found when he asked about the queen the answer was always the same.

"She is mending well."

But that was not enough for him. He wanted to touch her, to ease her pain, to lay his hands on her wounds and heal them with the force of his love.

Finally, the midwife, lamp in hand, knocked on his door, and coming inside, wreathed in shadows, said that he did not look well.

"I am well enough," he told her, "but my heart shows in my face and my heart is torn and ravaged. I have brought such agony to her. If

I could go back, I would love her from afar. I would never knowingly hurt her because she is my life."

"Sir, perhaps you would think it is not my place to speak, but you would be wrong on that account," she told him. "What I am going to say will sound fantastic, and perhaps a bit insane. But Czarinaea tells me you grew up with a mother that was obviously a seer. She tells me also that you believe that you have lived before and will live again when this life is done."

"Yes, that is so. Please do not tell me she is dying, please..."

"No, that is not at all what I have to say. She is going to be just fine."

The tension in his shoulders released and a smile lit his handsome face.

"Then tell me anything, and I will listen from my heart."

"Yes, I believe you will," she said, settling her bulk on a bench and leaning toward him. "More than two hundred years ago, in another lifetime, I was the mother of Czarinaea. In that life I sent her on an important mission. I have come to realize that both of us have much to learn from this experience. It is not for her to know in this life that I have before been her mother. For now it is only important that she listen to the guidance that she receives from her friends. And also that she continues to count on her unseen friends, those that have come to her in dreams and visions."

As she spoke, the mid-wife took on a younger appearance, and her eyes became radiant points of light. Startled, the prince heard music as her voice took on a hypnotic rhythm.

"You have been together before," she told him. "Czarinaea and you have been lovers in another life. You are flames of an eternal fire, twin peaks of light. When you meet it matters not what the mind wants, but what the flame desires. *Twin flames*, I call it, for there seems to be no other explanation for the fiery nature of the love, lust and commitment that rages between these two when they come together.

"Ah yes, it shakes up lives," she continued, "But there is also something wonderful that happens... something that touches those around them. There is such a power in this kind of love. It moves in waves out from the lovers like a pebble disturbing a pond, as it weaves its message into circles of forever. It will become stronger in each life."

Seeing astonishment and yet hope in his eyes, she added, "Yes, you will meet again in the next life."

"My lady, what you say makes so much sense."

"Call me Diana," the mid-wife said, and gently took his hand and went on with her story.

"To come together fearlessly is to open to the will of the Goddess," she told him. "It is *she* that knows the why of it. It is not for us to know. Walk with Czarinaea through the garden of this love and see its beauty. Do not look at the devastation. But know that chaos is the handiwork of the Goddess *setting things right*. It is what you learn in each lifetime that is important. It is that…that you take into the next life. No matter how brief the span of time you are together, much can be learned."

When Stryangaeus looked up the mid-wife was gone, although he had no memory of her leaving. The words *'setting things right'* kept going through his mind. He knew that there was a grand plan working here. He could feel it! It was like a gossamer web around him when he became very quiet. It had its own energy and seemed to pull and tug. It did not frighten him, but amazed him.

"Yes," he said out loud as he went back to the very beginning, "I felt it, but did not understand."

Hearing footsteps outside his door, Stryangaeus thought perhaps the mid-wife had returned. He went to open it and a dark clad figure ran down the hall. Spies, he thought. Indeed, he was in a very precarious position.

❦

On the morning that the warriors and council held the service for the dead king, the first before his body left for its forty day precession through the out-lying areas so that his people could pay their respects, Czarinaea was too 'ill' to attend. Of course being a Mede, Stryangaeus had not been invited, so with everyone at the ceremony, Diana secreted him into her lady's chamber.

Czarinaea's hand flew to her mouth to stifle her squeal of delight before she leapt into her lover's arms, the merging so sweet she found it hard to draw back. But feeling his ribs created concern.

"How long is it since you have eaten?"

"No, no food," said Stryangaeus, "I can nor eat. I needed to see you, to hold you, to know that you were alright."

"Diana," Czarinaea spoke with concern in her voice, "would you fetch mead, fruit and cheese, oh…and some meat, he will eat, I will see to it!"

The sadness that they felt for each other's pain flooded the room. Their bodies seeking relief from the sorrow, merged. No words were spoken.

❧

Time shattered, shards of it piercing their weary souls as they clung to each other. Flames of desire reaching heights and depths of their passion that had not been reached before.

The mid-wife had come and gone. Czarinaea had happily fed her lover as they laughed over his *forgetting to eat,* and yet the insatiable appetite they each had for the other.

In the early morning hours, the prince, holding her gently and stroking her hair, began to explain his plans for the future.

"I'm going to abdicate my title as prince. It is one given me reluctantly by the king due to the wishes of the people. Then I will cede my rights over to the half- brother of my wife," he told her. "I know that we have agreed upon peace, and I know also that this will bring war again. The King of the Medes will not take lightly to my deserting his daughter."

Alarmed by his words, she awakened fully, sitting bolt upright.

He begged her for silence with his eyes and lips.

"No, absolutely not!" she exclaimed. "You must not abdicate!"

"He has paid me handsomely to take her hand in marriage," he continued, having to look away from her piercing eyes, "Most of the dowry is still intact. I will offer it to him and say also that it is possible that I cannot father a child. Perhaps this will still some of his anger. His daughter will tell him that for the last many months I have not come to her bed. Mayhap that news will help, and perhaps after a good deal of time your people will accept me."

Once again, Czarinaea tried to speak, but he pressed his finger gently against her lips and proceeded in a rush, as if he did not do so, the words would not be said.

289

"The peasants know of our love and seem to applaud it. I think many of your warriors respect me, and it is possible that after a time we could marry."

The prince experienced tightness in his chest, and his face and lips felt numb. Diana was right, he told himself, he must not look for devastation, for they did indeed need to love and laugh together, whatever the future held.

"Let neither of us speak of it now," she said fighting tears. "You have spoken your heart to me. To all that you have said, my heart says yes. But there are many considerations. For now we are together. We so need to feel the love that has shaken both of our worlds. We need to relax, play in the sun and share time together. Preparing for this marriage between our people gives us a reason to meet. Then we will speak of the future."

⁘

Czarinaea called a meeting of the council by sending word that they would break their fast together in the meeting room the next day. She also asked the head councilman Mareus to have thirty warriors that he trusted attend. It was an unusual request but he was happy that she was well.

Czarinaea knew that there were only a couple of councilmen and a small fraction of warriors of importance that were ready for her head. She had been very good to the staff and to all of the warriors and now she reaped the rewards by knowing what was going on in the locale. She knew, too, that she had no fear of death, which gave her an edge in this game. And a game it was! There might be warriors that would want her position. They would want to fight her for the title, and many would look at the larder of the king with greed. If that was what they had in mind, so be it. Her feeling sense told her otherwise, so she decided *to keep her wits and move forward* as her mother had taught her.

Loud voices rang out as she moved gracefully toward the meeting room.

"How say yea?" shouted Appotheus one of the councilmen as he pounded heavily on the table. "This one who claims to be queen has committed treason, and came upon her title by killing our good king."

A very small number agreed with him. The rest came to their feet vehemently claiming Czarinaea their queen, just as she quietly took the seat that up until that time had belonged to the king.

Her elegance and poise could not be denied, and aware of her quiet demeanor, each man turned, in rapt attention to the proud woman sitting before them.

"I sit at the head of this table not because I have killed the king to have this seat, but because he chose me as his queen, for I carry the Royal lineage. He chose me also because of my skills as a warrior. Your king did not pick lightly, for he had many a dalliance, but waited until he was seasoned in knowing what he wanted in a queen, and then he chose me."

Pointedly, she looked around at each man at the table, and then looking behind the councilmen to the warriors that filled the room, she began to speak again.

"I have schooled many of you in the art of riding and the skills of battle," she continued. "Some of you have mentioned that my strategy skills are lacking. Though I do not believe that, I do know that is why kings and queens have a council, to organize and to help them with strategy in warfare."

At that, the councilmen sat straighter in their seats and the warriors seemed to lean forward.

"I know that we have among us talented organizers and great strategists," she told them. "And surely you have all noticed that I am quick to learn. I have not yet needed to lead a battle, but I know that I can. Just as I know that our clan and our holdings will grow with our strategy and our wits. I am a warrior, yet at the same time I wish peace for our clan. I wish to look out at meetings like this and see many a happy and prosperous Scythian."

Czarinaea hesitated, looking at the faces of each of the men at the table, and nodded to the warriors that stood leaning on the wall, some holding their short-bows.

Rising, she proclaimed, "I did not come here to kill your king! I came to be wife and warrior. And that I did! You know the circumstances that brought about the king's death! You have heard honest and decent men tell you of the day that has changed all of our lives. I stand before you, not as a woman but a warrior and your queen."

Drawing her sword, she laid it on the table before her. "I claim title!" she cried. "I am an Emetchi by birth, but I claim title to the Scythian Queen-ship because I choose to live and die as a Scythian... be it sooner or later! And I claim title because it is my right!"

She gave them a moment to think before she continued.

"So," she went on, looking again at each councilman in turn. "The title is mine or you put me to death and carry me back to my homeland and set my body beside my beloved grandmother who had a vision when I was born. The vision told her that I would *lead a great people*, and that I would die a good distance from my homeland. Shall we set her vision in motion, or is it my head you want? I will wait upon your decision. But I will wait here as you take your vote. I want to look into the eyes of my accusers and see those who would choose vengeance... over greatness."

The silence in the room was thick. No one moved or uttered a sound for a few moments until Mareus finally spoke.

"We shall take a vote," he declared. "I vote that Czarinaea remain our queen, for I have seen nothing but honorable action on her part. Who will move to vote with me?"

Pandemonium broke out as a great many shouted, "Long live the queen. Long live the queen!"

When the vote was tallied, there was not one in *open* opposition.

Chapter 9

As she walked away from the meeting room, Czarinaea's face was a mask held in place by will alone. The few people to whom she stoically nodded on her way seemed puzzled by her demeanor, and did not try to engage her in conversation.

Her experience of seeing mists of color around all the men in the meeting threatened her sanity. What took her attention the most was that while seeing the colors, she also seemed to be getting information about their thoughts, their honesty or lack of it, and of the fears that seemed to plague them. The information helped her, for as she spoke to them, she narrowed in on the areas of worry for many of the men. But none the less, it was overwhelming. Arriving at her door, she told the guards they could leave.

"I have just come from the council meeting and seeing as I still have my head, then I must officially be your queen," she rebuked them when they seemed confused. "So it is not a request! You are good warriors. Thank you for taking care of my safety. Go and join your friends for there is now no need of your services at my door. I am well and can take care of myself."

The guards bowed low and backed away, crying out in unison, "Long live the queen."

Czarinaea knew they were genuinely overjoyed at the outcome. She had always treated them with respect and she knew they were loyal. Both happily joined the celebration that was forming in the streets. Bakers, artisans and warriors alike were singing praises to their new leader. There would be many times during the long night of celebrating that she would have to show herself and throw gold to the crowd. Otherwise they would enter the court and carry her outside on their shoulders.

As she entered her room, she listened as the revelers welcomed the guards that she had just dismissed and then, seeing Stryangaeus at her door, flew into his arms. Freely sharing with him all that had happened, the council meeting, and the colors she had seen around the men, the thoughts she had picked up on, and the feeling of pride as she truly understood what it was to be a queen. And of course the elation that she would never again have to be wife to Marmareus.

"Come lie with me and tell me more about the colors you observed around the men, for something seems to be bothering you about it," he told her.

"Though knowing their thoughts helped me with choosing my words, for I truly believe I averted an argument between the men by knowing which fears to address, I know not what it means," she said, taking his hand. "I used to see pink around my sister and sometimes I would see color around flowers or trees, but not like this. Do you think there is something wrong? I have received two severe blows to the head. Could there be something wrong with my vision?"

Stryangaeus was mesmerized by the golden sparks in her eyes and knowing how important this was to her, he silently asked guidance of his mother and he repeated what he heard.

"Some people are born with the ability to see auras. Some come to it because of great reverence to the Goddess, or meeting a lover that opens their heart. Trauma to the body or soul can also be the catalyst to open the prophetic eye. Fear not. Let the colors guide you. Study what you know about a person and what color they are. In that manner you will know a stranger's intent by his color. You will be able to tell if a person is angry, even when they say they are not. Most importantly, you will be able to tell who is truthful and who lies."

"You seemed entranced just now, changed in some way," Czarinaea said when he offered her the advice he had received. "Though I liked what you said, where did it come from?"

"I am just as surprised as you," he told her. "I asked my mother to guide me and I guess she did. Perhaps we can ask another time for more information. Would you like that?"

"Yes, very much, but I have other things on my mind right now."

His sensual smile let her know that he was thinking exactly as she was.

"And so my queen... what now?" he asked as she removed her tunic.

"I will entertain you in style!" she replied. "We will plan the royal marriage that has been discussed to bring peace to our people."

"But what of you and me..."

"It is not time to talk of it yet. We are to laugh and play, for surely we deserve some happiness just as the next person does. There is always time for duty. Now my prince, it is time for *this*."

And then, as the crowd outside celebrated her victory, she celebrated her womanhood. Each time the crowd called her to the window, she came back to bed more exhilarated, and passion would renew itself, until finally the crowd became tired and the prince laughingly begged for mercy.

Their days were filled with laughter. They swam naked and rode like the wind. When they raced she would beat him every time. He loved her spirit, her smile, her body and her heart. They filled each other's senses, and the love in their hearts overflowed to all who came into contact with them.

There was no hiding their love. It was just a matter of time before she would need to make a choice. She sensed this, and also knew that the choice of her heart, though the one she wished to follow, would not be the path the Goddess had chosen for her.

The royal wedding would happen in a few short months. For now, they had reason to put their heads together. Propriety would or could not dictate differently. The council seemed only concerned that there were many plans to put in motion. Preparation for these events accounted for the many meetings and numerous encounters that they had enjoyed.

Czarinaea stopped abruptly as they were walking a forest path. When Stryangaeus asked what was wrong, she put her hand up to quiet him. She continued standing there until an eagle took flight from a nearby tree.

"I could see her aura," she said excitedly. "She is going to be having young soon. I knew that from her colors. I mean, it's hard to explain. I don't just see the color. I get information too, just like your mother said through you the other day. I had a dream last night. My spirit guide showed me the waterfall I built when I was young. She did not say anything in the dream, I guess because years ago I told her never to talk to me again. But the water fall spoke to me. Oh, I would never tell this to anyone else! Do you think I am crazy?"

"I think you are incredible! Tell me what the waterfall said."

"That everyone comes in on a wave of color, and because of that they need to learn the things that color will teach them. There are different colors, seven I think, because that is how many tiers there were in the waterfall, each with its own shade. If you understand the color, you understand the person. You, for example, are green, which means you would make a better peace maker than a warrior. Though I suppose anyone would know that," she added, teasing. "After all you tend not to kill your enemies but make love to them!"

"What color are you?" he asked, his eyes glowing with merriment.

"My color is yellow, though I keep wishing it was gold. It means that I am to learn strength, and leadership, also integrity.... Perhaps I just need to accept help from my guide, even if I am still a *bit* angry at her. She could answer many questions about the colors I think. Let's go back now. It's getting dark," she said, squeezing his hand.

The next day, when they lay by the river throwing pebbles into the depths, and watching the waves of ringlets as they moved out from the center, the prince reached for her and brushed his finger gently over her lips.

"Do not say the thing you have come here to say," he said, wetting his index finger and tracing her lips, then lazily running his hand down her bodice. "I cannot bear it. Besides, there is nobody I want save you, no life I want that does not have you in it. There is no reason for my heart to beat unless it beats for you."

As they merged together softly, silently treasuring each caress, he buried his face in her hair and then moved down to her breast. She broke the silence with a sound of such pain, that he covered her body and drank in all her energy so as to take the pain away. Giving herself over to him, she could not imagine such sweet pleasure and deep pain coming together, touching them, playing with them, haunting them. She thought that his love was so much more important to her than being queen. And yet she also knew that she must tell him to go back to his people. How could she do it? She prayed to the goddess to give her strength.

He looked deeply into her eyes, dark eyes with sharp pin drops of light shining up at him. The pureness of her love radiated, and vibrated still, though the height of their love-making had abated. It was as if he could still feel the orgasmic waves moving over him, stoking the fire in his heart even though, at present, the fire in his loins was calm. He laid his head upon her belly, and she stroked his hair. Each felt a peace that defied words, and they both knew that it would move them toward each other, lifetime after lifetime, seeking the completeness that no other lover could ever offer.

At the river they swam, laughed and made love for a long time. Lying side by side he stroked her shoulders, massaging her sweet curves as he sensuously moved over her back to her buttocks and thighs. He continued down her calves to her feet. Bending her leg at the knee, he took her foot in his hand and he massaged deeply as she sighed in pleasure.

"I have noticed that the people around us smile and laugh more when they are near us," he said. "They are participating in the cocoon of our love. I have also observed there is no measure of time when we are together, *yet I know that time is not my friend.*"

Stryangaeus was contemplative as he spoke the next words.

"I have allowed myself to suspend thoughts of time, but I have been noticing that it seems to be collapsing in on us.

Wanting to hold on to time, he turned her over, fervently kissing her feet and with his tongue, he traced her high arch and moved to the ankle. Enticingly using his tongue he lingered on her thighs and leisurely moved to her mound.

"I taste my seed and I taste your wetness," he murmured. "Each excites me, because you have opened your body to me, opened your passion, which in turn draws forth seed from my body and becomes part of you." His hungry mouth pressed against her mound and his tongue teased her till she could no longer stand the pleasure and begged him to enter her.

"No, I will enter you when I taste your new pleasure of me." He placed his tongue over her womanhood and soon felt hot liquid fire coming from her depths. He entered her, moaning as he felt the heat and instantly exploded, calling out her name.

The next day, she woke him at the first hint of daybreak.

"There are no down feathers that can take the place of your belly," he said sadly, raising his head from his pillow.

"You know what we must do," she said, her eyes downcast. "I'll not have it on me that you deserted your good wife and gave your future kingship away. I know that you are willing. You honor me by that willingness. Yet, it is because of honor and duty that I must decline. I asked you once before to go, and never turn back. I had such strength until I saw you again. Much has happened because I was weak. Yet I cannot say that I am sorry for the time we have had. It will carry me through a lifetime of duty and an empty bed. Take leave of me now. Make this new day the one that will allow destiny to take its course."

He could not look at her for fear that he would weaken. Once dressed and at the door, he bowed deeply.

"My queen," he said, "My body takes leave of you. My heart never will."

⁓❦⁓

Two hooded figures lurked in the hallway but the prince did not notice as he walked heavily back to his quarters. Once there, he slept fitfully until the serving girl knocked on his door to offer a meal. Declining, he went to the chair next to the window and stared out with empty eyes. Dusk stole the light quickly, reminding him of how black his world would be without Czarinaea. After a time, he decided to send for the livery boy to ready his horse for the journey home. Perhaps the blackness of the night would swallow him up and he would not have to live out his days without her.

As he rose up out of the chair, the heaviness in his chest became a crushing pain. It was as if his heart was in the jaws of a large and vicious animal. He stood still to catch his breath, waiting for the pain to abate, but instead it became so intense that he dropped to his knees. He clutched his heart and thought, *it does not want to continue beating without you……my queen.*

The two men that had been following him earlier, listened at the door, and hearing nothing, slowly entered, both with drawn knives.

The prince's body was lying on the floor, his hands pressed to his heart, a smile upon his face.

"Someone has beaten us to it," one of them cried.

"There are no wounds," the other said, bending over the body.

"Then we must take advantage of the circumstances," the first spy said. "Find a quill and some of his parchment paper."

"Here are the writing tools." Snickering, the taller of the two handed what he had found to the other. "How have you learned the skills of writing? No one from our clan knows the skill."

"You fool, it is not I t'will put my hand to it, but the councilman that paid us for the job. He learned from his travels, and keeps it secret. We will be paid double when I tell him of my plan. "Wait here, and let no one in... no one. Do you hear me?"

Pleased with himself, he scurried out of the room as fast as his short legs would carry him, counting the extra coins in his mind. He was sure that the councilman Kaeus would give him a full pardon for his crimes and extra in the boot. What luck he thought.

While the companion he had left behind waited for his return, someone called through the door, "Your friend awaits you. Come, I will take you to him. You have done well. There will be extra coin for you. There is no time to waste, hurry!"

As soon as he had left the body, a dark figure quietly opened the door to the room where the prince lay, and dropped a small empty vial on the floor, after which he tucked a note into the cool, still hand of the prince.

The next day, the mid-wife went to check on Czarinaea, for they had become very close. Czarinaea loved the motherly fashion in which she was treated by this wise and unusual woman. She missed Lotzar and every time she thought of the loss, it caused her to stop breathing. It helped that she had the loving attention of this woman she trusted completely, and her nurturing ways had made her think of sending for her mother; for it was time that she healed the harsh words she had spoken. Though it had been just short of three full cycles of the sun, it seemed like an eternity.

Upon leaving after their visit the mid-wife asked, "Is there anything more that I can do?" "Will you check on Stryangaeus?" Czarinaea asked her. "We have said our goodbyes, and I know that he will abide by my wishes. I have steeled myself from all feeling, for that is the only way I can do what is right for my people. Yet this past eve my dreams were of hooded figures and intrigue. The intrigue seemed to be against me. But though I hardened myself for the task ahead my heart pained me, physically hurt. Then the pain abruptly stopped, and now my heart feels like lead."

A short time later the mid-wife entered without knocking. She looked distraught and had a note in her hand. "I will have a private audience with the queen," she said, pushing the councilman who had followed her out the door.

"What has upset you so?" asked the queen.

"Please sit down Czarinaea. Czarinaea did as she was bid and the mid-wife handed her the note. "Here, read this. And tell me. Is this the handwriting of Stryangaeus?"

"I do not know!" Czarinaea said, shaken. "I have never seen his words on parchment. The Scythians as well my clan do not have the ability of writing, though some of the Medes do. Can you read it to me?"

After the note was read by Diana, Czarinaea was stunned. As all color left her face she said, "Stryangaeus is dead? That cannot be."

Diana sat quietly letting her absorb the news. The deathly silence in the room she knew was an indication of the void he left in Czarinaea's heart. When the queen spoke, ice coated her words.

"His note accused me of murdering my husband, mocking his affections, and ruining his life? He wrote that his death is on my hands. It cannot be so!"

Insisting that the note be read again she furiously wiped at the evidence of her tears. It did not make sense to her. Her full lips drew tightly across her face, rage seething just beneath the surface. If he were to write her a note she was sure it would have begun, *My Queen*, but this note was simply addressed to Czarinaea.

"Never would he have written that! Never! How is it that the hound Kaeus was at your heels when you entered?" she cried angrily as she jumped to her feet knocking the chair over. "***Did he see this note?***"

"Yes, he did. I went to the door of Prince Stryangaeus as you asked. I knocked but got no reply. When I felt a cold shiver run down my back I knew something was amiss. I decided to enter, and just as I did Kaeus came out of nowhere and entered, saying he had business with the prince. We found the prince on the floor and he read the note over my shoulder, I'm afraid, and found an empty vial on the floor! Something is amiss for sure. My feelings tell me this is all wrong. Czarinaea, you know him well. Would he take his own life?"

All her fury, rage and pain closed in on her, and as his death became a reality she blindly reached for the table in front of her. A deep blackness drenched her words as they were pulled from the depths of her being.

"He was a warrior and one of the bravest men I have ever met. He did not feel he had much to live for, yet..."

Unrestrained tears ran freely down her face, dampening the note and blurring the evil lies.

"Yes, I know him," Czarinaea said with conviction, "and I know he would never hurt me! That is why I am certain he did not write this. They have killed him to get back at me. The councilmen Kaeus wants Apothuse the warrior to have the throne. For power they would indeed kill! But then to insult the good name of Stryangaeus in this way..."

"Take me to him. I must see Stryangaeus... now!"

"But, my Queen, you are not yet healed," Diana said, taking her hands. "This could set you back!"

"This has set me as far back as there is," the queen said, pulling away from her. "Death would be welcomed, because life holds no meaning. I knew I was not fair to him, telling him to leave. But there was no other way. I knew that I had to be content to hold on to the memory of him. Knowing that he walked the earth, knowing he breathed, laughed, and sang... that gave me pleasure. Now what will there be? Take me to him, I need to..."

She swayed as she stepped forward and the mid-wife grabbed her elbow to steady her. But when they reached the room where the body lay, Czarinaea indicated that she wished to go inside alone, and that Diana should stand guard so that she was not interrupted.

Finding his body lying on the bed, she lay down beside him and covered them both with the rich wool blanket. Then, speaking in a soft voice, she began to tell him the story of how they had first met, including every detail she could remember, when she first opened her eyes, his voice, the songs he sang to her. After more than an hour she began to sing, softly crooning the songs he had taught her until, realizing that she had never sung to him while he lived and now he would never hear her sing, she rose and made her way to the door, her heart imprisoned in hate.

"I will have years to mourn him," she told Diana as she exited the room, "but for now I will see to the men who killed him. I will call a meeting today and we will see! If Kaeus and Apothuse killed Stryangaeus they will meet me in the orbeus. There we will settle this. There is no way to lose for me, for losing means I join my lover."

Two young girls sat on a stone fence at the edge of the city, enjoying the magnificent day.

"All of the city is talking about it!" said the older girl, feeling worldly speaking on such matters. "He killed himself for love of her."

"But I heard that she called out the councilman that found his body and challenged him and another councilman to meet her in the orbeus, saying *they* were responsible for prince Stryangaeus's death! Can you imagine such goings on?" declared the younger of the two as she shook her head.

"I can imagine! The nobles have such pride." declared the older one with an air of authority.

"Do you know what happened at the orbeus? Did they take her challenge?"

"No, it is closed to us. It is for warriors alone to settle disagreements with each other. I've heard two stories though, and one is rather strange."

"Oh! Tell me that one first!" her friend begged her.

"It was told to me," she whispered, "that the queen called a meeting, but the councilmen swore, on the lives of their families, that they did not kill Stryangaeus. Sitting opposite them in the center of the meeting room, her eyes fixed on a point over their heads, she questioned them. My mother got the story from a friend who said it was *very* eerie. This friend of my mother, he works at the big house and knows all the councilmen by name. He said when the queen was through asking the questions, she claimed that they were *guilty,* but she did not think they were guilty of actually killing the prince. Then she left the room, saying that she did not want their blood on her hands, and told the councilmen they could deal with it how they chose."

"But what did they choose?"

"Kaeus and Apothuse begged to be judged by the *warriors.* They claimed that they were only interested in protecting the people from the enemy, and were just keeping an eye on Stryangaeus. Tis rumored that the warriors voted to send them away with no horse or weapon to defend them, but no one seems to know for certain.

"But what is the other story?"

"That she fought both of them in the orbeus...*at the same time,* killing them dead!"

"Noooo....do you think that true?" squealed the young girl, "and then what?"

"Because it is closed to all but the council, no one knows for sure..."

"Couldn't the queen just have had their heads," interrupted the young girl, "if she believed they had anything to do with her lover being killed?"

"That's so... she could have. But she is, they say, determined to be fair in all cases, and no one knows for certain who killed him. Besides, it's so much more romantic to think he killed himself for her. After all, if he was such a good warrior how would they get close enough to kill him?"

"That's right, Tis so. Anyway, the songs say he killed himself for love. And surely the bards know, for they know everything!"

And with that romantic notion, both girls sighed.

Chapter 10

Silence was not a good sign and Czarinaea had heard nothing from the Medes, even though it had been weeks since she had sent the body of the prince back to his people, accompanied by a messenger that would relay the information that the prince had died of natural causes, and that she and all her people morn his loss. And so, when no response came back with the messenger, Czarinaea, knowing that there would be some response sooner or later, took the precautionary measure of doubling the guard.

Czarinaea strolled in the walled garden, thinking wistfully of her lover as she looked up at the full moon. When her hand strayed to the emerald on her neck, a vision in which she saw herself with her sister, Myrina, took her breath away. She could hear herself saying "He will ne're love again… and he will kill himself for he cannot have me."

But she knew that if she gave herself over to these thoughts, she could not do her duty, and she was having a hard enough time just getting from one day to the next. Turning to leave the garden, she found Diana watching her.

"Queen, may I be so bold as to address you, to speak on matters until this moment not yet attended," the midwife asked her.

"Of course," Czarinaea replied, "for you have proved yourself to have my concerns at heart."

"Tis true more than you know." Clearing her throat, Diana chose her words very carefully. "I am in your debt for I have enjoyed the graces of your home, though I am no longer needed here."

The queen laughed. "If you need to start out thanking me in such a manner as you have never worn before, mayhap I should rescind your permission to speak."

"It is good to set you to laughter even if it is at my expense," Diana replied. "I should have known that you would soon see through me.

Well then, let me begin. Just now as I entered the garden I saw enormous pain on your face. Can you speak of it? It is important or I would not ask."

Czarinaea sat on a bench and looked out over the garden. The moments lingered. She did not speak

"You have kept very busy since the death of Stryangaeus," Diana said solemnly. "You have shut down your feelings, your memories, and your heart. You do your duty as queen; no one can fault you that, but there is no life coming from your body. And soon there will be no body, for you refuse your meals… or move the food around on your plate as if you look for something hidden there. Mayhap trying to solve the riddle of life?"

"So," Czarinaea interjected heatedly, "Can *you* give me the meaning of life? Or at least some reason why I am here? Truly life is a riddle, but something I care nor to solve, for it holds no interest for me. I cut my mother out of my life and I lost a child! I put my friend's life in danger, thinking of my needs over hers, and lost a friend!"

"Yes, and at the very bottom of the well you have dug for yourself, you find you have refused to love your mate and then you lose the man you love," Diana replied. "You have dug the well deep enough, but tis usual to find water at the bottom. Water is purifying. It cleanses the heart… or you can drown in it."

It was not clear to Diana if her words could be heard by the queen, but wanting to pierce through her wall of anger, she continued.

"You could choose to think you have no luck in these matters, or you could recognize what is before you. You can continue to close down your heart, using the reason of losing all that you have loved, or you could be enriched by the greatness of the love you have received."

Diana inched closer, seeking Czarinaea's eyes.

"How many people that you know have been blessed with a greater wiser mother than yours?" she demanded. "You have told me she is bold and honest. When she makes a decision it is for the good of her people. Know the fruit by the tree Czarinaea!"

Sitting down heavily on the bench, Diana continued. "No one person that I know has had so trustworthy a friend as Lotzar. She left her family to be by your side and was honored to do so. Look to your friends and know ye who you are! And last but not least…no one person that I know save you, has been honored by the love of a man like Prince Stryangaeus. He gave you his heart and offered over his crown. But you could not take a man from his wife or a prince from his people. And so you refused him in life and now you refuse him in death? I say again, he gave you his heart and offered you his crown. Know ye that love given unreserved speaks well of the giver... and lives always in the heart of the receiver!"

There was a long pause while she waited for the queen's response. And when it came not, she continued.

"What say you? Do you close your heart and his great love comes to naught? Or do you realize what greatness you have before you? The power of all that you have ever learned is in this moment."

Diana looked sadly upon the woman before her, a woman who had been her daughter in another time and place. The mid-wife, who had been known as Goddess of the Moon had accepted life on life's terms, knowing the importance of this very moment. If her words could break through the wall of pain and anger of the woman standing before her, then her assistance during this pivotal moment in history would allow women to look on those that had come before them with pride.

"You wanted to go to the temple. Instead you have come here to be the queen of a great and powerful people. I wanted to marry, yes, and to have children. Instead I went to the temple to learn the arts of healing. I thought I knew it all, but this earth has many secrets." The midwife laughed, but it was not a joyous sound.

"I have brought many children into the world and seen love from afar. I come in front of you now with teachings of the temple. How hear you these? As judgments, as censure? Or do you not hear them at all? All that I have said to you I have said in love, so then my part is done." The mid-wife rose to go, then turned back for a moment and said, "Each thought you think or word you say produces fruit and yields itself in your world. So do not think thoughts you are not willing to wear... or say words you are not willing to eat."

Somehow those words jarred Czarinaea to full attention, as she remembered something Stryangaeus said that his mother had told him. "Become interested in watching how life is set in motion, yet dwell not in the watching but in the living."

Suddenly, the trees in the garden became more vivid, the colors of the wild flowers brightened, and she noticed the melodious songs of the birds. For a moment, she thought she felt Stryangaeus sitting beside her, and remembered what he had told her about the rose. "The petals are in groups of five to remind us of our humanness -the fact that we touch, taste, hear, see and smell. Under the petals, here on the base there is a star. Some of the Goddesses teach that we come from the stars, and that the rose is on earth to remind us of that. The divine scent spirals us to higher truths. Some priestesses use the scent of the rose to give prophecy."

Pulling the small vial, that had been given to her by her lover before she left Media, out of her pocket, she inhaled long and deep. It is indeed a glorious fragrance, she thought. Stryangaeus, I must know that you did not take your life. I cannot carry this burden forth with me.

And then she heard his voice clear and crisp.

"Czarinaea, you know in your heart what is true. What does your heart tell you?"

Reaching up for the emerald on her neck, the sadness that was etched upon her face spilled over into words. "I am sorry that you are dead," she told him. "The world is lesser because of it. What I have been forgetting is that I am more because I have known you. I hurt your memory by not accepting the part you played in my life. You taught me to love. I am sure you did not open that door for me to close it again because you are no longer on this earth. You opened it for me so that I could be a great queen to my people, and rule as my mother does from a place of love."

Slowly, unclasping the talisman from her neck, she held it in her hand, and finding herself stifled by her emotions, told herself to breathe. Only breathe. Word after word caught in her throat, words of anger, words of love, and words of missing him. The most frightening words were of guilt, the guilt of being angry with him... and with herself.

"I was angry with you for dying because, as long as you were part of this earth, I could hope to have brief moments with you, to steal time. Time is one of the most precious things one person has to offer another. Our time was brief, but I will go a lifetime and not find fullness such as ours with any other man. So I vow that there shall never be another man in my heart, not because you have or ever would ask this of me, but simply that no other man can fill that place. So then...it is time for me to act as queen and meet with the councilmen to talk of the clan's future. I must see to my duties for they have honored me by wanting me as their queen."

Czarinaea stood tall, her back straight and proud. Color flowed across the expanse of her high cheekbones as she thought of their physical love, at the same time that tears misted her eyes. Clasping the talisman around her neck once more to remind her of the faith he had had in her, she left the garden with Stryangaeus' voice still echoing in her ear. *"We have been together before, and we will be together again."*

And watching her leave, Diana smiled, realizing that her work was done. And looking up at the moon she knew that she could now go *home.*

All around her, the councilmen spoke at the same time, some shouting to be heard above the din. Czarinaea had been sitting quietly. When she stood the room became silent.

"Good," she said. "We have much to decide. Now that I have your attention, let us begin. Sit, all of you, and so shall I. You are good men. What has put you into such an uproar? Mareus, would you please speak for the group?"

"Yes, my queen," he began.

"Czarinaea will serve," she interrupted him. "Addressing me as *my queen,* puts me in a place above you and that is not the case. Yes, I have become your leader. I will not forget that. I hope that someday when you say 'my queen' - mayhap at some official ceremony - you say it not only with respect for the office I carry but respect for how I carried the office. For a title should not be something you just receive, but an honor that is bestowed upon you when there has been an earning of it."

As the councilmen relaxed in their seats, Mareus rose, smiling broadly. "Czarinaea, thank you for considering our need to adjust to the circumstances," he said. "I would like to speak for the majority here in the room. There is much concern, and even fear about the silence on the part of the Medes. Many of the council think we should send a portion of the dowry back and suggest that with the funds a statue of

Stryangaeus be made and be placed in the center of their city in memory of his honor and his fairness in battle."

"And what do the other councilmen think?" she asked, with raised eyebrows.

"I ah… well…"

"No one will be flogged for what they think. Please speak."

"Well almost every man here wants peace. This is a prosperous time and we want to enjoy it with our families. T'is not that we have become cowards, simply that we are learning a better way. We like that you teach the men to pay attention to the oak tree, to stand straight and tall but never be afraid to bow, for this movement alone adds grace and agility to the mind. We are at the ready if war calls, but joining with the Medes in a royal marriage has many a bonus."

"T'is truth my queen – I mean my royal…" one of the other councilmen stammered, causing an outburst of laughter which broke the tension of the moment.

"Gereaus, we laugh not at you but the circumstances we find ourselves in," Czarinaea told him. "I think that we are all finding it funny that addressing me is the biggest point of the day, when so much has happened since the last moon. We focus on small unimportant things because the stakes are very high. We must act on this situation. We must be strong, yet not push. We must show great respect for Stryangaeus, for the man and for the life he lived. We must be careful not to approach the subject of his death overly much… for it brings up so many unanswered questions."

Nodding her head she looked at Vareus, Mareus's brother who, she had noted, was proving to be as loyal as Mareus.

"Let us focus on the marriage," she continued. "We will send a crier that will state that we are looking forward to the plans that Prince Stryangaeus had put in effect. The crier, one of our very best, will glorify his talents, as well he deserved. We will state that the marriage will not only bless our peoples, but that the name of Stryangaeus will be central in our peace treaty. The statue is an excellent idea. We will ask that their very best sculptor begin plans to oversee the workmen that *we* will send, therefore making it a joint venture and we will send gold in good faith to be given to the sculptor that they choose."

"Is it such a good idea to send workman into their camp?" asked one of the councilmen.

"It is a wonderful idea," replied the queen, "if they will allow it. I will ask for volunteers, each one of which will receive a large pouch of gold and new boots for the journey. We will pick men that have no care or knowledge of state policy, those that care not about being a warrior and are not involved in the council. That way, if they are under scrutiny they can give no secrets away. So, are we ready to follow through on the plan? How say you?"

There was a loud clamor of agreement and a banging of cups upon the table as the vote was tallied. Only two held out, grumbling that they would be seen as weaklings.

"There is one more thing we must bring up," Mareus interjected. "There is a rebel group high east of here. They have stolen a horse or two and taken a few children from the out-lying clan that will be going into manhood by the spring equinox. They also have taken young women to mate with. We need to know how to deal with this. We have sent warriors after them, but they are hard to find, for they disappear into the hills after each raid."

"Call a small group of warriors together," Queen Czarinaea said thoughtfully. "See that there are many good looking women as part of the group, or men that can pass as women. They are to look defenseless. Tell them to camp a day's ride high east of here in the hills. Once the rebels raid the mock camp, our warriors will know exactly what to do. See that the rebels are kept alive, at least as many as can be handled safely. Once they are brought back here we will learn more of their people and their ways. Perhaps we can become allies.

"And now, we are through for this day. I feel that we have accomplished much. What say you?"

The councilmen nodded enthusiastically and began to rise. There were a few startled faces for many were leaving without bowing their heads in deference to the queen. The king had always expected it, and had men punished for not treating him with the respect he felt he deserved. Those that took the time to bow their heads were startled to see the queen bow hers in return. Her heart was very full for these men that trusted her. She would not let them down. She would die for them if it came to that.

She remembered how hard she had fought against her mother about coming here. A strong surge of emotion overwhelmed her, and love for her mother filled her heart. She must, she knew, get a message to her of all that has come about, and she must also send a message to Lotzar's family and let them know of her bravery, as well as how much it meant to her that she chose to leave her family and come here. Taking one more look around the room, she thought that even though her mother would be proud of her, she would not be surprised at the turn of events or even how she had handled them, for as well as she knows horseflesh, she knows people. Czarinaea determined to send her a message on the morrow.

After a prosperous and jovial meeting, filled with camaraderie and congratulations to the assembly about their good harvest, the council then boasted about the well planned skirmish in which a few women and two new warriors had gratefully joined their clan. With their business completed the council decided to adjourn.

As Czarinaea stood nodding to the men that were filing out, a mammoth man, one side of his face disfigured by crisscross scars, and wearing a battered breast plate on which the Mede crest was barely visible, shoved his way through the throng. Two Scythian guards, attempting to hold him back were as ineffective as flees on a dog.

"I demand to see the king in the name of my people!" he shouted. "They have been robbed of their Prince. A prince they themselves chose!" Stopping in front of Czarinaea, he snarled, "Where is your leader?"

"You are looking at the leader of the Scythian people sir," said Czarinaea standing tall, one hand resting on the hilt of her sword, "and you have disrupted our council. An apology is in order."

"And just who the hell are you?" he hollered, spittle sprayed from a cavernous hole in his face as he hovered over her like a solid oak tree. "Well speak up woman!"

The sound of his voice vibrating off the walls caused every man in the room to reach for his weapon.

"Stand down," Czarinaea cried. "I think it would be wise for you to tell me who *you* are, and state your business before my men have you for breakfast."

"Your men are as incompetent as sick dogs!" he said, spitting on the floor. "How can they be men if they have you for a ruler? It can't be so! Your king is so cowardly he hides behind a woman's skirt, for he knows I will gut him for killing my prince! I challenge the true leader of the Scythians to meet me in battle. As custom dictates, he may choose the place and the three weapons he will use. Does he accept this royal challenge?"

"*I hear you*," Czarinaea's voice was steady and smooth, "and I accept your challenge."

"You fools are not taking me serious," he shouted as he slammed his fist on the table in front of Czarinaea. "I cannot fight this woman!"

"I am not a woman," she told him. "I am a Scythian warrior. And you sir will live to regret your challenge."

Looking at her, it seemed for the first time, his laughter was as obnoxious as his shouts and his challenging manner. "Perhaps the spineless Scythians don't understand a challenge of this sort," he growled. "It, of course, will be a fight to the death."

"If that be the case," said Czarinaea, throwing her head back to stare up at him, "then I am sure that your family will miss you. Mareus," she said to her lead council, "call out more guards and let them escort our guest to the appropriate quarters. Oh..." and addressing the hulking man that stood in front of her she said, "And it would be helpful if we had your name when we bring your breastplate to your king with the regrettable news."

And with that, Czarinaea swept out of the room as the council and additional guards surrounded the angry man and led him to the prison barracks.

Once done with overseeing their hulking guest to his quarters, Mareus and his brother noticed that two Medes had been shackled by Scythian guards and were sitting quietly by the door of the prison. They explained that they were slaves sworn to fight by the side of Ceilapeus the Slayer, and had entered camp with him in search of the leader of the Scythians.

"Are the Medes not aware that the king is dead," Mareus questioned, "and that we have a new leader?"

"To be honest sir, there have been wild rumors of a lady king," said the smaller of the two, bobbing his head in deference to Mareus, "but Ceilapeus has been so infuriated by the death of the one person who had ever given him a kind word, that his ears have been closed to any such news."

"T'is true sir," said the other slave, knotted rope hindering his handless arm as he attempted to scratch his filthy face.

313

"How is it again that you are to assist this Ceilapeus?" said Vareus while looking them over in complete astonishment, "He doesn't seem to need…well anything other than a bath and some manners…"

Clearly seeing the slaves as no threat, Mareus interrupted his brother to ask if they had eaten, and when they told him that they had not, he ordered the guards to untie them and have someone see to it that they were fed, and *bathed!*

The two brothers, glad to be away from the overwhelming stench wafting off of the slaves, knew they must seek out the queen to put a stop to the insanity of the challenge.

"On the contrary, it is not only my duty," said Czarinaea addressing the council the next morning, "but I could not remain your queen with good conscience if I did not accept his challenge," adding as she smiled at a mighty warrior in the back of the room, "I am most honored that you would offer to fight in my stead, I know of the bounties you have brought to our court, but I must decline. Of course we, all of us, will try and dissuade *The Slayer* from his folly, but…"

The din that accompanied her announcement was so deafening that she put her hand up to stem the deluge of voices raised in opposition, and the volume slowly decreased until at last she could speak.

"Gentlemen the rules of the royal house are clear," she told them. "It is up to the leader to answer the call and I have done so! What then is all the dissension?"

"Dearest Queen, you must allow someone fight in your stead. We cannot do without you," said Mareus, his eyes reflected the fear that was being felt by every man in the room, though his voice held nothing but loyalty.

"I have told you in the past to address me as Czarinaea. I have not held my office over your heads. But in this instance I do. At sunrise tomorrow you, Mareus, along with your brother and the rest of the council will announce to… have we learned his name?"

"Ceilapeus the Slayer," answered Vareus.

"Well then," Czarinaea continued, "it will be announced to Ceilapeus…*the Slayer* unless someone can talk him into rescinding and apologizing, that the time is noon, three days hence, the place is in the arena, and the weapons will be chosen just before the challenge begins."

"My Queen, you mustn't do this..." pleaded Mareus, his words faltering as Czarinaea strode purposefully from the room, telling one of the guards to send a stable boy for her horse.

Noon on the dreaded day arrived. The blazingly bright sun was not co-operating with Mareus's black mood. Neither the council nor Czarinaea's house staff had seen much of her, and as she approached the crowded arena, sound receded.

As Ceilapeus lumbered toward the center of the ring, the guards that had been sent to retrieve him were having a hard time keeping up with his long stride.

"Choose your weapons," he barked at the queen, his cavernous mouth an open pit of decay.

"I choose Lightning," said Czarinaea.

Dismayed and confused voices drifted from the crowd, but as a stable boy led a huge armored Arabian stallion into the ring, the crowd opened a wider circle to allow room for the animal.

"No one said anything about horses!" shouted Ceilapeus, "everyone knows a battle of this nature should be on the ground."

"I am an Emetchi" she told him. "My horse is my weapon. You, sir, may have your pick of the stable, ride your own horse or stay afoot, but shall we get on with it."

Glaring at her, he shrugged and went toward the stable for his horse. Upon returning Ceilapeus vehemently complained about his horse not being a weapon and he was stoically told by Czarinaea that he could ride if he wished *and* he could choose an additional weapon. Mareus then began to explain the rules and showed them to opposite sides of the large arena.

Ceilapeus sheathed his long sword and clutched a barbarous looking chained club as he clumsily climbed on his dappled steed. As he settled in, one of the slaves that had come into the encampment with him handed him a battle worn shield and the short sword he had requested, which he put in his belt. When the slave offered words to the Slayer, he spit and kicked at the man, nearly running him over with his mount as he took his place on the south side of the ring.

Reaching behind her back to check on her dagger, Czarinaea declared it as her second weapon. Mareus handed her a shield and the sword she normally used in battle, acknowledging it as her third implement, she gracefully grabbed her horse's mane and slipped comfortably astride.

A stag horn alerted the challengers to rush toward one another, hoofs rending the air as dust rose from the parched ground blurring the field as the opponents flew at each other with cries of battle on their lips.

An evil smile crossed The Slayers gaping mouth as he powerfully swung the barbed club above his head and aimed at Czarinaea as she charged by him, missing her only because she had disappeared from her steed. In total confusion he reigned in his mare and looking back over his shoulder a booted foot struck him squarely in the face, nearly unseating him. Then, not much more than a blur, Czarinaea flew past him standing backwards atop her stallion.

Wiping blood and bits of blackened teeth from his mouth and nose, his eyes widened as he watched the queen back-flip, and landing astride she suddenly reigned in her animal and as the stallion pawed the air, Czarinaea unsheathed her sword and headed directly for him.

Putting up his shield too late, he sustained a deep wound to his side. Losing sight of her for a moment he was thrown from his horse by the force of her weight as she flew through the air hitting him and wrapping her legs around his throat, they tumbled to the ground.

Raising her sword above him with both hands on the hilt, she cried, "Hippa, hippa" and, brought the sword slowly toward his neck, just short of running him through she held the sword aloft.

The onlookers cheered wildly, some shouting, "Kill him! Kill him!"

Dazed, blood clouding his eyes, the Slayer demanded, "You claim to be a warrior! Finish me! Otherwise you are just a cowardly *woman*!"

Czarinaea pushed herself away from his bulk, rising with care and contemplating his words. A *vision* threatened, and for a moment she just leaned on her sword. But as the crowd sang her praises, she slowly walked toward her stallion and began to check him for wounds.

"Czarinaea, behind you!" shouted a chorus of voices.

Crouching while instinctively reaching for her dagger, she threw it, hitting Ceilapeus directly between the eyes. He died, hate written on his face and clutching his hidden dagger in his hand.

Dazed she slowly retraced her steps back to where he lay. Knowing what was expected of her she lifted his head from the dirt, the *vision* that had threatened earlier blackening her sight; she reached blindly extricating her dagger from his forehead. Standing, one booted foot on his chest holding the dagger high for the onlookers to see, her other hand extended outward to quiet the pandemonium.

"I am a Scythian by choice," she said. "Taking his head, though it is your custom —is not mine! But that is not the issue at this time. His body will remain intact. It will be sent back to his people with another declaration of peace! I will not let this misguided man ruin what we have worked so hard for.

"The Medes will be told that he died a warrior," she continued, "with the belief that he needed to defend his prince's name. But that his prince needed no defense, for a crime had not taken place… simply the untimely death of a man who will forever be a prince in the eyes of his friends as well as his enemies!"

"Hail Czarinaea, Queen of Peace! Czar-rin-nee-a! Czar-rin-nee-a!" cried the onlookers.

"Czarinaea, are you all right?" Mareus asked as he rushed to her side. Leaning on him, her color turned ashen as the *vision* took hold.

A heavy bearded man was on top of her, his breath was noxious enough that it could have ignited a torch and his clothing reeked of urine and salt air. She was aware of hard wooden planks and a rocking motion under her body, as if she were on a ship. It was clear that this man had every intention of raping her. When he was in the act of pulling down his britches, she chanted magic words, and a wraith-like spirit appeared that frightened him beyond words. Pushing himself off of her, he screamed and began to run about blindly, trying to escape the frightening creature that pursued him, he flung himself overboard.

"I have been injured," she said quietly to Mareus, unable to shake off the vision, "it is my shoulder. Make no mention of it. Walk with me to my quarters. We shall see what's to be done."

As they walked side by side, the crowd congratulated her and Czarinaea tried not to wince as the lively well-wishers clapped her on the shoulder. Going back to her room seemed to be at a snail's pace and the images in her mind were unrelenting.

Crouching in a dark hole, hearing vermin scurry around her, she whispered to a young man who she knew to be a cabin boy, "We will never speak of this," and he solemnly agreed before rushing up a darkened ladder and closing down a hatch. Bleak darkness surrounded her...

Darkness threatened as Vareus held her down and Mareus pulled her arm up and pushed it back into its socket.

"You offered Ceilapeus his life this time, where-as in another life you were responsible for his death," said her spirit guide, "You have balanced your karma with him, but his karma remains with him for another lifetime."

"Mareus," she said, in an attempt to distance the vision and yet understand it, "do you believe you have lived before?"

"My Queen, of what do you speak?" asked Mareus seeking out his brothers eye as he said to him, "call one of the house servants, Czarinaea needs help to undress, and some rest perhaps."

"No. No, I am not delirious," she spoke sharply, "I...Vareus....leave us please. And do not call a servant! It is not a woman I need, but a strong drink," and reaching for the hand of Mareus, she said, "and a good friend."

Once Vareus left, the friends put their heads together and spoke for hours on past lives, spirit guides and friendship.

Finally a messenger came from the Medes thanking the Scythians for sending both the prince and Ceilapeus back to them. The honorable Mede king said he would accept the offer of a statue depicting Prince Stryangaeus, and he set the wedding date between the Scythians and the Medes to take place in six moons. It was a relief to all of the council and warriors when the royal proclamation was read, and they sent workmen and artisans as had been promised. The groom had convinced the council it would be good for him to go along. He was looking forward to meeting and spending time again with his betrothed, whom he *knew* to be quite comely.

"Tillisa," Czarinaea said, keeping her voice soft while speaking to her timid new servant. "It is perfectly alright to look me in the eye when we speak. I recognize that you were taken in a raid and made a slave in the past, but you are perfectly safe here in…"

"Hippa, hippa!" came a loud but familiar cry from the front of the house. Czarinaea rushed to the door just as her mother burst enthusiastically through it, dropping the gifts she carried, and opening her arms wide.

"Are you not happy to see me?" laughed Antilene in Czarinaea's ear as they embraced.

"I think this hug should answer that question!" Czarinaea said, squeezing her mother harder.

"That is true, but you are crushing my ribs. Unarm me so that I can get a good look at you! Good, you have turned out well, and this," she said pointing to the spacious home, "this is truly magnificent. I would have you show me to my room, but I am hungry for words and wine, and a bit of food would be the very thing for a wearied traveler."

Czarinaea called the servants, who her mother dismayed by giving them each a bear hug, lifting the smaller women off the floor, and clapping the men hard on the shoulders.

⁕

Just a few days had passed, however, before all of the servants were vying for her mother's favor, she having endeared herself by learning all their names and asking about their families. How could she, Czarinaea wondered, ever have shut this vibrant woman out of her life? But when she tried to apologize, her mother told her never to feel guilty about honest emotions.

"I was stern, because I had to be," she said, "and I will not apologize for my sternness. I expect no more from you. You have always been a good daughter. Even in your anger you did the right thing. This was destined. I am so sorry about Lotzar, however. That is a part of your life I wish that I could change. She was a great friend, a woman you could trust and talk to as women do. That is why I came. I have brought you a special gift, a woman from our tribe, to assist you in training the men or the horses."

"Where is she?" asked Czarinaea. "Why did you not bring her the night you came?"

"I came on ahead with one of your warriors. I was too excited to dally on the road. We came straight through."

"Train my men?" asked Czarinaea, just realizing what her mother had said.

"The training I speak of is in horseflesh, horse talk and stunt riding. Your men are seriously lacking in the finer arts of understanding animals. Some of the horseflesh they have here should never enter into a battle. They are not trained to assist their rider."

"Yes…" Czarinaea hesitated before saying, "I suppose that is true. Must you leave right away, or will you stay to implement these new things?"

"The woman I brought will follow your orders, and she will help you to teach them and you can help her find a mate. She drives me crazy with talk of mating and children!"

"Oh, I see," Czarinaea said, laughing. "You are pawning one of your amorous young women off on me. It will be another mouth to feed. And yes. I see your motives now."

"Do you indeed, my dear? Do you indeed," her mother observed with a smile. "Well, she is impatient. I should warn you of that. In fact, if she has her way she shall have a child nine moons hence. See that she finds a good man. I will leave that to you." Antilene's face became very solemn. "Will you tell me about *your* good man? I've heard the rumors of course. But I think as a mother, I want to know that you were loved."

Czarinaea leaned her head to one side, her face sad but radiant. Finally she spoke.

"I think that a better way for me to answer you is to say that *I loved*. I want to thank you for teaching me how to give my heart! I did not want a man in my life. I did not grow up with that thought, or with the sight of you and a mate together."

Czarinaea reached lovingly for her mother's hand. "But small memories have lingered from the time when I was young and heard you comforting Lotzar's mother one day about losing the man she loved. You spoke about men who were special, who were gifts from the goddess and knew how to worship a woman. You said that they were few and far between, but that, when a woman finds one, she should recognize the gift and give homage to the man in every way she can. You told her that she was right to love him, and she now had the gift of a child. You knew what you were talking about. I could feel it. You gave her some very good advice and she healed and became a wonderful mother just like you. Are you happy with the warrior king Myrina married? I hear she lives at quite a distance."

"Oh, no you don't" her mother challenged her. "You cannot change the subject asking me about your sister. Won't you tell me a bit about *him?*"

"I am not yet ready to speak about him, but please know it is not that I do not wish to talk to you, just that I cannot speak of it yet! I am so happy that you are here. When do I get to meet this woman who will help me train the men to understand horses better?" Czarinaea laughed.

"Hello, hello!" came a voice from beyond the door.

"Now that is perfect timing," her mother said. "It is Egeria, the addition to your staff that I have been bragging about!"

Tellisa hurried to do her job and led Egeria to where she and her mother sat. Noticing that Egeria had the same saucy walk that Lotzar had, with hips swinging and a big smile splashed across her precocious face, Czarinaea thought, Yes, she will do just fine!

Chapter 12

Czarinaea awoke suddenly from a fitful sleep. Reaching across the bed she called for Stryangaeus, and hearing no answer, remembered, her eyes filling with tears as the loss of her lover became a heavy cloak engulfing her. Her mind racing with unbidden thoughts of all the things she could have done differently for both her friend Lotzar and for the man she had loved, she clutched her pillow to her and tried to stifle the sound of her sobs. All that she had learned in her life did not leave room for weakness, and she believed grief a weakness. Visions of her friend dying before her eyes and of her lover dying alone plagued her. Try as she may she could not stop the onslaught of grief until finally, she cried out, one single primal sound that brought her no comfort.

*Stryangaeus' voice was soft but true, "My queen, my beautiful queen, it is time you grieved… but it is **never** time for guilt."*

Czarinaea spun around, eyes wide at the sound of his voice. "How… how can this be?"

Reaching for his hand, as she had done in the past, she felt his fingers grip hers, and crying out, "I've missed you so," flung herself into his arms.

"Come," he said, "lie down beside me and let me hold you."

"What did you mean when you said there is never time for guilt?" she asked him as her tears slowly subsided. "There is so much I would have done differently! Lotzar did not have to die. And you! The guilt I feel over our love… over causing your death overwhelms me!"

"The expression of true grief unburdens the soul, but guilt is false and it creates burden," he told her. "You felt there was no way for us to be together when I was alive. By holding onto the guilt and not grieving, you continue to hold on to me. It's as if by not accepting my death fully you can hold on to the love we never had the chance to experience."

He took her chin, gently lifting it up so that he could look directly into her eyes.

"My love, I cannot move on until you accept my death. Your guilt connects you to me, creating a false sense of security. Grief, tears, pain, anger…they are all normal emotions to feel when someone you love has died. You lost your best friend, your child and your lover all in a matter of a few days. Yet you have not truly wept or allowed yourself to feel the pain, or to speak of your loss. Anger is the only emotion you allow, anger at your spirit guide for not warning you in a dream or in a vision."

"How did you know?" she asked. "I…"

"That you are angry because you were not warned? That is obvious, for you have been having visions and dreams all your life about the bigger happenings that would take place. You depend upon these things. They are like a rudder on your boat, and they failed you."

"Yes!" yelled Czarinaea as she wrenched herself out of his arms and rose to pace the room. "How could she not tell me? What… was she too busy to let me know of these life changing events? Flitting around doing goddess things, too busy to let me in on my own life! Yes, I am angry! I don't care to have prophetic dreams or visions anymore. She can just keep everything to herself! I cannot be bothered!"

"That is the guilt speaking," he told her. "You……

"No, it is anger! You said that I should be willing to be angry, well I am!"

"Anger is good. But with whom are you angry?"

"At her of course! The dream maker, the vision maker!"

Czarinaea threw herself on the floor in front of her pallet. Putting her head down, she sobbed into the covers as Stryangaeus gently caressed her hair.

"You are angry at yourself," he told her gently. "Guilt is anger turned inward.

"What was the name of the goddess that calls herself your spirit guide?"

"What difference does it make now? I am not speaking to her!" pouted Czarinaea.

Stryangaeus smiled lovingly at her. "I have never seen you pout. That's good, we have reached another emotion."

Czarinaea was very quiet. She turned away from him chewing on her lip and she delved into her feelings. After a while she reached a conclusion and slowly tried to put it into words.

"So when I am pouting... I am feeling sorry for myself?" asked Czarinaea. "Is that what you mean? I am angry with Desimena because I feel **I am the victim**, not the ones that I have lost... but me! It is easier to be the victim because I was ill prepared for the loss, and I am not willing to admit I was ill prepared for anything!"

Czarinaea struggled to remember her most recent dream. "My spirit guide said last night that there was a pinnacle of balance between pride and humility, and **acceptance** was the key. I didn't understand what she meant. But now I see that grief humbles you. Grief is the nadir- it is the opposite of the zenith, the summit. When you allow yourself depths of despair you are permitted a glimpse of the summit. Yes, I see now," she continued in a rush of words. "You cannot claim the summit before it is time, but you can slowly climb its treacherous heights with acceptance. But it is so hard to accept your loss... Please help me with it," she implored.

"To go on effectively, you must start believing in yourself again, and to do that you must have faith. Your faith needs to be placed on your dreams and visions. If you stop having faith in them, than how can you have any faith in yourself?"

He reached for her hand, and lovingly brought it to his lips. "Do not forget that your visions told you about me long before we met, and those visions have helped you in many ways. If you refuse them you are in effect saying to your guide, 'if you don't always let me know what is coming, I don't want to participate in life.' That would be a shame because your lust for life has always been such a beautiful thing to behold."

Czarinaea looked up at him and he bent down to kiss her, a soft loving kiss. His image started to fade.

"No, I am not ready for you to go yet," pleaded Czarinaea.

"Believe in yourself, my queen. Believe..."

"No!"

"I must go... your council comes for you. There are hostilities brewing and they need your advice. Gather all the warriors and wait on the bluff overlooking the eastern valley. Do not attack the intruders until I tell you, and there will be very little bloodshed."

෴

Following her lover's advice, Czarinaea led an advance on the intruders, in which not one of her men was lost, a move that brought a quick end to the insurgence and allowed peace to reign again.

Czarinaea spoke earnestly to each and every man that they had captured. Some were hostile and unruly, even in defeat, so she sent them on their way minus their weapons. Most she convinced to stay by telling them of the prosperity they would enjoy as her subjects, and expounding on the just laws and the systems they had set in place, such as rewarding their faithful warriors with gold.

Reflections of her encounter with her lover earlier that day danced around her as she hurriedly walked the last few steps to her dwelling. When at last she closed the door to her room, grateful tears streaking her dusty cheeks, she spoke aloud the appreciative words which flowed freely from her heart.

"My prince, your guidance was welcomed, as many lives were spared," she told him.

"But what I have learned today is that there truly is no death, and that you will always be with me. Your loving words and your trust in me will be a beacon, holding me fast and true to the course I have chosen."

The room filled with the undeniable aroma of roses. Czarinaea's heart brimmed with love as she reached for the bottle on her dresser. Smiling she said, "And when I think of you, I will always smell the sweet fragrance of roses."

Chapter 13

Czarinaea loved hearing Egeria's laughter which was full of ripe emotion that rose to the surface like air bubbles created by a lively waterfall. Dutiful to her mother, as always, she had found a suitable man for Egeria, although in uniting two such stubborn people, she had spent time she could ill afford.

Now, unpacking a picnic meal, she listened to the two horse trainers bantering. They teased each other unmercifully, but didn't seem to be willing to admit that they loved each other. How wonderful it must be, she thought, to be in love and not have to decide between your people or your lover. But she must not think like that. She was feeling more like herself again, which at this moment meant that she felt not only whole, but hungry!

"Czarinaea," Egeria called, "Kaleus is telling me that I cannot train a horse to dance, especially Karina, as he thinks she is too clumsy. Perhaps we should wager his last earnings on it. You could hold the gold for us. We will set a time limit to allow the wager to be fair. What say you?"

"Yes," said Czarinaea, "I think a wager is good. But perhaps the stakes are too low."

"Well… what would you suggest them to be?" Kaleus said, as he pulled his unruly brown hair away from his handsome bearded face and busied himself tying it in a knot.

"Kaleus, what do you want the most from Egeria?" Czarinaea asked.

"Ahh… I don't know, that's a difficult question," stated Kaleus as he kicked the dirt with his leather boots.

And so Czarinaea turned to Egeria and asked her the same question, hoping to shame one of them into answering.

"What would you say if I wanted nothing?" the girl retorted.

"All right then, I'll set the terms," said Czarinaea looking thoughtful. "Kaleus, if Egeria wins then you leave your post here at the stables and leave the clan. If you win, then Egeria goes back to her people and you may run the stables as you did before she came."

The trainers looked stunned! Both started talking at the same time saying that the terms were way too harsh. Czarinaea looked nonplused at their arguments.

"It is an order! I have heard each of you say more than once this morning that you wanted everything as it was! For now let us enjoy the meal that I have brought. I have goat cheese, mead and acorn bread. Let us eat, for you each have much to do."

Both Kaleus and Egeria were silent during the meal, but when it was finished and Czarinaea indicated that she was to leave them, Egeria asked to accompany her. Once on the path leading to the house, the girl said, "What are you thinking? You know that I can teach any horse to dance, so why would you make such a wager? Do you want Kaleus to leave?"

"I don't. On the contrary, I think he is quite valuable to the stable, therefore to the clan," said Czarinaea with a sly smile.

"Then... I do not know what you are up to," Egeria told her, clearly confused.

"I guess you will just have to wait and see," Czarinaea said, looking rather smug.

⁓❧⁓

When Czarinaea arrived at the house, she sent for Mareus, and excitedly told him about her new ideas for the royal wedding. They put their heads together and began to talk about a street festival and horsemanship event.

Czarinaea enjoyed her friendship with Mareus and began confiding in him that she missed her mother since she had gone back to her people. Then, eagerly, she told him of her plans to send word to her mother to dispatch five young women to them to perform stunt riding for the festivities. Having made plans to meet the next day after she had more time to meditate on it, Mareus left to meet and speak with the councilmen.

❧

The next morning, Czarinaea, refreshed, went out into the garden to greet the morning sun. As the sun crested over the low hills of their land, its golden orange glow filled her with hope. After the festival, she would take a trip to visit with her mother, so that she could tell her that she had been loved. She was now ready to share the greatness of what she had with Stryangaeus. By sharing it, by allowing other people to know of the magnitude of his love, she would be allowing it to live on.

Looking lovely in her light green tunic, with the soft folds hugging her body, Czarinaea greeted Mareus with a huge smile.

"Mareus, you know that I have had many visions," she said, ignoring the unmasked hunger in his eyes, "I have made no secret of it. My visions have always come to pass. The men are restless. Except for this last skirmish, we have had no battles to fight. Peace is easier on the body than war, but it is harder on the mind.

"I have asked for guidance and I believe I received it," she told him. "Two things are important. We have agreed that we need to schedule the royal wedding and the festival at the same time. The wedding comes first of course. Then we will start the festival the next day. And secondly, there are a few important clansmen that need wives. If we do nothing to supply these men with wives, some will go off on their own, pillage and take a woman by force which will cause skirmishes and loss of lives. I am thinking to ask my mother, not only to dispatch young women for our festivities, but ask that she hand pick those that wish to have a mate. That way, this festival will supply many needs for our clan. This is getting more exciting by the moment. And think of all the profits for our tradesmen. Why…"

"Yes, yes. I can see it now!" Mareus exclaimed. "But I did not mean to interrupt. I can see you are fairly bursting to tell me the rest!"

"We can have races with prizes. I *know*….true the women will win those," Czarinaea added as she saw Mareus roll his eyes. "But our men can have a contest on the short bow. I will have a very special bow made of the finest wood. Every Scythian worth his weight will drool at the beauty of it. They will have to use the newly constructed bow to shoot, and whoever wins the contest will get to keep the bow."

When the new servant entered with refreshment, presumably made bold by her few weeks with the queen, she looked Mareus directly in the eyes, asking him if there was anything else he needed, making it all too clear that she did not mean refreshment. And although he told her no, it was apparent that he found her attractive.

Czarinaea noticed the exchange and hoped that he would follow through. Tillisa was perfect for him, and perhaps a nudge on her part would help. Or perhaps, she thought, seeing the girl wink at Mareus before swaying off, she does not need my help.

Tellisa's wink brought a bit of color to his face, though it did not stop him from observing her flirtatious hips exiting the room.

"Well…" Czarinaea chuckled, looking directly at the bulge in his leggings. "You mentioned bursting earlier…"

And then, not able to contain herself, she laughed so infectiously that both of them ended up with tears in their eyes, and Czarinaea was forced to bite her lip to cease what had become uncontrolled laughter.

"Thank you Czarinaea," Mareus said, bringing sobriety back to their exchange, "for caring so about us. I was concerned at first. I thought it might be that you had stayed with us only because of the threats he held over your head. But – well, after his death I knew that you would be a wonderful queen, although I was not sure how deep the scars were of your husband's brutal treatment, and the loss of your child. It was a great deal to put behind you. Did you have a vision of being queen before you came here?"

"Yes, early on," she told him. "I could not understand it at first. But by the time Marmareus died, I knew all of you were *my people*, I was no longer surprised at my concern and love for the clan. When I left my homeland I was angry with my mother, and I had such hate in my heart for my new husband. I could not imagine caring for his people. I don't know when it happened. Slowly… I think all of you won my heart."

"I think you know that I wish it was I that won your heart," he told her earnestly. "But I will never put that before you. I have too much respect for what you have given us. I just thought I would let you know. I will always be here for you."

"You are a dear friend, and have been that since I came here, but you are also invaluable now as a trusted brother," Czarinaea said, hugging him. "I care for you deeply. As I told you before, you are a wonderful man. I am honored to know that you will always be by my side. We are family! I think we need family, perhaps more of it is in the works for you. Go now, we have much to plan."

The next few weeks flew by. The wedding was a grand affair, and coupled with the festival that went on for days was a great success.

Kaleus asked Egeria to be his woman right after she had pleased the onlookers with stunts aptly done astride Karina, looking anything but clumsy, and he teased Egeria unmercifully, saying that he only asked her to be his woman so that he wouldn't have to leave the clan, because she had indeed won the wager. A taunting reply hovered on her lips, but he grabbed her and whispered, "You are indeed the better horseman! I hope that doesn't get in the way of your giving me fine sons and a daughter *just like you.*"

Somehow those words sealed her lips, and her heart. Egeria kept her saucy words to herself but said instead as she held him close, "Perhaps I am a better horseman than you," the girl replied in a whisper so loud that even Czarinaea could hear" but I think you can still teach me a thing or two."

Chapter 19

Czarinaea and her horse rode as one through the green meadow. Wind whipped through her long dark hair, and her eyes shone amber in the golden rays of the rising sun. When she urged her steed to go faster, he effortlessly began to gallop at lightning speed until suddenly he rose from the ground. With Czarinaea holding tightly to his mane, trembling with rapture, they flew over the lush verdant fields of her homeland where, in the distance stood the Temple of Ephesus, the bright sun shining behind its glistening pillars. Suddenly, dark clouds ominously began to appear before them, hiding the sun, and the temple vanished from sight. With an anguished cry, she let go of the mane and fell, tumbling over and over into the darkness.

Only then, engulfed in the silence of deep despair, did she hear a deep velvet voice calling to her. *"Soon, I'll meet you in the temple garden. Soon... I promise you."*

"No...no, don't go," Czarinaea cried. Her body drenched in sweat, her heart pounding, she awoke to find Mareus sitting beside her on the bed, holding her hand.

"Have I slept long?" She asked him, her voice thick with effort.

"A few hours," he told her. "It was needed after such a battle. You should be proud of today's accomplishments. The village of Kronos has been liberated from tyrannical rule."

When she attempted to get up, Mareus gently put his hand on her shoulder.

"You've taken quite a blow," he explained. "I am sure that the man you bested in battle wondered how you stayed astride your horse after his onslaught."

"Call the council....I..."

"You thanked them Czarinaea, you thanked all of them as we rode back to Tanais."

"Who brought me to my room?"

"You… you stripped off your armor as you made for the bed." Mareus picked up a small earthen bottle and pointed to a garment that was lying at the end of the bed.

"You picked up this bottle and robe from your chest before you lay down. Would you like Tillisa to help you into the garment? It is very beautiful."

"It is very old!"

"It has weathered the test of time as you have my queen. I…."

Mareus, choked on the words and tears coursed down his withered skin as he hung his graying head to hide his pain.

"Stryangaeus gave it to me when I was his prisoner, as well as the Attar of Roses in the bottle. May….may I have it, I wish to put it on."

Mareus opened the bottle and smelled the fragrant scent.

"There is just a bit left," he told her.

"Ah…that is perfect, for I will not need it after today."

"No!" he cried. "You must not say that! You must not!"

Tellisa entered the room and put her arms around her husband to comfort him. She loved Czarinaea greatly, and knowing that her husband would be devastated once his best friend left the world, she held him as he wept. At last alone with the woman who had brought her such joy, Tillisa dressed her wound and, at her command, rubbed all that was left of the Attar of Roses over her body before helping her into the garment that Stryangaeus so adored.

"Thank you, thank you for serving me so faithfully all of these years," Czarinaea murmured, her breath labored. "And th…thank you for loving my friend."

Tillisa gently put her arms around her mistress. "It is I that needs to do the thanking. You cannot know what you have done for me, for my sons, for my husband…and for every woman in the clan…you cannot know," she sobbed openly, burying her face on Czarinaea's shoulder.

Once alone, as she had asked to be, Czarinaea picked up her mirror and looked at her withered skin and the streaks of gray in her long tresses. And then lying back, holding the empty vial, the faint aroma of which took her back into Stryangaeus' arms. She could feel his gentle touch. He was singing a song to her.

◦⋇◦

Floating above her body, she was surprised to find that a beautiful goddess was calling her name.

"Where is Stryangaeus?" Czarinaea asked. "Who are you?"

"My name is Desimena."

"Oh... I see. I hear Stryangaeus," she told her. "But I cannot find him."

"He is waiting for you," Desimena said in a soft voice. "Are you ready to go now?"

Czarinaea gazed down at her body and hesitated. "I have dressed myself for him. I have looked forward to this day."

"Follow his voice," the goddess told her. "He is waiting for you. You have done well, Aradia."

"My name is Czarinaea," the queen said, looking more closely at Desimena, "though the name Aradia is very familiar. I know you. I have seen you in my dreams and visions. You first came to me when I was a little girl at the waterfall."

"I have always been with you. I am very proud of you Aradia. You have learned the lessons that you chose for yourself in this lifetime. It is a remarkable feat."

"What lessons did I choose to learn?" asked Czarinaea.

"Forgiveness - Love of Mother- Courage- Commitment to the greater good, and last but not least, you have learned the balance between Pride and Humility. But we will talk about this in more detail another day. Now it is time for you to make a choice. You have served your people well. You would not be deserting them if you leave now. It is time for you to have a rest."

"Yes... I am very weary. His voice soothes me. He is singing! Can you hear it?"

"Oh yes. Heaven rejoices for your love," Desimena told her. "Go now. Follow his voice."

And with one last look at the body she had discarded lying below, Czarinaea moved off into a whitish-blue tunnel.

◦⋇◦

"My queen, how beautiful you look. I have so much to show you. Oh, how I have missed you. Come give me your hand," said Stryangaeus.

She reached out her hand and clung to him as he pulled her deeper into the tunnel and into his waiting arms.

"My queen, my queen, I have missed you so."

"My love," Czarinaea said, "I have held you in my heart each moment of every day. All that I have accomplished was because of your love and your goodness. Look… do you remember this vial?"

"Yes" he said, slowly smiling. "And I remember what I told you when I gave it to you. I showed you the bottom of the rose and I told you that the star shape was to remind us that we came from the stars. There is no aroma in the entire universe equal to the rose. It is a sacred gift from spirit to keep us open upon the earth to the world of the unseen. There is a love story about two beings from different star systems joining together in love and gifted with the first rose bush upon the earth. Sometime I will tell you the story," he said as they walked hand in hand.

"Don't ever leave me," she told him, her eyes glistened with love. "I adore your stories, and oh, how I have missed your voice."

"I have never left you. You have heard my words of love in your ear."

"That is true, my love, but this is much better, for the sight of you fills me with wonder and the smell of you delights all my senses. I'm sorry I have taken so long to get here," she said.

"There is no time in spirit," he assured her. "Our separation was but a moment here, even though a moment without you in my arms feels like an eternity. Is it possible that you are even more beautiful than I remember?"

"It must be this place, for everything is shining. Everything feels new."

They sat down on a carpet of emerald grass by a pond. The birds nesting in a nearby tree welcomed them with their song. Rabbits stopped in the field and a squirrel approached and crouched beside them.

Later, when they were lying in each other's arms, she told him first of the fullness of her life as queen, and the difference knowing him had made in the many decisions put before her each day. Then she told him of the emptiness of living without him, the long lonely nights and worse…day break… knowing that at day's end she would grieve again his loss. Many times it was a struggle to remember all that he had taught her so that she could somehow get through the night and face the next day with courage.

"*The taste of your lips, there is nothing that compares,*" *he moaned, holding her tighter.*

Hungrily, she merged with him in a bonding of **souls** *united in a love that passed the bounds of space and time. Radiant colors cascaded from their bodies, and multihued waves of energy lit the lush and fertile garden. Fish danced in the water and the animals moved closer to experience the depth and breadth of their love.*

⚜

"*Soon we will meet with Desimena,*" *Stryangaeus told her, and it was clear that he was choosing his words carefully.* "*We need to review the lives we just lived, and make preparations for the next.*"

"*No...! I do not want to go back yet!*" *Czarinaea cried, dismayed.*

Laughingly he reached for her hand and bringing it to his lips, he playfully tasted each fingertip before kissing her palm.

"*Oh...Aren't you the least bit excited and curious to again experience a physical lifetime with me?*" *With an irresistible smile he teased,* "*Won't it be interesting to see if you recognize me...this time?*"

⚜

"*Ahh child,*" *crooned Desimena upon greeting Aradia the next day,* "*how beautiful you look. It never ceases to amaze me how you glow when you have been with Thomas.*"

Seeing the confusion in Aradia's eyes, Desimena said, "*That is the sacred name we have given him on this side of the veil, as it means twin. His acceptance of this name as his prime energy will help him to delve deeper into the spiritual mysteries of life as he moves into each incarnation. Just as your prime energy, the name Aradia, meaning bright orb, creates the need for you to shine in each life and to never be afraid of being a leader.*

"*Well...as I was saying even in this luminescent atmosphere your radiance after being with Thomas is obvious.*" *Desimena contemplated her next words,* "*Although I have never been tempted to live in a physical body, I can understand the draw to the physical when* **twin flames** *are involved. I applaud your decision to quickly go back to earth, because I can see the benefits that will be garnered as you further explore what it means to allow the divine flame to ignite within the human body.*"

335

*"I have never heard the term twin flame before," Aradia said, "yet I felt the chill of truth when you suggested that Thomas and I **are** twin flames. Will you tell me more?"*

"No," replied Desimena, "it is best you receive the information first-hand. Your lesson for today is to meditate on what it means to be a twin flame. We will meet again tomorrow and you can share with me what you have come to understand."

⚜

"And so, what have you learned my child?" asked Desimena upon greeting Aradia the next morning.

"I have spent every moment since we parted in silent reverence of the feelings that I encountered as I asked Goddess to give me insight into twin flames. It began just after you left me when I sat quietly listening to the waterfall in the meditation room. As I relaxed, in my inner vision my world became pure white. Out from that white moved a fiery ball of blinding light that took my breath away. The bright ball encompassed me and I felt myself becoming a circle that had no beginning and no end. The circle bent and contorted into many shapes, but always became a circle again before it changed into another intricate and beautiful design. I was each geometric pattern, yet I always remained the circle.

*After a while I, the brilliant orb, separated into two halves. But I was each one. As I looked out from me, I saw another me, a mirror like image, yet one was male and one was female. But I was both! I did not understand how that could be. As I pondered that question I watched as the orbs began to make love. The entwining was incredible because I could observe and yet **feel** the intensity of **love beyond words**…*

Then the orbs moved further and further away from each other. Color began to be added to each circle, some colors bright and others muddy. Asking, I received an instant understanding that the bright colors were lessons completed and the muddy colors, karma that needed tending to. When the circles moved toward each other again and merged, some colors would brighten and others darken.

I could see that sometimes the orbs helped each other become clearer when they were together and sometimes the colors became brighter when the orbs separated. But again in asking, the answer was instant. Twin flames always offer growth, even if it is one igniting the flame for the other, even while their own flame diminishes, because that was the agreement from the very beginning.

Agreeing that their blending will always create growth, in one or both of them, they also agreed that it would always add love to the world by and from their love of each other. And yet… cosmic law dictates that each half needs to define its own identity before it can unlock fully the joint spiritual potential of their twin flame existence. I understood that this was because there was a mission agreed upon by the twin flames, that once completed would enhance the divine identity of their souls."

"You have done well, dear Aradia," said Desimena looking pleased, "and now I can share with you that you will explore all aspects of love and passion in this next lifetime. You are now ready to experience the **Sacred Green Ray**-It holds the energy of the Sacred Heart of the Goddess. Passion, desire and creativity will be taken to a whole new level as you merge with Thomas during the act of love. It will open you to the experience of **unconditional love** and no matter what path you choose neither of you will ever be the same again."

Aradia paled. "I am daunted by the knowledge of twin flames shared with me in my meditation. I am afraid that I might not be worthy of the task set before me."

"Aradia," said Desimena, "I take it that no matter that you are unsure you will still move forward, for that is your nature. I have taught you all that I can for now. It is time for your decent…"

"Wait… what other lessons will be opened to me by choosing the Green Ray?"

"The name of the Goddess of the Green Ray is, **The Enchantress that is the seed and the Eternal flower,**" said Desimena as she clasped Aradia's hand. "You will have a chance to resolve opposing forces, within and outside of yourself. If you can do that, then you will understand what it means to be the seed and the eternal essence in the same moment.

"Love well, and trust in this next lifetime my child, and you shall unburden yourself of more of what you have created by the harsh spell you placed on Thomas in your first life together. I will be with you always," smiled the goddess. "Call on me and I shall be there."

"Thank you Desimena," Aradia replied. "You told me that I learned the balance between humility and pride in this last lifetime, but I am not so sure. I did not call upon you often. I was very stubborn. In this next lifetime I shall remember to ask for your guidance."

"Yes, but now you must remember to hold on to the name you have picked," Desimena told her. "It stands for all that you have chosen to learn in this up-coming life."

Aradia was drawn to a small hut on a peninsular bordered on one side by the Sea of Azov and on the other by the Black Sea. She saw a strong, stunning woman that was in a great deal of pain. The female warrior that she observed did not make a sound as the mid-wife worked to bring her child into the world. Looking down at the proud and loving face of the woman who was about to give birth, Aradia realized that she was to be born again. And happily she moved into the womb to begin the journey of a new life.

~Moments later… Alyanna was born ~

Turn the page for a preview of *April Rane's **Alyanna, Amazon Priestess*** - volume two of the Aradia Chronicles. Look for the new release in October of 2013~

Alyanna, Amazon Priestess

Up-coming books in The Aradia Chronicles

Alyanna, Amazon Priestess
Andalusia, Goddess of the Sea
Alistrina, Warrior Princess
Goddess of the Golden Moon

Volume Two
Book Four
Alyanna, Amazon Priestess

Thought is another name for fate; choose then thy
destiny and wait for love brings love
and hate brings hate. ~Henry Van Dyke

Our story begins approximately two thousand
one hundred years ago on a rock-strewn
peninsula that is bordered to the west by the
Egean Sea and its mystical islands.
To the east lies the sparkling turquoise
Sea of Marmara. Hellesponte
Straight carries boats and curious men between the two seas,
bringing change to the women known as the Amazon's.

~It is here that Aradia is born again, and
she takes the name of Alyanna,
which means noble, vibrant, and cheerful.

Chapter 1- Part one

Alyanna observed the women of the clan as they went about the chore of preparing the midday meal. Sitting in the same position for hours, allowed only to move her eyes, was not the hardest test she had ever been given, but certainly the most boring. She had barely ten years, and had been training to become the leader of the clan for three suns. Nisca, wise woman of the clan reminded her often, "Goddess knows when you are ready, it matters not how many years you have."

Thea, the clan's leader, slowly emerged from her hut. She seemed intent on giving orders to some of the women in preparation for a hunt they had been preparing for. Stealing a covert glance at Alyanna, she placed the stag horn to her lips. The sound would call in the outer guards, and alert the next watch to take their post on the outside perimeter of their encampment. Her seeming inattention did not fool Alyanna. As another stolen glance came her way, she watched a soft pink aura form around her mother. Yes, she thought, mother sends me love, even now when she is determined to not interrupt my lesson.

Surveying the large circle of thatched huts, and women young and old bending over smoke laden fires, Alyanna realized that she had many mothers and many teachers but no friends. She had never laughed and played with the other girls. She had never whispered secrets or giggled over a funny story shared with a best friend. Surely, it was for her own good, she thought, she must not get too close she had been told, for then she would not be able to rule with equity. Nevertheless, she looked on with the longing of a child, watching the other young girls sitting together weaving flowers into each other's hair.

Alyanna's eyes followed the girls at play, bringing back the memory of the day she was running through the woods and she *took wing*, as she liked to call it. Phadra had spotted her and brought the story back to the other girls. "Alyanna flew above the ground, bounding through the woods like a rabbit with wings," Phadra had told them, her frightened voice carrying through the huts like wild fire. The story served to make the young girls all the more distant. The women of the clan bowed their heads and averted their eyes a bit more each day and seldom did they address her without adding Emetchi, a title of respect which held the secret of The Royal Line of the Sky People. It was said it was passed down through the blood, *only* from mother to daughter, never to a son. Many times Alyanna had begged for added information, but the old ones of the clan would say nothing more.

When Alyanna had gone to her teachers, asking why others couldn't lift off the ground as she did, the great ones told her the story of the ancient priests and priestesses who roamed the forest before there were horses. "They ran/flew through the woods as if they had wings. But the ability has been lost to most because people are afraid of what they don't understand," said Nisca. "You have wings! The girls are just jealous. Pay them no mind. It is not your business that they are jealous, only that they have respect for you. Jealously is an empty bucket that is heavy to carry. But respect is a bucket that though it has weight, it is easy to carry. It is up to you to load up their buckets with thoughts of honor and respect. In that way they have no room for jealously."

Alyanna felt blessed to have such honored teachers, but she had not yet seen her wings, but sometimes she felt as though there were wings on her feet. She wished she were deep in the woods at the moment, for there she had many friends and she always felt safe. Alyanna loved watching the wood nymphs play and talking to the fairy world. They loved her too, and had told her she had the sight even before her wise teachers had made reference to it. It was then that she realized not all people could see colors around others, and that not everyone had visions. Unfortunately it did not make her feel special.

Alyanna had been told at the beginning of today's lesson, that it was important to have the ability to be very still when you needed to outsmart an enemy. Also to train your eyes to see more, weather it was being aware of an interloper long before they entered camp, or finding truth in the eyes of an enemy, and lies in the eyes of your comrades.

Cramping in her legs reminded her that soon the sun would set. It would be the best part of her day. She had been told to search the sky at nightfall for the *horse and rider*. If she succeeded she would advance to the next level of training. Every time she moved on to the next level there was a celebration, and lots of food. Best of all, there was a performance enacted in her honor depicting the up-coming level of initiation. During the performance Alyanna would receive special herbs to expand her mind, so she would retain the most from the presentation. The herb tea made of blue vervain made colors more vivid and sound more acute, and it opened the inner eye to see that which had passed and what was to come. The young girls performing did so with excitement and passion, and the information always spurred Alyanna forward, giving her clues as to what was expected of her next.

Alyanna brought herself back to the moment and looked toward the sun as it was setting over the mountains. Vivid rose-colored clouds clothed the golden sun, displaying the colors of the heart and mind. The soft tones of pink when found around a person, tree or fairy, warmed you, and from it you felt love. The deep, sharp or muddied tones of gold when around a person's head gave information about the quality of their mind. Yes, Alyanna silently chuckled to herself; she had learned much from her teachers. But now, as she observed the colors of the setting sun she realized they would bring a beautiful day on the morrow.

Just as the sun set, Alyanna was given another drink of tea from one of the young maidens. No words were exchanged, but she knew she was to close and rest her eyes, so that by dark she could lay back and study the sky for the latter part of her test. Breathing very deep she looked forward to the internal light show that was usually a benefit of the tea. Closing her eyes, she went within.

Instead of the vivid shapes and colors she normally saw, a vision of an island appeared in her mind's eye. Seeing a sensual and ravishingly beautiful woman, she realized it was she in the future, it gave her quite a shock. She was very tall, taller than any of the women in her clan, slender but shapely. For a moment, she worried that if she had no bulk, she would not make a good warrior priestess. But then feelings of being a woman washed over her young body and flooded her mind.

As she watched, a giant of a man appeared in the vision. It was obvious by their stance and weapons that she and he were going to battle with each other. Yet he was smiling. At that moment, the vision faded and she desperately tried to call it back. Alyanna had had many visions, but she could not shake the unusual feelings that had come with this one. It was not just a vision. She was there. She was a woman with a woman's desires. Her heart knew this man. What she felt about him was contrary to all that she had heard of the treacherous evils of men. She wondered, why then would she do battle with him?

Night slid around her body, stealing the remnants of her jumbled thoughts. Reluctantly she forced herself to the task at hand. Lying back she opened her eyes, and began searching the sky for the *horse and rider* that was part of her test. Presently she fell asleep, and dreamed the horse and rider were in the constellation known as the Big Bear. It was said to have a tail, though everyone knew bears have no tails. In her mind she heard the name Mizare, for the horse, and Suha, for the rider.

When she awoke, she looked toward the constellation of the Bear. In the part known as the tail, right there in the middle, she spotted a small star off to the left that she had not seen before. It was so close to the bigger one, that most would easily overlook the double star. She had found the horse and rider, passing her test; she was sure of it! Going back to sleep with a huge smile, she reveled in the fact that tomorrow would be her day. There would be a festival in her honor. Strange, the other young girls could honor her, but they could not, nor did they want to be her friend.

A half smile was on her face as she awoke. Standing above her Nisca asked, "And the strange smile, it is for what purpose?"

Alyanna brushed the sleep from her eyes. "Mizare is the name of the horse and Suha is the rider... they are here." And she drew on the ground the Bear and tail and pointed out which star had the rider.

"And so you are ready for your festival," said Nisca with a huge grin.

"Oh yes, and for my special day I would like to go down by the river and be like one of the fishes. I will return when the performance is about to begin."

"Come when you hear the horn," Nisca said, trying to look stern, "You need to be dressed by the maidens for the sacred ritual."

Alyanna stood up, a rare look of defiance upon her face. Producing a large leather pouch she said, "I have my fur skin from the big cat and my special robe. I will adorn my hair and oil myself. It will be more sacred that way. When the girls dress me, there is jealousy as we spoke of before."

"Have you prayed to the Goddess Themis on this account," asked Nisca? "After all, it is the custom to have the maidens dress...."

"I know," Alyanna interrupted, "but not following through with custom will not interfere with my going to the temple. I will be the youngest warrior priestess ever crowned in The Temple of Themis, for I have seen that in a vision."

"So be it then, who am I to argue with a vision," said Nisca with a hardy chuckle.

When the horn sounded, Alyanna had just finished oiling her body. Her robe lay in readiness, as well as the skin of the big cat and the flowered wreath she had made for her hair. Quickly stepping into the robe, she put the cat skin over one of her shoulders and placed the flowers on her head, all the while singing the praises of Ma-Bellona and Themis, beloved goddesses worshiped by their clan.

"A-lee-an-na, A-lee-an-na, the women and children chanted her welcome as she was escorted to the dais, where a special chair awaited. During the performance she was enraptured, partly because of the herbs, but also because it depicted a friendly leader, always laughing with her clan and turning a blind eye when her friends stole from others in the group. The performance truly answered her questions of why it was so important that others saw her as a leader. For no one listened to the ineffective queen that was being portrayed in the play by Phadra, and the clan lost everything when it was invaded by a rival tribe. Alyanna also received a deeper understanding of how she could help and guide others more effectively when she was revered as an oracle and their queen.

Awakening in her bed, famished after sleeping for nearly three days, she gorged herself with helping after helping. Eating enough for a month, or at least her teachers teasingly told her so, as her ecstatic mother looked on with pride. It was obvious that Thea, never wanting to be a leader looked forward to the next few years as her daughter matured and continued to take over the reins. Thea would then be able to spend her time teaching and playing with the little ones of the clan. She missed that, other duties always seemed to get in the way.

After Nisca and the women of the council left their hut, Thea remarked to Alyanna the noticeable difference in her stance.

"Yes," said Alyanna, "I have always been uncomfortable about the fact that I was taller than the other girls of my age. But today I had a vision of the future. I will not stop growing for quite some time it seems. And that is good, for apparently someday I will do battle with a bear."

Perplexed her mother questioned, "A bear?"

Alyanna did not answer, her eyes glazed over as the same island, its peculiar setting, and the bear of a man that she had seen earlier appeared. The vision washed all thoughts of where she was, or who she was with from her mind.

Strange stirrings of being a woman charged her body with heat, and she instinctively touched her breast. Her nipples ached with a hunger she did not understand, as stimulating currents ran through her female parts. Feeling a yearning that was all too familiar, yet she had never felt it before today, she thought, *at least not in this lifetime.*

The Sacred Rays

The Seven Color Ray or Sacred Ray system is not a new concept. I received an initiation into this belief system thirty years ago upon reading the works of Helena P. Blavatsky as well as Alice Bailey. These incredible women penned their books in the late 19th and early 20th century, being the first to bring the knowledge of the Color Rays to the West. Reading these books pushed me to delve deeper into the mysteries of the rays. After a series of profound meditations on this subject I found that I was able to tap into my own color ray information, which gave me a clearer understanding of the lessons that would help me evolve as an individual. Shortly after, one of my spirit guides began to channel the information for others.

The ancient occult belief of the seven rays has appeared in many esoteric philosophies as far back as the 6th century B.C. It has been part of the Western culture as Gnosticism and part of the Hindu belief system since the post-Vedic era. In Rome it was part of the Mithraic Mysteries and in the Catholic Church it can be seen in its texts and its iconic artwork as early as the Byzantine era. Some esoteric Christians speak of the Virgin Mary as the Goddess Theotokos, who filters the divine spirit of the Holy Ghost through her, which emanates the spectrum of light that we know of as the Sacred Rays.

I read somewhere that the Goddess Theotokos stands at the portal of time and from the center of her being pours forth Seven Sacred Rays, each ray a vibrational bridge to earthly worlds, and each bridge holds the lessons that allow you to grow spiritually. I wish I could share with you who wrote this sentiment, but I have since lost the knowledge of where it came from. But I do remember clearly that at the end of this beautiful writing were the words-

"Know thy color and you shall know thyself."

349

APRIL RANE

Below is just a partial listing of the lessons offered through the frequency of each color.

1. <u>Red</u> is the color of the Ray of Sacred Purpose and Will

The Goddess of this Ray is called
Enchantress of the Wheel of Life and Death

It is the objective of this Ray to supply power and passionate intensity to evolve all beings upon planet earth. The *life force* of the human body is emanated from the frequency of this Ray. *Entities born under this Ray have the ability to ignite others with passion and to assist them in finding a purpose or direction in life.*

~ **The lessons** that will be offered to a soul that chooses the Red Ray will be of the nature of security. They must learn to accept their families as they are, or loss of a family member early on, recognizing that their family of origin was picked by them to assist them in the lessons of the Red Ray. They will need to learn to express a passion for living, and recognize they will be challenged in some way to learn survival skills. They will need to discover how to become responsible, and to live an honorable life.

On earth when the soul refuses the lessons offered by this Ray- it negates life and chooses anger over love-lethargy over passion- malice over honor.

Key words: Do unto others as you would have them do unto you.

2. <u>Orange</u> is the color of the Ray of Sacred Love and Wisdom

The Goddess of this Ray is called
The Enchantress of Cosmic Attraction

"It is the objective of this Ray to condition life with Divine Love, and to instill unity within all creation. The *love force* of the human body is emanated from this ray. It is this ray that presides over the life force of the entire universe. *Entities born under this Ray have the ability to unite opposing forces and instill courage in others.*

~ **The lessons** that will be offered to a soul that chooses the Orange Ray will be to form sacred unions of trust and honor within relationships, to honor the continuation of life and to gather wisdom by loving or understanding their enemies.

On earth when the soul refuses the lessons offered by this Ray– it negates love and chooses hate over understanding-moral turpitude over integrity- non-involvement over intimacy

Key words: Love thy enemy

3. _Yellow_ is the color of the Ray of Sacred Action and Intelligence

*The Goddess of this Ray is called, **Enchantress of Records**.

It is the objective of this Ray to give articulation to Divine Intelligence. This ray provides the underlying intelligence of nature. It is the force that *animates* human thought. Its purpose is to reveal the Mind of the Goddess within the consciousness of humans. This is the ray most associated with karma, for it holds the memory of all that has ever been, what was, and what is to be. *Entities born under this Ray have the ability to be leaders, and through their intelligence and their passionate nature they can inspire others.*

~ **The lessons** that will be offered to a soul that chooses the Yellow Ray will be to form self - esteem and personal honor, to develop integrity, to learn the difference between strength and courage and to recognize life as a precious gift.

On earth, when a soul refuses the lessons offered by this Ray – it negates honor and chooses mistrust over trust– dishonesty over truth-limitation over self-awakening.

Key Words: Honor Oneself

4. _Green_ is the color of the Ray of Sacred Harmony through Conflict

*The Goddess of this Ray is **The Enchantress that is the Seed _and_ the Eternal Flower.**

It is the objective of this Ray to create a sense of beauty and balance within all manifest life. Earth is a polarized experience. The function of this ray is to find resolution to opposing forces. Abundance is offered through the Green Ray and is achieved when the individual finds appeal and harmony in its everyday surroundings. *Entities that are governed by this Ray have the ability to see and understand both sides of any difficulty, therefore they make good mediators.*

~ **The lessons** that will be offered to a soul that chooses the Green Ray will be to form a nature of compassion and love for humanity. To develop a sense of true justice for those who have chosen to be enemies as well as those who befriend. It is left to them to develop a sense of tranquility in the face of adversity and to always lead with an open heart.

On earth when a soul refuses the lessons offered by this Ray– it negates compassion and chooses aloofness over empathy - bitterness over forgiveness - indifference over loving concern.

Key Words: Forgiveness is Divine Power

5. *Blue is the color of the Ray of Sacred Knowledge and Will*

*The Goddess of this Ray is called **Enchantress of Knowledge**

It is the object of this Ray to illuminate the Divine through the pursuit of spiritual knowledge. In other words, *Know Thyself* and the universe will unfold before you, allowing you to discern Truth from lies. This Ray teaches –thy will be done- through an understanding of karma. *Entities that are born to this Ray have the ability to open the gates of knowledge –thereby gaining wisdom and understanding, with which they can assist mankind.*

~ **The lessons** that will be offered to a soul that chooses the Blue Ray will be to form a gentle nature and to use their intelligence to observe and/ or to teach without criticism. This Ray needs to develop a sense of pride with humility.

On earth when a soul refuses to learn the lessons offered by this Ray- it negates awareness and chooses apathy over perception – indifference over mindfulness – talking over listening

Key Words: Thy Will be Done

6. _Indigo_ is the color of the Ray of Sacred Idealism

The Goddess of the Ray is called **Enchantress,
Flame of Spiritual Desire**

It is the object of this Ray to bring vision and spiritual desire to those that are receptive to it. The Third Eye Ray reminds humans to gaze upwardly, to reach and to aspire toward a higher essence. *Entities that are governed by the Sixth Ray tend to devote their lives to ideals that lift humanity into the realm of Spirit.*

~ **The lessons** that will be offered to a soul that chooses the Indigo Ray will be in what manner and to what end they will use the gift of clairvoyance and prophecy that is bestowed upon them.

On earth when a soul refuses the lessons offered by this Ray– it negates intuitive sight and chooses tunnel vision over clarity – darkness over light – censure and criticism over approval.

Key Words: Seek Only Truth

7. _Purple and White_ are the colors of the Ray of Ceremonial Magic

The Goddess of this Ray is called **The
Enchantress of the Magical Word**

It is the object of this Ray to bring order out of chaos. This Ray provides the energy for humanity to translate spiritual ideas into tangible realities. This can be achieved through the power of the spoken or written word. *Entities with a Seventh Ray Soul are rare. They are true magicians who can create positive change in humanity through their magical words, made manifest by their actions.*

~ **The lessons** that will be offered to a soul who chooses the Purple Ray will be to learn to live in the present moment and let spirit rule the body so that the body can respond to the directives of the higher self.

On earth when a soul refuses the lessons offered by this Ray- it negates the *future* by choosing to live in the past over the present - the mundane over the miraculous — chaos over order.

Key Words: Live Only in the Moment

Deep spiritual insight can be obtained from psychics and channels that have the ability to tune into the knowledge which is revealed by the Sacred Rays. Many times this information can clear up the mystery of why some things come easy and others are very challenging, or why specific abilities seem natural and others almost impossible to accomplish.

I find that Sacred Ray readings are best done in person, but on occasion can be accomplished over the phone. For information or to schedule an appointment, go to www.aprilrane.com

CPSIA information can be obtained at www.ICGtesting.com
Printed in the USA
LVOW040819181012

303231LV00002B/41/P